Praise for
LOVING PEDRO INFANTE

"Give thanks to Denise Chávez for writing such a swell book. . . . There are few writers with as warm and generous a heart."

—*The Washington Post*

"A fabulous book."

—*USA Today*

"A terrific novel full of *abuelita* wisdom and raunchy cantina wit. . . . The language is bawdy, sometimes downright *sucio*, but expressive in a way that pure Spanish or English couldn't be. A liberating Chicana coming-of-a-certain-age tale, rooted in a profound love for *la gente*, the book gives us heroines we didn't know we had and makes us understand that love means embracing flaws—our own as well as those of others."

—*Publishers Weekly*

"Chavez's spicy storytelling reminds us that women today, fictional and real, have other options."

—*New York Times Book Review*

"I didn't want this book to end. I haven't had this much fun since the last time I watched a Pedro Infante movie."
—Sandra Cisneros, author of *The House on Mango Street*

"A *teatro* of a book . . . you won't be able to put it down. . . . Chávez's *picante* story of love affirms the whole of our lives. For this alone she has earned her place at the most elegant table of American letters."
—*San Antonio Express-News*

"Ebulliently vivid. Chavez remains a pleasure to read. Her women retain a fiery individuality, an irrepressible spirit in the face of a world with few Pedro Infantes."
—*San Francisco Chronicle*

"Chavez brings her readers a funny, often harsh, but always real look at life in a small town. She writes with the authority of someone who's been there, and who understands. And, through her witty dialogue and often pointed social commentary, Chavez also teaches us a little something about life, love and, most importantly, Pedro Infante."
—*Morning Star Telegram*

"A rollicking fun read, a girls'-night-out good time. . . . Packs a cultural punch, offering eloquent insights into the joys, trials, tribulations, and tragedies of borderland life. In an earthy, spiritual and poignant way, her works convey the essence of what it means to be multicultural, straddling and embracing worlds, borders and cultures."

—*SunLife*

"Chavez's conversational writing style and the way she slips between Spanish and English is refreshing, like reading a note or eavesdropping on the bus."

—*Philadelphia Weekly*

"You never know when Chavez's harsh world may erupt in sudden jubilation, when its strivings and disappointments may mimic a state of grace."

—*The Miami Herald*

"Chávez has her forefinger firmly raised to measure the hot cultural crosswinds sweeping the southern borderlands, vividly capturing the region's eroded topography; the subtleties of its cuisine, fashion, and music; its pervasive religious ardor; and deep dependence on the leavening richness and peculiarities of family life."

—*The Arizona Republic*

DENISE CHÁVEZ

LOVING

PEDRO

INFANTE

a novel

WSP

WASHINGTON SQUARE PRESS
PUBLISHED BY POCKET BOOKS

New York   London   Toronto   Sydney

This book is a work of fiction. Names, characters, places and incidents are products of
the author's imagination or are used fictitiously. Any resemblance to actual events or lo-
cales or persons, living or dead, is entirely coincidental.

 A Washington Square Press Publication of
POCKET BOOKS, a division of Simon & Schuster, Inc.
1230 Avenue of the Americas, New York, NY 10020

ISBN 13: 978-0-7434-4573-3
ISBN 10: 0-7434-4573-2

First Washington Square Press trade paperback printing March 2002

10 9 8 7 6 5 4 3

WASHINGTON SQUARE PRESS and colophon are
registered trademarks of Simon & Schuster, Inc.

For information regarding special discounts for bulk purchases,
please contact Simon & Schuster Special Sales at 1-800-456-6798
or business@simonandschuster.com

Cover design by John Gall; cover art: detail from the poster for the film
Viva Mi Desgracia courtesy of Roberto Rodríguez Ruelas

Printed in the U.S.A.

Pa' Las Comadres
Las Eternal Fénix

And

For all fans of Pedro Infante,
those who smile on hearing his name,
those who loved him, love him still.

And to those new fans,
welcome to the Club.

¡Que viva Pedro Infante!
¡Que viva en la inmensidad de los cielos!

"¡Ay, qué trabajo me cuesta quererte como te quiero!"

"Oh, what an effort it is to love you the way I do!"

Es Verdad

PART I

LA VIDA

NO VALE

NADA

¡Híjole! In the Darkness

In the darkness of El Colón movie theater, larger than life and superimposed on a giant screen, Pedro Infante, the Mexican movie star, stares straight at me with his dark, smoldering eyes.

It is here in the sensuous shadows that I forget all about my life as Teresina "La Tere" Ávila, teacher's aide at Cabritoville Elementary School. Maybe that's why I like Pedro's movies so much. They make me think to stop thinking or stop thinking to really think.

It is here that I prefer to dream, seated in the middle of the people I call family. To my right is my comadre, Irma "La Wirma" Granados, and next to her is her mother, Nyvia Ester Granados.

It's dinnertime on a hot July night. I should be at

home, and yet I find myself lost in the timeless transparency of El
Colón watching Pedro Infante in the movie *La Vida No Vale Nada*.
Pedro plays a melancholic loner named Pablo who keeps leaving
any number of possible lives behind, and all sorts of women who
might have loved him. He's a good-hearted vato who goes on these
incredible life-changing borracheras whenever he feels overwhelmed, which is pretty much most of the time.

Ay, Dios mío.

Pedro's lips part slightly with that naughty nene—little boy—
grin of his as he breaks into a song.

¡Ay, ay, ay!

Pedro knows me. He knows I crave his arms. His touch. His
deep voice in my ear, his knowing hands on my trembling body.

Híjole.

The great flames of my dreams billow up to meet the flickering
screen, as a wave of intense light consumes the sweet, painful and
familiar song of my untold longing.

¡Uuuuuey! The man has me going. Revved up like a swirling
red, green, yellow and blue top, I can barely sit still in my seat. I
sit up straight, then shiver, then melt down to hot plastic, trying to
find a comfortable position. My legs are itchy, a sure sign of the
troubled state of my mind, my restless body. There is no relief. I
admit, years after he died tragically in a plane crash, I'm in love
with Pedro.

Who isn't?

In the movie, Pedro-as-Pablo meets Cruz, the widowed owner
of an antique shop in the market and he carries her groceries
home for her. He offers to stay on to help and that is exactly what
he does, cleaning up, fixing things, getting the shop back on its
feet. And he can't help but notice how voluptuous Cruz is, despite
her black widow's dress.

After exchanging glances that would have worked on any other
woman, Cruz still can't admit she loves Pedro-as-Pablo. But she's
thrilled to know he wants her—his lust naked, unadorned. Only
when she's behind closed doors in her room can she admit the
terrible truth.

What can I tell you about Pedro Infante? If you're a Mejicana or Mejicano and don't know who he is, you should be tied to a hot stove with yucca rope and beaten with sharp dry corn husks as you stand in a vat of soggy fideos. If your racial and cultural ethnicity is Other, then it's about time you learned about the most famous of Mexican singers and actors.

Pedro was born November 18, 1917, in Mazatlán, Sinaloa, and died in 1957 in a horrible plane crash in Mérida, Yucatán, when he was forty years old and at the height of his popularity. He was the biggest movie star in the Mexican cinema of the forties and fifties, what is called La Época de Oro del Cine Mejicano. Many know him as "El ídolo del Pueblo." Some people even call him the Dean Martin of Méjico, but he's more, much more than that. He was bigger than Bing Crosby or even Elvis Presley.

Pedro's real life was just as passionate as the one he played on the screen. There was his first girlfriend, Lupita Marqués, who bore him a little girl. And then there was his long-suffering wife, María Luisa. Then came Lupe Torrentera, the young dancer he met when she was fourteen and who bore him a daughter, Graciela Margarita, at age fifteen. Lupe was the mother of two of his other children. And, of course, there was Irma Dorantes, the young actress who starred in many of his movies and became the mother of his daughter, Irmita. The marriage to her was annulled the week before his death.

In between these women were many other women, some whose names we remember, many we don't. And one can never forget his mother, Doña Refugia, or Doña Cuquita, as she was known. She was really the first woman who truly loved Pedro. Pedro was the type of man who took care of the women in his life, from Doña Refugio to María Luisa to all of his mistresses. Either he had a fantastically rich and good life or a hell of a complicated one.

If I'd had a chance and been born earlier and in a different place, I might have tried to take up with Pedro as well. But I was born in Cabritoville, U.S.A., on the Tejas/Méjico border near El Paso. The closest I'll ever come to Pedro Infante is in El Colón on a Thursday night. In here time is suspended. In here I want to imagine the impossible, to leave, for an hour or two, my life behind.

Nyvia Ester sits behind a woman who keeps talking when Pedro-as-Pablo does something cute on-screen, or makes ojitos with his beautiful eyes—which makes us all sticky and hot like the popcorn with butter that we're holding even though we know he's been dead for years.

All I need is a little quiet and a lot of darkness. And for the man across the aisle from me to stop smacking his dry lips and murmuring under his hot breath.

When Pedro-as-Pablo suddenly takes Cruz in his arms there is a profound and sacred silence.

Then I hear a sharp intake of breath from Nyvia Ester. Irma sighs, a barely perceptible sound of pure pleasure. I slide down in my seat, my head momentarily resting on the plastic chair back, then nervously rise with dreaded anticipation of what is to come. This is the scene where Cruz gives Pablo her father's gold watch. I can't take it. I know what's going to happen.

It breaks my heart every time Pedro-as-Pablo leaves Cruz in the middle of the night after she's given him her father's watch. Later, she wakes up to find him gone and she runs down a set of dark stairs calling out his name. But he will never come back.

Pedro-as-Pablo is the type of man who will never be faithful to one woman. It's not that he doesn't want to be, he just can't. He can't stay with Silvia, the prostitute he befriends. Eventually he earns enough money as a baker to free her from the brothel owner she's indebted to, but when she finally finds him to thank him and hopefully spend the rest of her life with him, to her surprise he doesn't want her.

More adventures, more women, a life out of control. Pedro can't stop loving and leaving women.

Now raucous with laughter, the man across from me applauds

as Pedro-as-Pablo awakes to find himself in bed again, now with Silvia.

Not even Cruz could stop Pedro-as-Pablo, make him stand still, find a life of peace. He loved her, but it wasn't meant to be. There is no rest for someone as rootless as him. Only drinking will ease his pain. Silvia is someone he pities. Marta? Ay, she's a minor distraction. How can Pedro-as-Pablo love anyone when he doesn't even like himself?

The temperature inside El Colón is ninety degrees. The main floor and the balcony are packed with people of all ages, families hovering close to each other, young lovers, older couples resting like torpid flies near the water cooler. Outside, it's hotter.

The married men wander down to the concession stand to get a Coke and stare hard at the young girls, chiflando in that soft appreciative way with their breath, a small outtake of air releasing the sexual tension, while their wives slink down in their seats, grateful for a little peace as they pull down their bunched-up panties. Someone takes out a much-used plastic bag full of tortas, someone else a crinkly paper bag full of ripe mangos. The floor is testimony to the fierce hunger that the darkness arouses. Candy wrappers stick to it along with chewed-up stalks of sugarcane with mashed fibers that nobody wants to look at too closely. Crumpled soft drink cups and popcorn boxes are tucked between seats, wads of tired gum are glued underneath.

Voices call out incessantly to the actors on the screen, without any hesitation or embarrassment, as if the audience knows them, are friends, even family.

"Te quiero, Pablo," Cruz tells Pedro-as-Pablo.

The woman behind us tells him as well. "Y yo te quiero a tí, Pedro."

She's getting on my nerves. She knows all the lines to the movie and she repeats them to herself.

I know all the lines, too, but don't say them out loud.

In the darkness of El Colón, Pedro Infante could do it all, and he did. He sang, he rode horses, motorcycles, cars, buses, and he walked away from tragedy unlike anyone else. No one strode away from all these women, those men, their selfish attachments, all those inappropriate and terrible situations as Pedro did in *La Vida No Vale Nada*.

"Popcorn?" I whisper to Irma, who motions that the tub is with Nyvia Ester. Both of us know we may not see it for a long time. Someone is going to have to go back for the free refill pretty soon and it's not going to be me.

The popcorn at El Colón is greasy and salty, as it should be. Irma says it smells of hot oil, of maíz, of sweaty hands turning tortillas in small obscure villages, of present lives lived in a past tense, of ancestral struggles, of the humid breath of small children, of old, dying animals resting near crumbling adobes, of too many lives struggling for a modicum of hope. Leave it to La Wirms to try to understand the sociological and cultural meanings of different kinds of popcorn.

I say it's the way they do the butter. Gobs of it without regard to cholesterol.

Please don't ever give me a bag of day-old popcorn that isn't warm enough to melt butter. There is nothing I love more than something greasy and salty unless, of course, it's something hot and greasy and salty. Or fruity and crystallized and so sweet your teeth curl in.

I've got simple tastes, ordinary needs that become extraordinary in the dark. What do I know about ancestral yearnings?

And yet this is why Irma says we're here, years after Pedro's death. "We're fulfilling the destiny set out for us, Tere, by those who came before us, the multitudes whose black-and-white dreams have allowed us to dream in color, whose misery and grief, longing and hopes have fueled our tomorrows."

"Whatever you say, comadre," I whisper to her in the dark. "I'm okay with that theory. But, mujer, just look at the man! I don't care how many years he's been dead. I still want to taste him."

"¡Ay, tú!" Irma says.

But I know she knows what I mean.

And she knows I know what she means.

When I watch Pedro's movies I'm watching the lives of my people, past, present and future, parade in front of me. Pedro Infante could have been my father; he was my father's age when I was born. He's the man we want our men to be. And he's the man we imagine ourselves to be if we are men. The man we want our daughters to have loved. Pedro's the beautiful part of our dreaming. And his looks still have the power to make my woman's blood heat up like sizzling manteca on an old but faithful sartén. Just watching him on the screen makes my little sopaipilla start throbbing underneath all the folds and tucks of cloth on the old and creaky theater seat, just give me some honey.

He had a beautiful body. He lifted weights, which most Mejicanos didn't do at the time. When I think of the Mejicanos I know, I hardly think of them with barbells. They're not the exercising type. They're too busy working outdoors fixing the techo or cleaning or working en los files or running after their own or someone else's children or planting vegetables in their backyards.

When you saw Pedro boxing or riding a motorcycle, you knew he was a man ahead of his sluggish time. Physically robust, he did all his own stunts, whether it was fighting with Wolf Ruvinskis, the hunky Mexican actor who showed a lot of his chest during that era of moviemaking, or hanging on for dear life on the top of the old bus that took him down the dusty and interminable road to La Capital and into Cruz's waiting arms. Pedro loved more women than you can count, which is about the best exercise you can ever get.

He was incredibly handsome in that way only Mejicanos can be. I can't explain this to you, only a Mejicana or an intuitive gringa knows what I mean. The handsomeness and sexiness come on you slowly and then hit you between the eyes. The more you contemplate a man like Pedro, observe his mannerisms, stare into his eyes, delight in his unique smile and strong arms, trim waist and good legs, and watch how gentle and yet self-assured he is with people of all ages, and see how much they love him, you will begin to understand a little of what Pedro Infante means to me, and the other members of the Pedro Infante Club de Admiradores Norteamericano #256.

There was only one Pedro Infante, and he was a real man, and I'm very picky about men. It's a good thing. Not like Graciela Vallejos, Irma's walleyed cousin, who looks at men like driftwood she can just pick up whenever she wants. Nor am I like Irma, who's a little too finicky and rarely goes out on a date.

Irma never likes anyone, they're too this, too that. Too *desde*. That's the word my comadre uses for too *you know what*. For example, "Our President, Tere, he's just too *desde*. And what about his wife, she's just too, too *desde*. And not only that, but the press, why it's just been too *desde* about *desde*, if you ask me."

To Irma, most men either smell like Lavoris or pollo frito, or they're only interested in a woman's nalgas or her legs or her chichis and they can't spell worth a damn, which really bothers her. She also hates a man who writes like a third grader. She rejected a CPA she met at La Tempestad Lounge, our weekend "stomping ground," after he gave her his business card, having scribbled his home phone number as a child would, his fingers clawed around the pen while his other hand held a cold can of Coors.

"You can imagine what he'd be like in bed," Irma said. "All fingers and none of them coordinating. And not only that, he was a Coors drinker. Hasn't he heard about the boycott?"

I never seem to think of things like that, things that can make or break a romance, like if the guy has a nervous tic that will eventually become irritating, or if he smells too much of aftershave that masks sour body odor. Irma notices the way men smoke or what they say about people who smoke, or cross or don't cross their legs, the way they comb their hair, if they have hair, and if they don't have hair, what they think of themselves without hair, how they tie their shoelaces, if they have shoelaces, or if they wear sandals, and what their toes look like in the sandals, and the way they drink their beer. She won't tolerate a smoker or a serious drinker, just like me. I can understand that, what with the alcoholism in her family.

There have been a few people I know who have been drinkers, too. Tío Santos, my mother's brother, for one. He always had a cold beer in his sweaty hands. And then there's Ubaldo Miranda, my best friend in the fan club, besides Irma. He shouldn't drink, but he does. He's been seeing a therapist in El Paso for years at Catholic Family Social Services on the sliding scale, pay as you can, and I think he's finally beginning to understand why he drinks. If you were molested during a Quinceañera when everyone was in the big sala having fun and you were in a dirty rest room with your older cousin Mamerto Miranda's churro apestoso forced into your mouth, you'd drink, too. Because you'd want to dull the pain for giving up hope.

But I don't want to get all philosophical on you just because it's dark here in El Colón, or because it's late. Although I have to say dark and late are my best times for thinking. I'm always carrying on this dialogue inside my head. I talk to a Tere Avila who isn't gastada, apagada y jodida. The other Tere, the dream Tere, still has sense and hope. I keep trying to help her out and spare her pain, but she just can't hear me. She's too busy watching the movie of her life unfold in front of her.

I turn to look at my comadre. In the flickering darkness I can see her wipe her eyes. The scene with the watch has gotten to her. Irma is a friend like no other.

My first husband, Reynaldo Ambriz, was never my friend. The only other longtime friend I've had has been Albinita, my mother. She gives you a hundred percent of herself when she just stands in the door looking at you, with such love and hope.

Irma's other best friend is her mother, Nyvia Ester. That's the kind of person Irma is. Who would go to the movies with their mother every Thursday night and look forward to it each week, and not only that, but have a wonderful time? I look forward to it, too, but in a different way.

I wouldn't consider Nyvia Ester my best friend. To me, she's a little scary, but I still respect her. Kind of how you would respect the Black Virgin if she were standing in front of you. That's Nyvia Ester: short, dark, tough. She's had a hard time since her husband left her. Any woman would have to be strong, especially if you'd cleaned houses for over forty years and sent all your kids to college on the money that you'd saved in a world where it's impossible to save, and didn't have a man to help, and no insurance, and you only went to the sixth grade back in Méjico.

The woman who likes to talk out loud to Pedro is starting up again. Nyvia Ester has tried to stare her down with those dark bulldog eyes of hers, and even made growling noises that only a pissed-off Mejicana can make, but the woman just isn't getting it. I don't have a problem with her loving the movie, but how can I be in the dark all anonymous when she's in the dark all noisy?

If it weren't for her, there wouldn't be anything better than sitting in the darkness of El Colón on a hot summer night with La Wirma. She holds my large Dr Pepper while I dislodge a stubborn kernel of popcorn from my back teeth.

"Pass me the popcorn, Irma," I whisper. What I really mean is wrestle the popcorn away from your mother. Nyvia Ester always ends up with the tub. When we get it back it's almost always empty. And not only that, but Nyvia Ester makes us go all the way downstairs to the first floor for refills, where you have to wait in line for about half an hour in front of a bunch of short, horny married men in super-tight Wranglers and Western shirts with rimmed BO circles and thick humpy necks like Brahma bulls who stand behind you making that whistling Ssst! Ssst! noise under their breath, which means many things, and all of them bad. No, señor, today it's not going to be me. I'm not going to refill the popcorn tub.

I can tell Nyvia Ester is really getting irritated with the woman behind us. She whispers, "Silencio, por favor," and the woman still ignores her.

"Sssh!" says Nyvia Ester.

"Sssh yourself!" answers the woman.

"Jew got a problem?" Nyvia Ester says too loudly.

Someone yells out, "Dile que se vaya al Diablo."

"¡Silencio, por Dios! There's children in the audience, watch what you say, cabrón!"

Things are getting tense. An old man, in what was once an official-looking white shirt and pants, slouches his way up the aisle and taps Nyvia Ester on the shoulder. He's the only semblance of an usher I've ever seen here. When it's really busy, he also helps out with the concession stand. Nyvia Ester stands up indignantly as a cacophony of voices yells to her: "¡Siéntese, señora! Down in front!"

Nyvia Ester turns around and tells the woman who started it all, "¡Vieja testuda sin vergüenza!" and sits down to applause.

The woman rises and everyone boos her. She sits down, momentarily defeated. The very polite, very hard-of-hearing viejito raises his voice, "Señoras, por favor, ¡cálmense!" Everyone cheers him. The movie grinds to a halt as the projectionist yells from his booth to tell the audience to shut up. People boo, whistle, yell and stomp on the gummy floor, flattening popcorn boxes and grinding popcorn into fine chaff. Eventually, like an old motor revving up, the movie resumes, words slurred and thick. Pedro-as-Pablo tells Cruz he loves her and everyone cheers. The viejito shuffles up the aisle to the back and trips over a young child in the dark. "¡Ay, mamá!" he calls out in pain. More noise. More shushing. More ugliness, but now coming from the back. Two young men get in a fight.

"¡Jóvenes infelices!" an older woman calls out, damning all youth. "¡Tontos!" a man echoes her sentiments.

The old usher comes up and asks them to leave. The two disgruntled young men leave, two skinny girlfriends with highly teased sprayed hair in tow, to settle accounts in the alley behind the theater.

Things finally settle down. Pedro-as-Pablo walks on a beach near the coast in search of his father, Leandro.

Inside El Colón you can watch el mero mero, el merito, nuestro querido, Pedro Infante, the world's most handsome man love the world's most beautiful women. Like him, you can live happily ever after hasta la eternidad. He is the man whose child we want to bear. He is the man we wish we could be. Ay, Pedro, most fortunate and unfortunate of men. Dead at age forty. Papi, we miss you still.

I don't care if the floor at El Colón is sticky and gummy and wet with too many spilled Cokes. I don't care if kids throw orange rinds and pieces of hard bolillo and popcorn boxes down from the balcony or that everyone is talking or singing along with the music and it's a hot summer night and my legs stick to the torn humid theater seats. I don't even care anymore that the woman behind Nyvia Ester is making so much noise. We're all children in the darkness. In here no one watches us and tells us what to feel.

Inside El Colón I am closer to my people than I will ever be outside in the stinging sun. We are a collective here, and strong. Nothing and no one can deny us that.

Each of us yearns for Pedro, for the world he creates: a world of beauty, physical perfection, song.

Just look at Pedro's expressions. No actor on the face of the earth has done more acting with his eyebrows than Pedro. Not to mention his arms, the most expressive arms I've ever seen! They're very manly, and this is played up with the type of shirts he wears, with short sleeves flaring out at the shoulder. He also sports a lot of sweaters, most of them hand-knit. In her autobiography, *Un Gran Amor*, Lupe Torrentera, the mother of three of Pedro's children, talks about knitting Pedro the sweater he wore in the movie *Pepe el Toro*.

Few men could get away with wearing a tight-fitting sweater or those loose suits so popular back in the fifties. You put a suit like that on one of our modern-day so-called movie stars and you have payasoville. Most men have lost their natural grace.

Whether Pedro's arms just hang there, fisted or still, they're full of meaning. He can stride, too. Even his legs are expressive, not to mention his feet. God help us if he takes off his shirt. Who would have ever thought a man's nipples could express anger?

"Ahuumm. Ahuumm." The old man in front of us clucks like a demented rooster. He has something stuck in his throat. For a while we think he's not going to make it, but then he rallies and spits out the offending glob in the aisle near Nyvia Ester. She is not impressed.

It's hard to concentrate with so much happening around us, with the noise of people laughing, crying, sighing, chewing, burping, hiccuping, applauding. Not to mention the meddling, cajoling, rebuking, interrupting, interceding and encouraging words that fly back and forth between the screen and the audience. But just looking at Pedro helps to bring me to a place of attention.

I admit, I've never been good at hiding my feelings in the dark. It's my undoing. I started dreaming when I was a little girl and I haven't stopped yet.

La Vida No Vale Nada is really a violent movie. Only you don't know how brutal it is until it's over.

At the end, Pedro-as-Pablo wrestles with Wolf Ruvinskis. Wolf wants sole possession of a squirrelly hussy named Marta. Go figure what Wolf Ruvinskis would want with a woman like Marta! She's been sleeping with Pablo's father, one of those aging Mejicanos who have to prove their barrel-chested manhood by either dyeing their hair jet black or taking up with a younger woman. She's been chasing Pedro-as-Pablo as well, but he doesn't want anything to do with her, even though she's always throwing herself down on the sand in front of him like a horny, beached mermaid.

Everyone gasps with fear as Wolf Ruvinskis punches Pedro-as-Pablo and then drags him into the salty water to drown him while the spurned and vindictive Marta eggs him on.

Pedro-as-Pablo seems to flounder as Wolf Ruvinskis violently pushes him under the lapping waves, but then he gathers himself and flings Wolf back onto the beach with a battery of blows that leaves Wolf in a broken heap on the sandy shore.

Meanwhile, back at the pueblito, Pablo's mother and siblings struggle in the most abject poverty. The two men, father and son, finally come to the realization that they need to get back home and take care of their kin. All is well. All is safe. All is as it should be. For the men. A 'lo Macho Bravo.

And yet, I am left with questions. I look around El Colón. Is anyone else upset?

What about Marta? What's going to happen to her? Does anyone care?

A glowering and bitter Marta casts a long glance at Pedro-as-Pablo as he walks away arm in arm into a hopeful sunset with his now-reclaimed father, Leandro, both men the bane of her small, useless existence. Wolf Ruvinskis sputters nearby, trying to catch his breath. Marta looks at him with disgust and resignation.

Even in the darkness of El Colón I want to change my dreams, Marta's dreams, but the movie credits roll.

La Vida No Vale Nada.

Pedro Infante. Rosario Granados. Lilia Prado. Domingo Soler. Magda Guzmán. Wolf Ruvinskis. Hortensia Santoveña.

Nyvia Ester picks up her purse and shimmies out of her seat with bobbing and teetering crablike movements, her bowlegs unsteady until she finds her land legs. Irma takes her mother's hand and assists her up the incline toward the door that leads to the stairs and the lobby. The woman behind us smacks her lips, hoists her large body out of her seat and disappears into the uncertain night.

The sound track flares dramatically, full of reckless abandon.

I sit in the theater a little longer, my eyes full of tears, sad tears, tears of hope.

My heart hurts the way it does when you can't love the man you want to. A man like Pedro.

P for Pendeja

I was cleaning house on a Sunday morning when Irma called to say, "Grab Sunday's *Cabritoville Chronicle*. Now sit down, Tere. Open up to the wedding section. B3. Middle of the page. It's Rogelia Baeza. She took a trip to England and met someone at Madame Tussaud's, and now she's Mrs. Melton Everson. They have an antique shop in London."

If Miss Baeza could get a man, anyone could. Rogelia Baeza ruled the typing roost at Cabritoville High. She was short, broad-faced, with a good, solid D cup on her. Her wide hips anchored her spindly bowlegged goat's legs on the ground. Her small, hooflike feet were unbelievably nimble. She moved without sound and would sneak up on you as you were quietly fff fvf vvv fff fvf vvv fff fvf vvv fvfing.

Only when she was already behind you would you realize she was there. Her husky, masculine voice bellowed in your ear, "Low wrists, low wrists!" To us, Rogelia Baeza was a woman of considerable power. Metate Face, we called her.

"Give me a break, Irma!" I exclaimed incredulously. "Give me a B-reak. You've got to be kidding. He's blond. He's handsome. He's from over there. She looks like burnt toast next to him. As a matter of fact, she's so dark you can't even see her features in this photo."

"She's standing in front of the sun or behind it, I forget which," Irma explained. "She's in the shadows. But it just goes to show: a face does not a woman make. Nor a man. It's what's inside. Any woman can 'get' a man if and when she wants to, but she doesn't need one, and especially if she knows how to type."

"Remind me later that you said that," I replied.

"I said it years ago in high school and I'm still saying it," Irma continued. "Woman does not live by Man alone. You've always had the wrong attitude, Tere, that's all there is to it. It's the way most women think, and that's what gets them in trouble. We've got to have the right man or no man. But *who's* the right man? And what about this idea: maybe some women don't even *need* a man. Or at least in the way that cripples them."

"My father should have been the right man, Irma. The right man for my mother and for me. But he wasn't. I don't think your dad was the right man for your mother either. So who the hell is the right man anyway? Besides, if there *is* a right man, maybe I'll still find him."

"So I guess that means we're still going to La Tempestad tonight?"

"I have my new boots from the White House. You wearing your red dress?"

"I'll pick you up at eight."

"Make that seven-thirty."

"Seven forty-five."

"A little before eight."

"I'll be waiting."

That's what I said to Irma La Wirma Granados as I closed the *Cabritoville Chronicle*.

Irma and I have been going to Tino's La Tempestad Lounge every Friday and Saturday night for too many years. It's a ritual we can't break. I don't know why we always go there. There certainly isn't anyone to talk to. We stopped going for a while, after Irma met and lost Sal, and I met Chago—my last boyfriend, who moved to California to do construction work—and he lost me.

We tried to find normal men in a more normal way and at a more normal place. La Tempestad is a spot where the crippled and maimed congregate to pick up women who don't mind a one-nighter with someone who lasts less than an hour. It was Irma who first realized we had to give up La Tempestad.

"The name fits, Tere. We're tempting a terrible fate in La Tempestad. I wish it weren't so, but it is. I see signs of death all around. There was a dead rat near the men's lavatory and a heap of dead cucarachas near the water fountain. What really cinched it was the broken mirror in the women's bathroom that had 'Puta Power' written on it in black lipstick."

I wish I were more like Irma, noticing details and signs and later putting them all together and formulating theories from the way a person kisses you goodbye on the side of the mouth instead of full on the lips. I tell Irma, "Comadre, you're psychic, I should start calling you La Hermana Irma, the way you can predict what's going to happen by the way someone lifts their coffee cup or how loud they burp."

"I'm telling you, Tere, we have to move on. I see a new life for both of us."

Well, that's all I needed. Irma knew the signs better than anyone. And if she felt we were played out at La Tempestad, two women in our thirties, still searching for The Man, that's all I needed to know. I read my horoscope every day and I'm kind of superstitious, too.

"So let's try the Holiday Inn next week, Irma," I suggested.

"Tere, I'm talking about going cold turkey."

"Cold turkey? Like no men, or at least no men we meet in bars?"

"Like let's start a book club or learn to cook."

That's when we took the Robert La Grange Five-Star Cooking Class at El Paso Community College and learned how to fillet fish and make ratatouille. The class saved our lives, Irma claims. But that was last year.

All I could think about was that if Miss Baeza could get a man, anyone could, even a divorced thirty-year-old who *still* couldn't type. I didn't want to get married; I'd already tried that. I was married once for about two years when I was eighteen. We were both too young. I thought Reynaldo Ambriz was a good guy; he thought I was more mature. I didn't like the way he ate his food, mouth open and chewing sideways. He didn't like my family. Since there was only Mom and me, who didn't he like? Irma didn't like him either. My mother liked him too much. He was quiet and liked to read in the living room late at night. One day he said he was leaving and he did. He took all his Stephen King novels, his baby-blue electric blanket and his red Lava lamp. We were really too young. It was a good thing we didn't have kids, not that it was really possible. Reynaldo's sex drive was low. He used to fall asleep on the couch and didn't like the way I smelled. Women scared him. He was afraid of menstrual blood. The last time we made love I was just starting my period and stained the sheets. Rey se puso bien weird.

"My God, Terry, what IS that?" Rey shrieked.

"Oh, just chill out, Rey," I said. "It's only blood. When you men cut your finger you get all freaked out. Women aren't that way. We just clean it up. You have to make a big production out of blood. It's just juices. Juices, that's all. Don't use hot water. Any woman can tell you that. Hot water and blood don't mix. I don't know about you men, you're afraid of juices."

We only got married because we were lonely and wanted to

have a house of our own. I was working at Penney's and he was
working at the White Swan Laundry. But he's a thing of my past.
An old sheet full of menstrual blood. A stubborn stain. Hot water
and blood don't mix. Anybody can tell you that.

What I wanted was a lover. Top of the line. Certified A-OK.
Not someone like Santiago "Chago" Talamantes, the last walking
wounded who'd crossed my path. Chago looked Asian, with a
long, droopy Fu Manchu mustache and eyelashes that always
pointed slightly downward. He had a headful of thick black hair,
my onetime god with his chiseled obsidian profile, his snarling,
sexy, upturned Pure Vato lips.

"Have you noticed that many Mejicanos look Japanese or Tibetan or Indian or Asian, Tere?" Irma asked me later that afternoon when she called to see if she could borrow my black shawl
that goes perfectly with her red dress. "They're a resounding case
for the world's long-standing mestizaje, the mixture of many people's blood."

"Come again, comadre?" I asked her. "What brought all this on
anyway?"

"I was thinking about Chago. I ran across some pictures of
the two of you. I was struck by his resemblance to the Dalai
Lama."

"Who?"

"He's only a World Holy Man, that's all. Exiled spiritual leader
of the Tibetan people."

That's how I came to learn about His Holiness the Dalai Lama
and how I really never wanted to hook up with Chago Talamantes
ever again no matter how handsome he was and no matter how
holy his roots were.

I had finally recovered from Chago, that psychic vampire, the
world's tallest Chicano, one who could barely spell his name,
hadn't I? At least I prayed so.

Dear God,
Help me find a good man
(Not too good.)
Someone who can talk.
(Not chat.)
Send me someone with cojones who likes to dance.
(Everyone knows that dancing can cover a multitude of sins.)

PS Oh, and don't let him have too much body hair.

La Tempestad

Later that evening La Wirms and I were squeezed into her tiny pink bathroom in full battle gear, ready for a night on the town.

¡Híjole! we looked good. I wore a short, tight, black imitation-leather skirt, black textured panty hose, a maroon tank top and long white tie-up boots, on sale from the White House in El Paso, sixty-five percent off. Irma had on her favorite red dress. La comadre has a beautiful bust. I should know, I've seen it unsheathed. The men are always coming on to her, but when she opens her mouth, most of them run away. She's more intelligent than most of the population of Cabritoville, El Paso, and Juárez combined. She says that there are so many mensos around here that she surely is Mensa material.

We stood so close to Irma's bathroom mirrors that they were fogged with our breath. I wiped one with a pink Kleenex and then pitched it into Wirms's fuzzy Pepto-Bismol-pink wastebasket. Irma has a thing about pink. As we traded places, Irma went for a long view in the big mirror over the washbasin, while I did a final close-up inspection of my face in the smaller medicine cabinet mirror, noticing that I hadn't plucked the black hair on the right side of my face. I motioned to Irma with a red-tipped Love's A'Popping-nail-polished finger, then pointed to my face. La comadre gingerly handed me a pair of tweezers without a word. That's what I love about La Wirms, she always knows what I'm thinking.

I had my usual Friday night doubts, and Irma knew it.

"Cabritoville's too small. It's a sad thing to realize that we're about to waste ourselves on a few mangy, played-out dogs at La Tempestad. I don't know why we spend every Friday and Saturday night there. Especially after you saw the Signs."

"You're the one who wants to go back."

"I thought it would cheer us up. Maybe someone new will walk in tonight."

"There isn't anyone new or alive who's walked through La Tempestad's doors since what's-his-name, the movie star, stopped there that one night to get a quick beer on his way to Santa Fe."

"What *was* his name?"

"He wasn't your type, Tere. Did you notice he was wearing clear nail polish?"

"Ay! You let me dance and then make out with him in the walkway behind the bar for about twenty minutes in between sets of Bennie and the Barrio Busters when you saw right off he was wearing clear polish!"

"I didn't approve of him the moment I set eyes on him. But you lost your head. Again. One minute you're sitting next to me tapping your feet to 'Mamá Sí Puedo' and the next minute I lose sight of you. I had no idea you were doing what you were doing in the hallway behind the bar. If I'd known, I would have dragged you home."

"I have to get out of this town."

"¡Ay, tú! I love it here. I'm not going anywhere else."

"Well, if you're not leaving, I'm not leaving."

"If I'm meant to find someone, and I'm not looking, he'll have to find me within the city limits. So why are we going out anyway?"

"I'm still in recovery from Chago Talamantes. The man wore my confidence down. I just wanted to see if I had any flickering of life left in me. And besides, I heard the band—Los Gatos del Sur—was good."

Irma teased her hair one last time, tugged at the waist of her red dress, adjusted the white strap of her brassiere up a notch and looked me in the eye.

"You ready, Tere? I'm ready. I'm turning off the lights. I'm driving, okay?"

"I tell you, Wirms, a woman just can't go out and dance a few cumbias and then come home without the gossips in the neighborhood getting all agüitadas and snarly-toothed and coming after you with their vindictive mental machetes and harsh words. Everyone in town—make that the fan club, make that Ofelia 'La Bitch' Contreras—is a busybody who has to know the down-and-ay-so-dirty chisme of everyone's lives except their own. Everyone knows exactly how many months after your parents married you were born. Everyone knows who your daddy's parents were, if they were good people or not, and to whom your mama lost her precious, coveted virginity and at what age, and also if the desgraciado was your dad. As a matter of course, everyone knows if you're sleeping with anyone on a regular basis. They probably even know if the sex is good or not."

"Cabritoville's a good place to live, Tere, and you know it," Irma said.

"That is, if you're married and have no sex life," I rejoined.

La Wirms pulled the long, fine pink hair of her Troll doll key chain into a point. "You and I have roots here that go so deep we'll never get away from them."

"That's what I'm afraid of, Wirms. Oh, I like Cabritoville enough. It's a good place to live if you're a vieja chismosa like Ofelia Contreras, who loves to talk about the lowlife she's married to who works at White Sands as a car mechanic, or if you're happily married and have kids in Little League and band and like to make banana crème pies in your spare time and your husband belongs to a bowling league like Sista Rocha. But for any woman who has the misfortune to be single and dating, Cabritoville is twenty years behind the times. The women still wear cat-eye glasses because they think they're 'in' and the men still use Brylcreem with water to keep their hair neat. A night out on the town is going to La Tempestad or the Dairy Queen to get a Dilly Bar."

Cabritoville would be more boring for me, too, if I weren't always part of the gossip. Ever since Reynaldo and I got a divorce, I'd been fair game for Ofelia Contreras, one of our fan club members, and her sidekick, Elisa Urista. According to them, I was the type who was always "de parranda," looking for a good time anytime, anywhere, and with anyone.

Maybe it's because my eyes are very light brown. Or because when I was in school I got mostly B's and some C's and won the award for Most Likely Not to Become a Nun. I'd like to see Ofelia and Elisa in thigh-highs dancing a 'lo todo dar to Los Gatos del Sur.

And yet, there's something dangerous and exciting about living on the "edge" in Cabritoville, though the "edge" at La Tempestad was little more than the same bit of frayed rug I trip on every time I'm there.

I heard an unpleasantly familiar voice in the darkness.

"Yoo-hoo, Tere, Preems!" Graciela called out as she came toward us, a bourbon and Coke in one hand.

Graciela hugged her cousin Irma for what seemed like half an hour. It's hard to imagine Irma is related to Graciela. I mean, like flesh and some blood. Downright unbelievable.

I tried to look the other way, but there was no place to hide. Besides, she had us trapped in front of the fishpond. I peered downward.

The fishpond is in the middle of what is called the Golden Sunset Room. It's home to one old leathery-looking goldfish that should by now have been poisoned by all the pennies people have pitched in there for good luck. Panfilo Zertuche, the tired old goldfish, named after our chief of police, "Tuche" Zertuche, was feeding on what looked like some old chile con queso by the looks of it.

La Tempestad was hopping when we got there. It was a Friday night and that in itself was reason to celebrate. Besides the regulars sitting in their usual spots in their familiar poses going over their all too common diatribes about guns, the state of America's youth, religion and the difference between Mexican-Americans, Chicanos and Latinos, there were two handsome cowboys dressed in hats and Western boots, one in a classy red-and-black shirt with silver lapels, the other in a dark-blue jean shirt with a mother-of-pearl belt buckle at the bar talking to Pollo, the bartender. His wild little mochito of hair in the middle of his chin gave him the appearance of a curious monkey.

It was still early and there was an air of expectation. Each time the door opened, everyone in La Tempestad turned to look. Tonight was the night to find Ms. Right or Mr. Wrong. Los Gatos del Sur slammed out a hot version of "El Rey" and that was about as good an entrance song as you can have in Cabritoville. The only disconcerting element was Graciela Vallejos, who stood in front of me, blocking my view of the room, the band and the two cute cowboys.

"I got a table for us near the band," Graciela said, turning to me.

"Near the band? Why not in a quiet corner so we can talk?" I answered with irritation.

"Now don't start up, Tere," Irma cautioned.

I hated to be seen with Graciela. She had the audacity to go up to men and ask them to dance with her. She could never just sit still in her seat that one, oh no, she had to jump up like an over-heated chihuahua and make a beeline for the most available-looking man. Sometimes he was the most unavailable man in the room, like Justice of the Peace Gallegos, sitting next to his jealous wife, Florinda, or a group of Iranian students from the university who sat across the room from us but whom we could smell all the way to the ladies' room behind the bar.

Graciela led Irma and me to the table. Someone whistled at us, and we turned around to see Munchie Mondragón, a former boyfriend of Graciela's, who was up on the stage with Los Gatos del Sur.

"Hey, Gracie!" he called out to Graciela, who ignored him.

"What are you doing up there, Munchie?" I shouted.

"I'm filling in for the guitarist. He got sick."

"Oh," I said, and waved. Munchie was around five feet four in his stocking feet and full of bar charm. Only in daylight did his faults become apparent. Graciela continued to ignore him and hurried around to her seat; it was evident that she had failed to get an extra chair for me. I had to weave this way and that way through a number of tables full of noisy drunks, all of whom I knew: Dolores Morales Duncan and her boring husband, Doug, Chepa Sosa and her sister, Angie, both of them hard-drinking spinsters, La Señora Vescovo and her son, Pepe, who looked terrified when I accidentally brushed his arm. When I got back to the table, Graciela had ordered drinks for herself and Irma, but not for me.

"Don't you love it, girlfriend?" Graciela said, turning to me. "La Tempestad. The atmosphere. The color, the noise."

"Atmosphere? You want atmosphere, Graciela?" I said. "Go to the Caverns Bar in Juárez. Now that's atmosphere."

I kept up a steady stream of conversation. Graciela had unfortunately jarred my memory.

"I used to go to the Caverns all the time with Chago. It was one of his favorite places. He wasn't a fancy type of guy, but he liked the elegance of those stalactites that hung down from the ceiling, the small round tables with candles and the bowl of gardenias that the waiter would bring us. Yeah, ole Chago, he loved nothing better than being there at the Caverns with all of Juárez and El Paso and Cabritoville swirling outside those fake, built-up, gold, stone walls. The small cloakroom which looked like something out of a Humphrey Bogart movie in which a woman comes to your table selling cigarettes in a wooden box she carries around her neck. Now *that's* atmosphere. What you have here, at La Tempestad, is the sad side of three desperate women who should be in their pajamas at home watching *The Tonight Show Starring Johnny Carson.*"

"Have you looked at those gardenias in daylight, Tere?" Graciela sneered. "They're all old and brown. Some atmosphere you're talking about. I'd hate to see that place in daylight. Probably full of cockroach casings."

"What the hell is a cockroach casing, Graciela?"

"The shell that a cockroach leaves behind when he molts or sheds or whatever he does when he leaves his whatever behind. You can smell them."

"I'm going to the ladies' room, anyone want to come?" Irma said, getting up. I could tell she was ready to go home, and we'd just gotten there.

"The Caverns isn't all it's made out to be, Tere. It's like illusion."

"Hey, I like illusion," I said.

"You would. The worst thing about the Caverns is that on top of its wilted gardenias and fake stalactites, you have to climb all the way up a rickety flight of stairs to go wee-wee where you're forced to read the writing on the stall doors. Chuy y Lucha. Chuy y Margarita. Chuy is a Puto."

"Check out the bathroom walls here at La Tempestad: La Gracie y el Munchie Forever."

"Very funny, Tere," Graciela said. She lunged at the nachos cart that was passing by, bringing two heaping plates of nachos back to the table.

I couldn't stand the smell of grease, but Graciela snarfed the chips down with relish. She was happy, I could tell. She was her

old, usual resongando self. Criticize this, bitch about that. She reminded me of certain fan club members, Ofelia Contreras, Elisa
Urista, Margarita Hinkel, to name the worst.

But where was La Wirms when you needed her? I strode up to
the bar to order myself a drink.

"Tere Ávila! What'll it be?"

"Give me a minute, Pollo," I said as I leaned on the bar, my
body angled toward a revolving silver globe that mirrored dancing
couples flashing by, wild swirls of constant color and movement. I
kept time to the throbbing, pumping rhythm of Los Gatos.

A large, middle-aged woman almost lost her footing near the
pond and tipped forward, a full plate of nachos in her hand. She
caught herself in time, but dunked the plate into the murky water.
When she lifted it up, it was devoid of food, washed clean.

I laughed at the poor woman and caught a glimpse of myself in
the large gold mirror behind the long wooden bar which reflected
the entire room, and what I would call early Mejicano Mercado
bar decor: lots of old serapes from the market in Juárez made into
accordions that fanned out on the walls, neon Budweiser and
Coors signs (they knew about the boycott, but didn't care as long
as they sold beer), and a mishmash of old stained sombreros,
posters of Baby Gaby and Al Hurricane, a signed photo of Trini
López and one of Willie Nelson with a crew cut, photographs of
Tino "El Cuate" Sotero, the owner, with his wife and kids, Tino
with the mayor, Tino in the dark black suit, red sash and white
feather headdress of the Knights of Columbus, Tino as a pilgrim
at the Basilica of Our Lady of Guadalupe in Méjico, Tino at Cae-
sars Palace in Las Vegas.

Pollo was mixing his special concoction, something he called
the Devil's Machete, for Graciela, a woman who could drink any
man under the table.

I felt a tingling in my body. I knew I looked good in my white
boots.

Double-stepping his way close to me with a bobbing turkey
gait, Tuche spun his ruca round and round, then pulled her in
close as they segued into a slow and sexy version of "Mujer." His

wife, La Vivi, peered over his shoulder to flirt with Simón "El Squeaky" Suárez, who worked at the courthouse. El Squeaky was a good dancer and that's what kept him still running around the stockyard.

I stood at the bar for about twenty minutes talking to Pollo about the merits of pulque.

"You see, Tere, gringos don't understand high unadulterated sugar content the way we do. Look around you, you can see Raza going back and forth between the two tastes, sugar and salt. Gringos are babies in pañales when it comes to sweet and sticky, not to mention rubbery and slippery. I'm talking pulque here. That's where gringos really are babies. They're afraid of the slime factor that makes pulque the medicinal almost-psychedelic natural drug it is."

During that time, Pollo sent several Machetes to Graciela along with numerous glasses of water with a twist of lemon to Irma.

Graciela worked as a cashier at the post office and no Machete ever kept her down the day after. Liquor never seemed to faze her. She could drink and drink and still find energy to cumbia up a storm to anything Los Gatos del Sur dished out.

I drank a couple of Tecates and after the last one I remembered I hadn't eaten lunch. From far away I heard my own high voice reverberate against the walls of my super-elevated consciousness as I moved in the direction of the women's rest room.

"Hit me with your best shot, Pollo. A Black Russian!"

The long walkway behind the bar which led to the rest rooms was crowded with photos of Tino and his family. A large, overweight man washed his hands in a sink in the middle of the walkway that smelled of urine. He nodded to me and I moved on. He had asked me to dance earlier and I refused.

When I got back to the table Graciela looked at me, all bug-eyed and unpleasant. She hadn't changed in the two weeks I felt I had been gone.

"So when did you start drinking Black Russians?" Graciela asked me.

"Since when I got sick of Cuba Libres and Daiquiris, that's when."

"I don't know how you can drink those sweet drinks," Graciela said, squinching her nose like someone had secretly let out a pedo at the table.

"Look, don't get all critical with me, Graciela Vallejos. I don't know how you can drink all those Machetes. And while I'm at it, I've been meaning to ask you, how could you dance with that foreign student during the whole second set last week? I could smell him from here. You came back apestando like a goat."

"Are you calling me a cabrona, Tere Ávila Ambriz?" Graciela huffed.

"No, I wasn't. All I said was that your boyfriend smelled."

"It was Popeye Rosales and his brother, Wimpy, who were the real culprits. They'd been working in their father's dairy earlier that day and hadn't washed up."

"Okay," Irma said, and meant it as she moved to sit between us. "Will the two of you stop before you get started?"

"My boyfriend, I wish, Tere! That wasn't Fayed, that was Wimpy you smelled. Wimpy bumped into us on the dance floor. Fayed smelled like English Leather. We made a date to meet here tonight. He's going to bring his friend Mohammed."

"Oh, no, you don't, Graciela. Don't you be sticking me with any blind dates."

"Since when are you such a pendeja, Tere?" Graciela said, ordering another Machete from Lupe, who was making the rounds taking drink orders.

"Well, so I am a cabrona. I live in Cabritoville, don't I? The problem with you, Graciela Vallejos, is that you're too desperate to find a man, with that bug-eyed scan you have when you're scoping out single men. Irma, if I ever have that look, shoot me."

"Come on, you two, make up. Graciela, tell her you're sorry!" Irma implored, trying to make peace. She hoisted up my tank top, which was slipping down on the left side.

"Thanks, Wirms," I purred. I was feeling no pain.

"The least you can do is meet Mohammed," Graciela whined, pushing her chair away from the table.

"I do not date strangers," I told her firmly.

"Fayed had really white teeth. I told him so, and he said if you think I'm handsome, you should see Mohammed. Mohammed was a model in Paris, but he decided to get a degree in agriculture at State and then go back to Iran and help his people. He and Fayed are like brothers."

"How about we call it quits tonight, Irma?" I said with disgust.

I could see that the evening was going nowhere. The two chulito cowboys left suddenly and all the fresh air they blew in was now filled with stale cigarette smoke.

"Let's throw in the old toalla. I haven't put out the garbage. And besides no one has asked us to dance. It's like dead here," I said, getting up to leave.

"Why don't you stay with me, Preems, I'll take you home later," Graciela urged Irma.

"I have to drive Tere home, Prima. I brought my car," Irma said, grabbing her purse.

"Call her a cab, Preems," Graciela said, looking straight at me with her twisted Looney Tune eyes. She pulled Irma's purse from her and held it to her chest.

"I'm not going to call my comadre a cab, Graciela. No, I think we should all leave together. Now give me my purse," Irma said.

"Women don't hang out at bars alone, Graciela. It doesn't look good. Numbers, that's what you want," I said, trying to rationalize with her. "And besides, who's here? There's Louie 'El Baboso,' Jimmy Twitlinger, aged setenta y pico with a bum leg, Mysterious Carl, who sits in the corner near the men's room by himself, Popeye and Wimpy, old Juan Galván, in his cast from his car accident, who else? A few other tipos who look like they just came in from the Alaskan Pipeline."

"I don't see why you can't wait a little while, Tere. Fayed should be here soon. After all I've done for you!" Graciela was throwing a tantrum there at the table and people were starting to notice. I motioned for all of us to sit down.

"Like what?" I whispered vehemently. "Irma and I are always

dragging our sad butts around because you won't leave the bars until after last call."

"You'll be sorry, Tere. Mohammed could be the one for you. I mean, maybe not forever, but for a little while," Graciela said, trying to appease me. It wouldn't work.

"If I was really looking, I wouldn't be *here* at La Tempestad, Graciela. Who did we ever meet here that *mattered*. I mean, *really*."

"Irma *did* meet Sal. They *did* have a great love."

"Yeah, and then he died. Better she'd never met him. I told her to stay away from truckers. They'll only break your heart."

And with that, Irma burst into tears. It *really* was time to leave. I grabbed Irma's purse from Graciela and handed her a tissue. Sal was a trucker Irma met several years ago at La Tempestad. They had fallen in love. But then Sal had died.

"I'm sorry, Irma," I said apologetically. I hadn't meant to hurt her.

We never spoke of Sal, that was our unspoken rule.

They were going to get married. If he hadn't died. A big man like him allergic to bees. It's a story out of *The Enquirer*. He was trying to clear out a nest when they attacked. Afterward, the Animal Control people weighed in twenty-two pounds of bees that had been responsible.

"You okay, Wirms?" I asked sheepishly. She was tough, no two ways about it. Most women would never have recovered from the blows life had dealt La Wirma.

"I'm driving," Irma said at last.

"Oooh, look at that cute guy across the room." Graciela pointed toward the entrance.

"That's Wimpy, Graciela. Put your glasses on, girl. When Wimpy starts looking good to you, it's time to call it a night. So let's go already, Wirms. Give me the keys, comadre, I'm driving."

"That isn't Wimpy, Tere. Sheesh, I know who Wimpy is! I'm talking about the guy in the tight jeans. He's standing next to the Budweiser sign."

"Let me put my glasses on. Shit, girl, I just got prescription bifocals. So who are you talking about?"

I put on my glasses and had a good long look.

"Oh. Ohhh. The short guy in the very tight jeans that hug his huevitos like a mother hen nests an egg? I don't know him. I've never seen him before. No, he's definitely never been to La Tempestad. Do you know him, Graciela?"

"Would I be pointing him out if I knew him, Tere? If I knew him I'd be across the room now instead of talking to you."

"Do you know him, Irma?"

"Him? Oh, that's Lucio Valadez."

"Lucio Valadez!" Graciela and I said it at the same time. I knew about him, she didn't.

"That's Lucio Valadez?" I said with surprise. "The last time I saw him he was in junior high. So where has he been?"

"Away," Irma responded.

"Away, I know. But where away? Mmm-mmm," I said, scanning every inch of his tight little cuerpito. "I don't know *that* Lucio Valadez. I knew a skinny runty-assed kid who got sent away to the military school in Socorro."

"He's married, Tere. Maybe he's separated, I forget, and he has a daughter," Irma said. "He lives in El Paso."

"Okay. So let's go, Irma. I'm tired. It's been a long week." I said, wanting to stay, knowing I should leave.

"Every week is too long for you, Tere. The problem with you is that you don't know how to have fun," Graciela said in that drippy, catty critical-assed way of hers.

"Dammit, Graciela! You call coming to La Tempestad every Friday and Saturday night looking for available men and seeing Wimpy and Popeye trying to get it on with some stupid pendeja who doesn't know how jodidos they are, fun? Let's go. I'm driving, Irma."

"No me chingas, girlfriend. Los Gatos del Sur haven't even played 'Tiburón' yet and you're making me leave. Some friend you are, Tere Ávila!"

"Let's get out of here, Irma," I said, taking her arm.

"Ponte águila, Tere, peel those big brown eyes of yours because the man of your dreams might just be about ready to come up to you and say, 'Orale, chula. You want to dance, babes?' And where the hell will you be? Putting out your garbage!"

"Don't start in, Graciela. It's late. And Tere's right, we have to go," Irma said with finality.

"Ay, pues, if my Preems wants to leave, we'll leave. I'll follow you in my car. But, chihuahua, Tere, the night is still young for the very young!"

Graciela stuck her tongue out at me and turned one of her eyelids inside out like the boys used to do in grade school, with the eyelashes flipped inward.

"Remind you of junior high, girl?" Graciela said in that haughty way of hers.

"I'm going home, Irma, you coming?" I said with disgust.

"Of course I'm coming, Tere," Irma said. "We brought my car. And I'm driving. I have the keys." The Troll doll was doing his little twirly let's-go-home dance.

"Ay, mamá, Los Gatos are starting up with Tiburón. 'Tiburón, Tiburón, Tiburón, Tiburón.' I can't leave now, I just can't. 'Tiburón, Tiburón'!" Graciela got up, threw off her silk overshirt and headed toward the dance floor.

To Graciela Vallejos, nothing ever mattered more than dancing to "Tiburón." She just had to shake those flat nalgas, piernas galgas and hacky-sack chichis of hers to her favvvorrrittte song! "Tiburón. Tiburón, Tiburón, Tiburón." Pobrecita! She had no dignity whatsoever. I watched the girl shake those Jell-O-jointed limbs of hers as she sashayed herself as close as she could to Mr. Huevos. It was as disgusting a display as I have ever seen.

Irma and I looked at each other. We were stuck in the Golden Sunset Room of Tino's La Tempestad Lounge, at least until the end of "Tiburón." Another Friday night in Cabritoville, U.S.A.

My Thirties

That was last week.

Tonight my mom got sick and asked me to give her rollo at the Cursillo she was attending.

A Cursillo is like a popular underground religious movement within the Catholic Church, a grassroots weekend retreat sort of thing that's really taken off with La Chicanada. A rollo is a plática, a spiritual talk. My mom's talk was on charity.

"Can you go in my place, m'ija, and read my rollo?" Albinita asked weakly. I didn't have the heart to tell her no.

"I won't know anybody there, Mom."

"Sure, you will," she said. "You know my comadre Ermelinda, she's a friendly face."

Yeah, like a mummy from Guanajuato.

"And there's Ubaldo. You know Ubaldo."

"Ubaldo Miranda? Member of the Pedro Infante Club de Admiradores #256? *That* Ubaldo? He goes to Cursillos?"

"He serves the wine at Mass. He's a deacon."

He's a closet alcoholic, I thought. He's gay and his boyfriend, Mr. Cornubia, runs the Dairy Queen. Also, he's one of my sometime best friends. But I didn't have the heart to tell Albinita anything. After all, she *was* my mother.

"He's very devout. El mismo Cristo. He looks like Christ with his dark beard."

More like an anemic, spindly-assed version of Kris Kristofferson with long random pelitos here and there, clumping to simulate a beard on a nonexistent chin. But who was I to argue with my mother, a living saint?

"I wish you would think about God sometime, Tere. He thinks of you."

✹

I went to the Cursillo. I had to.

The meeting was held in an old parish hall with yellow linoleum. Early garage sale decor. A framed poster of God in the famous Salman painting, the glass cracked, in an ugly wooden frame, a handmade retablo of the Sacred Heart of Jesus surrounded by barbed wire, two curling prints of San José and what could have been either St. Anthony or St. Jude, a very old statue of San Martín de Porras, his saintly black face chipped and showing white ceramic underneath. A set of hand-painted Stations of the Cross made by someone with their hands tied behind their back. A number of six-foot folding tables formed a giant U. I sat in the back near the door, beside a leaky swamp cooler. Behind me on the wall was a stack of holy cards. I picked one up and read it.

PRAYER OF ST. TERESA

Christ has no body on earth but yours.
No hands but yours.
No feet but yours.

Yours are the eyes through which must look out
Christ's compassion on the world.

Yours are the feet with which
He is to go about doing good.

Yours are the hands with which
He is to bless people now.

Oh shit. I had to get out of there, and fast.

A small older woman wearing a tattered mantilla seemed to be
in charge. She motioned me forward. That was my undoing. It
was going to be hard to escape.

All sorts of overheated middle-aged women around me were
talking in tongues. Suddenly, from out of nowhere appeared three
women who surrounded me. One of them was La Comadre Ermelinda, who took my arm and led me up to the altar. She whispered something about a testimonio. I tried to pull away but the
two other celestial bodyguards had me cornered. A tall, rangy-
looking woman was wearing a De Colores T-shirt and kept repeating the words, "Thank you, Jesus." All eyes on me now, I coughed,
then sputtered that I was Albinita Ávila's daughter. This led to another round of sha-na-na'ing and "Praise you, Jesus." I moved
away to protestations from Ermelinda and a heavyset woman who
looked vaguely familiar. I found a nearby folding chair and
plopped down. One of the bodyguards tried to put her hands on
my head in prayer, striking out any latent demons. "No, no," I repeated, as I slunk down in my seat. There was a communal sigh of
disappointment. Everyone had expected more from the daughter
of Albinita Ávila.

The air was sticky-sweet with the sweat of damp women in a
state of heightened religious ecstasy. It got to me, especially since
I wasn't sure what I believed in. I was mad at God, and God was
cold and indifferent to me.

It turns out I knew more than a few people, but they weren't
what I call friends. They were mostly old ladies, friends of my
mom, who needed the maleness of God because they were losers,

all of them, divorced, single or in bad marriages, with husbands who drank and knocked them around every weekend after the bars let out at two, or who had sons who rifled through their purses for drug money.

The black-lace-covered gnome accosted me with eyes that said you are not worthy, heathen bitch, to read your sacred mother's talk to us, the divine elect. Someone with a thick accent, Hermana Somebody-Don't-You-Think-I'm-Holy, finally read the rollo.

I got up as quietly as I could but I accidentally knocked over my metal folding chair. Ermelinda motioned for me to stay. I looked around desperately and then coughed. I pointed to my throat. She nodded. Sore throat? Yes, I mimed. Too bad, her eyes said. Yes, I thought, too bad. I tiptoed my way out to the back, stopping in the bathroom to check my makeup. My eyeliner was smeared. I put on some fresh lipstick.

So who do I end up with later that evening? Graciela. Like a sleepwalker, I later found myself heading toward La Tempestad. It couldn't be helped, could it? A homing pigeon, that's me. Tere "S.H.P." Ávila. Stupid Homing Pigeon. Nothing better to do than end up at the Golden Sunset Room.

"I'm dropping dead, girlfriend, it's La Tere. Hey, Tere, put out your garbage yet?" La Tuerta called out.

I didn't have the heart to ever make fun of that skewed look of hers, those eyes that wandered off, as if looking for spiritual or at least physical consolation from some force around the corner, just out of range of her vision. Just once, just once I wanted to look her straight in the eye, one or the other, both if I could, and tell the twisted bitch to lay off, lay low, just lay down and die! But I couldn't. She was almost kin. Or at least kin of almost kin, making her, dammit, kin!

Graciela and La Wirms were sitting at a table with three men. Graciela proved herself right in at least one thing in her life. Mohammed was probably the most handsome man I'd ever seen up to that point in my life. Handsome? He made Omar Sharif look like week-old menudo. Like lengua left out in the hot sun. Like queso fundido con moscas.

I started my thirties doe-eyed, moon-faced and full of expectation. The men were dreamy, lazy-boned, half-cooked meat on a spit, without expectations. Some were good, some were bad, some were good and bad and some were just BAAAADDDD, meaning Good.

When I think of my so-called youth, I think of strobe lights and restless energy. I have an image of Graciela, Irma and me sitting there at our usual table near the band, watching the front door for a clue, some sign to see if we should stay or run. We're waiting to see if someone would be coming in shortly, to carry us away to a better life.

Later, no one special having come through that heavy door, I can feel myself lurching down the dark hallway of La Tempestad, like a newborn calf, all snorty and trembly-legged.

My goal was nearly always the rest room, but it seemed two miles away, as I bounded forward in that drunken stride that takes you so far you feel you've overstepped your own self and gotten there before you have any right to. Your other self will stand there in front of you as the slow self comes up, wondering at the other self who stands there, so proud and defiant.

Every week I swung the door open to the women's pale yellow bathroom at La Tempestad, peered into the dimly lit room, then reeled forward, propelled by some unseen force. In slow motion I rolled toward the one toilet stall that had a door. I seemed to float down, then woke up as I landed with a hard plop on the chipped ceramic seat. I grunted and thought: never again. I really didn't like drinking or getting drunk, so why did I do it? Why? Every time was the last time, I swore to myself, cursing the owner, Tino Sotero, for never having enough toilet paper.

My time in the bathroom seemed eternal, a charade of slow-motion gestures, ludicrous actions barely completed. My face in the cracked mirror was flushed, my cheeks were red, my lips pursed in anticipation, of what I wasn't sure. Eventually I left the safe harbor of this nocturnal nest, a newborn reeling out into the world, with dreams from the womb life of the unborn innocent. A nearby couple two-stepped to a slow clingy waltz, the kind that lovers love, as mismatched pairs of bodies rubbed and undulated against each other, eel pastry, empanada de anguilas, in the dim, sexually charged ambiente of the only place Cabritovillians could taste the forbidden fruit, on the other side of a man-made pond, in the deepest recess of the Chihuahuan desert, a place untamed and free.

I always was ahead of my time. Or so the guy thought who once asked me to dance at Jasmine's Quinceañera. Jasmine is Irma's favorite niece. I'm talking about the guy who averted his eyes when he talked to me. We were dancing to "Behind Closed Doors," and I noticed he was all nervous and sweaty-handed.

"How can you look in people's eyes? Aren't you, like, embarrassed?" he asked.

"What? I can't hear you."

"Isn't it hard to look in people's eyes? I haven't ever met anyone who looked into my eyes the way you look into my eyes. It's scary. Why are you looking into my eyes?"

The guy's name was Sonny. Have you ever noticed that the most popular nickname for Chicano boys and men these days is Butch or Sonny? "Hey, Butch!" "Where's Sonny?" "Have you seen Butch and Sonny?"

Butch is a name that doesn't come easily to Chicanos and yet you find at least one Butch or Sonny in every Chicano family. It's not surprising that men who can't look you in the eye are named Butch or Sonny. But sometimes when men are looking straight at you, they're not seeing you either . . .

At thirty, you somehow think things are going to be different. You think you've already played out the old tired hand of being single, gone through all the deadbeat boyfriends, the crazy lovers, the creeps. You've already spent half your waking life in the dark of the Golden Sunset Room of Tino's La Tempestad Lounge during countless unhappy Happy Hours and what seems like every Friday and Saturday night since you were in pañales sipping watered-down rum and Cokes. You've just about decided to never drink a Cuba Libre or a Daiquiri again, ever. You can't tolerate the taste of rum or vodka or even tequila (which is probably the last taste to go). You think if you ever have to sit at a table again with Irma and her man-hungry tuerta cousin, Graciela Vallejos, one brown eye going this way, the other half-green going that way, looking desperately for a Man—you might just as well walk out to Highway 478 and lie down on the road until someone with a flatbed of jalapeños comes by to run you over.

You're a deer caught in the headlights of that mating hunger. It's a terrible and degrading place to be if you're a woman in her thirties who's attractive and intelligent and still cruising the bars. Irma and I never had the look that Graciela had, eager and too full of wild desperation, driven by the idea that a man, any man would bring her happiness.

There are too many stories, too many dreary endings, too many men, young, old, inexperienced, experienced. Mama's boys, boys without mamas, men who could dance, men who couldn't and flung their sad bodies around like insects stuck with invisible pins. Pobrecitos. And pobrecita me, I can see that swinging door flapping open to a dingy room full of muted yellow light. That was me in my thirties.

The Big P

The next time I saw Lucio Valadez he was strutting his way across the cafeteria of Cabritoville Elementary School in straight-leg jeans so tight they could have been sprayed on over a pair of dyed pigskin Luccheses.

Holding a tray of tacos, beans, fruit salad, a carton of chocolate milk and a clown cookie, he moved through the heavy, child-thick air. I thought to myself: If Pedro Infante were here at this very moment in the cafeteria of Cabritoville Elementary School holding a tray of tacos, beans, fruit salad, a carton of chocolate milk and a clown cookie, that's exactly how he would walk.

Confident, without fear. Puro chingón.

At least until he got to the folding metal tables where the third graders were sitting. He bent down, straddled the low bench where his daughter Andrea was finishing her clown cookie and milk, the tacos and beans untouched. Lucio's Luccheses came up in the air as he almost tipped his tray over in an attempt to slide into the childproof seating. He landed on the dark linoleum with a thud. I was doing duty as assistant cashier for a Parents' Day luncheon, an annual ritual founded some years back by the principal, Mr. Perea. Andrea had come in earlier and found her way to her class table, without the company of either parent.

Lucio was late, as most children were happily beside one or both of their parents.

When her father arrived, Andrea seemed surprised, momentarily delighted, and then her face turned dark. She was pouting. I couldn't hear what he said to her or what she answered; the cafeteria was a din of children's voices, with an undercurrent of parental admonitions: "Aren't you going to eat your food?" "Why did you eat dessert first?" And "Watch it, watch it, you're going to spill your milk."

I liked the way Lucio seemed to move into Andrea, one of those smooth-slidy maneuvers where a child doesn't even know she is being led. He chucked her under the chin playfully, then tickled her under the nose. She broke out into a broad grin, and as she did, Lucio brought out something from his pocket. I couldn't see what it was, but Andrea's face filled with joy. She hugged her father hard and he hugged her back, holding her for a moment. It reminded me of the tender moment in *Los Tres Huastecos* where Pedro the bandit brother is putting his child to sleep. He goes into the other room, but she keeps calling him in; to bring her water, to tell her a story, you name it, all those ploys kids use to keep themselves from falling asleep.

I could see Andrea and Lucio go round and round with their familiar, well-loved game, he encouraging her to eat, she refusing, he prodding her a little more, she pulling away, he cajoling her, she reneging a little, he promising her the moon, the stars and some candy or a toy, and she, relenting at last, taking a few paltry bites. When she did, he beamed to the invisible crowd in the Cabritoville cafeteria, an imaginary audience of hundreds who knew he was the proud father of the one and only and deeply loved Andrea Valadez, the world's most perfect and beautiful child, destiny's princesa, who looked more like his side of the family than her poor mother's. And it was she, and she alone, who would be the only true love of his life.

I saw him look at her the way I wished my father had looked at me. They were so happy, so complete unto themselves. And it was then, with that love stretched between them, like invisible wires, that I resolved to find someone who would love me that way, the way Lucio loved Andrea, a 'lo todo you are my sunshine. My only sunshine. Someone who loved the brat and the woman that child had become.

When lunch was over and the bell rang, a harsh sentinel calling us back to our other lives, I saw Lucio take Andrea's small hand in his own, see her move into him and hug him as if she were saying goodbye forever. He smoothed her soft blondish hair out of her face, the way a lover would, and kissed her softly on the forehead, the way Pedro the bandit kissed his daughter, reckless rebel that she was, holding her as close as he could, before the world and all the other women in it intervened.

It was then I fell in love with Lucio Valadez.

If I'd known then that years later I'd still be a floating educational assistant, I would have stuck out typing with Miss Baeza.

When you "play the field" in Cabritoville, the field is pretty rough terrain. After a while, you're branded with a Big A, or in my culture, a Big P, for Puta.

I've mentioned all the dreary, bleary-eyed nights at La Tempestad. What I haven't told you about is *why* I hooked up with Lucio.

I could give you the short answer, that I was jodida by birth, but that's too simple. The long answer has to do with who I am, and where I live.

My mother had two brothers, Santos and Onelio, the one who died from his World War II injuries. Santos was married, but he didn't have any children. My father, Quirino, died of nothing. Albinita just found him dead in bed one morning. He might have had a heart attack or a stroke, it's hard to say. No one did autopsies in 1955, at least not in my neighborhood. The only autopsies were the ones we kids did on dead animals we'd find in the street. Smashed frogs, grasshoppers with missing legs, a blackbird without eyes, that sort of thing.

"Quirino! Who made up your father's name, Tere?" Irma asked me often.

"Just what's so dang unusual about my family, Irma? What about your family, them and their crazy names, your sister Pio, 'short for Pioquinta,' and of course, your brother Arthur, nicknamed Chichi, and his son, Chichito, little Arthur. What about your cousins, Gloria Cebolla and Kika Mota?"

It's a relief not to have any sisters or brothers—too many people to worry about. I mean, if they were people you really liked and agreed with, or even had anything in common with, that would be a different matter. But let's face it, most of us have nothing in common with our relatives. I mean, I'd sooner trust a stranger than a relative when it comes down to it. Don't ask me why. Maybe because I've seen the hell Irma has had to go through.

I'm grateful I have a small family, because I have fewer people to disappoint me. And, in turn, I have fewer people to disappoint. The people I call immediate family I have come to terms with, and I have forgiven them. Or at least I am still trying. It hasn't been easy. I realized some years ago that I had to free them to free myself. I released Quirino, my dad, for dying and leaving me and Albinita.

I should probably forgive my grandparents, all dead, as well as all the antepasados while I'm at it, for giving us the genes that made us putas and cabrones.

And then I should thank them for giving us the healthy genes that made us dream ourselves to be better, stronger and more loving than we are.

Forgiveness isn't something that comes overnight—unless you want it to. Most of us have to plod through the mierda to finally come around that maldita rincón.

Me, I'm working on forgiving my first husband, Reynaldo. Not for leaving me, but for being mean in the leaving. There isn't too much to tell you about my history other than the broken record of hurt, forgive and try to forget, hurt, forgive and try to forget.

The only real family I have, besides Albinita and Irma, are the members of the Pedro Infante Club de Admiradores Norteamericano #256. And the characters of Pedro's movies, whom Irma and I know as well as or better than we do our own kin.

Irma and I keep the names and descriptions of all the characters of Pedro's sixty-three movies, some of them shorts, with a synopsis of each movie listed in a red notebook, and we compare notes.

For a while now, Irma and I have been studying the Blond Factor in Pedro's movies. One day I started noticing that most of the heroines and leading ladies were rubias, blonds real or not real, but blonds. That's not to say Mejicanas aren't or can't be blond. There are many, many blonds who are Mejicanas. But Mexican-American blonds are suspect to me, and I can tell a dyed-blond Mexican-American any day of the week.

I need to start doing a blond count in Pedro's movies.

In *Los Tres Huastecos*, even the little daughter is blond.

I love *Los Tres Huastecos*. It's one of Pedro's sweetest movies.

Plot:

Pedro plays triplets. One of them is a priest, one of them is a military man and the other is a cardplaying, tequila-swigging, no-good no-account rascal with a blond three-year-old daughter who turns out to be okay in the end, but not before a lot of fraternal cross-dressing.

Analysis:

Now that I think about it, there are tons of blonds in Pedro's movies. You do see women with dark hair, a number of them, but it's the blonds who dominate.

But something else happens in *La Mujer Que Yo Perdí*. María, La Indita, whose father was Pedro's grandfather's manservant, is a full-blooded Indita and speaks in Nahuatl. She falls in love with Pedro, whose name is Pedro in the movie. Pedro is hiding out after being falsely accused of murder. Pedro, of course, is in love with a rich blond who lives in town. Well, I could tell from the beginning that a possible romance with María would never work. La Indita is of another class; she should stick to her jealous Indito boyfriend. It's not surprising that she steps in front of a speeding bullet meant for Pedro and then dies in his arms. La Indita had to die; she wasn't blond. Which is pretty ratty.

"You can learn so much about Mejicano culture, class structure, the relationships between men and women, women and women, men and men, as well as intergenerational patterns of collaterality in Pedro's movies," says Irma.

"What was that, comadre?"

"The movies tell you what Mejicanos embrace and reject in their lives," she translates for me.

La Wirms will always be my teacher, I know that. I love the fact that she says all the things in my mind that I can never verbalize. When I hear her talk, it's like I hear myself talking if I could talk the way she talks.

"You and I should have a Ph.D. from watching Pedro's movies, Tere. We know more about Raza than Raza. If I ever go back to school it's to get a degree in Mejicano culture. Then we could teach little Mejicanitos with brown faces who can't speak Spanish, and little gabachitos who do, what it means to be Mejicanos. And Mejicanas. And, in turn, to be human."

"Híjole, Wirms, you said it, girl. If everyone understood what culture really is, we'd be so much better off."

When Reynaldo Ambriz, my phantom hubby, left for Pico Rivera, California, to see what he could do out there in the laundry industry, I stuck it out at Penney's for a few more years until I just couldn't stand the housewares department any longer. Then I saw an ad in the paper for a cashier at Tafoya's House of Tile. I thought to myself: I can do that. I had cashier experience and I've always liked handling money. I took myself over there to Tafoya's and got the job. I stayed there a good five years until Mr. Tafoya had a heart attack and his widow decided to shut down the business. The Tafoyas were good to me, and Mrs. T. gave me a letter of recommendation to the Cabritoville schools, attention her cousin Emilia, who, it turned out, was retiring in June as a Bilingual Ed teacher.

When the House of Tile closed I found myself in the school office talking with the principal, Mr. Perea, who knew my dad. I wasn't a college graduate, but my lineage was credential enough. That's how I got a job as an educational assistant.

I go in every day at 8 a.m. and leave about 2:30 p.m. The hours are good, and the pay is okay, just a little less than the House of Tile, but it doesn't matter. I live in a one-horse-two-dog-mangy-one-cat town in a little house next to my mother's bigger house. I don't have to pay rent, and I can go over to her place and eat anytime I want. If I get to school early, I'll have a cup of coffee with the kitchen crew: Uvalia, Dora, Nancy, Felia and La Chole. We'll sit around, have a glazed doughnut and talk about men. Do you want one? Do you have one? Do you need another one? Why?

"I don't know why you and those women you work with spend so much time talking about men," Irma said over what had once been a full plate of enchiladas Christmas style at Sofia's Mighty Taco.

"We have fun," I countered. "And besides, what else is there to talk about?"

"How about art, culture, literature? All most women do is talk about men. Have you ever stopped to think how boring that is,

Tere? Why can't we talk about ourselves for a while? What we want, what we dream, independent of and apart from men?"

"You're in one of your moods. I can tell."

"I want to end this meal in peace. The world doesn't revolve around men, as much as you think it does. Pass me a napkin and let it rest, Tere. How's school?"

"I had a sixth grader at school tell me her fourteen-year-old boyfriend wants sex. She kept saying how big he was. Big? Well, I knew right then and there she'd already had sex with him. I told her to forget him."

"So you're giving out advice, are you? Since when do you have the credentials?"

"I have a degree in living, comadre."

"I guess you do, Tere," Irma said, laughing and wiping her mouth. "So are you ready, or what? Let's go. I have to get to the Flying W. I'm doing the books there now."

"That seedy-assed motel run by that tall albino gringo?"

"I assume you're talking about Mr. Wesley."

"Is he the W of the Flying W?"

"He's very nice, Tere. But you wouldn't know a nice man if he bit you on the ass."

"No nice man ever bit me on the ass. That's what I'm talking about."

"Give me the check, comadre. It's my turn. You can take me out to Dairy Queen for a Blizzard after the next fan club meeting."

Now, I have to say that when I hit Cabritoville Elementary I didn't know the workings of a child's mind, but I came to know and respect kids. Talk about deductive minds. They can scope out caca before you can say what did you say, and they're honest in ways that adults aren't. If you have bad breath, a child will tell you. There's no deception with kids, no lies, no don't look in my eyes, you're making me nervous.

I also want to debunk your understanding of the macho/macha myth here once and for all. Maybe then you can leave me alone at the enchilada dinner when you come up and whisper to me about what I should do, shouldn't do, or how I live my life. A small town like Cabritoville is full of too many old goats, male and female. I want to go on record saying that to be macho/macha isn't so bad, sometimes. That's if you're macho or macha in the right way. That's if you look at the Mejicano definition of macho. Macho for Mejicanos has to do with strength and pride and ability to carry out responsibility. It doesn't have to do with what the English language has done to a people.

In English, macho means demanding, unbending, chauvinistic, condescending and downright ugly. My culture has suffered from too much translation. That's why we have a generation of Chicanos named Butch and Sonny, and a generation of Jennifer Maries, Vanessas and Shirley Anns. What happened to all the beautiful women's names in Spanish for children? Neria. Esmeralda. María de La Luz. Angela de La Paz. Reina. Altagracia.

Just listen to the music of those names and you'll know what I'm talking about. If we've created a generation of super-stud Coors drinkers and forget-the-boycott grape eaters and half-baked Hispanic party boys, we've also created their partners, women with sculpted hair, artificial bodies and giant nails, wearing ironed jeans from the Popular Department Store, all answering to names like Kimberly Anne Guzmán and Lisa Jane Velásquez, pronounce that Goose-mon and Velaskweez.

It took an Iranian to teach me what culture was. I'll tell you about Mohammed later. He was a gentleman and a scholar and he deserves the best. It's because of Mohammed that I became a full-blooded Mejicana.

But just mention anything Indian or Iranian or Middle Eastern in Cabritoville and people wince. The same goes for curry. Cabritovillians will eat fat runny chicharrones until they're coming out of their ears. They'll relish their lengua and cabeza and tripas and they'll suck on pickled pig's feet and fried chicken skin with tomatillo sauce like there's no mañana, but you talk about curry and their eyes go dead.

They don't know what do with anyone who isn't white or Mejicano, and even then, they barely have the social skills to hold a conversation. I've been to too many family dinners, mostly Irma's, that I thought were awful. The tíos sit in the TV room with all the aging boy cousins who will later gather in the backyard with their Coors while they talk about the titty bars in El Paso, especially Prince Machiabelli's. It's always Prince Machiabelli pa'ca and Prince Machiabelli pa'lla.

The women flit around the kitchen like deranged moths preparing ugly food that you wouldn't feed an ailing dog. Things like frozen French-style green beans with those onion rings from the can. They're not so bad, but you know, try something else once in a while! What about the canned yams with the marshmallows? Or the tasteless macaroni salad and the potato salad that you know they bought from Ronnie's Bag-and-Carry, or in bulk from Cost Cut'em in El Paso. Spare me the hard taquitos and the Velveeta cheese dip—I like it, too, but enough is enough! No more cream cheese and green chile cheese roll-ups or chili chicken wings and Swedish meatballs and the baby weenies in red sauce. Ya basta with translated food, Americano or Mejicano!

I don't know anyone who really cooks anymore, except maybe Irma and me. I told Irma that I have never seen such ugly food as I saw at her brother Butch's wedding! It's a good thing Irma and I like to cook. To us, life is full of good food and pleasant conversation about things that matter. You think any of Irma's family talks about books, ha! I have never seen a book in her sister Pio's home. And not only that, Pio proudly admits hating to read. Her husband is the mayor of the town and not one book in sight. It's frightening. If it weren't for me, Irma probably wouldn't go to her family's dinners, she finds them so boring. I tell her, let's go together, we'll observe the human drama, and really, Irma, your uncle Pablo is getting old. We don't pick our family, Irma, I tell her, we pick our friends.

Analysis:

Cabritoville, U.S.A. A border world with a never-ending horizon of women struggling to find a place to rest in the shade of dreams that are dying like the cottonwoods too far from the river.

Cabritoville, U.S.A. A twilight world of men struggling to be men, men refusing to let other men be men, and women to be themselves. Border crossings right and left, someone at the checkpoint telling you you're an alien, that you don't deserve to live here, not now, not ever. Someone telling you that you're illegal, and not only that you are illegal, you're a number. A person without a face. One of thousands. Just another alien to be removed. Count to date: 1,956.

Name: Manuel.

Name: José.

Name: María.

Name: Lucha.

Hometown: Cabritoville, U.S.A.

I know you so well and I try to forgive.

⁂

Cabritoville, home of too many white boys whose names I don't remember. Too many brown boys whose names I do. And I've dated both. I hate what I see as prejudice from anyone, no matter what color skin. Come to think of it, the most prejudiced people I've met have been my family and Irma's family. I have to admit I have been prejudiced myself at times. I thought Rogelia Baeza was dog meat and no one would ever want to chew on her bones, but I was wrong.

I hate it when white boys or any-color boys look at a Mejicana or any ethnic woman and think to themselves: All my life I've waited for someone like you. You're the woman of my ethnicless dreams. The gypsy lover of my passionless life. Come to me, hot ethnic mama!

I've met a few of those men, mostly early on, thank God.

What kind of town/state/country is this where if you have an opinion there's always someone sneering at you—some lazy, uncreative, nonreading, noncooking aunt, uncle or sleazy male cousin or boring female friend of your aunt's that keeps getting invited to the family Thanksgiving and Christmas dinners despite the fact that they're about the dullest, most dysfunctional human beings on God's blessed earth.

These people are high on the Bovine Factor. It's a rating system Irma invented. Bovinity translates into dumbness, although I've heard cows are really smart. Now, I don't want to be accused of insulting cows. I love cows. Irma and I just don't like dumb people. We've rated Bovine personalities for years and I have to tell you we've seen them all in Cabritoville, especially at Irma's family's gatherings.

When you live in a place named Cabritoville, it seems the caca is all around. You can smell the cows from the Hernández dairy everywhere in town. Pobrecitos esos animales. How'd you like to be in a factory giving milk all day long? How'd you like to have your pechitos yanked right and left every day in the hot sun? I feel sorry for the little babies, huddled up against their mamás, fighting for a little shade, to get their feet out of the mud, their sad muzzly cabecitas stuck between the metal grates for a little bit of alfalfa, todo sequito from sitting on the side of the road for years while people like me drive by to shop at the White House in El Paso. And then when you see El Wimpy and Popeye spending the money they made on the cow families at La Tempestad, it's enough to tear your heart out.

Putos! I'll go on the record calling them Putos.

Sometimes I feel like one of those cows out in the hot sun, waiting for the shade that never comes. That's how it is—hurt, forgive and try to forget.

There we'll be, Irma and me, at a family gathering, except we're the only family we care about, I'll look at her and she'll look at me. And then one of us will draw a Big P in the air. No one knows what we're doing. They just think we're flicking flies. And then she'll draw a Big B in the air, adding a couple of exclamation points. We'll giggle as everyone looks at us. And then we'll look back at them as if butter wouldn't melt in our mouths.

Irma's family are people who sit. They gravitate from chair to chair, from one resting place to another. They aren't people who stand for long. They don't like to talk much either, and especially about anything serious. I have never understood why people get offended when you really try to talk, and that, of course, means having opinions.

It wasn't until I met Mohammed that I learned people could get together to debate ideas and talk politics or art or literature without having someone get all pedo and storm out of the house with threats to return with a gun.

I've had the misfortune of discussing Pat Robertson and the 400 Club in a family setting and was accused of being drunk. So now I just sit back and watch the family soaps. I tell Irma, let them all just do their Ávila-and-Granados-mecate-neck-choking-unconscious-jerky-can't-hold-a-single-rhythm-dance and I'll plug in and out when I choose. My family and Irma's don't irritate me as much as they used to, thank God. I realize they're only people, just like anyone else. A little more jodidos than the usual batch, but what's new?

I haven't met too many interesting people at Granados family functions, but there were a few memorable ones. There was that handsome older man at Butch's wedding whom nobody could quite place. Irma thought he was from California, a cousin of her mother's sister from Fontana. Butch and his new wife, Elva, didn't know him. Everyone thought he was a pariente, someone's relative. I sure did, or I would never have let him into my room later that night.

We had been making sly ojitos all during the wedding and then at the dance. And he could dance, let me tell you. He was a little stiff in the hips, but not so that it would detract. As a matter of fact, it gave him an unusual dip at the right times. He had a firm grip and a control I like to see in a dance partner. I never got his name. But there were plenty of ojitos, and he did sit next to me at the wedding buffet. Once, I brushed his hand under the table. It wasn't hot and steamy because of the tamales they were serving. The stranger was very popular and he was funny, whoever he was. "You mean he's not a relative?" I asked Irma Sunday morning after my shower, but by then, he'd already checked out, and try as I did, I couldn't get his name. He was registered under Pacheco Plastics. No town. No phone.

Mr. Pacheco Plastics was in his mid-fifties or early sixties, very distinguished-looking with white hair circling his face, not too short, just long enough to run your fingers through. He had beautifully polished golden brown skin without any visible pores, a skin that drives most women wild. And he had a full mustache, mostly black. Irma started calling him Mr. Bigote. I wish he'd left his calling card or his phone number.

After the dance, I went up to my room and there was a knock. Staring through the peephole, I saw the Dancing Bigote. What to do? Ignore him? Let him in? What? Well, frankly, comadre, I told Irma later, I was delighted. Without a word, I went to the door, looked into those big brown Azteca eyes of his and turned off the lights as I led D.B. to the bed. He was a mature man. I didn't have to explain anything to him and he didn't need to explain anything to me. What a relief. It was Fusion.

Leading to confusion. Who was Mr. Pacheco Plastics? You mean he wasn't your mother's cousin from California? He was a salesman staying here at the hotel who glommed on to the wedding? No me digas, girl. You have got to be kidding. You think my goose is cooked? Ay, diosito, Irma, if you tell a living soul, I swear to God I will never cook you anything you like de La Julia Child. Promise me on Pedro Infante's grave that you will not tell a living soul that I just admitted the most delicious *Modern Maturity* that I have ever laid puños on into my room at the El Paso airport Sheraton and that he crawled into my king-sized bed and that afterward we watched *The Tonight Show*.

So why am I telling you all this? Because maybe your dream

man will come up from out of nowhere and then he'll just disappear. Or else the one you think is your dream man turns out to be a nightmare.

"If you tell anyone about the Dancing Bigote, Irma, I swear on *Mastering the Art of French Cooking* I'll tell them about Delmore Benavidez, who was your chulito for months until you finally went to bed with him that fateful one-and-only night," I said to her as we were hunched over some sopaipillas at Sofia's Mighty Taco later that week.

She knew I had her when I mentioned Delmore Benavidez.

Look, I didn't see him up close as Irma did, so I can't tell anyone the truth of the matter, but I have no reason to doubt my comadre. She made me promise I wouldn't tell anyone he had the world's smallest flauta, ring size 5.

Better Delmore with his beautiful thoughts and fine language than some guilt-ridden separated-from-his-wife hung-like-a-horse man, that's what I say.

Better than Blue Jay, the aging, but still good-looking hippie we both met at La Tempestad the winter of 1969. Both Irma and I slept with him and we didn't know it until later. He was rete chulo, him and his hard kisses, his tight little body, his small hairy hands, his nalgitas bien tight. (I have continually fallen for these short, small-backed men. With them, you feel like you're hugging a child, and the truth of the matter is, you usually are.)

I wonder how I've managed to live over thirty years on this earth without anyone seeing and then commenting on the Big Black P plastered on my forehead. Probably because of the Giant B on their own.

Analysis:
Cabritoville, U.S.A.
The potential is not the reality.
Rating:
Ya, ¿pa' que?

PART II

ANSIEDAD

Aquella Noche

Aquella Noche was the first time Lucio and I made love and everything that should have been right went wrong. I'd been waiting for this moment for a long time, ever since I'd seen him at La Tempestad. And yet, I had no idea things were about to happen. It's a good thing I didn't know, or they might not have happened. That's if you want to look at it that way. If you want to look at it another way, it might have been best for all concerned if things hadn't happened at all. But they did.

The first time I saw Lucio was at La Tempestad. The second time was at Cabritoville Elementary. The third was at the Knights of Columbus Fourth of July fireworks display at Álamo Park, near the river. There was noise everywhere: homemade bottle rockets exploded behind us, a group of little girls was making giant alphabet letters in the air with sparklers, and down the street, higher and more potent than the Knights of Columbus' sad little duddy bursts, came a fast whoosh and blast of trenos the likes of which Cabritoville had never seen. Some vatos had gone to Sunland Park to buy the Black Scorpion SuperMega $79.95 box of firecrackers and were firing them between tokes near Sofia's Mighty Taco and the cottonwoods near the acequia. Híjole, I hoped they wouldn't set anything on fire, especially those beautiful big trees. Gabina, my favorite tree, in particular. It had been a dry spring, with little hope of much summer rain.

The night was a pyrotechnic free-for-all. There was something frightening about the way Cabritovillians loved their loud, cheap thrills. Irma and I had gone together to see the fireworks, but she didn't like the noise and went home early. I knew everyone there, the usual lackluster dry, dusty and bovinic crowd from La Tempestad, only this time with their wives and children. I was about ready to leave when I saw Lucio. His eyes locked like headlights onto mine saying: Mami Mami Mami. Mine kept blinking back: Papi Papi Papi. Mohammed and I were a short and sad history then. Chago was a recurring alien abduction nightmare. I thought to myself: Who's to keep us apart?

Lucio was standing alone near a big álamo. When he came up to me I could smell the liquor on his breath. Ay. He was drunk. It was a quick call. The dice came down hard and fast.

"So, what's your name?"

"Teresina Ávila. Named after the saint."

"Who?"

"Santa Teresa de Ávila. The Spanish saint."

"Oh. So you a saint, or what?"

"Hell no, you?"

"Do I look like a saint?"

"So what's your name?"

"Lucio Valadez."

"Nice to meet you."

I felt the heat rising between my legs. In the background I heard Los Lobos playing La Bamba. "Yo no soy marinero. Yo no soy marinero. Por ti seré. Por ti seré. Por ti seré. Bamba. Bamba. Bamba. ¡Bamba!" For you, Papi, un barco de oro. I tried to catch my breath but I couldn't. It didn't matter, because I wanted to die right then and there just like Irma's tío Willie from California, who came home after too many years away. He died singing and dancing in the middle of a party outdoors, the music blaring and resonating like a giant drum inside a lowrider car that thumps-tha-thumps its way down the street leaving you vibrating in place. Tío Willie just keeled over and he was gone.

Lucio invited me for a drink. I offered to drive. Only when we got into my car did I realize he meant for us to go to his room at the Sands Motel, No. 17. His home away from home.

Bueno pues. Ni modo.

It was already over before it was over.

And that, Tere girl, you puta cabrona, was the beginning of it all. Try and listen this time, girl. Just this once.

Aquella Noche I hadn't shaved my legs. My legs were stubbly and dry and now that I think about it I hadn't washed down there since the night before. Things happened so fast I didn't have time to worry about how clean I was or if I smelled down there or if my legs were like sandpaper or if my heels were soft, it being summer and all and you know how hard and cracked your heels get after months of wearing sandals. (When I have a pedicure in Juárez you should see the heel skin they shave off of me!) If I'd known I was going to make love to Lucio I sure would have thought about my feet. Not that they touched the earth much that night, but what if they had? What if they'd rubbed up against Lucio's baby skin? He'd have met Lizard Woman in the flesh. But would he have noticed?

Aquella Noche I didn't have time to think if I'd plucked my nipple hairs or my chin hairs or the one black one that grows on the right side of my face near my sideburn, that one wild hair I have to keep checking on. I was too overwhelmed to think about any of those things women worry about when they're about to make love to a new man.

Aquella Noche I was an unclean dog in heat. I was a wild woman, but not in a good way. I wrestled with Lucio but didn't give myself fully. I was afraid of my body and of not being a good enough lover. I was frightened to be with him because I already loved him and I didn't want to love him any more. I never wanted to touch him because I knew once I touched him it was all over. It would never end until it ended and even then it wouldn't end. I was tired, out of sorts, and not on the pill. I left my diaphragm at home and I was afraid of his sperm crawling up inside me too soon. But was it that? I just wasn't prepared physically. I remember this one horrible moment when my head was draped downward over the footboard of the king-sized bed, my legs up in the air like I was pedaling the way Irma and I do to her Flabbercise tapes. Lucio was mid-bed hovered over me and I just kept thinking: This isn't happening. This isn't happening. I'm not prepared. I'm ugly and I'm holding back. He doesn't love me. He can't love me. I love you, Lucio, I love you but I'm not prepared. I forgot to shave my legs. My diaphragm's at home and I'm not here a hundred percent. I'm sorry.

"Was it good for you?"

As if that wasn't bad enough, I looked up to see an ant crawling up my right foot. It stopped in the middle of my big toe. I tried to whisk it off with my hand, but that's when Lucio lurched and cried out. I shook my foot ceilingward and Lucio climaxed. If you were to ask me a hundred years from now what I remember most about that night it would have to be the pain. Ant bites can really hurt.

Aquella Noche. I can't remember a thing about how Lucio felt inside of me. I wish I could. A thousand times I wish I could remember how it felt that first time. I've played the scene in my mind a thousand and ten times and all I can see is myself hanging over the bed, the blood rushing to my head. I'm in a sexual stranglehold with a man who is moaning and I'm worrying about my bikini line. There's something awful about this kind of memory. This wanting to play the scene over. This dreaming the scene fresh, the knowing the time is gone and you were not at your best.

This is the problem with Lucio and me, always has been. I wasn't perfect, and I wanted to be. And he wanted me to be. But it was the imperfect parts of me that pushed him away. This is what I've always felt. He liked me for a while, every once in a while, and he might have even loved me in those whiles, but it wasn't a thing that lasted, just like an orgasm. Lucio liked it when he was inside of me, inside my head, my heart, my sex, and when he pulled out, I was there in front of him, glowing imperfection. A woman with bad posture, imperfect teeth, someone who couldn't afford nice clothes then, still can't, someone a little bowlegged from the other side of his town. I didn't have a college degree. I smelled like food and work and children. I loved him too much and that haunted him and made him wince and turn around and keep walking out that revolving door that brought him back to me so many times only to have him walk away again.

Aquella Noche I wasn't mentally prepared. Lucio caught me off guard. He said he liked me, did he say he loved me, or wanted to love me? I can't remember his words. My hearing was off. My sight was blurred. My heart was racing and I couldn't breathe. My stomach was in a knot and kept talking back to me: "Stupid cabrona, tonight's the night, but it can't be. I'm not prepared."

Aquella Noche my mind was weak and Lucio's was strong. We weren't equals. I was the woman fucked and he was the man standing over me as I was draped over the bed like a costal of green chile, a wet gunnysack without support. I kept thinking I was going to fall over, my position was so precarious. It was a cartoon fuck. I couldn't breathe, my limbs flailed like a rag doll's. I felt foolish and stupid and undignified. Every second I thought: I'm holding back. I can't give myself to you. Your wife is across town. Your mother is dying of cancer down the street. Your young daughter is one of my favorite students at Cabritoville Elementary. I can see her wide brown eyes in front of me. Your wedding ring glistens by the flickering television light. And someone is selling a revolutionary mop on the television. I can't breathe. I'm suffocating.

Aquella Noche I was a wet toalla, an old towel, thinned by use, too many wipings. I wanted Lucio to commit to me, to say FOREVER. To say: Tere, you are the air and the wind and the sun and the rain. To say: Mujer, I'm leaving Diolinda, she isn't perfect, oh, she's beautiful, do you think I'd pick an ugly woman to be the mother of my child? She's bright, she's talented, but she doesn't understand me. She's a good wife blah blah a good cook blah blah a good mother blah blah a good daughter-in-law blah blah blah, even my mother likes her and that's saying a lot.

I can't remember all of Lucio's words but they went on and on as he told me about his day life his night life his love life his mind life his dream life and how starved he was, like a hungry man on a desert island having to drink salty water to try to stay alive.

Aquella Noche I wasn't spiritually prepared. I'm a Catholic and I always will be. I don't go to church too often but when I pass a church I cross myself. I also go to Mass every now and then to keep in practice. I'm always thinking about becoming a better person. Death is always close to me. Just behind Purgatory. I'm good to people, I don't hurt them. I'm even-tempered, a nice woman. I talk soft and give respect. I'm never angry out loud, yelling for no reason. I'm afraid of Hell and looking for Heaven, I believe in Limbo and that the souls of small children go to the same place all animals go that have died by the road, to that Blessed Heaven of Innocent Creatures, the Highest Heaven, each mansion named and called forth by a merciful God.

Aquella Noche I wasn't prepared to sin but damn I did and damned I was and damned I'll always be since then. I'm sorry. I say that phrase out loud to myself whenever I get to thinking too hard. I'm sorry but I couldn't help it. I didn't want to stop it, and even if I had wanted to, it wasn't possible. My fate was sealed. My sin decreed. Aquella Noche. Aquella Noche.

After we made love and Lucio fell asleep, I tried to pry his wedding ring off. I wasn't going to steal it. I just wanted to see how tight it fit and if the skin on his finger had grown around it. I had to know if there was gunk or food in the grooves. To my dismay, there was no movement with the ring at all. It was on there good and tight. Lucio was snoring lightly as I left. My calzones were in my purse. There was no way his wedding ring was ever going to be pried loose.

I tell you, Tere girl, I've thought about that night too much. I used to remember all the details. The swirls on the red rug, what was playing on the television, the way Lucio felt, heavy, a little sweaty, his small back a surprise to me, I thought he was a bigger man. He looked larger in his clothes. Naked, he was shorter than I expected and had a tighter build and was nearly my height and then again he was hard and I could feel the muscles on his arms, and his hands were beautiful, a little stubby but beautiful, the nails manicured but without polish, the light, fine hair on his hands so dear and soft and when I touched his hands I wanted to cry with joy and just lay with him in the bed and stay that way for hours, saying nothing, doing nothing, being nothing, thinking nothing, just loving him and becoming nothing but one nothing inside another nothing and that nothing not bothering with anything.

Aquella Noche I was nothing but in another way. It was the beginning of my nothing with Lucio, that nothing that went on for too long.

Aquella Noche. That night.
Aquella Noche. That night.
Aquella Noche. That night.

Mi Tocaya

I'm not at all like my to-
caya, the other Teresa, whose name I bear with sis-
terly pride and no small daring. Leave it to Raza
to be bonded to someone who has the same name
as you. I've never known a culture that has more
interrelationships between people who aren't bio-
logically related. In Spanish, you don't even have
to be related to be related. That's why I call Irma
my comadre, even though I'm not the godmother
of her child. I love her so much, I've made her
kin.

But as far as I'm concerned, I really don't think I
have much in common with my tocaya, La Santa
Tere. My tocaya was a woman eternally untouched
by mortal man, now she's forever deified. My
mother, Albinita, named me after her—Santa Teresa

de Ávila—una ethpañola bendita, una thanta de la iglesthia—a holy woman pure and simple.

For some time now I've been working my way through Santa Teresa de Ávila's autobiography. I don't know if I'll ever finish the book. It's not an easy read. Pretty hefty, pretty intense. But I can do intense if I put my mind to it. And yet, it's hard to read the book at a good clip. I've read the introduction about three times. I have to keep putting it down to think. But when I put it down, I forget what I've been thinking. The images in my mind get all fuzzy reading La Otra Tere.

Wirms gave me the book for my last birthday. At first I thought it was a strange gift. "When you're on a bumpy airplane ride, or sick with the Crud, or in the middle of a love affair—which can feel pretty much like the same thing—you should read spiritual things," Irma said on her birthday card.

As a result of my reading, I decided to make a list of all the ways I'm like my tocaya. Just to know where I stand. And to list the areas where I need to do work.

Ways Mi Tocaya and I Are Alike and Not Alike

Santa Teresa de Ávila	Tere Ávila
A woman.	Ditto.
Never married.	Married once, although I wouldn't call it Married Married. If that was married, I don't want to ever be married again.
A mystic.	Can't see anything worth shit, literally and metaphorically.
Una Ethpañola.	A Mejicana/Chicana born and bred! ¡Que viva la Raza!
Born 1515. Died 1582.	Live in today's world.

Had loving parents.	Have a loving mother. Father died long ago.
Loved her work.	Really need a full-time, better-paying job. Being a floating educational assistant is not a career, but then again, this is Cabritoville, U.S.A.
Spiritual Directors were men: García de Toledo, Pedro Ibáñez, Domingo Báñez, Francis Borgia, Peter de Alcántara and, of course, St. John of the Cross.	Spiritual Directors are women: Albinita Avila, Nyvia Ester Granados, Irma Granados.
Saw visions.	Never knew what hit me.
Depended on too many men to tell her if her visions were holy or the work of the Devil.	What woman hasn't been pronounced a witch/bitch by some man?
Didn't have children and didn't want them.	Double ditto. Although if I had a daughter like Andrea I might reconsider.
Had trouble with praying early on.	Never a problem. I seldom go to church, but just holding a rosary calms me down.
Sephardic/Crypto-Jewish roots.	Ditto.
Almost went through the Inquisition.	Have gone through the proverbial chisme mill of "interrogations" from the fan club members, especially Ofelia Contreras, a feverish mitotera who has nothing better to do than gossip and destroy reputations.
Medium height.	Ditto.

More plump than scrawny.	Ditto.
Three moles: one below the center of the nose, one over the left side of the mouth, third beneath the mouth.	Two moles on my back. One on the right side of my face near my sideburn with a black hair growing out of it that I have to keep plucking.
Didn't want to have anything to do with mortal men.	Only want to love and live with one mortal man.
Wrote her autobiography.	Haven't even begun.
Jodida by Doubt.	Ditto.
Graced by God.	Yeah, sure.
For many years longed to see God.	Who doesn't want to see God?
A saint.	No saint.
Finally saw God.	I'm still waiting.

When I get through more of the book, I'm going to consult La Wirms. She's read all the greats: St. Augustine, the Little Flower, Bishop Sheen, Billy Graham, Oral Roberts, Rod McKuen. She knows so much about saints and the holy life of trying to find your way home to God, she could teach a course at the State University. Seeking God 101.

I, on the other hand, am a woman living in sin, in the hinterlands of life, in the sticks of a place called Cabritoville, U.S.A. The man I love is married, he's rich and five years younger than me.

What was the attraction of Lucio? He was a child with a child. Only twenty-five years old when I first met him, he had Andrea when he was seventeen. There was something wild about him, reckless. I liked what I saw. For years I've been looking for the lost boy inside too many men.

Lucio is a part-time insurance salesman and a full-time car

dealer in El Paso. The dealership there is an extension of the
family-owned car business, Valadez Ford, in Cabritoville. Lucio is
married to Diolinda Pérez Valadez. They separate from time to
time and then always get back together. Their courtship was one
of those small, hometown, Mejicano things. He and she were
better-off Mejicanos, eligible college-bound kids who hooked up
and then never finished school. Lucio's father, Lucio Sr., ran El
Chorrito Bar for many years. He died of a heart attack about ten
years ago when he was on the roof of the bar checking the air conditioner. Lucio's sister, Velia Valadez-Schwagerman, runs the car
dealership, a dog-grooming business, and a hot-dog restaurant,
one called Dogs, the other More Dogs, all in a small strip mall in
Cabritoville. His mother, Cuca, otherwise known as La Vieja
Bruta (La V.B.), is dying of stomach cancer.

The Valadez family is wealthy in Cabritoville terms. They're a
family in a small town that owns many of the businesses. But you
wouldn't know it from the mother's stinginess and cheap ways.
What meanness exists in that family comes not from Lucio's father, Lucio Sr., but from his mother, La V.B. She has a reputation
as a ruthless businesswoman who'll die with the first dollar she
ever made tucked in her giant steel brassiere. Lucio isn't like her.
He can be charming and generous. He's also a good businessman
who's interested in life and people. He'd like to go back to college,
but says it's too late now; he lost his chance when he got into the
insurance business.

"But I can still learn, Tere. That's why I always carry a dictionary with me. Do you know what a 'pip' is?"

"Do you mean like Gladys Knight and the Pips . . . ?"

"No . . . ," he said, and this is where he opened up his Random
House Dictionary of the English Language and announced in a
loud voice: "Page 1010."

Lucio was always looking up words and announcing what page
number they were on.

"Pip. One of the small segments on the surface of a pineapple."

"So that's what they call those things. I always wondered. Not that I ever called them anything. If I had, I guess I would have called them nubs," I said.

"Nubs? What are you talking about, Tere?"

Actually, I'd never ever wondered what those things were called, but Lucio was a man who liked dialogue at certain times of the day, and he expected responses.

"Pip. That's a good word for the day," Lucio said with certainty. "The thing is to keep your mind active, Tere. To keep learning about the world. You know those word tests in the back of *Reader's Digest*? I'm going to start saving them for you so you can improve your vocabulary."

"Oh, okay," I said without too much enthusiasm. That's all I needed. To be carrying a dictionary around with me during the day, bulging in my purse with all the Kleenex and makeup. But if that's what Lucio wants me to do, I guess I'll just have to humor the man.

Lucio would have been a good teacher; it's too bad the insurance business got in the way of his education. He's always talking about his little girl, Andrea, who's in the third grade, and how he's teaching her how to do this and do that. He's a good father, that's one thing I'll say about Lucio. He spoils her rotten, but he is strict when it comes to her schoolwork. I imagine that he makes Andrea learn over ten new words a day as he's making me do. No telling what Diolinda has been through. He probably made her go through the Dale Carnegie course or the Evelyn Wood reading school. I don't know Diolinda, but sometimes I feel sorry for her. If he's like this with me, what is he like with her?

I see Andrea every day in the cafeteria or down the hall from where I work. She's in school here in Cabritoville because Lucio thinks the school is better than the schools in El Paso and that the small-town atmosphere will do her good. Andrea drives in with a chauffeur every day from El Paso. She's a poor little rich girl, but she still doesn't know it yet.

Andrea and all the kids at Cabritoville Elementary know me by name. They call me Miss Terry. I work with the Elementary kids, one day I'm in one class, another day I'm in another. I'm what they call a floater. But I'm a dependable floater and the staff likes me. One of these days, when there's a full-time opening, I'm sure to get a permanent job. A job that pays.

My hands get tired after a day of work. Other people get tired feet or achy legs or sore shoulders or stiff fingers. I get swollen hands from all the lifting, cleaning, folding, tucking, straightening, and unwrinkling I do every day as an educational assistant. I used to be a teacher's aide until someone Bigger and Higher Up decided to change my job description. Now that everyone has to be highfalutin—the garbage men call themselves waste disposal engineers and the movers from Bekins Van Lines call themselves relocation specialists—I'm an educational assistant. A teacher's aide. Call me whatever you want. Just let me do my work.

Ever wonder who cleans out the funky smelly grooves of colored clay in the little worktables where twenty-five second graders have made miniature Mother's Day flowerpots out of Play-Doh?

Do you ever wonder who rinses out the small white plastic watercolor trays full of ugly mixed-up colors that a seriously challenged group of young artists has created on the spot? Or who swabs down the trickles of red and blue paint from the sides of the toy stove and fridge to the left of the artwork tables?

Who sits with the disappointed, crying children after school when their parents forget to pick them up? And who is there to cheer them on those long, hopeful hours on Parents' Day when their mothers and fathers have forgotten to show up?

Who cleans off the throw-up and wipes up the pee?

Who sees the old bruises underneath the dirty brown T-shirts, the cuts, the burns, the dried blood in the ragged panties? I'm the one who sees those poor battered children, who wants to take them in her arms, who cries in bed late at night because she doesn't know what else to do.

I hear them, I hear their stories.

I listen to my kids when they are silent and when they make noise. I listen to them huddled into the corners of themselves. I listen to the still-fresh bruises and the nasty scrapes. I listen to the terrible haunting quiet of a child whose father beats her with a belt and whose mother hits her with a broom. I listen to what is never heard, what should never be thought.

I want them to say later on when they are grown, "Remember the lady from Cabritoville Elementary, Miss Terry, the one who was kind to us? The one who listened and respected us? The one who was strict, but nice?"

Once I wanted to be a teacher. But, as with Lucio, life got in the way of my doing what I really wanted to do.

Cabritoville Elementary has about three hundred students. That's not including the ones from Mesa Junior High across the field from us who are coming over here for their meals while their cafeteria/multipurpose room is being renovated. You know what that means for me: more work, hands so sore I have to soak them at home at night in warm manzanilla. Chamomile is what it's called in English. Tell me how manzanilla translates into chamomile; I'd like to know.

It isn't enough that I have to handle my twenty-five second graders, but sometimes the principal, Mr. Perea, will call me to the cafeteria to fill in. The Mesa Marauders keep me eagle-eyed, half of them without lunch tickets or even lunches. They try to sneak into the line and push my babies out of the way, or even worse, steal the little kids' lunches, yeah, from right under my nose. They jostle everyone all baggedy-raggedy in line with their pants all hip-hoppity, clutching bags of Lay's potato chips and Big Reds like a bunch of scarecrows blowing in the breeze. They're skinny the way many teenagers are, all angles and sharp edges, pulling and pushing their way through life.

You have to look at all those kids and wonder what they dream.

It's hard to imagine that someday they'll be thinking thoughts like mine: night thoughts in the day and day thoughts in the night.

They'll forget they're not supposed to dream in the sunlight and
make plans late at night when all other people want to do is sleep.

⸙

Having an affair with a married man is as risky as smoking in the
bathroom is for a teenager. You exhale through the window's mesh
screen hoping your mother won't catch you in the act. Later,
when you finally have to vacate the bathroom because someone is
yelling to get in, you hurl lame excuses of something attacking
your tripas, must have been the green chiles. You aren't sure you
can carry off the deception. But you have to; some kind of sick
personal honor is at stake. You think it'll be okay, that everything
will be all right, but then your mother comes in with her blood-
hound nose and her golden retriever eyes. You think you'd covered
your tracks. But you forgot the obvious. Your mother looks in the
toilet bowl and there it is, the butt you forgot to flush. You may
even have flushed, but somehow that butt kept bobbing up.

It's never easy, is it? Your problem is that you think no one can
track you both down, not his wife, not your best friend. And so
you become reckless. You take a hard drag of that burning cigarette just to see your all too human breath in front of you. You
hardly know what to tell God, much less your mother. You're in
love with a bright and vivid Lucifer. And he loves you back.

This is a private love. You're desperate and without dignity. You
drive to his house at all hours of the day to see if he's there, just
cruising, as if the circling round would bring you peace, as if the
knowing where he was would help you find some rest. You leave
disguised messages on the answering machine that never get answered, you keep calling him and there's either a busy signal or no
one's there. If Diolinda, the wife, answers, you hang up. If his
daughter, Andrea, says hello, you cry and vow to never call back.
But you do. And you hope she won't recognize your voice. Your
best girlfriend, Irma, finally says with disgust, "Ya, déjalo que descanse en paz, leave him in peace," but you can't. One year or forty,

it's all the same. You can't leave him, much less leave him in peace. You're still waiting for that phone call. For him to walk in the door to say, "Tere, I was wrong. I love you, chula. Forgive me, I was a pendejo, a fool."

My story is no white girl's musical. No que será será sort of thing. There's no Doris Day pillow talk, no Doris pouting up a storm because Rock Hudson accidentally saw her in her slip or kissed her lopsided on the cheek when she'd had too much champagne to drink and gee-I-really-should-be-getting-home.

This story is about late-night betrayals, the other man's other woman, and late-night phone calls from any number of Holiday Inn and Sheraton Hotel phone booths, your home away from home. It's been days since you talked con tu honey, so you find a corner in which to park your nalgas and seek him out in the dark with plenty of change. You whisper ay precioso that you love him, only him, that you have to see him, diosito, as you put another fistful of quarters in the phone.

My story is as true a story as they get. There's no turning back, corazón. If you don't want to get burned, don't get in the fire. There's always a dicho in Spanish that gets to the heart of the matter. Cada chango tiene su mecatito y yo tengo el mío. Every monkey has his little chain, so if your metal chain is too tight, listen up.

You want romance, go read a fantasy. You want mystery, go sit in church. You want peace, I hardly know what to say.

Most of my daydreams take place in the middle of the night. I'm in bed with Lucio making love. In fact, I've never been with Lucio in the daytime. We have our separate lives then. I know I love him. And I think he loves me, too. Especially late at night. Irma

says that to really love someone you have to know them. Morning.
Noon. And night.

Things like this should worry me, and they do. They're the kind
of things you know inside your head but put aside because you're
in loooovvvve.

"I never dream," Lucio bragged to me early one evening in our
room at the Sands Motel. Every town that I know of has a Sands
Motel. It seems crazy to me that I should end up here at the shifting sands.

"You never dream! That's like saying you don't read books, Lucio. Imagine not reading books! Of course you dream. You just
don't remember your dreams," I told him confidently.

"I really don't dream, Tere."

"You don't *dream?* My dreams are like movies, Lucio. They just
go on and on. I even dream about Pedro. The last time I was on
that beach in *La Vida No Vale Nada.*"

"I don't know why you go on and on about that man."

"Have you ever seen his movies?"

"No. I don't go to that movie theater. Only poor Mexicans see
movies there."

I wanted to say, "Oh, Lucio, what's wrong with you?" but instead I said, "You aren't feeling well, are you?"

"It's the heat. Now be quiet about Pedro and come over here.
He's not here and I am. You can move . . . afterward. We'll sleep
better that way."

"Yes, mi amor . . ." I said, patting his hand the way my mother,
Albinita, does, soothing me when she knows I'm irritable.

We made love and then Lucio moved over to the other bed. I
tried to engage him in conversation but it was impossible.

Forget Lucio, his mind goes dead after 10 p.m. Sometimes I
wonder what Lucio and I have ever really talked about. I should
secretly tape-record one of our conversations. It would go something like this: Him saying, "Uh-huh," at the end of every sentence, and me talking about deep things.

"Lucio, do stars feel?"

"Ummm."

"When little birds leave home, do they think of their mamas?"

"Ummm."

"Have you ever thought about how cancer gets started and why it stays with some people and not others? And why someone dies of a heart attack and someone else of kidney problems?"

"Ummm."

"Do wasps dream, Lucio?"

"Ummm."

"Why is it that when you dream about dead people they never talk to you? I mean, out loud, with their mouths?"

"Ummm."

"Speaking of dreams, Lucio . . . why is it that when you see a dead person you can hug them, but you can't look at their face too long?"

With that last long "Ummmm" I knew Lucio had fallen asleep.

I wish I could find someone to really talk to, and not about sports, or the weather in Cabritoville. We all know it's hotter than hell here, and duller than a Luby's on a Tuesday afternoon, but don't say that to Margarita Hinkel, our fan club member, whose husband owns the local Luby's franchise. And don't get Sista Rocha started on her latest story about Padre Gato, her parish priest, who poisons cats with antifreeze and then takes them to the river to dump them. And for God's sake, please don't ask Ofelia Contreras the difference between Catholics and Jehovah's Witnesses, which is what she is, or was, until she ditched the Holy Rollers and the Pope alike and took up with Pedro.

The problem is that, other than Irma and sometimes Ubaldo, I can't find anyone who'll listen to me when it matters, especially really late at night when I can't sleep, and want to just lie in bed discussing my dreams, like the one about the giant man circling this tiny shack I'm hiding inside of with a bunch of people I don't know, or how it's the end of the world and I can see this huge wave of water in the distance and I'm running up a mountain, or how I can see myself becoming a crow as I watch the beak emerge from my face. Oh, there are people to talk to you in the daylight, but who wants to really talk then? Daylight talk is harsh talk. What I want is someone to hold me close. And talk. About deep things.

If I had known then what I know now, I would have gotten up from that bed and its wet spot right then and there and walked away from Lucio Valadez, just as Pedro walked away from Marta on that stark, barren beach in *La Vida No Vale Nada*.

But I didn't, did I?

The movie tape had to play on and on.

Waiting is the most exquisitely painful part of loving someone.

If waiting is a penance, then I'd be a saint.

The Blue Dot

Irma and I were sitting in the Blue Dot restaurant out on Highway 478. The Blue Dot was named for the blue dot in the *Enquirer* magazine. The owner, Essie Torres, is a blue dot nut. The blue dot is rumored to bring you good luck. You're supposed to meditate on the blue dot and wave it over things and carry it in your wallet and sleep with it under your pillow. I've had my blue dot in my coin purse for over six months. As a matter of fact, it was about the time that I cut out the blue dot and started waving it around and praying over it that Lucio came into my life.

Irma and I sat in the corner booth of the Blue Dot. My back was to the door while Irma faced me so she could see who was coming in at that hour of the night. It was one of the few restaurants in

Cabritoville that were open after 9 p.m. on a Thursday night. We would have preferred to go to Sofia's Mighty Taco, but it was closed.

"So what do you want to do with your life, Tere?" La Wirms asked me as we hunched over grilled cheese sandwiches with extra pickles and coleslaw. The Tater Tots with red chile, what Essie Torres called "Spanish fries," still hadn't arrived. Irma had a way of asking off-the-wall questions.

"I know what I want and what I don't want, but saying it out loud has never helped me."

"If you had a wish right now, and you could have anything in the world, what would it be, Tere?"

"I want to live. And love. That's all I ever wanted, comadre. To celebrate a fiftieth wedding anniversary . . . With my kids down at the Elks or Moose, most likely the VFW, what with the escalating prices these days."

"You know what a female moose is? A cow. Except the women don't call themselves cows. They're called Women of the Moose."

"Well, I don't care if I'd be a cow or a moose. All I ever wanted was a family, no little house with the white picket fence, but a solid jacalito with huge adobe walls with nichos all around. A little plot of green grass—I know grass is asking for a lot in the desert—but there you have it. I want to sit outside in the hot evenings and eat sandía in the yard and laugh. There would be native plants and wildflowers and a few loving pets. Throw in a swimming pool and that's it. After living happily in my casita with my viejo and the kids, I'd want to celebrate our fiftieth with a very high High Mass and a renewal of vows, dressed in cocktail white, with an orchid corsage, followed by a second honeymoon trip to Las Vegas or Cancún.

"Picture this, Irma: My viejo and I get married. Our wedding is a quick trip to Juárez to see the juez. We get hitched border style, with one night of passion at the Cortez Hotel. I don't know why we pay for the room. We stay up all night making love. It's delicious. So what if the air conditioning isn't working and we feel like the hot and dusty alligators in the stagnant pool in the middle of the plaza next day at work. The next morning we have breakfast at the Kress's and lunch at the Oasis—a BLT for me and a turkey club with the works for him—and then we drive home. He never goes to bed, but straight to work. I go back to sleep knowing I have to work graveyard. We never really take a luna de miel because we are both working so hard, but hey, isn't love enough? That's the way it is and it was and weren't we happy then?"

"You know, that's all I ever wanted, too," Irma said. I noticed she had tears in her eyes and it surprised me.

"You okay, Irma?" I nudged.

"Sure, I'm okay, Tere. Just because a person cries a little bit now and then doesn't mean they're not all right. I'm human just like the next woman."

It was hard for me to see Irma's face because she was facing the shaky fluorescent light Essie needed to replace.

"You know, Tere, there's a darkness in you."

"There is?"

"You're what I would call a 'tragic beauty.' "

"I don't know what you mean, Irma."

"You're like Anna Karenina."

"Who?"

"She was a woman who killed herself for love. You remind me of her."

"Oh yeah? How do you spell that last name?"

"K-a-r-e-n-i-n-a."

I reached for my purse.

"What's that?"

"My word notebook. Lucio gave it to me. I'm supposed to learn at least ten new words a day. I'm building up my vocabulary. Although I have to tell you, comadre, it's been very hard. But I can tell you I'm nothing like Anna, whatever her name is. I'm not killing myself for love the way she did. I'm the type who would kill someone else *first* with my bare hands before I would kill myself."

I put the notebook away and looked at Irma. She had composed herself and was digging into the Spanish fries.

"Hey, Wirms, have you ever heard of Doña Meche? Ubaldo was telling me about her."

"Who is she?"

"She's a curandera off Highway 478. She can cure anything. Ubaldo had a planter's wart that wouldn't go away. And then Mr. Cornubia wouldn't leave him alone. The man was obsessed. I thought I might go see Doña Meche. You know, to ask about Lucio. I heard she's good."

"What in the hell do you want to see a psychic for, Tere?" Irma nearly shouted. "I can read the edge of your grilled cheese and tell you that Lucio will never get unstuck from his wife and child. It's sad, Tere, when you have to pay someone to tell you what they think you want to hear. I understand there's a deep need in you to find God. That's why I gave you Santa Teresa's autobiography for your birthday. But to seek out Doña Meche, no, I don't think so."

"I can understand what you're saying, Irma. For a while there I was calling the psychic hot line every day—that is, until I got my first telephone bill. But for your information, comadre, I am not a Doña Meche groupie. I have patience, comadre, and I can wait. I really can. I honestly believe Lucio will leave Diolinda. It's all a matter of time."

"You're hopeless," Irma said with disgust.

Irma and I had just driven in from El Paso, where we'd seen *Las Mujeres de Mi General* at El Colón. Pedro Infante plays a Revolutionary general, Juan Zepeda. He enters the city of Ciudad Martínez accompanied by his compañera, Lupe. She later bears him a child. After a lot of misunderstanding—including Pedro-as-Juan hooking up with his old flame, Carlota, who lies and connives to keep the two lovers apart—things finally end up happily. Well, as happily as they could in a Revolution where you're fighting soldiers and firing guns from the towers of the city while carrying a baby in your arms. At least the lovers stayed together at the end as they went down.

"Comadre," I said, turning to face Irma, who had Essie's famous green salsa all over her chin. I wiped it and began again. "Comadre, let's talk about loyalty."

"Loyalty?" said Irma, grabbing a handful of napkins and fanning them out of her prodigious bust. Prodigious—adjective. Extraordinary as in size or amount. Synonyms: amazing, stupendous, astounding. Page 1056. La Wirms's bust wasn't so enormous as it was wondrous.

"What I'm trying to say, Irma, is that all I've ever wanted from Lucio is the kind of loyalty that Carlota showed Juan Zepeda in the face of danger in *Las Mujeres de Mi General*."

"The problem with Lucio, Tere, is that he's tapado y jodido."

"It's more than that, comadre," I countered.

The real problem was Lucio's daughter, Andrea.

***

I was reading *Confidencias de un Chófer, el gran amor de Pedro Infante*, a serialized brown-and-white comic book about Pedro Infante's life. Lying on Irma's couch after work, in shorts, I dangled my bare feet over the back of the couch and then her doorbell rang. Irma was warming up hot wax so we could work on our legs. It was something she wanted to try. I was her guinea pig.

I was reading a conversation Pedro was having with his old friend Don Ruperto, who was ill. Pedro tries to console him by suddenly saying that Ruperto will surely outlive him. Neither of them knew how true that statement was! Only a week later, Pedro would be dead in that terrible plane accident, on his way to La Capital on business, carrying a pet monkey to Irma Dorantes ("Mi Ratón") and their daughter, Irmita. It was with irritation that I got up. Nobody, but nobody interrupts me when I'm reading, not even La Wirms. By now she knows better than to get between Pedro and me.

When I opened the door, I saw Andrea in front of me, and on the sidewalk, at the foot of the front steps, stood Lucio.

"Hi, Miss Terry!" she chirped.

"Andrea!" I said with shock. Lucio was as surprised to see me as I was to see him.

"I'm selling things for Christmas," Andrea chirped, pleased with herself. "I didn't know you lived here, Miss Terry."

"I don't," I said, looking at Lucio. "This is my girlfriend's house."

"Daddy," Andrea called, "come here! This is the lady I told you about, from school!" She waved to Lucio. Reluctantly he came over.

"Daddy, this is Miss Terry. And, Miss Terry, this is my dad," Andrea said with pride. With horror I looked down at my legs—my hair grown out for Irma's "experiment." I could see Lucio sizing me up in my raggy shorts.

"Hello, Mr. Valadez," I said formally. "Tere Ávila."

"Nice to meet you." Lucio said stiffly.

Lucio and I shook hands quickly.

Just then Irma walked in with a pan of hot water. When she saw us, she turned around, and left the room.

"That was Irma," I said to Andrea. "You want to come inside?" I asked.

"We really have to get going, Andrea," Lucio responded. "Your mother is waiting for us. And besides, it's late, Andrea. Can't you see the lady's busy?"

"Sure, Dad," Andrea retorted, in a tone of unconcern. She entered the living room; Lucio remained outside, near the door.

"You're selling things?" I asked awkwardly, sitting down on the couch.

Andrea handed me a catalogue of Christmas gift items: tins of licorice, glass containers of gumdrops, ceramic St. Nicks and a Nativity set in white chocolate. I thumbed through the catalogue quickly and then looked over at Lucio.

"Most everybody is buying candy," Andrea explained. "My mom, she doesn't like chocolate. I like it. And I like fish and my mom doesn't."

I kept returning to the peanut butter cups and pecan clusters.

But Andrea was sure of herself, self-possessed, a great sales-woman.

"You order now and pay me later when the things come, Miss Terry. Give me the number. There on the side."

"7736," I said. "The peanut butter cups. And 3492. The pecan log roll."

"I've sold a lot of pecan clusters. 3897. You want one of those, Miss Terry?"

"I'll take one of those, too," I said matter-of-factly.

"Where do you live, Miss Terry?" Andrea inquired.

"Not far from here," I answered, looking straight at Lucio.

I tried to hide my legs with one of Irma's large pink pillows.

"Do you want something to drink?" I asked.

"Nah, we gotta go now. Me and my mom and dad are going out to dinner. See you later, Miss Terry. Bye!"

"Goodbye, Andrea! See you." I called out. "Nice to meet you, Mr. Valadez," I said to Lucio, who shot me a glance.

"Same here," Lucio said without emotion. He put his arm around Andrea as they walked away. She looked up at him and smiled. He smiled back, then he tugged her hair. She hit his arm, pretending to fight. "Race you to the truck!" she called out. He let her beat him. I could hear their laughter inside the truck.

Andrea waved to me as they drove off. I waved back. Then I went inside.

I wished we all could have gone back into the house as Andrea headed to her room to do her homework, while Lucio and I talked about what we'd done that day.

But instead I sat on the couch, my legs propped up on a coffee table, as Irma came back in and swirled the hot wax in my direction. She then spread the honey-colored wax on one leg. I closed the fragile copy of the novela I'd borrowed from her. "Lea usted La continuación en la edición dominical de Confidencias de un Chófer," the last page said, teasing the reader into buying the next installment. But the comic book was published in 1957. No one I knew had the sequel.

To be continued.
The story of my life.

"The real problem with Lucio is that he's more Americano than
Mejicano. No one ever taught him who he really is and who his
people were and are. No granma. No granpa. No loving mom or
dad who knew where they came from and where they were going.
He's about as deracinated as they come," Irma said, without bat-
ting an eye. La comadre had it all figured out, as usual.

"Deracinated?" I asked.

I pulled out my Random House Dictionary of the English Language, College Edition. I carried it in a medium-sized plastic bag
I bought on El Paso Street at La Esquina, a store renowed for
huge tables filled with baskets of miscellaneous household items,
toys, hair ornaments, makeup, and ginseng. It was run by Koreans
and catered to the Mejicanos who daily crossed the border to
work and shop in El Paso. The webbed plastic bag was orange, red
and yellow, and it was the kind many women on the border used
because it was cheap, effective and colorful.

I read from the dictionary: "Page 358. 'Deracinated—adjective.
Isolated or alienated from a native or customary environment.' So
he's a Mejicano without the roots. Is that what you're saying,
Wirms?"

"*Do I see some cracks in your love for that stinking ratón, Lucio
Valadez?*" Irma said with exasperation.

"Let's just say I'm thinking about things. I have been ever since
we saw *Las Mujeres de Mi General*. It really affected me, Irma. I
can't get it out of my mind, just like the movie *The Head*. Did you
ever see that movie? This old dude wakes up to find he's just a
head. No body attached. He's resting on a stretcher when the mad
doctor shows him his head in a mirror. It was pretty chilling."

"We saw that movie together, Tere, don't you remember? When
we were seventeen. You had your eyes closed during most of it

and so I told you what was happening. Later we walked home because we didn't have a car. And you were so upset you threw up in that vacant lot near the Colonel Sanders."

"Okay, so that's what I mean. Loyalty. Trust. Through thick and thin. No finding yourself on a stretcher with a mad doctor."

"I think you're finally starting to see the light, comadre," Irma said with emphasis. "You're not stupid by chance, Tere, you're stupid by choice. When you fall in love with a married man, you have to be either a pendeja or a cabrona."

"I guess I'm both, Irma," I said. I tucked the Blue Dot, my bookmark, back inside the dictionary but not before rubbing it twice.

But I am a high school graduate and I'm proud of it. Not a college girl, though I did take a correspondence course with Tedley's Beauty College in El Paso and graduated with honors.

There are some gaps in my education, I admit. I was absent during the 7s, 8s and 9s. Multiplication tables, that is. Ask me what 7 times 8 is and I'll have to pause. Ask me what 9 times 6 is and I get shaky. Ask me how to spell "tomorrow" and I'll get feverish. The possessive? What possessive? Don't get me going about diagramming. I was never a good diagrammer. I wanted to be a good diagrammer, and I could have been. I liked drawing downward- or upward-slanting lines, but I had trouble with adverbs. Mine just hung in space. Same thing for outlines.

To me, the spooky possessive translates into Lucio Valadez. What I'm really trying to do here is diagram and outline my life for you. I'm looking for the words, but there's no dictionary I know that can explain the way I feel.

I'm a middle-of-the-roader. I watch from the sidelines. I'm not too religious. Too serious. Too conservative. Too judgmental. Too critical. Too backward. Too you-know-what-I-mean. Too *desde*. I'm an optimist except when I get in dark moods that usually have to do with low blood sugar or that time of the month or when I start thinking about Lucio Valadez. All I can really do when I get down is just wait it out and pray myself well again.

I know right from wrong. But knowing it hasn't helped. There is absolutely no way that La Santa Tere, mi tocaya, would have gotten herself into a mess like this with Lucio Valadez.

I know a good movie from a bad one, and I know enough to know I'm in a very bad movie. It's called *The Life of Teresina Ávila*, or *Outlaw Sex*. A story of unbridled passion. A woman. A man. Sparks. Eternal Fire. Damnation.

Pink Eye

The Sands is a dingy little motel off the beaten path. It's been a fairly good cover because of the drive-around location of the rooms, which are in the back near the river. You have to be standing in the water to see who comes and goes. And still, I'm nervous. Lucio's nervous. We're about played out here at the Sands but we keep pushing it. Last week Uvalia was in the lobby and she saw me going around the back. Her sister works at the Sands as a cleaning woman. I had to leave with excuses.

Lucio's excuses are legion. "I'm going out for a pack of cigarettes," he'll tell Diolinda, and come back three hours later after having met me at the Sands. How long can it take to get a pack of ciga- rettes? How long can you linger at the spa after a hard workout? How long does a dog need walking? How many times a week can you go out with the boys? And how long, puto, can I take the smell of another woman on you?

I didn't want to think about that smell. My smell on Lucio or Lucio's smell on Diolinda. I know what it's like to smell another woman on your man. I know what my smell is like, I often smell my arm in the soft spots, behind the wrist, or in the crook of the arm, that sensual zone few have ever touched. I imagine how Diolinda feels when she's smelled me on Lucio. Fortunately, Lucio says, Diolinda's sense of smell is permanently altered. She probably can't smell at all, especially after her last nose job. Her sinuses are screwed up. Something like that.

It's an Ávila family curse to have such a keen sense of smell. I can smell body odor from across the street, menstrual blood down the hall, chlamydia in an elevator and another woman on my man as soon as he walks in the door.

I was supposed to meet Lucio around four, in his room No. 17, at the back of the Sands, which faced the river. We thought we could hide behind the noise, the color, the craziness, in the preparations for his nephew Andy's wedding. Just for an hour or so. The "or so" was always the dangerous part.

Lucio paid monthly rent on the room. He still lives with Diolinda in El Paso. He only uses his motel room now and then when he comes home to visit his mother, Cuca, La V.B., otherwise known as Mother of All Cockroaches.

I parked around the corner at Sofia's Mighty Taco. When the coast was clear, I walked behind the drive-in restaurant. I peered in as Pinco Mondrales suddenly dropped a burger patty on the rubber mat, stooped over, dusted it off and flung it back on the greasy grill.

Sofia's was near the row of old cottonwoods that rimmed the small park by the river, near a tree-lined bend in the Río Grande where it was reputed La Llorona lived. The city fathers, currently a blustery, overfed, slightly constipated quorum of short older men, had named the spot Cortez Park last year in a citywide festival. The park honored Hernán Cortez, never mentioning, of course, his guide/translator/mistress, Doña Marina, La Malinche of the legend, una vendida who sold her people out to the Spanish conquerors. Ay, was the same act repeating itself? Was Lucio the conquistador and I the woman whose shame would go down through history?

The only thing that hadn't changed in all my years of growing up was the cottonwood trees near the river. They were old and still stately, despite the thriving mistletoe that had taken hold and wouldn't let go. Their shade was languorous, merciful.

As a young girl, I sat near the old cottonwoods, alongside smaller ugly trees whose names I didn't know. Each year the smaller, less graceful trees bore a strange fruit. The large balls had a pitted surface like little green brains. Some called them horse apples. A friend of Irma's who studied biology at State called them Osage orange. It didn't matter what they were. The balls were sturdy, useless, discarded. Meandering home the long way, I loved to kick the ugly, bruised fruit that no one ever ate.

I was a tall, skinny girl with banana feet, a flat, empty melon face, my heart as big as the sky, my dreams as green as the leaves on the enormous cottonwood I called Gabina. It was no one's name, a name I made up. I was that lonely tree, Gabina, a woman so full of mystery, a spirit so deep no one dared to see me as I truly was.

I often sat in the quiet dappled rooms of Gabina's shade, a young girl unappreciated by all men. My father was long dead and Albinita had no men other than God in her life.

I stopped to rest underneath Gabina in the hot afternoons. Long before Sofia's Mighty Taco. Long before Sofia's famous chimichanga deluxe with sour cream and guacamole. Long before Lucio Valadez.

And long before the discovery of Albinita's old diaphragm, tucked away in the shiny green plastic case that held hosiery, a few matching stockings, many with long, thin runners. The smell of my mother's feet assailed me, blended with that other smell. A woman smell I knew from entering the bathroom shortly after Albinita had sat on the toilet, her thin legs spread wide, hot, pungent urine trickling out of her dark space.

What was that gray plastic thing I found in Albinita's hosiery bag? I punched the little rubber hat. What are you? What do you do? How long have you been here? And with that question, I replaced the rubber circle and pushed it further into the stocking purse, in a corner next to Albinita's copy of *Lovers and Libertines*, a secret book only she was allowed to read, a book she kept there, for those times . . .

"Nor was it altogether chance that made her choose men who bled freely; they were invariably cut of the same frail cloth, for, untamed and untameable, she could never love strong men. Such men were too much like her—too independent, too masterful. . . . George Sand was too rebellious to be dominated."

Lucio was waiting for me.

"I brought you something, Tere."

"Oh yeah? What?"

"Biscochos."

"Biscochos? You know I'm trying to lose weight. Since I met you, I've put on ten pounds. It's all those Beer Nuts we eat in bed. Ay, I'm sorry. Thank you, baby, I mean it. I love the cookies. Who made them?"

"My mother."

"Oh, she bakes?"

"They're the best. I'll leave them here for you. So, what time is it? I have an hour."

I always forgot to have the Swamp Thing nearby, and just as we were about to consummate our secret unholy union, I had to stop and say insistently to Lucio: "Querido, wait a minute. Please, I have to put La Cosa in."

I went into the other half room, the shame room, to put the

Monster from Hell in before mi querido would have to see me, before he would be bothered, because it was my responsibility, it was my job as a woman to take care of IT, any number of ITS, there had been one before Lucio. It happened with Chago, but I never told him. He would have forced me to marry him, and I wasn't ready. But before I could even think of doing anything, I lost the baby. And that's when we broke up.

I hopped into the little room, moist breasts flopping. They were sudosos from Lucio's tongue, still full of his perspiration. One small dark wiry hair of his was wrapped around a nipple.

Alien, I discovered to my dismay, was in the glove compartment of my car, down the street near Sofia's Mighty Taco. That trip took five minutes and Querido Precioso Baby Boy wasn't happy. But it was all right. ¿Qué no, honey? No, it wasn't, because Lucio wanted to pick up La V.B. from her home and take her to the rehearsal dinner at the Holiday Inn. La Mosca Entremetida, the Interfering Fly Woman, her acid wings touching everything she came into contact with, was waiting for him.

But it was good I went out into the cold night air. Lucio had left his room key in the door lock, and there were some teenagers smoking marijuana out back.

I went to my car and got the damn pink holder from inside my glove compartment, where I kept it just in case, and made my way back to our room at the Sands. I turned on the damn lights to Lucio's gritos: *Dammit! Shit! What the hell!*

¡Ay! ¡Querido! Sweetheart! Honey! I called out as I stumbled across the room to my damn overnight case to where the damn Morrell's was and took out the damn Creature from Planet X. And tripped over Lucio's Luccheses, stubbing the same damn toe the damn second grader had stepped on Thursday, dammit, when I was at work, as I was every damn Monday through Friday, with a damn bunch of needy and unpleasant elementary school children, including the damn one who nearly broke my damn toe.

I limped back, took off my clothes and stood there, chichis sueltas y caídas, my breasts dead fish, my nipples slightly sore from Lucio's first crazy bites as I got back into bed. Lucio was out again and was snoring loudly.

I jellied the hell out of Rosemary's Baby, squeezing out the initial L for Lucio-Baby-I-can't-live-without-you-Papito-you're-the-only-one-really-the-only-one inside the plastic face. I folded the rim in, and tucked it into my body, a long-standing battleground, where it tried to find merciful darkness.

Dieguito, Lucio's little pee-pee, was limp as a worm from one of the old cottonwoods. I nudged him gently. Without a word, Lucio got on top of me. Dieguito suddenly came alive as Lucio's long-awaited kisses sucked the life from me and we ground ourselves into each other. We were a small island in the middle of the king-sized water bed. We sloshed and rolled to what each of us wished was a never-ending tide.

And not once, not even during Lucio's climax, did his mouth leave mine. No one had ever kissed me that way before. No one ever would after he was long gone. Lucio's mouth covered mine in delicious shame. Maybe next time there wouldn't be Godzilla between us.

There would be only soft, warm, pliant skin, the unmistakable bitter-tasting juice, the rollicking, roiling sea of our passion, and maybe, just maybe, a little tadpole would swim free to make a home in the pool of my sex and become a fish to swim free.

At six-thirty, after taking a shower that started off well and suddenly turned cold, with conditioner still clinging to my wet hair, I slunk back to the car, going home the long way, meandering through town, my vulva dripping hot Lucio juice. It was only when I got home and sat in my little beat-up red Hyundai in front of my apartment that I realized the horrible truth.

¡Ay, Dios de mi vida, diosito de mi corazón, chingao! I had forgotten my diaphragm at the Sands. No, it wasn't true!

Had I left the diaphragm in Lucio's bedroom/living room, whatever you called that all-purpose room we make love in and almost never sleep in, on the fake wooden table beside the king-sized water bed?

Did I leave El Demonio on the nightstand in its Pepto-Bismol-pink plastic case, a peeping flesh-colored eye reverently closed? I had to have left it in its case! There was some dignity to that. The maid would pick it up, without thinking, and throw it in the wastebasket, just another thing forgotten.

But no. Oh no! I'd left it exposed, oozing and swollen, roñoso, a running sore in the face of life, on the soap shelf in the dirty shower stall of the Sands Motel, on the flea-bitten dog-assed side of town behind the tracks. A dripping reminder of my darkest transgression.

The Sands Motel was one of any number of innumerable Sands Motels in the world, only this Sands Motel happened to be in the middle of my hometown, where it was hard to lose a diaphragm in the middle of the day and even harder to get it back at night before the morning cleanup.

I should forget about the diaphragm. Nothing important. Nothing irreplaceable. I'll just buy a new one. Size whatever. I'll go down to Planned Parenthood on the corner of Río Grande and Main and talk to Irma, who was doing their books. Irma would look up my records: birth control pills from age eighteen on, one irregular Pap leading to a frozen cervical tip, a harrowing case of mastitis, intermittent yeast infections that blew up overnight and just as quickly went away, and lastly, a thyroid scare that led to my leaving off with Dr. Cut'em, my regular gynecologist, his eyes opened wide with fear as he related tales of womanly woe: swollen chichis, dripping vaginas, vulvas hot and thick with pain. Cut'em had retired and now I'm a regular at Planned Parenthood, where I pay on the sliding scale. It's good that way, since my pay at Cabritoville Elementary isn't going anywhere too soon. No Dow Jones rising.

Irma will be kind. She'll understand. Getting a new diaphragm is like ordering out at Sofia's Mighty Taco. Just pull in around the back, I'll have the usual, a chile BLT with a side of fries. Hold the cheese. Oh heck, just give me everything.

Maybe I should just forget about getting a diaphragm. I'm not married now and I'm old enough to have a child if I want one. No one can tell me no if that's what my body wants. No sickly sniveling mother crying in the background, "Ay, ay, ay," no blustering big-bellied father yelling, "El honor de la familia . . . who do you think you are?"

God, how I hate folding that thing into my vagina. It has the texture of old rubber bands. When it's soft it becomes a wrinkly coin purse that winks at me as it buckles out. It smiles at me like the one tired gray eye of La Vieja Lerma, the cockeyed newspaper vendor with the silly grin, her baggy striped shorts and pink blouse a perennial clown's outfit as she ranges the median strip on Ranchitos Street.

It's a stupid contraption that I slip into my body on the sly. Hola, mi amor. How you? That's the way La Vieja talks.

I know the pain of sex the day after a night of too much lovemaking, my stomach knotted hard and tingling. With disgust I reach inside my swollen vagina to search and destroy. The slippery flesh-colored dome comes out with a pop, the sound of a tight watermelon cracking. I take the thing to the washbasin and rinse the yellow-white semen away.

I've tried pills, but I hate them. I always forget to take them, then I double up, knowing they are for the wrong days, hell, the *wrong week, knowing they make me feel sick and dry and irrita*ble. The diaphragm is worse, it's so premeditated an act of murder, except it's myself I'm killing. I'm allergic to the spermicidal jelly. It makes me break out; somehow it makes me break down. That's what happened to my cervical tip, too much jelly, too much lovemaking, too many hard humps on a too soft mattress with someone without a soul.

I hate the medicinal smell of the killer grease, even though there isn't supposed to be a smell. I hate the way the jelly feels, not something sweet like its name, apricot or raspberry jam, but something greasy like a fingerful of Morrell lard, sticky when I wash my hands making biscochos, remembering too late that the lard won't come off with water.

What is lard but animal fat? Which animal? What fat? With the jelly you wipe your hands on a toalla or paper towels and even then there is slimy-slick mugre between your fingers. That's how a man's sperm gets stuck—by a handful of unknown grease from a long-dead animal who didn't know that it would betray.

It's bad to have to use that thing I hate so much, even if the loving comes strong and crazy good to you from a man you can't live without.

I was always worried about someone finding Lucio and me at the Sands. Cabritoville is too small a town. We've already used up all the tricks lovers use to hide their love, and then some. We've met in all sorts of out-of-the-way motels from Cabritoville to El Paso, from El Paso to Juárez, rotating locations but always returning briefly to the shifting Sands.

Things have revolved around our frantic couplings, strangled late-night conversations from pay phones in the middle of any number of cold empty highways, and from the musty, smoke-filled lobbies of innumerable wayside motels and out-of-the-way truck stops.

Everything comes back to this: the shock of the missing diaphragm.

¡Aaaayyy! Why hadn't I left the diaphragm in its pink case on the room divider, a natural and logical action? I'd checked the drawers for underwear and slips, cameras, not that I'd put anything in there, had I? I couldn't remember. All I ever remembered needing in this room was the diaphragm. All I ever wanted to do in that room was make love to Lucio and then fall asleep in his arms. That was if he had the time to fall asleep and didn't have to do an errand for someone in his family, mostly La V.B., whose long and demanding cancer was only soothed nights with a little pint of whiskey from the twenty-four-hour Stop-and-Go.

Maybe someone could help me out. Uvalia's sister cleaned

rooms at the Sands. María? Marina? What was the name of the sister who cleaned? Marta?

I made my way into the sad-looking lobby. I couldn't find anyone. I pressed the buzzer on the desk. I practiced a speech in my mind.

Dear Marta:

You don't know me, but I know you. I mean, I know your sister, Uvalia. How are you, Marta? ¿Qué tal? I'm Tere Ávila, a friend of your sister's. Could you, would you mind looking, pretty please, for a used diaphragm in the shower stall of room number seventeen? Would you, I mean, could you—por favor—put it in a paper bag and leave it for me at the front desk? I'll come back and pick it up later. No, that wouldn't do. So I made up an imaginary scenario in my mind to explain the forgotten diaphragm to myself and Marta, the cleaning sister:

I, Teresina Ávila-Anglo-Fill-in-the-Name, a married woman, and Fill-in-the-Blank-Anglo-Name, my husband, a kind and loving man and our kids, Junior and Brenda Ávila-Anglo-Name, and Muffie, the Anglo dog, stayed at your motel. My husband, a nice, loving and supportive Anglo man who cooks, is at the wheel of our white Anglo van. He wants to get an early start. Denver is a long way off and Aunt Lula, *his* aunt, is waiting for us.

If I wanted, I *could* make my loyal Anglo husband a Mejicano, or better yet, a tolerant, hip and loving half Anglo/half Mejicano man, but no, to have an Aunt Lula meant you were the worst kind of Anglo, someone from Oklahoma, according to Graciela. The only thing worse, Graciela often said, the only thing worse than a Mejicana from Oklahoma, was a Mejicana who *thought* she was Anglo. Graciela had a thing about Oklahoma. Someday I'd have to ask her about it. Probably has to do with a man from Oklahoma she met at La Tempestad.

Only one old girlfriend I know married someone from over that way, south, west, east, north, any Anglo direction, and Boy Howdee did she now have an accent from over there.

"Terry, I'd jes love to come home to visit yu'all and Mama for Chrismus but I jes cain't. Dexter and the twins have me runnin' up one side of the crick and down th' other. And on top of that, there's a conflict with a Wildcats game. And *you* know how Dexter feels 'bout the Cats! Wish I could come. I have to tell you, Flat Prairie is hoam to me now. Cabritoville is a thing of the past! I tell you, Terry girl, I wanna come home, but I jes cain't."

Cain't? This was a born-and-raised-in-Cabritoville-dark-as-a-raisin-living-across-the-tracks girlfriend, María Refugia del Carmen Benavidez. Did she just say cain't?

Here she was acting like a white girl when all her Mejicano relatives had hokey-sounding puro Mejicano names like Plutarco or Chamala or Fila or Piro and they lived in Cabritoville and were married to Tumbia and Mecho, Chevito long gone.

I stood at the front desk ringing the buzzer for what seemed like ten minutes, until finally a tired-looking Anglo woman with dark worn-down rodent teeth came to greet me.

"Miss . . . I, uh, left something in a room, could you ask the cleaning lady, I think her name is Marta, if she could take me around the back?"

"What room was that?"

"I'm not sure. I think it was number seventeen. Yes, seventeen."

"Got any ID?"

"I was visiting a friend."

"Oh, was you? Who?"

"There was a party back there. I think the man's name was Mr., uh, Valadez."

"Mr. Valadeez don't have no parties. Not that I know of. He likes to read his books."

"There was a group of us. I know Marta, she could take me around back."

"Marta ain't here."

"Can I borrow the key? I left a bracelet. Took it off. Must have fallen somewhere."

"What kind of bracelet . . . Miss . . ."

"Mrs., uh, López . . . I mean Ávila, López-Ávila, I'm a friend of the Valadez family."

"Oh, come on now, just get on with you. Here's the damn key. I seen you before and don't think I haven't, missy. Go on back and get the hell thing you're missing. Now go on, and bring me back the key."

It's not like the diaphragm had my name on it or anything, but it was the principle of the matter. And the inconvenience of it all. And on top of everything, the shame.

The horrible fact of the matter was that everybody and their goat knew La Vieja Bruta as the reigning Queen of Cabritoville. And it didn't matter that the Goat Queen, La Gran Cabrona, was dying, she still had the power to change lives. All of Cabritoville would soon learn, if they didn't know already, that I was the no-body with the missing diaphragm. And now EVERYONE who knew Lucio or who knew about him would know as well.

I'd left the diaphragm in the moldy shower stall, the beige tile stained brown in the corners, the shower head a lone bugler pointing downward toward Hell. The dirty cream-colored shower mat was soggy and tangled with curly, wiry hair. Surely not mine, surely not Lucio's. The step up to the shower was slippery and soapy. No one ever cleaned these shower walls with antiseptic cleaners or lemon-scented ammonia. The shower smelled of old rusty water tubes. When you turned the shower on, the levers lied, the hot meaning cold and the cold meaning hot. I heard the deep rumble of trapped water, then the long metal squeal of re-lease, which reminded me that this wasn't home, could never be home. I was here for just one reason, one purpose.

I, Teresina Ávila, had lost all shame.

Marta, Uvalia's sister, would have had to pick up my diaphragm with a brown paper towel and throw it away, squinching her nose and trying to avert her eyes, thinking all the while: Cochinos, marranos, sin vergüenzas. Here I am. Me. Left to clean this filth. Fuuuchi, fuuuuchi!

Once inside the room, I made a beeline for the shower stall. Sure enough, the Swamp Thing was there, all wet and shiny-looking like an alien pod. I picked it up and put it in a small paper bag. I also picked up the bag of biscochos Lucio had brought me back from the wedding rehearsal. Might as well go back home and make myself a cup of dark, strong coffee. I tiptoed back to the lobby to give the rat woman her key back.

"Thank you."

"Yeah."

I set the two little paper bags down and handed the key back. I left as quickly as I could.

And when I got back to the car, I realized I only had one bag.

¡Ayyyyy! There was no turning back now.

¡Biscochos!

I took a cookie out of the bag. Too dry.

Minutes of the Pedro Infante Club de Admiradores Norteamericano #256

The meeting was called to order at 7:45 p.m. by Nyvia Ester Granados, president.

Members present: Nyvia Ester Granados, president; Irma Granados, vice president; Tere Ávila, secretary; Sista Rocha, treasurer; Catalina Lugo, parliamentarian. Members at large: Concepción "Connie" Vallejos, Elisa Urista, Ofelia Contreras, Merlinda Calderón, Francisca "Pancha" Urdialez, Tina Reynosa, Margarita Hinkel and Ubaldo Miranda.

We would have started earlier, but the lights went off around 7:15 p.m. when Sista Rocha's son, Carlos Jr., put some nachos in the toaster oven. Too many appliances were going at once: the washer and her daughter Raquel's hair dryer. We had to wait until Carlos Sr. came home from bowling so he could turn on the circuit breaker. The first fifteen minutes of the meeting was held by candlelight, which was very romantic.

The treasurer's report had to wait until the lights came on. Sista Rocha counted $24.59, which she pulled out from her brassiere. Things are at an all-time low. Former treasurer Onelia González-Johnson's son, Del Wayne, got into her purse and stole the membership dues to support his cocaine habit. We wish Onelia the best of luck in her new job in Amarillo, Texas. We were sad to hear that Del Wayne was sent to La Tuna Penitentiary.

A motion was passed by Catalina Lugo that Sista open a bank account as soon as possible. It was seconded by Francisca Urdialez, who wants to be called Pancha from now on.

Irma Granados suggested we should think about raising money for the annual pilgrimage to El Panteón Jardín de la Capital de la República for the Anniversary of Pedro's Death on April 15. Members who have expressed an interest in going include everyone except Concepción Vallejos, who wants to be called Connie if Francisca is going to be called Pancha. Connie has to have gallbladder surgery that month. She will report back to us if she can change the date of her operation.

Sista Rocha recommended we have an enchilada fund-raiser at the Knights of Columbus Hall. Ofelia Contreras didn't think it was a good idea making thousands of greasy messy red enchiladas just before Christmas when you have to make so many sugary messy biscochos.

Other fund-raising suggestions included raffling a velvet Pedro Infante painting by Ubaldo Miranda and having a Christmas Dance at Tino's La Tempestad Lounge.

Ofelia Contreras said that if we had a fund-raiser at that no-good bar and den of iniquity that masks as a lounge where men pick up women and I don't know what else, she was quitting the fan club.

Elisa Urista seconded the motion.

Voting was 8–5 in favor of the enchilada dinner, 12–1 against the velvet painting and 10–3 against the dance.

The fund-raiser ideas were tabled by Madame President until the next meeting.

Sista Rocha made sure all the unnecessary appliances were off and we watched *Los Gavilanes*, which came out in 1954. Pancha led the discussion.

Juan Menchaca, played by Pedro Infante, was a modern-day Robin Hood Mejicano-style a 'lo Zorro dressed in black. We discussed its pros and cons. Everyone was in favor of his taking the money from the patrones and giving it to the poor, everyone, that is, except Margarita Hinkel, who didn't feel the movie set a very good example for our youth.

Tina Reynosa said that because Margarita was rich and her husband was the manager at Luby's Cafeteria and she got to eat Salisbury steak, baked potatoes and iced tea anytime she wanted, she'd forgotten what it was to struggle. The rest of us have to take baloney sandwiches to lunch. Tina advised Margarita to stop talking about the rich and the poor.

Merlinda Calderón said that what got her was the fact that the mother, La Señora Menchaca, didn't tell her son, Juan, that Roberto was his brother, sparing everyone a lot of grief to come.

Ofelia suggested that there wouldn't be any movie if La Señora Menchaca had done that. And not only that, if Merlinda didn't know what was happening in *Los Gavilanes*, it was no surprise she didn't know that her daughter, La Rebecca, was hanging out at Sofia's Mighty Taco with a greasy-headed pachuco from Sunland Park who was full of tattoos and drove a red lowrider car with "Queen of the Night" painted in drippy black letters on the hood.

Merlinda called Ofelia the B-word. Madame President told everyone to SHUT UP.

Ubaldo asked if anyone wanted a shot of whiskey in their hot chocolate.

Madame President suggested we keep it clean. The vote was 12–1 against the shot of whiskey.

Madame President asked for a moment of silence as we remembered Pedro Infante and thanked him for bringing us such joy and happiness.

Ubaldo Miranda sang "Amorcito Corazón," one of Pedro's best-known and loved songs. He didn't sound at all like Pedro Infante, what with all the hacking and honking. He apologized profusely for his cold, but Madame President encouraged him to continue singing, saying that "even Pedro got colds."

Despite his cold, the fan club members felt he had a real feeling for Pedro's music. Tina Reynosa commented that Ubaldo's voice had improved. How come? Ubaldo was so moved he brought himself to tears and had to start over.

Even a man can love Pedro Infante, said Merlinda Calderón. All the fan club members looked at Ubaldo. Madame President told Tere to console Ubaldo, who was still crying.

Pancha suggested that Pedro Infante was greater than any other Mexican singer, including Jorge Negrete, who everyone thought was a little too thin, not enough meat on his bones. Tina Reynosa said that José Alfredo Jiménez had a beautiful voice, but put a paper bag over his face, would you?

Connie remarked that José Alfredo was only forty-seven years old when he died, pobrecito. Irma said he looked much older. Pedro was only forty when he died, Tina noted, and he still looked good.

Elisa said that Javier Solis was okay, more than okay, he was good, but you name them all, they were no match whatsoever for Pedro.

Madame President proposed a vote be taken to name Pedro Infante the top Mexican singer of all time. Irma Granados seconded the motion. All members said "Ay."

Madame President called for New Business.

New Business included Elisa Urista's update on current Pedro "sightings." Elisa reported there will be a special program on Univision that will go into the interior of Méjico to a small village to find a viejito who says he is Pedro Infante. She didn't have too

many details, but asked us to stay tuned. She will call the Juárez
TV station for information and will report back to us. We'll "chain
call" each other and plan on meeting at Irma Granados' apartment
to see the program on her wide-screen color TV.

New Business also included the motion from Ubaldo Miranda
that we connect with the sister club in Ciudad Juárez, Club de
Admiradores Mejicano #777, joining them for dinner and drinks
at the Kentucky Club for the next meeting.

The motioned was seconded by Tere Ávila. Voting was 10–3
against the "drinks" part at the Kentucky Club.

Lunch maybe, said Madame President, but we aren't going to
put up the bail bond money to get you out of jail if you take off on
us like you did last time, Ubaldo.

A committee was set up to look into an intercambio with the
Juárez club for an afternoon tea at the Museum of Fine Arts with
shopping afterward at the PRONAF Shopping Center and at the
Old Mercado.

The committee includes Nyvia Ester Granados, Catalina Lugo
and Margarita Hinkel, who has offered her large van to the group
as transportation, just as long as we split the gas.

Connie suggested we go early in the day to get pedicures at
Salón de Belleza Maritza and avoid the late afternoon traffic on
the Chamizal Bridge.

Pancha seconded the motion only if we could swing by the bak-
ery off 16th of September to get her pastel de tres leches that her
husband, Mikey, loves and a couple dozen of their famous boli-
llos.

The next meeting will be held December 8 at the home of Tere
Ávila. We will have a gift exchange. No gift more than five dollars.
Members drew names from an old sombrero Sista had on her wall
and took down for the occasion.

Sista reported that she bought the hat in a small shop behind
the Basilica in Mexico City. The shop owner told her it had been
worn by Pedro Infante. She had no way of verifying this, but she
bought the hat anyway as a memento of her trip to La Capital.

Madame President reminded members that the Christmas meeting will feature Mexican BYOB's (Bring your own Bebidas y Botanas).

Merlinda exhorted Ubaldo that he refrain from drinking liquor at this year's Christmas party. Remember last year? Everyone did. Merlinda said her rug would never be the same. A vote was taken to encourage Ubaldo to stop drinking. All in favor said "¡Ayyy!"

Tina suggested we close the meeting pretty soon, because she had to get up early in the morning for her son Sammy's paper route and how come we changed the meetings from Friday to Monday?

Madame President tabled this question until next week.

Ofelia seconded the motion that we close the meeting.

Madame President adjourned the meeting. She couldn't find her gavel, so she hit the coffee table with her hand, breaking a small blue vase.

The meeting was over at 10:35 p.m.

PS A few members stayed around for "goodies." Sista brought out her famous puchas, the Mexican wedding cookies only she can make. She's been making cookies for over a month for her daughter Raquel's wedding on December 1.

By the way, all members are invited. If you want to bring food, Sista still needs macaroni salad and any kind of Jell-O salad, especially the green kind with cottage cheese and nuts like the kind they make at Luby's (hint, hint!) that tastes so good, or the kind with the multicolored layers—that is, if you have the time to make it—and whatever else you can think of that goes with tacos. The wedding will take place December 1 at 4 p.m. at Sacred Heart Church, with the wedding reception starting at 6 p.m. at the Knights of Columbus Hall and going on until the 11 a.m. Mass on Sunday. Only kidding. Dress fancy. Be sure and wear your levanta chichis, said Sista. Music is by Los Torcidos.

Minutes for the monthly meeting of the Pedro Infante Club de Admiradores Norteamericano #256.

Respectfully submitted by Secretary Tere Ávila, Esquire.

PART III

EL
INOCENTE

Another Pedro-athon

"Do you want to watch *Arriba las Mujeres*?" Irma asked.

We were in her small pink kitchen taking food out of large paper bags from Safeway. We'd both given up going to La Tempestad—again—we didn't have formal dates, and as on too many other weekends when we didn't have a social life, we gathered at her place to cook up a storm. Tonight's fare included spaghetti, some fresh basil, a frozen plastic container of Hatch green chile and a platter of our favorite cheeses: Extra Sharp Cheddar for me, Monterey Jack for Irma and black olives for both of us.

Irma lives in a medium-sized two-bedroom house near Álamo Park, by the old cottonwoods near the river. It's a nice spot if you have to live in Cabritoville. I live near what passes as a downtown, behind the fire station and the Tastee-Freez.

The largest room in Irma's house is what we call the Pedro room. It's in the rear of the house and leads to her backyard. The main feature of the room is a large framed poster of Pedro Infante in *El Enamorado*. Pedro wears a huge grin on his handsome face, holds two cocked guns at elbow height, while behind him a group of masked men hold up a stagecoach, the bearded driver with his hands up in the air. Pedro's huge smiling face is to the viewer's left; and in the right-hand corner, looking a 'lo todo chingate baby I'm-too-hot in my bright red lipstick, is Sarita Montiel, the Spanish actress who was one of the few women during the Época de Oro who could hold her sexual own with Pedro. Híjole, the woman was beautiful. Irma has quite a collection of Pedro posters from the forties and fifties that she's bought over the years and needs to frame.

A large picture window in the Pedro room looks out on a small but neat backyard full of apricot, apple and fig trees. Irma is a gardener and loves her rosebushes and fruit trees almost as much as she loves Pedro Infante.

What La Wirms has done in the Pedro room is magic, it's like a living shrine, all rose-colored walls, the large television set flashing images of Pedro here, there, doing this, now that, the fruit trees silent and strong in the background, Pedro looking slyly at Carmen Sevilla in a poster from the movie ¡Gitana Tenías Que Ser!.

At times like these, life's too perfect and we know it. How much longer it will stay this way is uncertain. But at this moment we are an unconquerable sisterhood that says to hell with the world outside this room and beyond that too cool yard.

Sometimes after a long hot summer day of temperatures over a hundred, we'll go outside in the evenings and lay on a blanket under the trees and watch the shooting stars. We're both allergic to grass, and in spite of the blanket, we always come back inside itchy, prickled with the enormity of the many distinctive parallel lives out there.

Our favorite thing to do no matter the season is to have our weekly Pedro-athons. Irma will wear one of her two extra-large pink T-shirts, washed so many times the necks are frayed, with a pair of black shorts and pink plastic thongs.

She loves the color pink and most of her decor is just that, pink as all get-out: each room a different shade, from the raspberry-colored couch in the Pedro room, with its crocheted fuchsia comforter thrown carelessly over the top, to at least ten fuzzy pink pillows, the floral paintings on the walls Irma has painted herself, as well as her collection of pink Troll dolls, which line one whole bookshelf in the Pedro room.

And yet, there's nothing glamorous about these evenings. We wear our most comfortable baggy clothing, our hair in pink plastic curlers with gray foam rollers on the bottom in the back and sides to soften the pain of our self-imposed beauty regimen. We don't care who sees us, because nobody will. And that is what is so delicious about these nights of our beloved Pedro-athons. No men, no other women to distract, infuriate, or demand anything from us.

I wear a large white nightgown that I leave in Irma's room in a drawer she's given me. I'm known for falling asleep during our Pedro-athons, oftentimes as soon as my head touches my special pillow that I keep in my designated spot in the hall closet. Some of my best sleeping is done on La Wirms's long couch in the Pedro room during an exhausting and exhilarating Pedro-athon.

La Wirms lets me sleep until late the next morning. When I wake up, I'll go home to clean house during that Saturday morning busy time when you feel you should be doing important work. Sometimes La Wirms and I go out to breakfast at Sofia's Mighty Taco. Other times we make waffles or eat plain yogurt, which depends on whether Irma is dieting that week.

We can watch two or three Pedro movies in a row as we eat and talk about men. Which means I talk about Lucio while Irma listens. After that we fall asleep exhausted on Irma's huge megalounger in the Pedro room, stretched out on the world's largest sofa that takes up the rest of the space not used by her giant-screen color television set.

Irma has, by now, gathered an incredible collection of Pedro Infante videotapes. She taped most of his movies when they played on late-night television. Last year she was frantically busy for the Anniversary of Pedro's Death on April 15. We wanted to go to Méjico for the big celebration, but I couldn't get off work and she was studying for her orals. Nyvia Ester went with Sista Rocha, and they didn't come back until they wrung the rag dry, as Sista said. Next year, Irma and I will go to the panteón with the rest of the fan club.

"So, do you want to watch *Arriba las Mujeres* or not, Tere?" Irma asks, a bit impatiently.

Is the girl in one of her moods? I wonder.

"No, I don't, Irma," I reply with conviction as I take out her cutting board and start chopping onions, the kind that make you cry. I'm all right with this, since I feel like crying anyway. Whatever excuse is good enough with me.

"If you must know, Wirms, I'm feeling sad and betrayed by the world. I want to assert my male side. I think I need to hate someone. That movie is too tame for me, Irma. I gave it a C minus last time and I haven't changed my opinion. I really want to hate tonight. Any suggestions?"

"Are you in a hate-your-parents mood or a hate-all-men mood? Or just a hate-the-friggin'-planet mood? If it's parents, we could watch *La Oveja Negra* and *No Desearás la Mujer de Tu Hijo*. The father in that is very despicable."

"I'm in more of a hate-men mood."

"So you haven't heard from Lucio this week, Tere?" Irma said as she put the onions in a frying pan. She was working on her famous spaghetti sauce.

"Who said that? All I said was that I wanted to hate men. *All* men. And for no reason. Porque me da la gana. Just because."

"*La Vida No Vale Nada* should do it, then. Followed by *Los Hijos de María Morales*. After either of those two movies, we should build up a rabia that is unchained, girlfriend. What Pedro Infante and Antonio Badú do to the women in that pueblito in *Los Hijos de María Morales* should inflame us sufficiently. We can hate men as much as we want and then we'll be done. Or we can eat a quiet dinner and watch something sad, like *Sobre las Olas*, where Pedro plays the music conductor Juventino Rosas. You remember he loses Lolita, the woman he loves, and then dies before his true talent is appreciated. It'll make us cry. And after that, we'll fall asleep like babies. So where's the garlic? You left it out last time, Tere, and the sauce was flat."

"That's what I love about you, comadre, you always understand how I feel. Unlike Lucio, you know what I need and when I need it. So hand me the cutting board."

Just before our periods, for example, we always watch either one of two double features: *Nosotros los Pobres* and *Ustedes los Ricos* or *Un Rincón Cerca del Cielo* and *Ahora Soy Rico*, two back-to-back tearjerkers that turn up the volume on the menstrual blues. If we need to laugh, we watch *El Inocente*.

"I love *El Inocente*. Why don't we watch that," Irma said. "It might even cheer you up, Tere. God knows, you need to laugh. I can't remember the last time I heard you laugh out loud. Come on, it's one of Pedro's funniest movies."

Wirms was right. You just want to see *El Inocente* over and over again. Here Pedro plays a poor car mechanic named Cruci, who runs a Mexican AAA type of business helping stranded travelers. He gets a call on New Year's Eve from Mané, a rich young woman, who has him drive her to her parents' home in Cuernavaca. When they get there, the parents are gone. One thing leads to another, and they get drunk to celebrate the New Year. There's something so romantic about it, too, as unbeknownst to each other (!), they innocently fall asleep in the same bed after a night of drinking. In the morning her parents and brother find them sleeping together and make them get married. It's a terrible situation until Mané realizes she *really* is in love with Cruci.

"You know what I love about Pedro, Irma? He's not a wolf. Not like most men. When he fell asleep with Mané, there was nothing sexual about it. That's what I love about him, he never took any woman by force."

"He never had to, why would he? Just look at him. He's a gentleman, and if the matter did come up, the answer, as far as I'm concerned, would be yes. So what do you say we watch *El Inocente?*"

"I don't know, Irma. I don't feel like laughing tonight," I said, getting the cheese board out and wiping it off. Irma hated when I did this, as if anything in her impeccably clean house needed to be improved upon.

"How about *Los Tres Huastecos?*"

"Eh . . ."

"I know what you mean. A movie like *Los Tres Huastecos* could go several ways. You never know what sort of mood you'll end up in after watching it, so it's kind of risky. You could be irritated with the three brothers or pissed off at the Blond Factor or you might laugh your head off with the cross-dressing shenanigans, you never know. Now if you want to feel pensive and thoughtful, *Sobre las Olas* is a good call. Or if you want to see a movie that will encourage you to continue, despite all the odds, *Pepe el Toro* is the movie. I mean, in the movie, Pedro is still poor, his wife and twins have died in a car accident, his carpentry business has failed, and when he tries to earn money by boxing, he accidentally kills his opponent."

"So what will it be, comadre?" Irma asked me as she sharpened a large knife.

"Today is an angry yell-at-the-cabrón-sky-and-the-mother-puta-who-brought-the-pendejo-into-my-life-who-caused-my-blistered-heart-to-bleed sort of night. We have to go dark. Really dark. I haven't seen hide nor hair of Lucio's slick little cuerpito for about a week. No flowers, no messages, not even a measly call saying, 'Hey, it was great, was it great for you?' "

"I'm sorry, Tere. But there's nothing you can do. He's married and that's all there is to it. So where's the bottle of wine you got?"

"Don't get started, Irma. For your information, it's chilling in the fridge. Damn it, Lucio could have at least called and lied to me. 'Baby, it was so good. I can't wait until we can get together again and I'm in your arms. You're so good, baby.' "

"Lucio doesn't seem the type to call you or anyone else 'baby.' Not even a baby," Irma said. "I told you to get red wine."

"I forgot."

"You know I wanted red."

"And I wanted white."

"Red with pasta."

"Says who?"

"Only a million Italians and Robert La Grange in Chapter Ten of *Italian Cooking with Mama and Papa*."

"So shoot me. On one hand you're right, Lucio's not a big cariño type of guy, not up on the endearments scale. He's a man of action."

"Oh, so he doesn't believe in foreplay?" Irma said, slurping a long thread of spaghetti into her mouth. "Not quite done. I mean, for you; for me it's overdone."

"I never said he didn't believe in foreplay. Do you mind if we just concentrate on cooking? Where's the bread?"

"And I'm *not* curious. Not that I really need to know. I mean, you don't have to tell me everything. I'm only your comadre."

"We're not really suited when you come down to it. I'm a little bigger-boned, and I like my men a little longer, more stretched out and filled in. And yet, he's very developed for someone his height. Not that he's that short. He just isn't a big man."

"So is he at all *desde*?"

"No, he's not at all *desde*. He might sell insurance, but his hands aren't soft. They're the hands of someone who works away from work. And he doesn't have a panza from sitting behind a desk and getting no exercise. He's not dusty. Not one bit. Not like Mr. Perea, the principal at school."

That's another way Irma and I rate men. Are they dusty or fresh? Dusty is someone who looks gray and lifeless. Fresh is someone with blood still running through their veins, a little jugo left in the can, todavía con sabor, you get the idea.

"Yeah, Mr. Perea is dusty. If you saw him naked you could probably follow the outline of his tripas and count them one by one. He isn't bovinic, but he's dusty."

"So what does Lucio do, Tere? I mean, I know he's an insurance salesman, but what does he really *do*?" Irma said as she spinned out, a dancer in circular motion, to drain the pasta in the sink. She ran cold water over the pasta so it wouldn't stick, something she said she'd read somewhere. I disagreed with her on this, and refused to believe it was true. I always drained the pasta and then put it back in the pan without rinsing it. Two different styles, two different pastas. One gummy, the other al dente.

"Lucio only has the most successful insurance company in southern Nuevo Méjico and West Tejas. He's been 'in insurance' since high school when his dad put him to work in the Valadez Loan and Insurance Office. The loan part of Valadez Loan and Insurance dropped away with Lucio. He wasn't interested in pestering people to pay him for their arrears. He and Velia just bought Cabritoville Center, that strip mall that houses Velia's doggrooming business and her adjoining hot-dog restaurant. Lucio says he'll eventually open a branch of his insurance company there. Sure, his dad started the insurance business. But it was never the business it became after Lucio took over."

What I didn't tell Irma was why I really liked Lucio. You can tell your best comadre most things, but there are some things you can never share with anyone. Things that you usually didn't realize you loved about a person until they were gone from your life.

I liked the fact he wasn't shy when he was naked. He just strode around the room like he was completely relaxed being naked, not nervous, not looking at you out of the corner of his eye like most men, embarrassed and wondering what you were thinking about them, if their huevos hung too low or were too stretched out, or if they were too small or if their taco was okay. I say, who's looking at the chimichanga anyway? I mean, at least all the time. Where's the romance? Where's the music? Where's the mystery?

So enough with Lucio's chicken flauta, that's not why I kept winding up in his motel room at the Sands. I didn't like the room, but I liked him. I liked his smile and I loved the kindness I thought I saw in him. I remembered how he was with Andrea, how much he loved and cherished her. He made me want so much more than I had ever had. And he made me forget I had no right to such things, especially with him. He made me long for those things I never thought would be mine—like a home, family, someone to hold hands with those long, long nights, through the good times and in the bad.

"Well, here we are, Tere, two women without men," said Irma, fluffing up a large pink chenille pillow on her side of the couch. "And it makes watching *Arriba las Mujeres* just about perfect. That's the movie we're going to see."

Irma was starting her familiar nesting routine. She fluffed the sofa pillows, turned down the lights. The pasta was done, and the sauce was simmering.

"I don't really like *Arriba las Mujeres* as much as you do, Wirms," I said, getting out the wineglasses.

"It's one of Pedro's early movies, Tere. It predated women's lib, and by a lot of years. I love seeing Mejicanas boss Mejicanos around. It's rare enough in the cinema, much less in life. We'll eat well, then fall asleep and wake up with our hearts pure, hopeful again, ready for more chingazos and ready to give or take pleito. What do you say, comadre? And if you think about Pedro, you'll have the courage and hope to go on. How could a carpenter born in Mazatlán and raised in Guamúchil, Sinaloa, ever think of becoming Méjico's biggest film star and most favorite and loved singer? People called him 'El Peladito,' the Nobody, but he rose from obscurity and that's no small matter."

"You know, Wirms, I've never thought about it, but Pedro's right up there with Jesucristo and La Virgen de Guadalupe. Just thinking about both Pedro and Christ being carpenters makes me feel holy."

The plot of *Arriba las Mujeres* is simple: a young woman from a small town comes to the big city to learn the "feminine ways and guiles" of her compadre's two daughters, leaving her boyfriend behind, a loving country bumpkin, played by Pedro. The girl and her father find the house turned upside down, the wife and her two daughters wearing mannish clothing, and the father, a simpering yes-man to his overbearing and liberated wife, who wears a man's tie and a double-breasted suit. The movie had potential, but the dream of equality for women couldn't be sustained. Not then. Not now. Women always seem to lose out to men. They always have to give in or give up and save face or bend backwards to keep the peace. *Arriba las Mujeres* pooped out in the end.

Arriba las Mujeres is one of Pedro's early movies. It was made in 1943, and although Pedro's shy and a bit awkward in it, there's something wonderful about it just the same. You keep looking for Pedro, but he's never there. He's back in the pueblito, waiting for his novia to return as a grand lady who knows how to sew and knit and make tasty guisos out of nothing. We don't see him for much of the movie, though he does turn up near the end.

I got up for some potato chips Irma always keeps in a top kitchen cabinet, just in case we needed some junk food to offset the good food we were about to eat.

"Would you sit down, Tere. Your puttering is making me tired. The sauce is almost done and then we'll eat. Sit down and rest. I vote for *Arriba las Mujeres*."

"Are you sure?"

"*Arriba las Mujeres* it'll be, Tere. It might knock some sense into you, although I doubt it, you've gone too far down the road of no return. The movie was ahead of its time. A dangerous movie, or it could have been, if the women had continued to challenge their roles in that male-dominated society and not given in to the men at the end. Come on, it's a good movie. Just about right. What with me in Limbo and you in Hell. Or is it the other way around?"

"You in Hell? What do you mean?"

"Sit down!"

"Okay, I'm sitting."

"Tonight's the anniversary. Don't you remember?"

"What anniversary? Oh, you mean since I met Lucio?"

"Sal died three years ago tonight."

"I'm sorry, Wirms, I forgot."

"Sal and I used to like to watch *Arriba las Mujeres* together. We'd fight about women's lib—yes or no—and then we'd make up. I was thinking about Sal and me, and that made me think about Mr. Wesley."

"Mr. Wesley!" I said, getting up to check the sauce. "Mr. Wesley? You mean your boss Mr. Wesley, that viejito like an albino salamander, *that* Mr. Wesley, the old man, the widower, you're not telling me the old dusty dry stick whose books you're doing?" I was prancing around the room like an angry marionette. "Him? The guy who owns the old motel on Highway 478? What's it called?"

"The Flying W."

"The Flying W. Don't tell me."

"Mr. Wesley's a gentleman."

"And so is your father's best friend, all seventy years of him, Mr. Knights of Columbus."

"You have something against the Knights of Columbus, I swear, Tere."

"I do not. Just because the first older man that took an interest in me sexually was a Knight of Columbus. He was a friend of my dad's. Every time I saw him he came up to me and tried to hug me and get close. He found me attractive, okay? And when he had a little to drink at the fiestas he'd make a beeline for me. At first he scared me and then I found it flattering. I mean, he *was* handsome. And I guess I did find him attractive. I want to go on record saying I have nothing against the Knights of Columbus! Remember my mom's best friend Ermelinda's son, Casmiro? He was Knights of Columbus. Casmiro was one of the best and most inventive lovers I've ever had except maybe for Mohammed. It's amazing what you can do with a cheap dollar-nineteen paper fan from Walgreen's."

"Come on, Tere."

"So what's the Haps?" I said, looking straight at her. "Don't tell me Wesley has you under his spell. What sort of an attraction does a man in his seventies . . ."

"Mid-fifties."

". . . have for a woman like you in her prime? Tell me it isn't true."

"He's nice," Irma said, going into the kitchen and tasting her spaghetti sauce. I followed her in there, still incredulous.

"So is your grandfather."

"Oh, Tere, you never met him!"

"Your grandfather or Mr. Wesley?"

"Both. All I'm saying is that I never thought of Mr. Wesley as a Man Man until yesterday. Hand me the pepper," she said with an authoritarian voice. She had made the addition of spices to food an art.

"You just don't get it, do you? He's an old guy and you're young. I know Sal was the love of your life—gaaa, I didn't mean for you to start crying, Irma. You loved Sal. And Sal was a good man. For a trucker. Okay, so I have something to learn about truckers. Sal was a gentleman. You got me going all which way. Don't be confusing me, Irma. I only want the best for you."

"Just settle down, would you, Tere?" she said, quickly collecting herself. "I am not saying I have a 'thing' for Mr. Wesley. I am not dating him nor am I going to marry him. He's my boss, I work for him as an accountant. That's all. Open your eyes and look out into the world, there *are* gentle men out there. Good men, many of them. There's no reason you and I have to stay stuck in the same patterns for the rest of our lives. Lucio, by contrast, is a chump. It takes you so dang long to see things as they really are, Tere. You're the slowest learner in the world. I ought to know, I tried to teach you how to type."

"The one thing you didn't need to teach me was how to cook. Look, let's just leave it now. I won't talk about Mr. Wesley if you won't talk about Lucio."

"You said it, comadre. You know, it's amazing how you can go on living with only one idea in mind about a person and suddenly wake up to their reality. I mean like Mr. Wesley."

"Oh, so you're starting up again. I'll get the plates and you can tell me the whole bloody story."

Irma followed me into the kitchen.

"Yesterday was Secretary's Day. So I was in the back office at the Flying W and Mr. Wesley comes in. He startled me. We both laughed and that's when he invited me to lunch at Sofia's Mighty Taco for Secretary's Day. He apologized because he didn't want me to think I was his secretary, more like a 'colleague' he said. He's been a good customer. But this was nothing I expected."

"No! You went to Sofia's Mighty Taco? He didn't take you to the Cattle Baron? Or the Golden Corral? I mean, it was Secretary's Day, *after all*. You could have at least gotten a couple of margaritas out of it, or some blackened catfish."

"Come on, Tere, you know Pinco Mondrales makes the best red enchiladas in the world. That's what I had a hankering for. When we got there, Mr. Wesley had a corsage for me. Can you believe it?"

"No."

"An orchid."

"I bet Sofia's never saw orchids before yesterday."

"You always have to joke about serious things. It was an orchid corsage. That's enough spaghetti." She held up her hands for me to stop. "And give me more sauce. I don't want it to get all *desde*."

"Besides the orchid corsage, what happened?"

"We had a nice lunch, talking about the Flying W. But that's not what got me. When we were leaving, this old woman, in her late seventies, eighties, came in the front door. She was confused, and stopped in the middle of the room. Suddenly she let out this terrible gurgle. It was a horrible noise. I can't even describe it to you. It sounded as if she were drowning. And that's when Mr. Wesley got up and helped her sit down. She looked at him and there was a little flicker of something in her eyes. Tere, he brought her back from death. I saw it. Then he brought her some water.

And then he excused himself. The last I saw of him he was walking the woman to his car."

"Was she his wife?"

"Oh, Tere, he didn't know her. *No one knew her!* She just walked in. I felt so sorry for her, reeling in the middle of the room like that. God help us, I hope when we get to that point someone helps us sit down."

"And so they just took off?"

"He was going to take her to the hospital. Try to find her family. She had to have some family. God, I hope so."

"Enough with the basil leaves," I interjected. "The sauce is a chile-basil thing, not a basil-chile thing. Now sprinkle a few piñones on top."

Irma continued. "I sat there in the booth a while thinking about the woman. And then I thought about Mr. Wesley and how tender and kind he was, and to a stranger! And then I thought about my life and where I was going. I thought about the time I was in Sofia's Mighty Taco and this guy kept staring at me. Finally he came over. He was an architect from Albuquerque working on some project here in town. We got to talking. No, I didn't like him. A gabacho with big wild sandy bigotes. No shape to them. A few strands of Monterey Jack were hanging off the front of his mustache. And so whose Gulfstream trailer do I end up in later that night against all better judgment?"

"No!"

"Like it hasn't happened to you?"

"Okay. Okay. So do you want parmesan French bread?"

"Yeah. So there I was in that hot trailer with no air conditioning. I saw him a few times after that, but I didn't really *like* him. Oh, he was a professional man, but he made a lot of sloppy, sloshy noises."

"Don't tell me anything gross. We're just about to eat."

"Sound familiar? 'It's good. Is it good for you? It's good for me. Oh, baby, it's good for me.'"

"Ay, and so what does the architect have to do with Mr. Wesley other than these things started out at Sofia's Mighty Taco?"

"You don't know what I'm talking about, do you? I'm talking about mi tío Juventino and the Power of Love. That's what I'm talking about."

"You lost me there, Irma." I said. "So let's eat."

"That's all you can think about, Tere, food? What about love? What about dignity? What about respect? What about tenderness? Gentleness. That's what I'm talking about."

"What are you trying to tell me?"

"There are so many men who are gentle and loving. And you don't have to settle for anything less."

Irma and I carried our TV trays into the Pedro room. She took my hand and we said a silent grace over our chile-basil pasta. Irma wasn't one to call out loud to God, especially before eating.

"Why don't you ever say grace, comadre?"

"I say it in silence in memory of one or another of my ancestors. Today it's for mi tío Juventino."

"Who was he?"

Irma was up, getting the salt we'd forgotten. Then I followed to get the napkins.

"He was my mother's tío, so that would make him my great-uncle."

"Would it, Irma? I can never keep those things straight. If I had more relatives I might understand how so-and-so is related to so-and-so and why."

"You think lineage is hard in English? Try it in Spanish. Bisabuelo this and bisabuela that."

"Thank God I don't have many relatives," I said. "I'll let you organize those things in your mind and tell me what I need to know."

I was having trouble adjusting my table. Irma came over to help me.

"Mi tío Juventino was my mother's uncle. He was given a land grant to settle near the river. Hell, for what it was worth. A few houses, mostly desert. West Texas, does that say it all? Sometime I'm going to take you there, Tere, to visit my roots. I can tell you there isn't much there. What we know as sacred is subjective."

"Come again, comadre."

Irma finally sat down to eat, but then she remembered she'd forgotten one more thing—the olives. She left to get them, but took her glass with her and promptly forgot that in the kitchen. After she went back for her glass, she perched on the kitchen counter.

I wasn't very hungry all of a sudden and I put my plate down. I dropped my napkin on the floor, and when I bent over, I accidentally spilled my wine and had to go to the kitchen to get some paper towels. Irma cleared a space out on the kitchen counter, and motioned for me to sit down. Then she seated herself. The phone was on the counter, and while she talked to me, she untangled the cord, hanging it from the receiver and letting it twirl.

"Tío Juventino was the first in the family to come over from El Otro Lado. He helped all the others cross. Let me paint the picture for you: West Texas. Summertime.

"It was so hot that you were lucky to find a small tree offering what little shade it could. Sweat on your forehead, on the back of your neck, in your armpits, between your fingers and most surely between your legs. There was no respite from a scorching, merciless, red velvet sun."

I grabbed the phone cord.

"Just tell me the story, Irma! Why do you always have to be doing something with your hands? Can't you talk without moving?"

"Do you want to hear the story or not, Tere? God, you can be so obstinate!"

"Obstinante!"

"Obstinate! You always add the *n* at the end. And put down that damn dictionary."

" 'Obstinate—adjective. Adhering firmly or perversely to one's purpose, opinion, etc.; unyielding.' Page 918. That's you all over, Granados! So finish the story."

"Tío Juventino knew those parts like the palm of his hand. And he knew the little cave with the small spring, La Cueva de los Torres. It didn't matter if he rested for an hour or so. Then it was back to work with unbending stone, back to the mine, seven hundred feet under the earth. In the cuevita, the stone gave shelter; in the mine, it caused your back to ache, your kidneys to pull in, your liver to jump up, your heart to run wild, and your arms to want to lay themselves down and never get up.

"How long Juventino slept, no one knew. He was the father of twelve children, all of them without hope of a tomorrow. He was a man wrung out by having too many mouths to feed. His wife's mother lived with them, and a retarded niece of his whose parents had died. All of them in two rooms. El Otro Lado had followed them to this side. And it was during the Depression. It's no wonder his sister Josefa's child had been born retarded. Josefa always said her daughter hadn't gotten enough nourishment during that terrible time. ¿La Depresión? Give me a minute and I'll write you a poem, Tío Juventino would say."

I sat cross-legged as Irma regaled me with the story of her famous tío. Our food was getting cold, but we didn't care. We'd warm it up later. Both of us knew there was nothing better than a good story.

"When Tío Juventino finally awoke, it was night. Or so it seemed in the immensity of that darkness. Slow to rouse, he awoke on a sharp inhalation. There was a weight on his stomach. It was alive.

"What could it be?

"An animal?

"What kind of animal?

"Juventino's left eye opened slowly and then the right. Near-total darkness.

"What was it?

"Ayúdame, mi Diosito.

"The creature was still sleeping.

"Juventino felt the cold weight of leathery skin. A large rattler was coiled on his stomach. Unconcerned, passive, the large snake circled the moist warmth of Juventino's flesh. It's impossible to say how long mi tío Juventino lay there. It may have been a minute or an hour or days. Time stopped."

"But your tío Juventino finally managed to get away from the snake, didn't he, Irma?" I asked, getting up because my foot was going to sleep.

"I can't tell you how, Tere, but I know he did, because he lived many years after that. I never knew mi tío Juventino, he was long dead when I was born, but the stories about him survived. Whenever something extraordinary and unusual happened to someone in my mother's family, it was likely to have happened to mi tío Juventino."

"Did he ever talk about how he finally escaped?"

"All he said was that it was the Power of Love that saved him."

"How's that?"

"It's not what you think, Tere. He did pray to God to save him, but after praying to God, he took stock of the situation. He decided that God didn't have much to say about it. And if He did, there wasn't much time in which to say it. Tío Juventino meditated a while. What came back to him in that moment was the need to communicate to the snake the power of all-encompassing love. Love eternal. Love without fear. Love undiluted and unrestrained. Love from the highest self to the lowest and back again. He talked to the snake in his mind. It was almost like a waking dream. He cross-dreamt with the snake maybe. Or maybe the snake dreamt about him. It was a communication without words. Mi tío Juventino didn't have any explanation for it, other than to say, 'I loved the snake. And the snake loved me back.' "

"That's it? That's how he escaped from the snake?" I said, trying to walk out my cramped leg. I poured myself another glass of wine.

"That's the story of Tío Juventino and the Power of Love."

Irma picked up her plate and then mine and dumped our pasta back in the pan. She turned on the burner to warm it up.

"Are you ready for *Arriba las Mujeres*?"

"One thing I'll say for you, comadre, you sure do have the Stories!"

"There's a lesson here, Tere."

I kicked off my house shoes, spread my sleep sheets on my end of Irma's enormous couch and watched as Irma stirred our pasta. We were ready for another Pedro-athon.

"There sure as hell is, Irma. You can't sleep with just anybody you pick up at Sofia's Mighty Taco! The sandy bigotes full of cheese should have warned you. You should have seen the Signs. And as far as Mr. Wesley goes, personally I think he's very dusty."

"Isn't it funny what a movie does to you, Tere? It makes you laugh and cry and sing inside. And it makes you realize a woman can live without a man, especially if the man she loves doesn't really care for her. But beware if she *does* love the man. A snake is a snake, comadre. You can love them once, maybe even for a little while, but then you have to walk away."

"Ay, so turn off the lights already."

Putas ¿Y Qué?

Every family has its puta.
In our family, it's me. This only applies to our generation of Ávilas and Rámoses. In the other, older, more secretly jodido generation, there was no designated puta or puto.

In Ubaldo Miranda's family, he was the designated puto, although his long-suffering mother would never admit out loud that her baby son loved men, especially ones who looked like Pedro Infante in his later years.

Ubaldo and I were walking in Adams Park, named for an Anglo man who didn't live in our Mejicano/Chicano side of town, but he did much to help the neighborhood. He was someone who had grown up here speaking Spanish with his Mejicano friends. He loved the food, the culture, the bustling vibrant life of la frontera, his little edge of the world, the Chihuahuan desert that had burned its way into his spirit and left its mark. Cabritoville was his hometown. Each day he crossed that invisible membrane between the east side of town, where his store was located and the poorer families lived, and the west side, where the moneyed aristocratic families held court. Adams vowed to help all his brothers and sisters—black, white, Mexican, Asian, the living generations descended from all the ancestors who had settled but never tamed the West. It took a hearty soul to live in Cabritoville, and Harold Adams was a man of mettle.

At least that was the story invented by Adams and his family, a story perpetuated by a town that wanted to believe everyone got along, a story that had become a reality unto itself. The real reason Adams crossed from one part of town to another was that Lupe, the mother of five of his seven children, lived in that part of town, in a little house he bought for her down the street from his grocery store. It was a house paid for by the braceros who came from Méjico to harvest cotton, lettuce and onions, families of cheap farm laborers who needed flour, oil and a little bit of whiskey to keep going and who found what they needed in Adams' City Market.

"It's hard to imagine, Tere, but when Mayor Adams died, everyone in town went to his funeral. Of course, Cabritoville was only about three thousand people then. Not that it's grown by leaps and bounds. But we're probably one of the few places on this earth where people really get along. It's so damn hot and dusty here, you *have* to get along."

Ubaldo could be thoughtful when he chose to be, and he was very smart. I liked to listen to him talk when he was feeling mellow, not to the angry young man who hated everything about his life in a small hometown that held little promise for love.

Adams Park was nearly deserted, except for two cholitos in their baggy jeans near the cement bleachers that faced Sedillo Street. They were trying to light a cigarette in the breeze. It was around 7:45 on a Sunday evening and the sky was full of dark gray clouds coming in from the northwest. There was something mysterious about the impending storm. You could see the outline of trees against the vast immensity of unbroken horizon, dark against the blue-gray sky. It wouldn't have been surprising if one or another of the trees just pulled themselves out of the earth and walked away, they were so massive, so alive and full of restless movement.

"I wish it would rain all night and hard, Ubaldo," I said.

"Oh no, it can't rain too long or too hard," he countered. "My mom's in a floodplain and I worry about her house. It has to rain good, but slow and steady—not too long."

"Just as long as it rains."

"Have you ever noticed how much we talk about rain here in Cabritoville, Tere? Let's sit on that bench across the way that faces the álamos over there. We can see the storm coming in."

"I don't know if I want to sit near trees if there's going to be a storm."

"Girl, you are a scaredy-cat."

"You know," I began, emboldened by his remark, "I've always wanted to ask you, just how did you join the fan club?"

Ubaldo started kicking a large rock across the scrubby grass. The park was the size of a large city block, with scraggly patches of dry Bermuda grass, circled by a ring of old álamos. We stood in what was once the Río Grande as it meandered down the valley, before the river was diverted.

"I met Nyvia Ester at the Come-On-and-Drop-In," he replied. "She noticed I kept playing all of Pedro's songs on the jukebox. She's a character, but I don't have to tell you that."

Ubaldo pranced out doing his Nyvia Ester imitation: all floppy queen of the roost with an accent that hit you between the eyes.

"My mamá y papá come to the Jew-es to get ahead, not to hang our arms next to la plebe who don't want to work. Too many of my own people don't want to work. If they do, they work for some puto or puta, like the INS or the FBI or the CIA, which is another way of saying El Gran Puto, El Puto Mayor. ¡Que Dios me proteje del Diablo!"

And here Ubaldo crossed himself à la Nyvia Ester, a grand gesture ending in an exaggerated kiss to the lips.

"I hate that word," Ubaldo said, turning serious. "That's what my dad called me when I was growing up. And he called my mom a puta. 'Hey, puto! You, puto! Puta, yeah, you, come here!' He was nasty. My mom could have saved me so much time and so much pain if she'd talked straight to me as a kid and said, 'Your dad has problems. He's sick.' "

"Kids understand."

"Sure they do. Just as you and I didn't miss anything about our folks and how they behaved and how they told us one thing and did another. Anyway, that's how I got into the fan club. Hell if I care it's a bunch of old bats. I don't mean you, Tere. Not a brain between them. They won't have anything to do with me. You're the only fan club member I like other than Sista Rocha. She's like an older sister to me. And, of course, there's Nyvia Ester. Those old witches think it's perverse that any man would belong to a fan club for another man. Obviously they're tainted by living in the U.S. for so long. You see male Pedro Infante fan club members in Mexico all the time. What about all the mariachis who still love him and all the men from the Police Motorcyclists Union? They respected Pedro for the work he did in *ATM: A Toda Máquina*, in which he played a stunt-riding motorcycle cop who wins a place in the Escuadrón Acrobático."

Ubaldo was right. He was usually right, but no one ever listened to him. There was nothing wrong with Ubaldo that a stint at a Betty Ford wouldn't cure, if only he had the money.

His mother, María Luisa, had spoiled him badly. He lived with her if he didn't have a boyfriend at the time, usually some old dude who worked at White Sands Missile Range repairing army trucks or someone who worked all-nighters at the Zaragosa Port of Entry. I never tried to understand Ubaldo and his actions, and as a result, his actions never bothered me. He was a Mejicano/ Chicano gay man in a small, two-bit-flea-assed-lame-dog-covered-in-shit town full of hidden putos and putas. What we needed in Cabritoville was a major limpia of the cosmic kind.

"Let's walk some more, Ubaldo, before it gets dark, even if it does rain."

We crossed the open field in front of the bandstand. The cholitos were smoking cigarettes. They finally took off in the direction of the Rodríguez Meat Market—"We cut 'em, you cook 'em."

The bandstand was full of graffiti, much of it obscene. A lot of chinga-thises and chinga-thats. The typical Chicano mural was up there: animal, plant and mineral in the mythical land of Aztlán, except bigger and browner and uglier than usual. No doubt someone's cousin and their cousin and a few other cousins had painted it during the summer for the Cinco de Mayo celebrations, an event sponsored by either the Boys' or the Girls' Club or the LULAC youth.

A few frames of Chicano heroes highlighted the corners: César Chávez, the father of the United Farm Workers Union, Vicki Carr, born and raised in El Paso, and some other contemporary Chicano heroes whose faces were blurred and were now full of painted-on black mustaches, graffitied scars, blackened eyes and dripping eye sockets. They were now all legends to a generation of aging Chicano brown berets from the frontera who still believed in their dreams of justice and equality for all, especially for Chicanos.

Ubaldo stopped to read something around the back side of the deserted band shell that never had a band in it. It was a magnet for a group of tecatos and winos and otherwise "riffraffy tipos, babosos peludos sin dinero o jale who hang out at the Come-On-and-Drop-In and then go wee-wee in the bushes near the water fountain of Adams Park."

This is a direct quote from Nyvia Ester Granados, who worked in the kitchen at the Come-On-and-Drop-In a couple of blocks down the street and who had to deal with the crudo menudo crowd.

We walked by several large cottonwoods, relics of another time, their trunks brown, gnarled and full of carved graffiti, chalo crosses, lovers' initials scratched out in bark. Imaginary wind-whipped faces peered out into the growing darkness from the desiccated flesh of the giant trees. The rain seemed closer. You could smell it, and almost feel the anxious earth rising up expectantly, the plants straining for contact. A feral cat ran swiftly toward its shelter near the electrical generator that powered the park lights.

"Do you want to sit on a bench, Tere?"

"For a little while. I love this time of the day."

Ubaldo and I seated ourselves on one of the cement benches. Then there was an uncomfortable silence.

"Tere, can I talk to you?"

"Sure, Ubaldo. What is it?"

Ubaldo made a fist with his left hand, and cupped it hard with his right hand, a gesture of angry impotence.

"I knew something was wrong," I said to him. "You were drunk at the last fan club meeting. When you said you had a cold I knew it was more than that. And when you couldn't stop crying, I really got worried. And then you had that car accident, running into Mr. Reyes."

"You know I've been seeing a counselor in El Paso for a long time. He thinks it all started with my cousin Mamerto, who started messing with me when I was five."

"My God, Ubaldo!"

"He was bigger than me, and he threatened me."

"Why didn't you tell your mom?"

"He said he'd tell everyone I was a puto."

"Oh, Ubaldo."

"There wasn't anybody to tell, okay? And I thought I was bad, just like my dad told me I was."

"I'm so sorry, Ubaldo."

I tried to reach out and touch him, but Ubaldo had gotten up and was pacing back and forth. I walked over to him. He was staring at the wall in front of him. "Hey, Tere, check this out. I thought I saw something here. Can you read it?" He pointed to the wall. "Putas ¿y qué? Culeras. Si no les gusta, préstenos el culo, épocritas! Signed, Marisela."

"¡Híjole!" was all I could get out. "Why do people have to be so ugly?"

The wind came up. It was cooling down at last. Ubaldo had picked up a stick and was writing out words in the dirt. I peered down to see "I'm a puta" in front of him.

"What do you think of that, Tere? 'I'm a puta, so what? If you don't like it, lend me your asshole, hypocrite.' At least Marisela has the huevos most people don't have when it comes to being honest about sex."

Ubaldo flung the stick away. He was always restless, tapping his feet, bobbing his head, making some kind of music with his nervous body. He was a handsome man, but too thin, with the dark burnished eyes you see in photos of survivors from a prisoner-of-war camp, or men who've come out of hiding. It was hard to believe he was in his late twenties, he seemed so much older.

I had to admit I was attracted to him, the way women are attracted to men they will never know in any carnal sense, men who are disinterested in them sexually, men who are like lost brothers, brothers you want to hold, and give cariños to, if only they would let you.

And yet, Ubaldo and I did touch once in a way that nearly moved me to tears. Not the brother-sister punching he was fond of, or me knuckling him in the arm to say hurry up or come on or ay, tú.

It happened late one night after we'd gone to a movie. I drove him home because he didn't have a car. His last boyfriend had left him high and dry for some pip-squeaky pretty boy. When we said good night Ubaldo took my face in his hands, ran his finger over my lips and then kissed me softly. He then pulled back, giving me a hug that took my breath away. Suddenly, he was gone—inside his mother's house—and I wanted more.

"Everyone is a puto or puta if given the chance, Tere," Ubaldo said with too much ease. "Especially if given the chance."

"Well, I don't agree with Marisela," I replied. "The girl's raw. And I don't agree with you, or believe that you mean what you're saying. We're not born ugly, we become that way, later, after the world and other people have hurt us or we've hurt ourselves."

"She's so raw her skin is inside out," he added. "Well, I don't agree with her either. Hey, look at this. Someone's answered Marisela."

Ubaldo read the wall below Marisela's statement.

"Putas son ustedes . . . All of you are putas. Y si tienen un problema, díganos . . . And if you have a problem, tell us. Now, you usually don't find things like that in Cabritoville," Ubaldo said with wonder.

"Oh yeah? Well, try the rest room at La Tempestad."

"I'd like to, Tere, but I can't set foot in that joint. Not since Mr. Dairy Queen and I broke up. His brother-in-law owns the place, and Double Dip goes there all the time with his wife."

"Come on, Ubaldo. Why can't you be serious for once? I'm worried about you."

"Yeah, I know. It all makes me tired, doesn't it make you tired? When I think of sex or love, whatever the hell you want to call it, all I can think of is what a struggle it is to keep making yourself happy. Day after day. Year after year. One person after another."

"What are you going to do, Ubaldo? It's good you're seeing a counselor. That will help."

"I've had a lot on my mind lately. Life stuff. You know. Changes."

"So what's new about that? Everything is changes."

"This time I'm talking about Changes Changes."

"Changes?"

"Yeah, changes. Like maybe I'll just leave Cabritoville someday without telling anyone. I'll just disappear and I won't ever come back. I'll head south, Tere. To Mexico. Find me a Pedro Infante. He'll be a little older than Pedro when he died, mid-forties, fifties, sixties, hell, seventies. Handsome. With a good voice. I'm telling you now. If you ever find me gone, you'll know I've found my Pedro."

"Why would you do that, Ubaldo?"

"Not even if my mom is dying will I come back. I don't need to be here to love her . . . Hey, I'm just warning you. You know, in case someday you hear I've gone away."

"You're acting like you're crazy, but I know you're not."

"I'll find my Pedro or die trying. My new boyfriend lives in El Paso, but he's been offered a job in Dallas. Who knows? Maybe I'll move there with him. He's not the one, you know, but maybe in Dallas . . . ," Ubaldo speculated.

"¡Adió!" I said to him. "You said that last year and you're still here."

I loved to use that word of Albinita's expressing disbelief.

"Your mom's going to die," I said, immediately regretting it. "So who is he?"

Ubaldo was always going somewhere, but he never left town for more than a couple of days. And there he'd be at the next fan club meeting with red eyes, trying to stay away from the booze, crying himself to sleep because some mechanic or construction worker had left him plantado, with one foot planted in Hell and the other one in Purgatory.

"He's from an old family in Chihuahua. You don't know him."

"Don't tell me, he looks like Pedro."

"How did you know?"

"So am I going to meet him sometime?"

"No. Víctor doesn't want to meet my friends. He acts very straight."

"Oh, one of those. What does he do?"

"He's got a carpet business."

"He sells carpets?"

"No, he cleans them."

"Oh. Why don't you just go to Las Vegas or Disneyland for a week and get this out of your system?"

"I need to leave Cabritoville, Tere. Start my real life. It's a sad thing to acknowledge your best days have been spent in the back of a Bonneville during some short sweaty councilman's lunch hour or dry-humping in the vestibule of a cold church before Ash Wednesday services."

"Ay, Ubaldo. This town can kill you if you let it. But this is your home. I just can't see you living in Dallas."

"Hell, I've never known anyone my own age here! I always seem to end up with older men."

"Ubaldo, take it easy. Settle down. You don't have to leave Cabritoville."

Ubaldo wasn't listening. He looked exhausted.

I tried to put my hand on his. He was trembling, then moved away.

"I thought I'd go see Doña Meche before I left. You want to come with me, Tere?"

"Who's Doña Meche?"

"She's this curandera. I had this planter's wart that wouldn't go away, and when Mr. Cornubia from the Dairy Queen started harassing me, I needed help. She told me I would meet a handsome stranger, not too tall, not too young, not too dark, and that I was going away."

"So let's say you go away, how will I know you got there, I mean how will I know you finally found your Pedro? Will you send me a postcard or something?"

"Don't expect anything big. It'll be some small thing. Who knows what it will be? I'll surprise you."

"You promised, remember that. On Pedro Infante's grave."

"On the hope of seeing Pedro someday. That's better."

"All right then, on the hope of seeing Pedro."

"I'm on fire, Tere. I have too much passion. Just like Pedro. That's why I love him. He knew how to live."

"Did he, Ubaldo? I wonder. People like Pedro always burn out so quickly. That's not how I want to live my life. I want to be steady, inside, where it matters, not una ánima sola, a lonely soul engulfed in flames."

By now it was dark, the storm clouds having sneaked up on us.

"Ubaldo, we should be going," I said.

"Let's sit a little longer, Tere. Tell me a story."

"You want a story, Ubaldo?"

"A love story. I'll start it. I'm standing next to Pedro."

"He's beautiful," I continued.

"He starts to sing."

"Now you and Pedro are dancing on the beach from *La Vida No Vale Nada*. He holds you close."

"Really?" Ubaldo said. "How close?"

"Close."

"Real close?"

"Ayayay. Pegaditos. You're plastered together. Did you feel a drop, Ubaldo?"

"No, did you?"

"We should go. I felt something. I can hear thunder."

"It's far away."

"It's starting to rain, Ubaldo! Uuuy, quick! It's raining and we're two miles from my car! Run!"

"You run, I'm walking. I'll meet you there."

"Ay, I'm getting soaked! Ubaldo, hurry up!"

"Can't!"

"Can't?"

"Won't."

The thunder was closer now. The rain had moved in from the northwest, true to its early promise. I ran through the humid, charged air. Ubaldo lagged behind. Then there was a crack of lightning and he caught up to me, grabbed my hand, and we raced against the wind.

What Is It?

What is it about me that you don't love, Lucio?

Am I too much of a Mejicana, not Mejicana enough? Am I too poor, too uneducated? Do I think too much of myself or not enough? Am I too clinging or too independent? Am I too old? (I *am* five years older than you, but in the beginning you said it didn't matter.) Am I too ugly? Not that Diolinda is any great beauty, although some people might think she is—nothing but skin and bones, with two high, pointy, artificial chichis like unripe grapefruit, a mane of dyed black hair and a nose that keeps getting smaller. She *is* a career woman, I'll grant her that. She *does* have her Mary Kay franchise. Other than that, what possessed you to marry her? She's a spiritual dog, Lucio, a dog.

Am I too outspoken, too quiet? Do I think too much or not enough? Is it my voice, the way it rises and falls? Do I laugh too often? Is it my twisted bruja humor? Sometimes you're so serious, Lucio, you don't have a sense of humor. And you're driving me crazy with that dictionary of yours.

"Do you know what a perigee is?" he asked me only last night.

"Of course not," I answered. I had my limits.

"Page 987. 'Perigee (per'-i-je)—noun. The point in the orbit of a heavenly body, especially the moon, or of an artificial satellite at which it is nearest to the earth.' "

Oh, Lucio, what the hell do I care about a perigee? You're always looking up words. And I'm always trying to figure out their meaning. I care about you and you care about words. Why can't you talk to me the way I need you to? Why can't I hear you say the words I need to hear: I love you, Tere. I love you. And why do you sometimes tell me little white lies? And even some very black ones?

What is it that you don't like about me? Is it my posture, with the beginnings of a humped back? You've told me that I walk slightly stooped. Is it my clothes? (You didn't like my pink-and-orange velour pantsuit that I was so proud of, an outfit I wore just for you. Albinita gave it to me, and yes, I thought it was wonderful.) Do I dress too shabbily, too brightly, too tightly, too loosely? You keep telling me not to dress like a Mejicana in dresses from Juárez. What are you talking about? Mejicanos dress the way they can. Have you ever bought me a dress, Mr. Fancy Dresser? You like my chichis. They're real, every inch of them, so what does it matter to you what I wear?

Sometimes you can be so cruel, Lucio, and prejudiced against your own people. The way you talk about Mejicanos makes me so sad, as if you were higher and mightier than they, you who go around with a dictionary looking for the right words, words that will confirm that you are better and more worthy—of exactly what, I'm not sure.

Am I too short? I'm not that short, I'm a good height for a woman and especially for a man like you. You're not so tall. As a

matter of fact, you're short for a man. You have a small back and
no butt, not to mention no waist. Without nalgs. Very short. With
bird legs.

And you can be mean. I didn't want to notice it at first, but now
I see you can be mean. You're not mean in the way people can be
mean. You've never pinched or punched me. But you've never told
me that you love me when I know you do. You have mean
thoughts. And you make sounds. Wordless noises. That's mean.
You snort when I mail in my five dollars for my foster child in In-
dia, or send money to the Paralyzed Veterans for those cute little
greeting cards with the dogs and cats. And worst of all, you con-
stantly withhold your love from me. That's about the meanest
thing anyone can ever do. It's unnatural and goes against the laws
of God and nature. If anyone should go to Hell they should go to
Hell for not loving the way they could.

So what's wrong with me, Lucio? Am I too thin? Too fat? You
say you like me with some flesh. I'm soft and you like that, too.
You're always telling me how soft I am. I mean, I think that's good.
I'm soft like a woman and not soft like canned biscuits. (I happen
to like those types of biscuits and I'm sorry you don't. You can
make really good doughnuts out of them, too. All you have to do is
cut a hole in the middle. Fry them and then roll them in brown
sugar. But you've never tried them. You don't know what you're
missing.)

Do I have cellulite behind my knees or under my sobacos that
pooch out from my bra or a panza that hangs over my panty line?
(You're getting a small panza, you better watch it. I've never commented on it until now. It's only because you brought up my
panza one day when you were feeling cabrón, which is often these
days.) We all can't have washboard stomachs, women are supposed to be round. Are you afraid my arms will get flabby like all
the women who work at Sofia's Mighty Taco or the Menudo Hut?

Do I walk too fast, too slow, dragging my feet, or is it the way I
stand, one hip out, or with both hands on my hips? Like a radical
lesbian, you tell me. What do you have against women?

Is it the way I sleep, on my side, never on my back? Do I snore?

I have in the past, but I don't do it now. If you want to talk about
snoring, just look in the mirror. If you don't believe me, I'll play
you the tape I made of you snoring one night when I couldn't
sleep. I taped you so you won't say I'm making it up.

Do I have bad morning breath? You should smell yourself, Mr.
Always Criticizing. Everyone has bad morning breath, don't they?
I try to get in the bathroom before you wake up to make myself
up, but sometimes it's not possible. Now, we're not talking about
a lot of mornings here, Mr. Can't-Spend-the-Night-I-Have-to-
Take-My-Mother-Her-Bottle-of-Whiskey-So-She-Can-Sleep. And
besides, if you ever do spend the night, we usually don't kiss in
the morning. What you like to do is a quick side-by-side Funky
Monkey in which I always face the wall.

Is it the wrinkle between my eyes? Is it that worried scowling
look my mother told me would be there if I kept looking at the
world the way I did and do? Is it the permanent smile lines on the
side of my mouth like bigotes of flesh?

Is it my ugly hands, hands like my father's? Is it my large
knuckles, the dry skin around the nails I can never seem to get rid
of? Is it that I am my own chiropractor and can pop my knuckles,
my neck, my back? Is it that I love to read things you would never
read: *The Enquirer, The Star, The Weekly World News*? Is it that I
come from a background of poor food and eat things you would
never eat: Vienna sausage, potted meat in a tortilla, hominy from
the can, cold beans from the icebox and cottage cheese with pepper? Is it the way I mash my eggs, fried over medium, until they're
a yellow mess, sprinkling on lots of salt? (You told me it was disgusting the way I mashed my eggs. Amor, if only you could look at
yourself eating chicharrones, the fat oozing down your fleshy lips
as you suck the marrow out of a split bone. I've never seen a man
chupar meat the way you do, like an anteater.)

Is it the people I come from? The Ávilas, the Rámoses? Is it the
people I love, the people you could never love? Is it the fact that
you hate your parents, especially your mother, and the fact that I
love mine? Or is it that you are jealous of my mother, that quiet

little rabbit, always afraid and standing in the doorway wanting to know what I need? Is it the memory of your father, a hard and critical and arrogant man too much like you? Is it because your mother, Cuca, the one woman in this world who should have taught you mercy, failed you? Is it her that you see when you look at all women, especially me in those moments you hate me? Is it your sister Velia? Is it because she has nalgas wide as a semi and looks like you? Are you afraid I'm developing big nalgs? Is it the brothers and sisters I never had? The not understanding what it is to be "familia"?

Is it my messy little house on Bowser Street, the bathroom with spiders, the kitchen with ants? Is it the old posters on my walls: Janis Joplin, President Kennedy, Che Guevara, Pope John XXIII, Pedro Infante in *Necesito Dinero*? Is it my old pots, my crusty pans, the ancient stove you refuse to come near? Is it the shabby rugs I have, with hair from my mother's old dog, Diablo, who ran away? Is it the way I keep or don't keep the house?

What things have I done or left undone? Tell me and I'll fix them. Is it the food in my icebox that you commented on: Cheez Whiz, a bottle of cheap champagne? Is it the fact I say icebox instead of refrigerator? Is it the two meals I cooked for you, the first a gray mash of vegetables and rice, a meal I once loved (my comadre Irma gave me the recipe), but when I made it for you it came out bad? Was it the veggie burger patties I made the night it rained and my roof leaked on the insurance files you left on the old recliner that smells like cat pee, a reminder of my mother's cat that died, Angelita? Was it the black olives, sardines and onions you smelled on my breath the day you came over when I wasn't expecting you and was in the middle of mopping the kitchen floor with the old trapo I bought in Juárez that loses its ratty cotton chunks that harden underneath the kitchen cabinet corners? Was it the fact I was in my pink rollers in my mother's old battered baby-blue bata, that bathrobe you hate?

Is it my mirrors that are too old, the mercury nearly gone, especially the one in the bathroom in front of the toilet that you asked me to remove because you could see Dieguito in it when you made pee-pee? Was it that?

What is it, Lucio? Just tell me.

Is it the visible desire that I feel for you, the heat that comes out of the top of my head, a heat that envelops me? Is it the hot knot of my clitoris, dense as a rock, the pain that grows with the thought of you? Is it the way I cry when you are gone, my face ugly and red, my voice soggy with longing, my sad, sad way of looking at you when you drive away, a look that expects too much? Is it the way I wave goodbye, as if it was forever? Is it the great open space in my heart for you, the fierce yearning for your flesh, your back, your thighs, your kisses? Kisses I always dream about and can never fully remember until I kiss you the next time? Is it the way I love you, all hunger and bravado without shame—the way few women love a man? Is it the way I kiss you—the way women shouldn't kiss—in places that no one should kiss? Is it that? Is it the fact I want too much? Love too much?

What is it, really? Is it that I swore on my grandmother Chencha's grave that I couldn't live without your kisses to me down there? I didn't know what a real orgasm was until I met you, Lucio. If I couldn't feel your lips on me down there and up here and under there and over and around there and I couldn't come like that, a blue wall shuddering black . . . I'll just . . . I'll just . . . I don't know what. I'll just . . .

Is that it?

Please don't call me if you're not prepared to be my lover. I don't want to be your friend. If you call me, expect to love me the way I love you. Both hands on the burning wheel. You know my number.

La Tere

One Little Girl

I always feel sorry for the children in Pedro's movies. There's the little blond brat in *Los Tres Huastecos*, played by María Eugenia Llamas, who's demanding and gets on your nerves right away. She's spoiled to the core, and could handle a gun at such an early age. But I know it's not easy being the daughter of a bandit.

The child in *Angelitos Negros* was just plain pitiful. She knew her mother, Ana Luisa, didn't love her because she was black. It was a heartbreaking scene when the little girl put flour on her face to make herself white. Nothing she did could make her mother love her.

Pedro's teenage daughter, Chachita, in *Nosotros los Pobres* was a mess, too. She was pampered by Pedro, who plays a carpenter named Pepe el Toro.

Pepe had his reasons. He had to hide the fact that his sister was a puta. I mean, there's no getting around it. The woman had a bad life and Pepe didn't want to have anything to do with her. It was very sad when Pedro later revealed to Chachita that the dying prostitute was her real mother.

Once again, if Pedro-as-Pepe had only told the truth early on and to the people that needed to know the truth, a lot of heartache could have been spared. But that's not the way we Mejicanos do it. We don't know how to spare ourselves pain. I should know. And Pedro should have known as well. But no, he had to carry on as if Chachita was his daughter, causing her to grow up to be intolerant and shrill.

All these young children, most of them girls, lead troubled lives. There are boys in Pedro's movies, but they tend to die early on, like the sick baby in *Un Rincón Cerca del Cielo*, or El Torito, Pedro's son in *Nosotros los Pobres*, who is burned alive. Such painful lives and such horrible deaths. The little girls fare better in a certain way, if you want to call their lives easier. To be a woman in Méjico in the forties and fifties was a hard life sentence. Same goes for growing up in Cabritoville, U.S.A., in the fifties and sixties. I mean it, there are more uncomplicated ways to come into this world and to go out.

Boy/girl/girl/boy, all the children in Pedro's movies have a hard go of it, no matter the social class, the time frame or the color of their hair. That goes for all the women as well. No matter what age. Although if you had a Pain-O-Meter and randomly tested blonds and brunets, the blonds would probably come out with more favorable lives. Except Ana Luisa in *Angelitos Negros*. What she did to Pedro and to her little biracial daughter is unforgivable. The woman should go to an everlasting Hell for her sins—and they were many.

Even the newly born fare badly in Pedro's movies. How would you like to be dragged around like a stuffed doll while your stronghold was under siege? Poor little tiny baby girl in *Las Mujeres de Mi General*. Maybe that's why the girls are more evident in Pedro's movies. They hold up better under gunfire, they can yell and carry on; they don't have the same sort of dark destiny as most of the men.

When you look at the role of women in el cine Mejicano, they are still under the yoke of their fathers, their sons, their husbands and their brothers. I'd like to line up all the women who appeared in Pedro's movies and take a good long look at them. Híjole, there's an assortment for you. Pedro had his turn with all those women, and they had their turn with him.

And yet, Pedro had many ongoing and wonderful relationships with women. There's his friendship with Sara García. They really did have a tender friendship on-screen and off. Sara García loved Pedro and you can tell he loved her. And there was his off-screen friendship with Blanca Estela Pavón, his lead in *Los Tres Huastecos*, *Nosotros los Pobres*, *Ustedes los Ricos*, *La Mujer Que Yo Perdí*, *Vuelven los García* and *Cuando Lloran los Valientes*. When she died in a plane crash in 1949, he was inconsolable.

Pedro's on-screen male friendships were many. There was Luis Aguilar in *ATM: A Toda Máquina* and *Que Te Ha Dado Esa Mujer* and Antonio Badú in *Los Hijos de María Morales*. But just like his relationships with women, his movie friendships with men were hard-won and problematic.

Me and La Wirms never did do a blood sister cutting of the finger with our sangre oscura blending one into another. The closest we ever got to that was sharing a box of Tampax in high school that we stole from Woolworth's because we both were on the proverbial gara at the same time and the line was too long. We are so tight, me and La Wirms, that we even have PMS together. Except in this instance PMS stands for Pobrecitas Malditas Sinvergüenzas. That's what we'd call ourselves when we had our joint periods. I tell Wirms that La Puta has come and she'll confirm the visit.

If Irma and I think we had it bad growing up in Cabritoville, U.S.A., and we did, how could it have been for all those children in Pedro's movies? All those poor little chavalitos mugrosos pobrecitos in those isolated pueblitos and in the teeming city streets? We all grew up with dreams that Pedro's fabulous life could sometime be our own.

Irma has often discussed this subject with me and for too many long hours. La Época de Oro was a magical time in Mejicano film, but it also began the cycle of confusion that led all the way from Quirino to Albinita to Reynaldo and Mohammed and Chago and Lucio and then to me.

"When will the cycle of illusion end, Tere?"

"What are you talking about, comadre?" I said to Irma.

"I'm talking about the sins of the fathers and the mothers, the grandmothers and the grandfathers. About a race of people jodidos by celluloid dreams."

"You lost me there, Wirms."

"You know what I'm talking about, Tere, only you don't want to admit it. There have to be better ways to live our lives than on the jodido edge of obsessive love. Waiting for the dream lover who never comes, the knight in a shining Trans Am who can't stop looking in the mirror at himself or the mama's boy who's on welfare and talks on the phone to his mother every day while the food that you made him is getting cold. Have I mentioned the Pedro look-alike who is a married Coors-drinking INS officer and deported his mother yesterday? Pedro's life should be a lesson to us."

Didn't Pedro know he couldn't or shouldn't and that if he did, the life and things he loved would turn on him and eventually strike him down? Pedro had to know that he was the cause of his little boy dying of pneumonia in *Un Rincón Cerca del Cielo*. The reason he was so troubled in that movie was that he was so selfish. Didn't he know that, and didn't he have any inkling that he was to blame for all the bad things that happened in all his movies?

Ubaldo calls this karma. He's always talking about karma this and karma that.

I tell him Irma has an aunt named Carma. Short for Carmen. But he just looks at me like I came in out of the July heat after pulling weeds at high noon.

I say it's karma that Pedro died in a plane crash. It was also karma that Blanca Estela Pavón, one of his leading actresses and best friend, died in the plane crash she was in. I do think Pedro *did* die on that plane. After all, he wanted to die that way. He said, "Yo nací para ser aviador . . . Debe ser hermoso morir como los pájaros, con las alas abiertas."

Pedro was born to fly. "Quiero morir volando y que me entierren con música." He wanted to die flying, like the birds, with their wings wide open. And he wanted to be buried with music.

I didn't know what karma was until I met Ubaldo, just as I didn't know what a chadra was. He was always talking about how one or another of his chadras was out of kilter, how he had a psychic pain here or there and how he needed an aura balancing from Doña Meche, a sort of cosmic Tums that would do the trick.

"Ubaldo, what's a chadra?" I asked him during one of our late-night phone conversations.

"Chakra! Chakra! Get the right word, Tere. It's an energy center in the body. I'll bring you a book you can read."

"No, thank you, Ubaldo. I've got my hands full carrying around the damn dictionary that Lucio gave me. Wait a minute. Sure as hell can't find the word chakra in here. But hey, did you know a chacma was a large, brownish-gray baboon? Page 221."

"You're hopeless, Tere."

"I'm too busy living my life for karma or chakras, Ubaldo."

"That's what I'm afraid of, Tere. You've got to get a grip and break it off with Lucio. There's his daughter. Do you ever think of his daughter?"

Everyone always says that the mistress never thinks about her married lover's children. I have to tell you, that's almost all I think about.

Andrea Valadez.

One little girl.

If and when Lucio and I go our separate ways, it will be because of this one little girl.

Yes, my heart breaks for children, especially for little girls like Andrea.

Girls like me, well, our hearts are already broken. We came into the world that way and that's how we'll go out, still on the cosmic rag, trying to wipe away the bloody mess.

"¿Qué no, baby girl?"

I see Andrea every day. Like all the other children at Cabritoville Elementary, she calls me Miss Terry.

"Hi, Miss Terry, how are you today?"

Every time I look at her, it breaks my heart. She's a beautiful child. She doesn't look like Diolinda, no dark smoldering looks, high arch of the brow, thick lashes or high cheekbones and olive complexion. She's more her father's daughter. Slight, self-composed, sure of herself, even at her young age. A fragile, almost transparent beauty. Pale eyelashes and a small, delicate, heart-shaped face. She reminds me of a child you'd see in one of Pedro's movies. The precious, precocious child of the blond woman he married who lives in town. The granddaughter of the haciendado, not a little Indita cleaning woman who loves her patrón without hope or expectation. Andrea was born to a finer life.

And yet there's something of Chachita in her, something of the bandit brat, something of the lost and unloved daughter, something of the little siren, and too much of the little girl whose father is confused.

She wasn't supposed to see me kissing her father in the parking lot at Cabritoville Elementary.

School was over for the day. The kids were waiting for their buses. Lucio drove up in his white truck. He motioned for me to come over, then he asked me to sit with him a while. I was afraid, but I got in. Knowing that once I touched him, that was it. That it would be all over.

Lucio kissed me hard, the way Pedro kissed the brazen married woman who sought him out in *El Gavilán Pollero*. The first time hard, the second softer and the last time with great tenderness.

When I looked up, breathless, I saw Andrea standing near the bus. There was something horrible about the way she stared, a look of incomprehension, then infinite disappointment on her face.

Lucio looked up to meet Andrea's burning eyes. Then he pushed me away, his face darkened.

"Dammit, Tere, what have you done? I've told you a million times that I can't love you! I have a family. Now get out of the car. I have to take Andrea home. And don't call me. Whatever you do, don't call me!"

Little girls know early on who their fathers are. And we know how much they will hurt us. Just as we know our lover's faults. It's the women who betray us who hurt us so much more, because that betrayal is never expected.

Lucio got out of the truck and went to Andrea. He tried to put his arm around her, but she moved away and looked at him with disgust. No other woman, only Chachita, was capable of hurting Pedro as much when she gave him that look of pure hatred in *Nosotros los Pobres*. Andrea bit down on her lip and I could see she was holding back tears. She may have been a spoiled little rich girl, but now she no longer had a father she trusted. I walked quickly into the cafeteria. Lucio was visibly upset, and as they drove away, Andrea held on to the half-open window, her back to her father. Lucio would take her for ice cream or a toy, try to get her to promise not to tell her mother, I knew that. He would try to make it up to her, but he never could. And eventually, he would forget about it. But Andrea never would. And for that, I was so sorry.

Sorry for Andrea and for myself. We would stop looking each other in the eye and she would back up against the wall whenever she found herself near me. And she would never smile again at me the way she once had. There would be no more respectful "How are you, Miss Terry?"s.

There was no one to apologize to, and I needed to confess my sin to someone. I thought of going to see Father Ronnie, but he was out of town on Wednesdays, usually gambling at the Speaking Rock Casino in Ysleta, where he ran up a tab. I couldn't face old Father Gregorio, el ethpañol with the thick lisp who smelled like his dusty confessional and talked down to you in his constipated way, reminding you of why the Spanish Inquisition had taken place in Spain. Or Padre Gato, the stone-faced priest, who kills cats and then throws their bodies into the Río Grande. Holier than thou, O Lord. (The man delivered a terrible wake, often never mentioning the deceased.) How could I speak to any of them?

I decided to call Irma.

"Comadre, I'll meet you at La Tempestad at four o'clock for Happy Hour."

"What happened, Tere?" Irma said over the phone. She knew something was wrong.

"Don't ask me any questions now, comadre. My heart's on fire."

"We gave up drinking, Tere, remember? And besides, I don't want to meet you at La Tempestad. I told you I saw the Signs. I'll come by at five and we'll go for a drive."

"I'll be waiting," I said gratefully.

I hated to do it to Irma, but if anyone could handle it, she could.

Another Listen-to-
Poor-Me Story

"**I**rma, I've lost my center.
I want to kill myself!"

"Don't," she said without any real concern. "We'll
just drive around until you settle down. How about
if we drive down the back road to El Paso and then
we stop for an A&W root beer?"

"It sounds good to me. But how about we get the
A&W *first* and *then* drive down the valley?"

We drove to the A&W and ordered two large
frosty mugs.

"So what's going on?" Irma said.

"Andrea saw us kissing. Lucio and I were in the
parking lot. Oh, comadre, Lucio yelled at me to get
out of the car and to leave him alone. And now Andrea knows everything."

We were one of four cars at the A&W. Someone
in a dark green Impala waved to us.

"Who was that?" I asked tremulously.

Irma waved back. "I'm not sure . . . So what's going on, Tere?"

"I love Lucio, and I think he loves me. But I don't want Andrea to be hurt."

Irma turned to face me. She was upset, I could tell. She swigged down the last of the root beer, put down her frosty mug and looked me square in the eyes.

"You *think* he loves you. You *think* he loves you? It's not the same thing as *knowing* he loves you. And besides, he can't ever love you. He loves himself too much."

It's a good thing both of us had more or less finished our root beers, because Irma honked loudly and a much too old woman on roller skates came up to collect our tray. Irma gave her a dollar tip and we pulled out a 'lo todo don't-talk-to-me-now-I-don't-know-what-to-say.

She drove for about twenty minutes without saying a word, while I looked out the window at the passing farmland on Highway 478. The red chile crop was ready and lay there in the drying fields gathering potency from the earth. Most of the crops had been harvested: lettuce, onions, corn. Dirty cotton bolls remained in dry fields, waiting for the machines to separate them from the stalks. The trees hadn't started to lose their leaves yet, but they looked tired. Summer was nearly over and the heat had taken the life out of so many things. A resolute calm hovered over the long-overused land, which seemed to sigh with relief. It had been so long since I'd driven through the farms that lay south of Cabritoville, farms with names like Los Grijalva, and La Hacienda de los Dominguez, or simply Reyes, with hand-painted wooden signs over rickety gates that led into several acres of dearly loved, privately owned land. I was grateful to Irma for bringing me here, to a place we both loved.

It was a ride she often took her dying tío Pablo on when she could. Since he was confined to a wheelchair, it was his last connection to his former life as a chile farmer. He loved the freedom of getting in a car and being on the open road, as he peered down the seemingly endless rows of pecan trees and cotton fields, the bright blood-red chiles basking in the sun. Irma would patiently explain to him: "There's the old church, Tío, where you used to go to church with Tía, and remember that house? Your wife's cousin used to live there. And that's where the man was murdered. What was that story, Tío, do you remember?"

When Irma's tío Pablo was dying, this was the last road she led him on, in a guided mediation at three in the morning as he lay in his hospital bed, his sons and daughters at home sleeping soundly. It was her shift. And that's when the end came for him, with her, on that long stretch of highway going south.

When La Wirms and I are on that open road, we forget how much greater we are than our suffering.

Just past La Mesa we turned around, a little beyond Chope's Bar and Restaurant, and drove back to Cabritoville.

We ended up by the big álamos around the back near Sofia's Mighty Taco and by the park where Lucio and I first met. I saw Gabina, my favorite tree. She was still looking strong. For how much longer? I wondered. How long do trees live? I knew I had messed up my karma years ago. But if I hadn't, I wanted to come back as a tree. Just like Gabina. A large healthy cottonwood by the banks of a quiet river.

Irma had brought me here specifically because she knew it was my favorite place in all of Cabritoville, a place where I couldn't lie to myself.

There is nothing more beautiful and full of life than a healthy álamo with its shimmering leaves rustling in the wind, the play of light on stippled green, the quiet enduring strength of a life bending as it must. Irma had brought me here to gather what strength I could, in Gabina's tender, embracing shade.

She stopped the car and looked at me. She had that don't-mess-with-me-comadre look. I knew better than to interrupt her no matter what she was about to tell me.

She just stared straight ahead saying nothing for the longest time. And then she let me have it.

"You want to be with Lucio for all the wrong reasons, Tere. You know he'll never marry you, and that if you're his mistress, you'll be free. And that's what you've always wanted, Ms. Tere "Free As a Bird" Ávila. You want to be free of responsibilities, free of duties and free of obligations. Free to do whatever you please and with whomever. But what really gets me is that you feel you need him to validate your self-worth. Why, I don't know. You act as if he's from a higher class, as if class ever mattered to you. You just want the easy life, Tere. But the easy life is never easy. And being free isn't being in the middle of a sexual stranglehold with someone who will never love you. Someday you're going to wake up and realize you loved the wrong things, the wrong man, and that maybe it's time to get it right."

Irma's words hit me hard, and I burst into tears.

We held each other. If anyone had come by, they would have thought we were two lovers hidden in each other's arms.

Irma gave me a Kleenex and I wiped my nose.

"Thanks for the pep talk," I said, laughing through my tears.

"I just want the best for you, comadre," Irma replied.

That's what I love about Irma. She's a highly evolved human being. Her karma is good. Her chakras are clear. When I see her, I feel clearer and cleaner and not so jodida. Not on the ugly bleeding rag of life.

Okay, so I'm dramatic, pin me down. It was a dramatic day, a dramatic time, and I was feeling pretty damn dramatic.

All I needed to come back to earth was a plate of tacos—make that red enchiladas with an egg—which I had at Sofia's Mighty Taco.

To understand how I could ever imagine a life with Lucio Valadez, you have to know several things.

I really desperately and honestly and sincerely love him.

I sincerely and honestly and desperately crave him. He's my drug. My mind love.

I am desperately and sincerely and honestly jodida.

I honestly and really believe that if Lucio could gather himself up and get the strength, he would leave his wife, Diolinda, for me. I honestly and truly believe it's possible that Andrea and Lucio and I could live happily ever after, a happy little family, just like Pedro-as-General Juan Zepeda and Lupe and their child in *Las Mujeres de Mi General*. They're finally reunited even as they face a barrage of gunfire at the end of the movie. I want to believe that people who love each other can stop the speeding bullets.

I found myself explaining all of this to La Wirms, lapping up the runny egg yolk with an edge of hot tortilla at Sofia's Mighty Taco. Suffering has always made me hungry.

"Lucio's everything I want in a man," I said. "He's stable, from 'a good family.' I'm so tired of a having-to-struggle-so-hard life, like my mother's. I want marriage. Children. A home with a roof that doesn't leak. Is that too much to ask?"

La Wirms peered over a high heaped-up plate of Tostadas Compuestas, her usual, the finely grated cheese spilling over the edges. She glared at me with those icy-cold don't-you-go-there eyes of hers.

"Tere, stop it! Didn't you hear anything I said before? Wake up! Lucio's married. Don't you understand?"

"I'm trying, comadre, I'm really trying."

"We'll go dutch today."

"I was going to treat you, Irma, but that's okay."

I stared at myself in the mirror at Sofia's Mighty Taco. I sat across from Irma near the back of the room, close to the kitchen, in our favorite booth. It was a good place to sit if you wanted to just talk and not be interrupted. All the lovers sat in this corner. Everyone who had just had a good cry and didn't want to be found out too quickly hid here.

The enchiladas were hot, but I ate them with gusto, I surprised myself. That's one thing I'll say for Mejicanos, there's nothing like deep sorrow to give you a good appetite.

Tragedy seems to bring out the hunger in me. After a wake or funeral I can really eat, and it doesn't matter if the meal is maca-roni salad and weenies in somebody's backyard or a five-course French dinner. Not that we see much of those in Cabritoville. No one here ever sets a table with two forks. It's not necessary. In

fact, people here rarely use forks. We're finger-food people. Of
course, I prefer what Irma and I call real food as opposed to the
fake food we've eaten for years. I'm not talking about the fideos
and calabacitas and good home-cooked comida Mejicana that we
both love, I'm talking about the typical contemporary Mejicano
diet, which is composed of anything lardy/anything sweet/any-
thing salty that you find on the tables of Mexican-Americans who
don't like to think about cooking, much less cook.

All my best intentions to eat cleanly fall away when I'm in the
throes of passion or really upset. That's when I love Miss Deb-
bie and Colonel Sanders, prepackaged cherry Jell-O and mus-
tard potato salads at Canales' Grocery, bags of miniature white
powdered-sugar doughnuts and as many pan de huevos and gin-
gerbread marranitos as I can eat at one sitting.

Irma watched me as I single-handedly devoured an order of
four sopaipillas slathered with honey.

"You enjoyed that, comadre, didn't you?" she asked.

"You know what? As I'm sitting here in front of this mirror, I'm
thinking of the mirror scene in the movie *No Desearás la Mujer de
Tu Hijo*," I said.

Here Pedro is Silviano, the long-suffering son of a bully father,
Cruz, played by Fernando Soler. I don't think there's a greater vil-
lain in the Época de Oro movies than the hard-drinking womanizer
Cruz. Not only did he kill his loving wife, Bilbiana, slowly and with
malice; he had the audacity to think Josefa, Silviano's girlfriend,
was in love with him! In this big dramatic mirror scene, Silviano finally stands up to Cruz. It's a moment that will chill your blood.
Silviano shows his father his old, wrinkly face in the mirror. Someday Cruz has to wake up to see what he's done to Bilbiana and to
Silviano. He has to accept the fact that he is getting old and that
he can't control the lives of those around him. How long can a human being live under the yoke of another? And especially if that
person is your father or mother? Or worse yet, a lover?

"I can't help but think that I'm like Silviano and that Lucio's
like Cruz, comadre. I look in the mirror and see myself as a mop
of a human being. You've got to help me, Irma."

"Move in with me for a few weeks, Tere," Irma offered. "I'll keep you so busy you'll forget to feel sorry for yourself. Go home and pack. We'll have a Pedro-athon this weekend the likes of which have rarely been seen. We'll give each other pedicures. We'll cook up a storm. I have some new recipes we can try. And if that doesn't work, I'll call Father Ronnie over. We'll have a cookout."

Part of me wanted to go home right then and crawl in bed to die, another part wanted to track Lucio down and throw him on a bed—after a tall glass of Alka-Seltzer and a bath—and still another part of me wanted to be tied down until all the demons came out of me, an exorcism of unparalleled proportions. But Irma was right.

"I'll invite Ubaldo and tell him to bring his Ouija board. It's a long time since we've talked to La Llorona, comadre."

"Oh, all right. Although I'm not sure it's a good idea. Being that Ubaldo's a *desde* and Father Ronnie is a *desde*. I don't want to be responsible for corrupting a priest."

"Hardly! I've been wanting to see Father Ronnie's impersonation of Barbra Streisand. I've heard so much about it."

"It's about time you thought of going on a retreat. Your spiritual life has gone to Hell during this affair."

Irma had it all figured out. She would walk me through the burning coals. I was trying to break loose after several seasons in Hell. I needed all the help I could get.

It was time to let go. And God help me, I was ready.

I prayed.

Dear God:
I know it's been a long time since I've talked to you. I'm sorry.
I've been so busy thinking of too many things that aren't nice to
think about now. I'm not a bad person. I'm a good person. I love
life and I love children. I believe in justice and equality and in
Pedro Infante. What I've done weighs on me so badly, especially
when I see the hurt in Andrea's eyes. She can't look at me any-
more. I can't say I'm sorry for loving Lucio, and this is my
biggest sin. I wish I were more repentant, but I can't be. All I'm
asking for is a miracle like the one you gave me the last time I

went on a retreat. I didn't want to have sexual feelings then. I was there for healing. It wasn't good when I developed a lustful hankering for this hunky-looking man I'd met in front of the sixth station of the cross: The Face of Jesus Is Wiped by Veronica. I asked you to remove all evil thoughts from my heart. To take the burden of horniness from me. I prayed for release. I want to thank you, God, for making the man I was crazy about a priest. If he hadn't been, I would have jumped his bones after one of the late-night prayer sessions. I do believe we both wanted to make hot passionate love instead of talking to our inner chidren. I did get to wash the papi chulo priest's feet and feel his deditos between my fingers and hug him real tight and tell him that I loved him, but only like a spiritual brother. It really wasn't enough, I have to tell you. I've never believed priests should be celibate, especially the cute young ones with hard legs and lots of hair on their head. I did manage to finally let go of my evil yearnings, but it was difficult, and only came after a long night of tossing and turning. I want to thank you for having a middle-aged woman come up to me and warn me el precioso was a priest and that people were talking about us taking too many long walks. I had no idea el chulito was a man of the cloth and it was a shock. We still write to each other for Christmas. I understand from his last letter that he's left the priesthood. I finally admitted to him that I had the hots for him. He liked hearing that and said that maybe we could get together someday. I wouldn't mind washing something more than his feet. That's if things with Lucio don't work out. Which brings me to my real problem. I need a miracle. Now if you can only do something for me with Lucio like you did with that handsome priest, I really would believe in you. I'm not sure what I would believe, but it would be a start. Anything you can do would help.

    La Tere

I stared in the mirror. I had a smudge of red chile on my chin. The woman in the mirror stared back.

PART IV

DICEN

QUE SOY

MUJERIEGO

The Priest of Pain

In *Ahora Soy Rico*, Pedro plays a man named Pedro. There are a lot of similarities between Pedro in that movie and Lucio. The same sort of snootiness. The same sort of irritated turn-on-a-peseta flare-ups that become ugly once he doesn't get his way. The same kind of irrefutable heart-wrenching sexiness despite the flawed nature of the beast.

I've always been attracted to men who are mean and like to show it. Irma says it's because I've mistaken cruelty for strength, willfulness for free will and selfishness for pride in oneself. I say it's because of the jodida unlucky roll of the eternal black furry dice. And because I'm attracted to short, bossy men with small backs and tiny butts who have to wear their belts halfway down their knees because they can't find pants that allow for ultra-sized huevos. These Napoleons know how to kiss a woman and leave her reeling.

They revel in their meanness; they flaunt it the way a woman shows off a new dress. And as they twirl and prance before you in their most vain, pompous and self-assured bravado, you can't help but love them. They're bad little boys. Unreliable men. Terrible husbands. Distracted sons. Questionable fathers. Insatiable lovers. They drive you crazy. And leave you begging for more.

I hate to speak ill of Lucio, but he can be a shit if and when he wants to and yes, he mostly wants to lately. Same goes for Pedro-as-Pedro in *Ahora Soy Rico*. I feel sorry for Marga, his beautiful long-suffering wife. Not only does she have to put up with a man who tried to kill himself by jumping off a building when their little son died (but only managed to break his legs); he's also a wimpy-assed cojo who feels sorry for himself. What about Marga? She'd been caring for their m'jito day and night and taking in laundry and ironing, only to have Pedro go out and spend what little money they had on cervezas because he couldn't stand the fact that they were poor. Why did he have to drink until he was senseless? Why did he have to hang out with a bunch of fulanas de tal who only wanted his money? He should have stayed home and taken care of his family! Pedro-as-Pedro is responsible for his twisted, crippled legs.

I wish I had a dollar for each song Pedro Infante sings in a drunken voice. Which leads me to my theory of why Mejicanos love to drink. It numbs the pain and heightens it at the same time. There's nothing a Mejicano or Mejicana loves more than the burning, stinging pain of thwarted, frustrated, hopeless, soulful, take-it-to-the-grave love. Nothing gets us going more than what I call rabia/love of the te-juro-you're-going-to-pay-for-all-the-suffering-you-caused-me variety. We know the pendejo o pendeja is going to regret it someday. But just try to come crawling back, it'll be too late! Just eat your heart out, you had your chance!

Pedro is really good at these moments. More than anyone I

know, he captures the rabia/love we've all felt at one time or another. Hell, I know what that rabia/love is all about. Just call me Tere La Rabiosa.

I was washing my hair in No. 17 at the Sands. Pedro was singing "Mi Tenampa" in the background. Above the singing, I heard Lucio's voice, the one he uses when he's about to get mean. Something in me pulled itself up and stood at attention.

"Who's that?" Lucio asked.

Oh, he knew, but he had to ask.

"That's Pedro," I said. He was only being *desde*. He was so good at it. I knew the ins and outs and ups and downs of his reedy little voice. I knew his tender late-at-night kiss-me-Tere voice. I knew his early-morning where-are-my-pants voice. I knew his I-want-to-say-I-love-you-but-I-can't voice. (This was the most painful of all.) What I didn't yet know was which voice was about to come over the airwaves, like a defective radio. The static was never the same. It was always unexpected, and when it did come on, I wasn't quite sure what had happened or where the sound originated from.

Lucio was irritated.

"Can you turn that crap down?"

"Sssh! Everyone can hear you!" I whispered. My hair was wet and the water was dripping down my neck.

The way Lucio was yelling, you could hear him all the way to Sofia's Mighty Taco. Lucio's cronies were probably all sitting around trying to get Sofia to tell her stories about her last win in Las Vegas or the time she had to get rid of the stripper who wanted to show everyone her patriotic red, white and blue pasties.

"So who cares?"

"I care. You're not the one who has to sneak around. You, at least, are renting the room. You can show up with tools, boxes of books, notebooks. I have to slink in here like I'm the cleaning woman. Which I'm not, so pick up your chones, Lucio Valadez. You're starting to leave your underwear around again. And don't drape them over the television to hide the time. If you do that, at

least turn the crotch side in. You're driving me nuts. For your information, the song is called 'Mi Tenampa.' "

"I'm out here trying to read, Terry. I can't go through *Roget's
Thesaurus* and think with that man singing."

"So what are you thinking?" I asked with surprise. Lucio wasn't
one to share too many of his thoughts unless he was drowsy or
had had a few beers. I'd test him out. It was worth a try.

"I'm thinking things," Lucio said.

"Things?"

"Things. I can't always tell you what I'm thinking and why. Do
you have to know everything about me? Can't I have my own
thoughts? Just let me think alone."

By now, I even knew Lucio's think-alone voice. What I couldn't
tell at that moment was whether it was a think-alone moment or
an irritated explain-to-me-what-I'm-doing-with-you moment. I
didn't know if he was mad at me or Diolinda or Cuca or his work.
It was really hard to figure Lucio out sometimes.

"So, that's *him* singing?" Lucio said in a strained, high-pitched
voice. "He sounds like he's gloating over something."

"Who else would it be singing? It's who's always singing when I
listen to someone singing. It's Pedro."

I was irritated that Lucio had asked me a question that didn't
need an answer. I needed my alone thoughts as well and my alone
time to be just that: alone.

Of course, we weren't ever really alone in the Sands Motel
room. To me, there were always hundreds of people in there with
us: all the people who had slept, eaten, made love in there and
moved on. Like all of them, Lucio and I were travelers. Moving
from one destination to another, from one hope and then disappointment to another. We were desperate people trying to get
home.

I hated to be interrupted while I was washing my hair. It was a
terrible imposition. Lucio never gave me enough bathroom time
alone. He was always popping in there when I was plucking my
eyebrows or clipping my toenails. If he needed thinking time, so

did I. Men never understand how private a woman's bathroom time is. The French call it a toilette. And I mean it, toilette is the word. I tried to explain to Lucio the importance of a woman's toilette.

"Think about what your French teacher, Dr. Ganeau, would say about a woman's private bathroom time," I said to him, knowing that would do the trick. Lucio was always talking about Dr. Ganeau this and Dr. Ganeau that. This is proof that any small amount of college can affect your intelligence: Lucio thinks he understands French because he took a couple of semesters of French with Docteur Jean Pierre Ganeau, who said French was "the most civilized langue in the world."

"So what are you saying to me, Terry? That the bidet is a very French thing? I think so, too. When Dio and I were on our honeymoon in Paris, well, it was very convenient is all I can tell you."

"What are you talking about, Lucio?" I yelled back. "I couldn't hear you."

"A bidet, it's handy."

"What's a buh-day?"

"Come on, now, Terry, you mean . . ."

"I'll be out in a minute, Lucio. I'm busy in here. So, you don't like the song?"

"Well, so is he drunk or what?"

"What?" I screeched. I couldn't hear Lucio. The Sands Motel towel covered my ears. The towel was old, the victim of too many washings.

"Sounds like hell."

"Yeah, I like it, too," I said. It was one of my favorites.

I sang loudly in what Lucio calls my "ugly Mexican" voice. (Lucio hates that I can echar gritos better than he and that I know the words to all the Mexican songs he's never heard of.)

"You're a baby," I tell him. (He is five years younger and that's the only reason I sometimes feel compassion for him.)

Lucio's a child who is still spoiled by his mother. His father was such a worker ant, trying to make a living from El Chorrito Bar, he

didn't have time to get to know his son, let alone ever love him.
There is a great sadness in me for Lucio, and when I feel angry at
him for being so young and so uncaring, I remember how crippled
he is, just like Pedro in *Ahora Soy Rico*.

"Don't you have any other music, Terry?"

I couldn't hear Lucio at all now, the hair dryer was on high, and
as I dried my hair I sang out in a voice as loud and passionate as I
could, knowing full well Lucio was listening in the other room.
Our bedroom. Ha.

¿Cuál cariño es el que dices
que te dí con toda el alma,
cuando abriste tú conmigo
las persianas del Tenampa?
Tú qué sabes de parranda
tú qué entiendes
por pasiones?
¡Tú cuando oyes un mariachi,
ni comprendes sus canciones!
Parranda y Tenampa
mariachi y canciones
Así es como vivo yo.
Tú qué sabes de la vida,
de la vida entre las copas?
¿Tú para ser mi consentida,
necesitas muchas cosas!
Yo me paro en la cantina
y a salud de las ingratas,
hago que se sirva vino
pa' que nazcan serenatas.
Y una vez ya bien servido,
voy al rumbo del Tenampa,
ahí me agarro a mi mariachi,
y a cantar con toda el alma.
Parranda y Tenampa

mariachi y canciones.

Así es como vivo yo.

Tú qué sabes de la vida,

de la vida entre las copas?

¿Tú para ser mi consentida,

necesitas muchas cosas!

You get the drift of the savory pain. Nothing like it!

The sad thing about all of this was that I really loved Lucio. I was ready to open a vein for him in the bathroom, right there in No. 17, while he was in the other room hating me a little more each day.

I was beginning to hate him as well except I loved him so much that the thought of life without his love overcame my hate. But things were about to change. Lucio was moving to the Cielo Vista Apartments on Airway Boulevard in El Paso, near the airport. Sixty-nine dollars gets you in. That's where he wanted us to meet from now on.

"I have to get going, Terry," he yelled, and I heard him this time.

I went into the bedroom, jumped on the bed and covered him with kisses. Lucio responded the way he does each time I kiss him. With hunger and with passion. Everything was all right again. For now. No mothers or wives to bother us. "Mi Tenampa" aside, Lucio liked me at that moment and for many reasons.

But I wanted him to hold me and tell me all the reasons he loved me. To list them one by one: (1) Tere, you are beautiful. (2) Tere, you make me laugh. (3) Okay, you get the idea.

Lucio never answered my questions fully. He never played the games lovers play. He was too busy, and too businesslike. He didn't have time to lie around talking about why he liked me so much and why I was his consentida. He didn't understand the concept of having a consentida, a person you spoil and dote on, a lover whom you love to love and do little cariños to and for and whom you just wait on like there is no tomorrow. Tommorrow? To-morrow? I was never Lucio's consentida.

"What is it about me that you really like? Tell me."

"Ummm . . . ," he mumbled, fingering my breast. "This . . ."

"And? Let's try to get away from my breasts and thighs this time . . . Okay?"

"And . . . I really don't have time for this, Terry. I have to drive back home and it's starting to rain."

"Come on, Lucio, you never *talk* to me. We usually only get together at night and by then you're talked out. All you want to do is make love and then go to sleep. Or else you have to rush off and there's no talk there. So what do you like about me? You never tell me."

"I like your faith, Terry."

"My faith? What's there to like about being a Catholic? I mean, I know there's a lot to like. Purgatory for one. The existence of Purgatory is a nice thing for a religion to have. Purgatory gives us hope, despite all the odds, even after death. I like Purgatory. And then there's Midnight Mass. Midnight Mass is about the coolest Catholic thing. And I like it when the priest washes people's feet on Good Friday. I say we should wash more feet. We'd be better off. Good Friday, that's a good Catholic time. Easter's good, or was good when you were a kid, but personally I like Good Friday better. Ay, so what am I? An expert on being Catholic? I guess I am or I wouldn't always feel such guilt when I'm with you. And on top of that, I love my guilt. On the Guilt-O-Meter, I guess I'd have to say I'm a pretty good Catholic. But I'm not a bitter Catholic. There's a difference. Catholics always have good stories.

"Here I am doing all the talking again. Lucio, what do you like about me? Really like? Is there anything you love about me? Do you love me, Lucio? Because I love you."

"If I say I love you, you'll only want me to love you more and more."

My mouth was suddenly dry and I felt faint.

"I can never love you the way you want me to love you, Terry."

I could feel my heart tighten up and my lungs contract. I turned on my side and closed my eyes so Lucio wouldn't see I was in pain.

"You don't understand. I like the fact that you have faith. I mean, just listen to you. And I do, believe me. You're like a child. You believe the best about people. What more can I say?"

I rolled over to face Lucio.

"Well, that's *one* thing. Faith. Although I'm not sure what you really mean. What else do you like about me, Lucio?"

"One thing or two or three is enough for now. Don't talk anymore."

Lucio had his mouth on my right breast. He was a child, really. Did Cuca ever nurse him? I would have to ask him about it. Now wasn't the right time. I would try and find out later if Lucio was ever on formula. He seemed like a formula baby, his need to nurse was so great. When Lucio was quiet, I got quiet. When we made love, it was in silence and in majesty.

The thoughts that come to you when a man is sucking on your breasts!

The music played on in the background. It was a magical moment. Diolinda and Andrea didn't exist. Cuca seemed far away. I was fresh and clean and beautiful and now Lucio was quiet and happy.

Still, Pedro was in my thoughts. Irma and I had seen *Un Rincón Cerca del Cielo* and *Ahora Soy Rico* back-to-back at our last Pedro-athon. I couldn't get Pedro-as-Pedro out of my mind.

Could Lucio be doing a Pedro?

El Nene

Pedro Infante liked young
women. There was Guadalupe, "Lupita," the mother
of his first daughter; they were just kids when he got
her pregnant. Then there was María Luisa. They
never had any biological children of their own, although they adopted a child, Dora Luisa. María
Luisa was the only one of Pedro's loves who was
older than he. Then there was Lupe Torrentera, the
mother of three of his other children. She was just
fourteen when they met, and fifteen when she had
her first child with him. Margarita was the baby's
name; she died of polio at four months. He used to
go to her grave site every day. And then there was
Irma Dorantes, the young film actress, who had a
child, Irmita, with Pedro, and who later married
him, although that marriage was annulled the week

before his death. There's something terrible about the timing, you have to think Pedro wasn't in the right state of mind when he was piloting that fatal flight.

Prior to his death, Pedro endured several plane crashes, the most terrible being the one on May 22, 1953, near Zitácuaro, Michoacán, where he was almost killed and had to have a metal plate put in this head. The accident left him with his head opened from the middle of his forehead to his left ear. Lupe Torrentera was on that flight and survived with only facial injuries. It was a big scandal in Méjico, but still María Luisa went to the hospital right away and sat with him, offering him her cariños.

"Pedro was a daring child, one who never learned, Tere. I believe he had two separate personas," Irma said to me as we were pushing our shopping carts side by side at Canales' Grocery, "the adult and the child. And with the child, El Nene, you could never discuss things, because he would screw up his face and act the innocent. He was the kind of Mejicano who called his wife Mamá and meant it. At least that's what his wife María Luisa said about him."

"You would have thought that Pedro would have never flown again, Irma," I said to her as I stopped in front of the tomatoes.

"And while he was at it, stayed away from women, especially the young ones, who brought him all kinds of trouble. The kind of trouble you can never extricate yourself from as long as you live. Now that's a good word for you, Tere. Extricate."

"Extracate?" I said as I pulled out my word notebook.

"Extricate," Irma corrected. "Remember that word."

The night before, with nowhere to go, no place to be, no one to attend to but each other, Lucio and I made out like high school kids in the middle of a deserted road, tongue kisses so deep they almost made us gag. We stopped at every stop sign on that quiet late-night country road to neck and then drove a little bit further,

giggling and feeling foolish, too old for this stuff. We thought of
taking off all our clothes and making love by the side of the road.
We couldn't wait. We didn't have to wait. The time was now and
we knew it.

Albinita was at a weekend-long Cursillo. Lucio's family was out
of town. I invited him over to my little house, so he could see
where I lived, although I realized this would probably be the only
time he'd ever be with me there. It was too dangerous. Albinita
was a light sleeper. I couldn't bring shame to her by luring Lucio
home with all the neighbors watching from drawn curtains. The
neighborhood dogs were too *desde*. The rooster was erratic and
the hens were always full of nervous energy.

The morning after, I could hear the rooster behind Albinita's
house, Mr. Trejo shuffling down the street on his early-morning
walk to Denny's for his daily cup of coffee with his sidekicks, the
Sunshine Boys, and the sudden yapping of the neighborhood
mutts, all of them bored, with nothing to do, their errant masters
never home.

A few chihuahuas down the street had escaped and were
headed toward freedom, yammering happily. I was afraid to talk,
afraid to breathe, too lazy and too ecstatic to get out of bed to
even brush my teeth. I was worried that the moments would slip
by. I was too happy for words. And so I was mute as Lucio talked
to me in that crooning baby way, as he traced the outline of my
chin with his warm fingers, kissed my eyelashes and neck, lay
next to me cooing sweet things: Baby girl, and Terry, oh, Terry. I
nodded and made little noises and tried to answer his questions.
Did I love him? Nod. Did I want to be with him? Nod. Was I
happy? Nod. Nod. Nod. Yes. Yes. And still more yeses.

No words came out, only sounds of joy, sounds of the early-
morning sleepy me who couldn't believe Lucio Valadez was in my
bed, under my sheets, next to me. I was mute. Afraid to move.
Afraid to dispel the moment. Afraid to pee and needing to so
badly. I was afraid I had bad breath. I tried to turn away from Lucio, but there he was again, stroking my face.

"I wish I could love you the way you deserve to be loved. I want to give you everything and I could, Terry," Lucio said, as he outlined my ear. "But it's not possible now. Someday, Terry. Someday will be our day."

From the bed, I scanned the photographs that hung around the room on the simulated-oak-wood paneling: Albinita and me standing near her rosebushes for Mother's Day, both of us shielding our eyes from the fierce sun; my dad, Quirino, holding me up, two years old, as he waved to Albinita from a parked Studebaker; Irma and me looking downcast in front of El Colón, April 15, 1977, the twentieth anniversary of Pedro's death; Irma and me, dressed to kill for someone's wedding, 1969, both of us in hot pants; Irma, by herself, looking small and sad after Sal's funeral; four small photographs of Ubaldo inside a pay photo booth, looking bleary-eyed and full of booze after a night in Juárez with his latest love, each frame underlined in black with a word—Tristeza, Rabia, Ternura, Coraje; me, alone, in front of Gabina, my favorite tree, a picture taken by Irma one late-summer afternoon.

I wanted to remember the early-morning daylight streaming through the soft blue curtains as the harsh barking of the neighborhood dogs receded like an unpleasant echo. I wanted to hold on to the memory of driving blind, kissing Lucio every few hundred feet, drawing breath and life from him and feeling that dark dangerous passion, the thrill of his hot flesh. If I could do that, I would be able to go on, because that's what I needed, assurance that it was the man who loved me, not the selfish, needy boy.

I try to think of the good times, the times we slow-danced in our room at the Sands, him sidling up to me like a long hungry cat, the times we sat naked in the middle of the king-sized bed, encuerados, two jaybirds chomping on the grated cheese spread and Hi Hos he loved with plenty of Mountain Dew and Coke with a squirt of tequila and no care in the world at least for a

few hours, when I'd wake Lucio up with kisses after he'd fallen
asleep.

But these days I'm so full of hidden agendas and pendeja loca
escapades that normal is a midnight drive to El Paso for a fifteen-
minute Funky Monkey at the Cielo Vista Apartments. After the
forty-minute ride home, I'll put out the garbage or watch late-
night movies to see who is giving pleito to whom and why. These
shows get me, they're so *desde*. But at that time of night I'm feeling all *desde* anyway, so what the hell. I watch them and I feel
better. My life could never be as bad as the ones you see on television late at night.

Sometimes I'll water the yard, if it's my watering day: Tuesday,
Thursday or Saturday, before 8 a.m. and after 6 p.m. If I'm really
feeling *desde*, I'll water no matter what time or day. There I'll be at
one or two in the morning moving the hose to the side of the
house. And I'll be thinking of Lucio Valadez and wondering if he's
snoring next to Diolinda.

One night I couldn't stand being the Other Woman anymore
and decided to phone Diolinda at home to have it out with her. I
just couldn't take it anymore. My bowling was off. Lucio hadn't
shown up Saturday at our new love nest on Airway Boulevard, and
he hadn't bothered to call. I spent the night in El Paso by myself
and sat in the plaza early the next morning throwing pennies into
the alligator pond. I was so upset I ordered a huge plate of pigs in
a blanket at the Oasis and ate every single one, and I was still
upset when Irma and I met for our weekly Pedro-athon the next
Friday night.

But Irma fell asleep on the lounger, as she usually did during
Los Hijos de María Morales. She said she couldn't take any more
womanizing from Pedro and that she'd catch me later when the
movie was over. While Irma snored, I decided to phone Diolinda
and have it out with her.

After I called her I knew it was a mistake. When I heard Diolinda's voice, I hung up. I wanted to tell her Lucio and I were going to get married, although you might say it seemed a little
premature. Lucio hadn't even told me he loved me!

I called Diolinda back. Andrea answered. I hung up again.

I was stunned. I fell back on the couch, and then shook Irma awake. We had to stop the movie I was so upset.

The following Monday, Lucio tracked me down in the cafeteria after I broke down and told him I'd called Diolinda. He appeared at the side door by the teachers' parking lot looking like a mangy animal come in from the desert heat. He looked like he'd just gotten out of a woman's bed and needed a drink of water. I knew that look of his, eyes glazed and staring out like a wounded vulture. He was the biggest bird I ever saw with his full dark mustache that he sucked nervously as if it was cotton candy. He was working those hairs in and out of his twisted little about-to-lie-to-me mouth. It was a disgusting sight. All the bad things I'd repressed came up full force and I took a deep breath and started the Serenity Prayer, but before I could get past "God grant me," some of the pain I was feeling took hold of me.

Lucio motioned for me to follow him to the parking lot. I slunk out a few minutes later, hoping no one would notice. I saw La Chole from the cafeteria crew stare at me. She knew! Felia winked at me from behind the steaming platter where she was dishing out sloppy joes. She knew! Then Uvalia raised her hand and waved to me with her chubby fingers going this way and that, as if to say, "Hasta luego, honey. Have a good time." They all knew.

I had called Diolinda because I wanted to tell her that Lucio and I were in love. The truth of the matter was that he was sleeping with me a lot of the time and with her some of the time and maybe with someone else a little of the time. Lucio said he would quit Diolinda after he met me, that he would get a divorce, but I knew it wasn't true. For the life of me, I couldn't see what he ever saw in Diolinda.

"Don't you be calling Dio, Terry. She's my wife," Lucio hissed at me. "What's wrong with you?" He stood in front of me—an excited yapping dog. "Dammit, Terry, you leave Dio alone. Besides being my wife, she's my one true friend!"

"Since when do you have any friends who are women? You hate women! You told me you hate Diolinda. And your big-rumped sister Velia, nalgas like a couch, you told me you hate her, and not only because of her nalgas. You hate her personality. You hate the way she snorts and hiccups when she laughs, spraying baba all over the place. And most of all you hate La Vieja Bruta. That's all I've ever heard you call your mother. That and La Sangrona and a few other choice names. The only women you're friends with are the women you're sleeping with. And I guess that's me. Or is it me and someone else?"

The scene was ugly and getting uglier by the minute.

Something in me had broken up or out.

"Crazy bitch!" Lucio yelled.

"I hate you, Lucio Valadez, I hate you!" I screamed.

The words slipped out of my mouth and I've regretted them ever since, because that was the first time I articulated my pain. Lucio saw it, and it caught him off guard. For a moment I thought he was going to hold me. He reached out to take my arm and I hit him. Hard. Then he took me by the shoulders and shook me. My arms were flailing like the baby's in *Las Mujeres de Mi General*, where bullets are whizzing right and left and Pedro is holding his little daughter in his arms as he defends himself from gunfire. I hit Lucio again and again. He squared off, stood back and said simply, "I can't love you, Terry, not the way you want me to."

"Why, Lucio?"

"Because you want me to be with you all the time, and I can't. I just can't! I have a life of my own apart from you and I like that life, Terry. Goodbye. Please don't call me," he said as he spun around and walked away, one tight pressed jean pant leg swish-sliding against the other, his crocodile Luccheses kicking up rocks and leaving a trail of fine dust in the air.

Our yelling brought out La Chole, who reported back to the crew. Then one by one they all came out to the parking lot. Thank

God the lunch crowd had already thinned to nothing. La Chole said she was going to call the police, but I said no, no, no between hard tears. Dora brought me a glass of water.

"I'm all right," I gasped.

"You want me to get the security guard?" asked Nancy.

"Or Principal Perea?" whispered La Chole, all watery-eyed. She looked as if she had been standing over a tray of raw onions.

"No, I'm fine. Just let me sit here, Chole. Go on back to the kitchen, Dora, I'm okay. Really."

Everyone went back to work. I sat on the curb near the back door to the cafeteria. And it was then I decided to go to Santa Fe.

Graciela and Irma had planned on going for the annual fiesta, where they burn Zozobra, Old Man Gloom, a giant, white-sheeted effigy with huge black eyes and a black bow tie who groans and moans as the flames leap up to burn him. I had declined their invitation to join them earlier in the week because I wanted to be close to Lucio. But that night I called La Wirms and told her I was on for the trip.

"You mean you're actually leaving Cabritoville to be with me and Graciela, Tere?"

"I haven't seen much of you either, Wirms. Not since you met Mr. You Know Who. You're too busy for your girlfriends."

"Don't get started, Tere," she warned. "If you're going to Santa Fe to spite anyone, just don't go. We don't want any grouchy people along for the ride. Graciela and I want to have a good time. We want to go see the Miraculous Stairway. So do you want to go or not?"

"I want to go. That's why I'm calling you, comadre. Tell me about the Miraculous Stairway."

"Not one nail. This mysterious carpenter appeared and built a stairway for these poor nuns. They had this small space in which they couldn't figure out how to put stairs. Legend has it that the carpenter was St. Joseph. So get ready. We'll leave tomorrow after work. And try to leave Lucio behind."

"For your information, Lucio and I broke up."

"You broke up?"

"I'll tell you all about it when you pick me up. Forget it, Graciela will be there. I can't trust her. Does she have to go?"

"It's her car, Tere. And besides, she's my Preems."

"Yeah, I know. Blood is thicker than a good story. All you need to understand is that Lucio and I . . . we had a fight."

"Good."

"Irma!"

"I'll pick you up around three-thirty."

"Make that four."

"Three forty-five."

"A little before four."

"You better be ready."

The drive to Santa Fe was long and boring. Graciela talked nonstop about her latest boyfriend, whom neither Irma nor I knew. He was a lawyer from a wealthy family in San Antonio, Graciela said with pride. And he was crazy about her. She regaled us with stories of a possible impending engagement y no se qué no se cuando, a honeymoon in Tahiti or Las Vegas or Disneyland, she couldn't decide.

The miles were interminable as I stared out the backseat window into the great bowels of a lonely dark hell that led out of Cabritoville. The further out of town we got, the worse I felt.

We checked into the King's Rest Motel on Cerrillos Road and slept until noon the next day. We ate breakfast at the Pantry restaurant and in the afternoon we walked around the plaza and went to all the fiesta booths and the stores, where we couldn't afford to buy anything. Irma treated us to Frito Pies at the Woolworth's. We found a spot on the grass that wasn't taken on the plaza and planned our evening: an early dinner who knows where, the burning of Zozobra and who knows what with who knows who.

That night I got drunk at La Fonda Hotel. Graciela picked up these Santa Fe-style dudes a 'lo todo La Conquistadora in the plaza. You know the type: I'm Spanish. You're Mexican. The Mexican in them had invited us to go dancing at La Fonda while the Spanish part kept looking at us sideways like we were inferior human beings. Leave it to Graciela to befriend the least likely suspects in an unlikely situation. The three of us women had been dancing together off to the side of the Santa Fe plaza to a really bad version of Clapton's "Layla."

"So where you from?" one of the dudes asked Graciela.

"Cabritoville," answered Graciela, like butter wouldn't melt in her mouth. I would have lied. I didn't want Oñate and his two fellow butchers to know where we lived. Leave it to Graciela to blurt out the details.

"She's from Cabritoville and I'm from somewhere else," I replied.

"Where the hell is Cabritoville?" asked this short dude, who sniffed at me as if I smelled sour.

"You don't know where Cabritoville is?" I asked. "Where the hell you from?"

"Cabritoville's down south," Graciela purred.

"Oh," the three little Matrushka men said, each one shorter than the other.

"You look Mexican," the tallest said to Irma.

"I'm an indígena," Irma said in English. Then in Spanish. And then Irma said something in Nahuatl. Leave it to Irma to come out with something like that. I asked her about it later and she said she'd remembered the phrase from one of her favorite Pedro movies, *La Mujer Que Yo Perdí*. And here I thought she'd taken a correspondence course in Nahuatl! Irma was always taking courses by mail. Irma said she told him she was nativa just to piss him off. And then she showed him her armpits to let him know how really pissed off she was. I have to tell you, I was really proud of her.

Irma has this theory called Sobacage, from sobacos, armpits.

She says that men and women, men particularly, will show you their armpits when they need to physically express their dominance over others. It's a visual and sensory power trip, like cats or dogs leaving a scent.

"A man usually shows a woman or another man his armpits, Tere, when he's in some doorway, entering a room or a situation that he needs to control. Notice when a woman shows you her armpits. It's usually when she feels she's losing ground or asserting her male side. Observe when and where people show you their armpits, whether they're relaxed or angry, defensive or aggressive, and whether they show one or both armpits. You'll learn a lot about human nature, Tere. It'll surprise you."

When I saw La Wirms flashing both upraised armpits at Mr. I'm-So-Spanish-Just-Call-Me-Señor-Cervantes, I knew she was very upset.

I hate that north/south shit. The northerners can't understand that the Spaniards came up through Méjico. Who do they think they had babies with? What are we but a mestizaje, a mixture of all the people in the world? Especially Cabritovillians.

That night in Santa Fe, after several pitchers of margaritas that Graciela drank practically all by herself, it didn't seem to matter that we were Mejicanas and the no-name dudes were Spanish. Once you're horny, the lines seem to blur. But then it flared up again when Irma went to the bathroom and one of the guys, who finally introduced himself as Ruperto, started in about how they spoke real Spanish and their Spanish was the Spanish of the Spanish and how our Spanish was the Spanish of the conquered Mejicano pendejo, only he didn't say it that way, he said it like Mexicun but I knew what he meant. I was just thankful Irma was in the bathroom, or it could have gotten really ugly.

Ruperto went on about the words they use up north, the correct and ancient Spanish words and not the bastardized pocho Spanish we use. He kept on about Spanish this and Spanish that. Yeah yeah yeah—puto, I kept thinking. When Irma came back, Ruperto started in about how great La Conquistadora was, she being the Patroness of Santa Fe, and the beloved symbol of the Spanish conquest over the Indians.

Irma took a deep breath and let ole Ruperto have it.

"Very few people understand la cultura Mejicana the way they should," Irma said with authority. She was just getting revved up, I could tell.

"I'm the ambassador for Mejicano culture. My culture. I have to be. It's because too many people both here and elsewhere think Mejicanos are uncultured."

Ruperto and his cronies snorted. Irma didn't let them get a word in. She continued with gusto.

"What about the Mayan civilization? What about the pyramids? What about Monte Albán? What about Pedro Infante? María Félix? What about Cantinflas? Dolores Del Río? It doesn't matter if we're in or out of Méjico, we're always Mejicanos, with roots as deep as the cottonwoods near the Río Grande."

The good old Spanish boys looked at each other. This inflamed Irma.

"And if you don't know about the great culture and history of Méjico by now, then someone should make you walk with glass in your shoes all the way from the Zócalo to the Anthropology Museum as the pilgrims do December 12 on the Feast Day of Our Lady of Guadalupe."

"I was talking about La Conquistadora, miss," Ruperto said, half apologetically. He could see La Wirms was going high octane.

"La Conquistadora? That short, blood-covered lace doll? You want culture, let's talk about culture! Personally, of all the Blessed Mothers in the world, all of them being one and the same—only different—I think the Guadalupe is the best dressed. Have you seen the Spanish Black Virgin? Dios mío, that stiff formal dress. Uh-uh. And those somber colors, no way, she's definitely Spanish. I like the little fur trim on the Guadalupe. Her fashion sense is incredible. She isn't frilly like the Immaculate Conception or scary like Our Lady of Sorrows, or any of the other incarnations of the Blessed Mother, bless their little pure hearts, all white dresses

and blue shawls. No feeling for design. No pizzazz despite a few
stars or roses here or maybe a glowing diadem there. How many
of those women are standing in front of the sun? You tell me. Our
Lady of Guadalupe is the best dressed of all the Blessed Mothers,
bless them all. She's what I call high, very high fashion. Chalk it
up to Mejicano design. Mejicano culture. Love it and believe it."

Ruperto's mouth was hanging open. The two enanos were sling-
ing back their beers like there was no tomorrow. The "I'm Spanish, you're Mexican" crap ended right then and there with the
Guadalupe, patroness of the oppressed.

Graciela suggested we dance.

The band began playing and until then I hadn't realized Irma
was yelling at Ruperto across the noisy table. Father Frank Pretto,
the salsa priest of Santa Fe, started playing "Tiburón" in the background. It gave me the heebie-jeebies when I saw Graciela's wild
devil-come-here look. She was sidling up to one of the Españoles
and now there was no turning back. ¡Qué caray!

The guy who asked me to dance and whom I later ended up with
was in Oñate's Royal Court. Go figure. Earlier that day he was in
the parade dressed in Spanish armor with a big feathered headdress. A small man, but handsome in a Spanish way. Okay, so
maybe he was a descendant. Half-pints. I always seem to end up
with half-pints with small backs, hairy butts with hairy cracks, hairy
knuckles and hair sticking out from their shirts front and back.

The last thing I remember was making out in the back seat of
somebody's car with the guy from the Royal Court. Graciela was
going at it in the front seat with his sidekick, Fray Marcos. The
car windows were fogged, but I could see Irma talking outside the
car with Ruperto, who turned out to be a car salesman from
Bernalillo. He was trying to put his short Spanish moves on Irma
but she wasn't going for it. Every once in a while I heard what I
thought was a bad word in Nahuatl.

Mr. Royal Court was trying to run his fingers through my hair
but they got stuck in my wiglet. He kept telling me to take it off,
take it off, meaning the wiglet. I just wanted to say: Shut up, pay
attention. What does it matter to you if I'm wearing a wiglet or a

padded bra? Not that I was, but you know what I mean. You're lucky to be getting what you're getting. He was a good kisser despite his height. To tell you the truth, I can't remember his name.

We drove back to the motel and left early the next morning. Right around the Owl bar in San Antonio I fell asleep in the back seat of Graciela's Grand Prix with my false eyelashes on. Graciela woke Irma and me up when we got to town.

I blame Graciela for my eyelashes getting stuck. I had a horrible time unsticking them, and when I finally did, I pulled off a bunch of my own. It was all Graciela's fault. When most bad things happen to me, their madrina is named Graciela. My wiglet looked like a dead squirrel. I never could revive it, so later I gave it to Irma's niece Jasmine. She's the person to whom I give all my old guango stretched-beyond-the-limit textured panty hose and my pushed-out push-up bras. Ten years old, the girl is into dressing up. She doesn't yet know the price of being a woman.

Sometimes I think sadness is the downside of hating. And hatred is the other side of pure sorrow. Sweet and sour exchange only too well.

I admit I have too much hatred in me.

I finally got a chance to tell La Wirms about my fight with Lucio. Irma called me at home the day after we got back from Santa Fe to ask me if I could meet her at her house. Make it six o'clock more or less.

"Some men *do* deserve to be hit, and more than once," Irma said. We sat at the kitchen counter drinking pink lemonade. La Wirms knew a bad scene when she saw one, or in this case heard about one. Such debacles had ceased to move her. There was a steely chill to her voice. I knew her heart burned for me and she had to restrain herself from wanting to kill Lucio. "Are you all right? Lucio didn't hurt you, did he? Well, if you ask me, I'm glad you broke up. He isn't good for you, Tere."

"Let's go to La Tempestad, Irma," I said with false bravado. "For Happy Hour. Two for One on the Well Drinks."

"Just tell me what happened, Tere. As ugly and low-down as it was."

"The cabrón chewed up my soul and spit it out like a piñón shell and left my tamale husk of a spirit there in the parking lot of Cabritoville Elementary. I never hit a man before I met Lucio. I was mad as hell. I'm still mad as hell. Lucio just seems to bring out the pendeja in me, all the untapped ugliness. He makes me think ugly thoughts. And not only that, he makes me feel ugly. He's the first person who made me realize I could kill and not feel a thing. He doesn't love me, is what it comes down to. So what do you say we go get a beer?"

"Look, I have to get back to work, comadre. I'll pick you up early for the fan club meeting later this week. We'll grab a bite at Sofia's."

"I can't go, Irma. I'm too full of rabia."

"Oh yeah you can, Tere. Besides, you missed the last meeting. This week we're watching *La Tercera Palabra*. It's one of your favorites. You'll get to see Pedro play the innocent child of nature who realizes that the world is really evil when his teacher, Margarita, helps him to understand that his relatives have used him and wanted to declare him insane. Your sense of injustice won't be wasted. Believe me, you'll feel good afterward. See you at Sofia's," Irma said as she walked me to the door. I knew she was headed back to the Flying W. She had a dusty glow.

"Hey, so, Irma, what did you want to tell me?" I called out after her.

"It can wait, Tere. I gotta go."

Remember the scene in *Ahora Soy Rico* where Pedro-as-Pedro is singing a drunken song in a noisy cantina? He has lipstick all over his face from the two women who are sitting next to him. (You have to wonder how Pedro could possibly do that to Marga. Didn't he know she really loved him?)

I didn't want to be one of those two drunken women with the smeared lipstick. Neither did I want to be Marga, stuck at home waiting for her man.

Nor did I want to be like Margarita in La Tercera Palabra, spurned by a child/man who should know better.

I drove home, confused, and when I tried to go to sleep that night, I couldn't. I moved to the living room couch. I opened Chapter 1 of the autobiography of Santa Teresa, La Santa Tere, and sooner than you can say "Lucio, do you love me?" I fell into unconsciousness.

I had a dream in which I flew high over the top of my little house to Lucio's bedside. Far below I could see Lucio and Diolinda sleeping. I stood next to them in the deep blue darkness. You know that dark blue? Dream blue.

I watched them sleep. They didn't know I was there. They seemed so peaceful together. There was nothing I could do to take Diolinda's place. Lucio had made his choice, and try as I could, he would always be faithful to her. An unspoken vow of unfaithful faithful that only they understood.

That dream faded into another dream. In the second dream Lucio had his fingers up my vagina. Okay, I admit it, I wanted more. It felt so good. I loved him touching me like that. I wanted to make hard love to him right then and there on that dark going-nowhere country road.

"You liked that, didn't you?" he sneered.

I decided not to tell Irma about the dream. She and I usually reported our dreams to one another. But lately we'd stopped. I missed that. Besides, the dream was mine. Other than Lucio scorning me with those squinty pig eyes of his, it was a pretty damn good dream.

The next thing I remember is flying up in the air and then coming back to earth. A dark presence surrounded me. I was afraid. I stabbed at the shadow figure with a sharp knife that I held in my hands.

I often dream about stabbing people in my sleep. It takes all my strength to stab, and when it's done, I feel so empty. These dreams had disturbed me so much that I finally had to tell Irma about them.

"The stabbing is a symbolic way of letting go, Tere. In your dreams, you have to kill Lucio to find release."

"So who says I'm stabbing Lucio anyway?"

"I'm glad to see you finally making some progress," Irma said with relief.

"I am?"

The next morning, after my nightmares, I flashed on Pedro-as-Pedro in *Ahora Soy Rico*, who was man enough for the two women who sat by him.

Pedro-as-Pedro *was*, I thought. Lucio? Now *that* was another matter. Was he man enough for me, Diolinda and La V.B.? I kept thinking of Pedro, of poor María Luisa, who could never have children, of Lupe Torrentera, of Lupe's children, of Irma Dorantes and their little girl, Irmita, as well as Pedro's mother, Doña Refugio. The man had his hands full. And for the women in his life, it was worse.

A silent prayer occurred to me.

Dear God (Female),
Take care of us women. Women with hopes. Women with
dreams. Pendejas jodidas. You know who we are.
  Amen.

Doña Meche

It was around ten o'clock on a Tuesday night. I sat trussed up in bed, the twelve-foot extension cord wrapped around my thighs. Ubaldo was on the line. He'd called to check in on me. I'd missed the last fan club meeting and Nyvia Ester had forced him to take the minutes. He planned to leave them on my doorstep in the morning.

"What you need is therapy, Tere," Ubaldo said with certainty.

"Says who, Ubaldo?"

"Says me. Hey, I've been there. I know what jodido suffering is. I know what it is to love a man who doesn't love you and to love him so much you hate him."

"Ubaldo, I just don't know. I mean, I know you

find the Catholic Family Social Services in El Paso like the very best place to unload yourself. Forget I said that. I know you really like Mr. . . . What's his name, the Catholic guy from New Jersey who's like your soul mate and all that?"

"Damn you, Tere, you have a way of deflating and making fun of stuff you know nothing about. And it all stems from your insecurity. For your information, Miss Doesn't-Believe-In-Therapy-and-Could-Use-It-So-Badly-Because-Her-Head-Is-So-Far-Up-Her-Ass, he's from the Bronx."

"What's his name?"

"Robert Dinguelaire."

"How do you spell that?"

"Just think Bob Dingler. You'd be in good hands."

"That's what I'm afraid of."

"We've been seeing each other. I mean, I've been seeing Bob for over a year now, and yes, he's helped me. He has tremendous faith in God. He's a good man, tough on me, and I need that. So, do you want me to make an appointment for you?"

"No. If I wanted to, I could go to the Prayer Group here in Cabritoville. The Cursillo crowd is waiting for me to turn my life around. But I'm not ready yet to give my life over to a bunch of humid apostles praying Jesus home."

"Ay, girl, you are a mess! So what happened?"

"Lucio and I had a big fight. We're not speaking. I went to Santa Fe for the fiestas, got drunk and made out with someone from the Spanish Royal Court."

"Is that all?"

"Oh, and one more thing. How can you tell if your man has another woman?"

"Smell him. He'll start smelling a little pasado."

"Off? Like sour bread? Old bananas?"

"Yeah, like that. It's really hard to tell with a man who's used to lying and cheating and is really good at pulling the dirty lana over a good woman's eyes. That means you."

"You never liked Lucio, Ubaldo, did you?"

"Pues, girl, you can't say que no te dije. I told you once and once more, he's a 'you know it because I already said it.' But now you know for sure."

"Yeah, well maybe. Maybe. He just seems distracted. He says he's just tired. That he's overworked."

"But he smells of another woman, doesn't he? Admit it!"

"I knew it the night it happened."

"I heard she's a travel agent at AAA," Ubaldo said.

"¡Ayyyy!" I sighed. So it was true! "I don't know how to say this, Ubaldo, but I feel violated. Like someone hovered over me when I was sleeping, lifted up my nightgown and then punched me in the stomach. I feel like Lupe in Las Mujeres de Mi General. It wasn't enough that Pedro-as-Juan Zepeda got confused when Carlota, the Blond from Town Who Married the Rich Old Man, Fermín, for his money, lied to him and told him that his girlfriend Lupe didn't love him anymore. He didn't know she was pregnant with their child until after Carlota had him in her clutches. Damned if Lupe would let Pedro-as-Juan know how much she loved him. Carlota ended up killing Fermín, with Pedro-as-Juan taking the rap. Ay, that Carlota was a bitch at the end."

"I don't know why you feel like Lupe, she doesn't sound at all like you. You didn't have a child with Lucio, thank God, and no one ever lied to him about you."

"Someone had to. Ay, what did it matter that Lupe loved Pedro anyway? Look what happened to them at the end! Bullets flying this way and that. All I can say is that meeting Lucio was my Mexican Revolution!"

"Suffering has made you a poet, Tere. But you've got to get a grip on yourself. I'm calling Bob."

"No, no, make me an appointment to see Doña Meche. If it has to be anyone, Doña Meche it is. You can come along, if you want."

"No way I'm messing with your Dark Forces. It's not good to blend our chakras."

"Nothing's darker than a Catholic therapist from New Jersey, if you ask me."

"The Bronx."

"Get back to me about that appointment. I have to get off the phone, Ubaldo. I need to call Irma."

"If I were you, I'd take a hot bath, two aspirins, and go to bed."

"So what's the woman's name?"

"Alice Something."

"¡Ay! Good night, Ubaldo."

"Good night, Tere."

I had to take off work to make my appointment with Doña Meche the following Thursday at 1:30 p.m. When I got to her house on Superstition Lane, I knew it was a mistake. No one goes to see a curandera for the first time in the middle of a hot day, without preparation of some kind or someone to stand in for you. I needed Ubaldo or Irma, someone to brace me for the shock of baring my soul to a complete stranger, especially one who reportedly had tremendous powers.

Doña Meche's house was in a cul-de-sac at the end of an old subdivision called Hacienda Acres, in a poor section of town. There was nothing fancy about it. As a matter of fact, you could say it was a lousy neighborhood. Although to hear it from Ubaldo, Doña Meche was one of the richest women in Cabritoville. He claimed she loved to invest in the stock market. Oh yeah? Well, invest in your neighborhood, and your yard, girl!

My Ávila nose could smell the fumes from the nearby city dump. A row of leaky sandbags were propped up against the cracked fake adobe. Clearly, the house was in the floodplain, by the look of the brown-rimmed watermark that circled its exterior. When I accidentally kicked a sandbag near the door several large black cucarachas scurried away. No one would ever believe that once this land was an arroyo segueing into the not so mighty Río Grande.

The house badly needed stuccoing. The door was off its hinges and the buzzer was ripped out. I knocked several times on peeled dry wood. And then again.

A woman came to the door.

"Doña Meche isn't there," she said in a low, lush voice. "She never works on Thursdays; it's bad luck."

Sure enough, my appointment was on Friday, but I had come a day early. It's happened to me before. I'll be there for the party and wonder why the parking lot is empty.

"Can I reschedule?" I asked the woman. She had bright red hair, the color of Mercurochrome. The hair has nothing to do with nationality; you see it on Mejicanas, Cubanas, Latinas and all types of women from all kinds of cultures and nationalities, at Bonanza City riffling through bolts of oilcloth, or stepping into the rest room at the Cabritoville laundromat, while ten dryers spin their faded T-shirts and stringy bras. Any nationality that likes loud, clown-red hair can have that hair.

I could see an old truck in the front yard, make that two old trucks, as well as a bunch of old lumber—what looked like an old crossbeam to one side—and a lot of ill-tended cactus.

"You want to come inside?" the woman said kindly.

"I'd like to leave a message for Doña Meche," I replied. "If I could."

Despite the clutter outside, the house was homey within. I stepped into the living room. A huge old cat with mangled ears got up to leave.

"Everybody wants to see Doña Meche about one thing or another. She has to rest her mind and heart. She works very hard. It's demanding work. You can imagine, can't you?"

"Well, no. But I hear she's good."

"It's not her, it's the spirits she talks to. Sometimes they want to communicate and sometimes they don't. Listen, I feel real bad. You coming here and all. Why don't you come in and sit down."

"Does Doña Meche live here?" I asked the woman, who by now had taken off a faded scarf from her head, turned off a loud vacuum cleaner and offered me a seat in the small living room. She was wearing a large kitchen oven mitt over her right hand decorated with red chiles that she waved around when she spoke.

I made a place for myself on the ragged couch next to a worn but impressive collection of stuffed bears of all sizes. The largest of them, and the newest, bumped up against me. I had to hold it to sit down properly. I felt foolish, but I was bound and determined to talk to Doña Meche about Lucio. She was the only one who could help me now.

"Just sit down right there. I'll get some paper. Would you like something to drink?" the woman asked, as she bustled around the room putting throw rugs back in their original spots and rearranging furniture to where it belonged.

I looked around the room. It wasn't dirty dirty, but it was shabby. It wasn't that things were in a terrible state, they were just old, shopworn, a little tired out, like the inside of a worn pocket that's held a lot of softened Kleenex and old metal keys. The hardwood floors had probably once been very nice. All the house needed was a little work, some paint, wax on the floors, new furniture, new curtains, some flowers here and there.

"What do you have to drink?"

"Now, let's see. What do we have? Milk? Water? Pineapple juice?"

"I'll take some pineapple juice."

"Why don't you just go into the kitchen and get yourself some juice. There's ice in the freezer and the glasses are in the cabinet above the stove. I'll finish up vacuuming here."

I went into the kitchen. What else was there to do? The cleaning woman wasn't threatening. She was nice and she was busy. It was like getting ice out of Albinita's old freezer.

The loud mechanical whir of the vacuum cleaner echoed in the background. Another cat, a large, irritated and disgruntled calico, scampered away, interrupted in its sleep. He or she obviously didn't like strangers. I found the glasses just where the cleaning lady told me and opened the freezer. One lone frosty ice tray was squeezed atop a package of frozen beef tripe. The freezer was crowded with plastic containers of all sizes that held what looked like chile and meat, probably pork. Reddish fat rimmed the top, as discolored grayish meat floated near the bottom. Doña Meche loved her menudo!

"I think I'll just have water," I called out to the woman. She couldn't hear me, the vacuum blaring in the other room. I filled my glass with water from the tap. The calico whirled by again, this time hissing in my direction.

I sat on the couch and watched the woman finish vacuuming. There was a determined intensity to her labor. She was enjoying her work.

"I'm so sorry Doña Meche wasn't here today. You can come back tomorrow," the woman said, wiping her hands on a rag. "She'll be in then. Here's some paper and a pen."

"I don't know if I can come back tomorrow. It was hard to get off work. I need to see her today."

The cleaning woman came up and looked at me with concern. Then she sat down on the edge of the couch. A large black cat appeared, eyeing me warily from behind a nearby chair.

"Nothing is ever hopeless. Doña Meche can help you. Come back. She can look at someone, see into their heart, and know their pain."

"Oh," I said, then burst into tears. I hadn't planned on crying, but when the cleaning woman took out a large wad of Kleenex that was tucked inside her sleeve and gave me a clump of crumpled tissue, I broke down.

"What's wrong?" the woman asked kindly.

"I'm sorry."

"It's someone, isn't it?"

"I need to talk to Doña Meche," I said, trying to get away from the woman's stare. It was unnerving in its intensity.

"What is it?" the woman asked, and I felt myself let go.

"He doesn't love me anymore," I said without shame.

"It's not that he doesn't want to love you. He can't. But life is like that, we can't always be with the people we want to love."

"And why is that?"

"It isn't in the plan. Your paths are different. You had to come together to know that."

"But I love him. Why doesn't he love me?"

"He can't be with you. Not in this lifetime. You have to let go."

"I can't."

"You have to."

"I need to talk to Doña Meche!"

"She'll get back to you. She's very good about that. She cares. And she knows what's going to be. Be patient."

"What can I do?"

"Come on, have a drink of water. When you do, the little angels will come down to help you go on. Drink, you'll feel better."

"Tell Doña Meche that Tere Ávila came by. I'm a friend of Ubaldo's. Ubaldo Miranda. Please have her call me, as soon as she can. I've left the number on the table. I'll be waiting."

"Doña Meche will get back to you. She'll help. She knows how."

"I'm really grateful. I didn't mean to bother you. I just wanted to . . . I thought it was . . . I'm sorry. What's your name?"

"Amparo Luz Aranda de La Cruz."

"Thank you."

"Can I give you a hug?"

"I'll be all right."

"Yes, you will. I see the angels all around you, helping you."

"Tell Doña Meche I was here."

"She'll be in touch . . ."

I closed the door.

Doña Meche wasn't in.

Not in that incarnation. In her incarnation as Amparo Luz Aranda de La Cruz she was. When I got home, I called Ubaldo. He had just gotten out of the shower and was probably standing there dripping wet in a soggy towel.

I was angry. I told him that I'd gone to see his beloved Doña Meche but she was a sham.

"You're mistaken there, Terry."

"Well, I didn't see her anyway. I saw her cleaning lady, the woman with the toxic red hair. She was very nice, that's more than I can say for Doña Meche."

"Tere, that *was* Doña Meche!"

"What are you talking about, Ubaldo?"

"The woman with the bright red hair."

"THAT was Doña Meche? You have to be kidding!"

"Would I kid you about Doña Meche?"

"That woman, the woman vacuuming that shabby little room wearing an old bandanna on her head, the woman waving an oven mitt in the air, that was Doña Meche?"

"That was her."

"Five feet two, maybe. A little on the plump side. A hangy mole on one eyelid? Big chichis?"

"Doña Meche."

"¡Ayyyyy!"

I never called Doña Meche back. There was no need.

All I can say is that it's really hard to trust someone with a freezer full of old pork.

Cloning Pedro

"All of you Womyn, you are all strong, potent female souls. Look into your hearts, and see the strength of the ancestresses within you," Sister Something Full Moon said with authority.

"There's no reason to cling to the destructive aspects of our imagined self. It's time to let go of any impediments, whether they be your family or your past or present attachments."

"Does this include old lovers?" I asked.

"Especially old lovers. They're more family than family," Sister said to me sharply as she scratched one dripping sobaco. I hadn't looked at too many women completely naked and when I looked at her I couldn't concentrate. I tried to look away, but it wasn't easy.

We were in a sweltering hut in the middle of the west mesa. My chichis were dripping with sweat, my legs pretzeled tight as I tried to undo the past, transform the present and project a new future. La Wirms sat next to me in a mute heap. It was her idea that we join the Full Moon Lodge.

It was a good idea that didn't work. My body twitched and itched, but full release was not forthcoming. I felt so jittery, I wondered if we had disturbed a nest of ants. My eyes were dry, empty of tears. I wanted to cry, but frankly I was too tired. The effort that it would require was too much to ponder. All thoughts were gone from my head. I just wanted to get the hell out of there, and as soon as possible.

I could tell Sister Full Moon hadn't liked me from the moment she set eyes on me. I was too *desde* for her. She was one of those Anglo-shaman types with thin, frizzy, permed blond hair who'd moved to the desert to be close to nature but who secretly hated the weather and the people and would always refuse to learn Spanish and would always pronounce Juárez "Wha-rez." On top of everything, she didn't like men and most women. Especially women like me who liked men. I was too *desde*. Underneath her dislike of me, I felt she was drawn to me sexually. And because I was everything she hated in women, her feelings toward me were completely ambivalent. I often got this reading from women New Agers. They didn't know what to do with me.

Yet I understood what Sister meant—although at that moment I was hungering for Lucio so badly I couldn't see straight. Despite my false bravado and outward strength, I felt it rapidly disappearing in that seething, suffocating hut.

"Let's meditate on those people who have embedded themselves in our vaginas and won't let go. We attempt to cry them, laugh them, scream them out, but still they cling to the folds in our sex."

"Yeah," I heard myself say weakly, with a voice I hardly recognized as my own. Wirma looked at me limply. She was so wiped out herself she couldn't speak.

"Womyn! Womyn! Unloosen those sex folds. Release the knot

of sexual oppression, the stranglehold Dream of the Giant Cock."

It was then that someone in the hut farted loudly.

"It's a beginning. And that's all I'm asking for," Sister said through the steaming haze.

Irma looked at me, and in slow motion, like an animal with a diminished will, made a small but distinct p in the air, followed by a smaller b, and it was then that we both lost it. The hut shook with our laughter, the laughter of two overcooked but not half-baked women who had come through the other side of the jodido cosmic fold without Sister's help, much to her chagrin. Our feeble laughter grew stronger, bounced off the mud walls and resounded in the sultry night.

The sweat lodge helped for a while, but then the old ghosts came back to haunt me. Wirms and I did get a good laugh out of it, two stupid Mejicanas going to an albino gabacha witch.

Just about the time when I thought things couldn't get any worse, La Chole called me at home. I'd left work early with a headache and was resting in bed when the phone rang.

I thought it might be Irma checking in on me. Or Ubaldo. Or maybe it was Lucio calling to apologize.

"Tere. It's Chole. I'm here at work. Someone's waiting for you here. No, it's not Lucio. I know you don't want to talk about him. I'm sorry, Tere. It's not him. There's a man here who says he's a friend of a friend."

"Is this a joke?"

I knew it wasn't a joke, because La Chole never jokes. She has no sense of humor. She's a completely rational human being, a simple one, but a compassionate one. If she said my long-deceased dad was there in the cafeteria, then my dad had to be standing there.

"So what's the man look like?" I asked with a certain weariness.

"He's very handsome, Tere. Oh, not like Lucio. He looks a little like what Pedro Infante might look like if he was alive and in his late fifties. Only he's not too tall."

"Uh-oh. What else do you know about him?"

"Well, he's not talking much, not even after Felia gave him a cup of coffee and a cinnamon roll. Hot from the stove. He asked for you by name and keeps saying he needs to see you. I thought I'd better call you, even if you're sick."

"I'll be right there. No, better yet, have Mr. . . . What's his name . . . ?"

I could hear La Chole yelling to Felia and then I heard Felia yelling back. These women were gritonas, no discretion whatsoever. I imagined everyone in Cabritoville could hear them.

"His name is Mr. De La O."

"Okay, put him on the line," I said wearily.

"Hallo?" I heard a man's soft voice on the line.

"Mr. . . . Señor De La O? It's Tere Ávila."

"Ay, sí, Señorita Ávila."

"Mr. De La O, I understand you want to see me."

"I have to talk to you. Ubaldo, he's a friend. He tole me about you."

"Do you know where Sofia's restaurant is? I'll meet you there in half an hour."

"No . . . Sofia's Mighty Taco?" and here I heard La Chole in the background giving directions. "Oh, uh-huh, okay. I'll be waiting for you, Señorita Ávila. I'm wearing a blue suit."

"I'll be there. Goodbye. Put La Chole on the phone, Mr. De La O. Thank you. Goodbye."

"Goodbye to you."

"Thanks, Chole."

"Don't you worry about Señor De La O. We'll take care of him. And take care of yourself, mujer, you're running around like a chicken without a body. Stay away from brujerías, Tere. I told you not to go to that gabacha. It's a wonder your hair hasn't fallen out, and you haven't been bleeding tadpoles from your cosa during that time of the month, or barking like a dog. Que Dios te bendiga, Tere. And I mean it."

I needed that blessing. I got dressed and dragged myself over to Sofia's.

I was so surprised to hear from Mr. De La O that for a while (about twenty minutes) I forgot all about Lucio Valadez.

Sometimes life's details add up and make you forget your abject personal misery. Anything that could make me forget how betrayed, lonely and unredeemable I felt was a blessing. Even a stranger who turns up without warning.

So who was Mr. De La O?

Víctor De La O was the son of Melitón De La O Borunda and Estefanita Cruz. Once from Chihuahua, Chihuahua, now living in El Paso, Texas. Víctor De La O was Ubaldo's lover.

Víctor was waiting in the back booth near the kitchen at Sofia's when I got there. Instinctively he knew where to sit. He looked pretty good, too, just like La Chole said. A 'lo todo Pedro.

De La O looked up as I came in the door. Right then and there I knew he was Ubaldo's consentido.

De La O motioned to me with his eyes to come over. Pinco Mondrales looked up sleepily from the cash register, where he was getting change. He sometimes did double duty as cook and cashier. Sofia came out running from the back with her face bright red. She waved to me and mentioned something about "running out of gordita masa." I couldn't help her.

I moved in the direction of my favorite booth and realized I should have called Irma to report in to her. She would have wanted to come along.

I was Irma's failed case study, more lovesick every day. I begged off seeing Irma often now, she was so busy with Mr. Wesley. I couldn't tell her that her happiness was making me sick, although she knew how I felt.

No, I would tell Irma later about De La O. Who knows, maybe I wouldn't ever tell her. It was about time I had secrets. Especially from Irma. What did she need to know about De La O anyway? Why did anyone need to know? Why did it matter that Ubaldo was in love with someone who looked exactly like Pedro?

I'd heard that Pedro had come to Cabritoville to perform in the forties. Nyvia Ester had seen him in the flesh. Quirino and Albinita might have seen him, too. It was possible De La O had heard him perform.

I could see the movie magazine headline in my mind: *Woman Discovers Man Who Says He Is Pedro Infante's Clone. DNA from Exhumed Corpse Reveals It's True.*

❁

Víctor's naturally wavy hair was swirled to the left side, like Pedro's, where it peaked in a high pompadour near the forehead. He had intense dark brown eyes and a strong nose and beautiful lips.

Víctor wore a dark blue suit with a navy blue tie full of white coronets. He was one of those men who still used handkerchiefs and placed them in the pocket of his suits. He looked as if he'd stepped out of time. And he had.

I'd never seen someone so elegant grace the red plastic booths of Sofia's Mighty Taco.

He stood, introduced himself and then waited for me to sit down. It was gentlemanly.

I sat across from him, in jeans and a T-shirt that read: "If It Feels Good, Do It." Suddenly I was embarrassed by my clothes. They were so unsuitable. How could I have been so stupid?

De La O didn't seem to notice what I was wearing.

I felt like I had walked onto a movie set. Teresina Ávila—make that Teresina Valadez—in *La Magdalena*, in which I played Mary Magdalene.

Open to shadows. A Garden of Gethsemane type of place, but set in a pueblito in the interior of Méjico during the Revolución.

Lush, flower-filled gardens with a high stone wall draped in vines. A wrought-iron bench. La Magdalena sits in darkness. There is an intense crescendo of noise. We can't tell if the sound is human or animal. It's as if a million creatures are all breathing and exhaling at once. We can hear the roar of the ocean, the wind whipping up the sand, a wailing, deep and profound. To our left is a long, interminable line of people moving toward the horizon. They wind down a most desolate and lonely road. From our vantage point there are thousands upon thousands of people marching forward through valleys of ash.

Behind them is a burning mountain. It is bright red, the color of lava in the terrible darkness like the ASARCO cement plant in El Paso, whose tall smokestacks spew toxins in an overcast sky. When I was little, we once drove by there and I remember seeing the earth glowing red with torrents of hot ash and molten lead.

The people are restless souls who wander blindly forward, confused by the prospect of eternity in an unknown land. Later, a man comes out of a clump of trees and walks toward La Magdalena. He has been in the shadows all the time, watching her.

At first we can't tell who the man in the shadows is. But we know he is a man marked by suffering. He is the Christ.

Then La Magdalena turns to him and says with great love:

"I am your Mary Magdalene. Come, let me wash your feet . . ."

The movie fades out, the long line disappears and De La O sits with his back to the booth, facing out. He's come to ask my help. He's moving away. He doesn't want Ubaldo following him. He says it's over, done. Can I help? "You know Ubaldo. He's your friend."

I sit facing the long mirror in front of me. Pinco needs to clean it. The neon sign outside beams SOFIA'S MIGHTY TACO. I see the figure of a man in the shadow of the cottonwoods. Another person moves into the light. Close-up to eyes, wide open, full of hope.

Mexican Kabuki

The body holds the oldest memories. The spot on the lung recalls the cough of long ago, the one that came from dark desperation. The foot that still hurts from the fall in the yard, late at night, if you move it the wrong way. What were you running away from? The shadowy ink marks from the pens you accidentally stabbed into your thigh, your upturned palm, veritable stigmata. The white scar, the skinned knees of childhood, the accidental burn, the many scrapings, the itches that became more than they should have been. The hand, nails, face, legs and breasts of a woman full of the unmistakable memories of flesh.

Lucio had begun sleeping with Mary Alice, a woman from Tres Arboles. She was a travel agent at the AAA.

Cabritoville is too small to have a mistress, then leave her and then not have everyone on alert, waiting to see what would happen next. People were looking, as well, to see what I would do. But I had people looking out for me. Albinita was ever faithful. Irma was vigilant. Ubaldo wasn't around, but I knew he wished me well.

"It can't be love, Tere," La Chole said at work one day out of the blue. I was standing in line getting my tray of food. I had an early lunch and was headed afterward to playground duty.

"If you want, preciosa, you can come to my house. I'll give you a special rubdown with salt and we'll pray together, not like the so-called limpia that the White Witch gave you. That Cochinada from Hell. What do you expect from someone who's a used-up hippie with leftover psychedelic candles made with mota and a thousand unicorn tattoos?"

"I didn't know you gave limpias, Chole," I said with surprise. "I thought you were Baptist."

Chole gave me an extra serving of mashed potatoes and winked at me.

I made an appointment to see her that night. But first I had to talk to Irma.

"After the sweat hut, I'm not sure you should be messing with anything else," Irma said with caution in her voice.

"I'll take anything I can get at this point, comadre. But I need to talk to Lucio first. I miss him too much. I know he's only seeing this other woman on the rebound to torment me. I know he doesn't love her. He can't."

"Tere, it doesn't matter what Lucio says or wants. It's your life, what matters is what *you* want. And you don't want him. He no sooner stops seeing you than he takes up with someone else, another puta, fill in her name. Oh, I didn't mean it that way. What I mean to say is: let him go. Honestly, the way you two drag it out! He calls you, you call him, he needs you, you need him. He doesn't need you, he makes you cry. He's a dog and you're his stinky, chewed-up toy that he slides all over the room. If I were you, I'd be happy that he has another woman so you can just ease out of the way. Now it's safe to call him a cabrón to anyone's face and mean it."

That turgid night, after a half-Baptist, half-leftover-Catholic, part-voodoo ritual following a vigorous massage and rubdown with salt, including candles in the darkness at Chole's house, I drove home the long way and saw Lucio's car at the Sands.

Should I stop? Drive on? What to do? Should I knock on the door, confront him? Would he be alone, or would he be with her? I couldn't say her name.

Heartsick and shivering, I pulled over, with still-wet hair from my purification ritual. I had Lucio's birthday gift on the floor of the car, a black turtleneck from the Popular in El Paso, along with a stuffed toy for Andrea.

I didn't want to see him. I couldn't. And yet, I had to. Oh, God help me, I felt lost. What to do? I was sick with grief and doubt and worry and angry at myself for still wanting to be with him. How could he have taken up with the other woman? Why hadn't he explained things to me, have told me he didn't want to be with me anymore, that he'd found someone else? And what about Diolinda, Andrea? Was he leaving them as well, or only me?

I questioned my sanity. Was something wrong with me? Why was I drawn to such an uncaring, selfish human being? And why was I parked in the darkness of the Sands, waiting to see if Lucio would come out of his room, if the curtain would be moved back, if the window would be opened, if I heard voices, male and female.

It was a pretty despicable place to be, groveling for love, in a cold car, without a shred of honor. And yet, I had to talk to Lucio. It had been three weeks since we'd argued. I'd tried calling him nearly every day, but he never accepted my calls. Once, we spoke briefly, but then he got mad and hung up on me.

I knocked on the door, hoping Lucio would be alone. I had no idea what I would do if anyone other than Lucio was there. I woke him up, and he looked tired. Surprised to see me, he stood behind a dead-bolt lock, barricading my entrance.

"Please, Lucio," I said, "we have to talk."

"It's late, Terry."

"We can't go on this way. I really need to see you. Just for a little while. I know you're tired, please, Lucio."

"Wait there. I need to get dressed."

It took Lucio a long time to come back. I was embarrassed and ashamed and worried someone would see, hanging around like a sick moth.

Finally, Lucio unbolted the door and took my arm. "Do you have your car?"

"Yes, Lucio."

"You drive, Terry, I'm still asleep. And besides, I left the light on in the truck and the battery is dead. I need to call AAA and have them jump the damn thing tomorrow."

"I don't want to drive, Lucio. Why don't you drive."

I threw Lucio the keys to my car and he threw them back to me.

"I'm still asleep. You drive."

"All right. Just move those gifts. Happy Birthday, Lucio."

"You didn't have to."

"I know it. There's something for Andrea."

"Andrea? Terry, you can't be doing that. I don't want to get her involved."

"She's already involved, Lucio. She knows about us. She won't talk to me at school anymore. And she used to like me!"

We got in the car. I turned to face Lucio. In the blinking red fluorescent lights of the Sands Motel he looked demonic, charged with an unearthly energy. His voice was harsh, strange.

"Why didn't you call me before you came over?"

"You never answer my calls anymore, so why should I call? So you can hang up on me, or lie to me again and tell me that we have to stay away from each other because you have to be with your family? So tell me about La Puta."

"La Puta? Who are you talking about?"

"I know about the woman from AAA. Tell me about her. When did it begin? And what are you going to do now, Lucio?"

"Pull over there, by the trees."

I pulled over by the river, near Gabina. I wanted to fold myself in her darkness and sink into the earth. I couldn't see Lucio's eyes in the shadows.

"What do you want to know, Tere? I care for her and I care for you. I didn't mean for this to happen. I didn't want to hurt you. Or Diolinda. And I don't want to hurt Mary Alice. She's a wonderful woman."

I turned the motor on then and, through tears, peeled out of the parking lot near the rest area, almost knocking over a metal picnic table.

It was a wild ride through Cabritoville. And I'm sure somebody saw it. A recap of the evening's events would be in the *Cabritoville Chronicle* the next day, no doubt. *Crazed Cabritovillian on the Rampage Damages Property and Has to Be Subdued. Educational Assistant Apprehended and Handcuffed.*

The more Lucio tried to soothe me, the more upset I became. I started throwing things out of the car window. His cigarettes that lay on the dashboard went first.

"Terry, stop! What the hell are you doing? Pull over. I'll drive. Take me back to the Sands. This is crazy!"

It was then that I grabbed his leather jacket, which lay on the seat between us, and threw it out the open window of the speeding car.

"Dammit, Tere, my Ray-Bans were in that jacket! Stop the car.

Turn around, turn around! Christ, how could you do that, Tere? My Ray-Bans! My Italian jacket! What the hell is wrong with you?"

We found the Ray-Bans all right, though it wasn't easy in the darkness. I ran in and out between oncoming cars, their horns blaring.

One of the temples was bent, but Lucio said he could straighten it out. The jacket was another matter. It had tread marks and would probably never be the same.

"Take me back to the Sands. You can't be driving around Cabritoville like this. I care for you, Tere, I do. The thing with Mary Alice just happened."

"Yeah, sure."

"You never listen to me. You're always talking. And she's gentle."

"Bullshit!"

"You're so rough, Tere. You don't need me the way Mary Alice does. She's a beautiful woman."

The Factor was in Effect. I tried to remember what she looked like. I had gone to the AAA to check on prices for the upcoming trip to the panteón on April 15. Fosa 52. Lote 156. Mary Alice was short, a bit on the chunky side and blond. Petite she wasn't. She was a nalgona chichona with fleshy sobacos. She was bound to be a lot bigger than Lucio. He kept sidling up to big women because he was a small man. She would engulf him. Probably already had. I don't know who I felt more sorry for. Me, him, Mary Alice, Diolinda or Andrea.

"She's beautiful, inside and out. But it's more than that . . . ," Lucio droned.

"Why can't you love me, Lucio?"

"I can't, Terry. Don't ask me why. Let's not start this again."

I pulled the car over and got out. I walked around the side and opened Lucio's door.

"Get out of my car, Lucio Valadez! Out!"

I pulled on his sweater, some Italian piece of shit. Everything he owned was Italian, except his chones. "Out!"

Lucio threw his birthday gift at me and I threw it back at him.

"Goddammit, Terry! You are so bathetic!"

"What the hell does that mean?"

"Look it up!"

"You're so cruel, Lucio."

I wailed as if I'd lost a family member. That is, if I had any family that I really cared enough about to wail that way about. Probably only Albinita. Then Lucio took me in his arms. We rocked back and forth and smoothed each other's hair, as if we were children who'd fallen down in the grass and hurt ourselves.

And then Lucio drove me to my house.

After an hour of recriminations, mostly mine, Lucio had the audacity to borrow my car to go over to La Puta's to cut off the affair (that's the term he used) because it was only decent and Mary Alice deserved the best.

And I, Tere P. Ávila, let him drive away in my car! I figured that this would be the straw that would break that chingao ugly camel's back.

Lucio left me, with promises to return soon.

As soon as he left, I found my dictionary and looked up the word "bathetic."

Bathetic—adjective. Sentimental, gushy, maudlin. Maudlin? Tearfully or weakly emotional.

Oh, Lucio.

Instead of coming home directly, Lucio ended up staying there all night. Around two in the morning, I got into the bathtub and soaked for what seemed weeks, as I called out to God and especially Our Lady of Guadalupe, who deserves to be prayed to, in all ways and at all times, especially when you need a mother and no one is near.

I was a little worried about spending so much time in the bathtub and all in one night, but the situation was so dire that it required extraordinary means.

I prayed to all the female saints, especially the ones wronged by mortal men. I called out to all the Holy Souls in Purgatory, espe-

cially to the women with the longest terms, the women who had
to kill out of self-defense. I chanted the names of the unborn fe-
males in Limbo. I raised my voice in an incantation to all the ancestors, all the way up to the great, greater and greatests, mostly
all the maligned women that I could remember, including my
mother, my grandmother, my great-grandmother, and my great-
great-aunt Lorena, whose Mejicano husband, Roque, had abandoned her and her small son, Roquito, in Chihuahua, Méjico.
(Great-great-aunt Lorena had come all the way to Cabritoville to
find Roque, living with a half-gringa/half-Mejicana by the name of
Luz Alarid Jones, and took up the fight of her life. Roque finally
did come to his senses and left off with the puta Jones, but from
all Lorena's reckonings, he was never the same, in bed or out.)

I prayed fervently to all the Angels, especially my four guardian
angels, the ones I called Marío, Noe, Armina and Marina, the
three lesser and the major one, the one that always stood behind
to my left, in all her luminous eight-foot glory. I whimpered, then
screeched, then moaned in the hot steamy tub until 4 a.m. I
promised God that if She let the cabrón come back one more
time, just this one gift, this one mercy, this one consideration, I
would remain faithful forever. All I wanted was for Lucio to stay
with me until I got over whatever I needed to get over.

When Lucio finally returned, around 7 a.m., we stayed in bed
for you-count-'em hours making love, pumping bones until I was
dry inside and the only thing that kept me lubricated was the animal fat. I was sure I'd get an infection from the grease. And not
only that, I was mad at myself for stooping so low as to have a
sexual lockdown. I called in to work and told them I was sick. I
wasn't about to tell them that I was trying to save a relationship.

The whole evening and the next day was like a bad movie.
Much darker and stranger than even Pedro's movies. It was Mexican Kabuki. Lots of flailing, animal grunts, deep, gut-wrenching
gritos, gyrating and twisting limbs, violent action and reaction and
imagined death by spears, arrows and knives. We were lovers
doomed from the start. And we knew it. In all of Pedro's movies,

there's always a glimmer of hope. Not so in mine, *La Madgalena*.

I was sure I had injured myself physically. I knew I'd damaged my psychic self as well, after having called out all the spirits that would probably never come back in the same way again. But the incantations and prayers worked. Lucio promised to leave Mary Alice. And then he promised to talk to Diolinda. And then he promised that he and Andrea and I would get together.

It was the best lovemaking of my entire life.

That was a week ago.

Now I was holed up in bed in my apartment. Albinita was my nurse. Irma came over every day to see how I was doing. Lucio never called. He didn't know I was sick. Sick as a dog. I had an illness without a name. The doctor had called it "the Crud."

Strep throat was part of it. A terrible weakness was another part. The real part was terrible terrible depression. I wondered if I had pneumonia. Or something that came on from taking too many baths in one day.

Of course I had to get sick. There was no other way. My body was telling me many things all at once.

I couldn't talk because of the strep throat and it was just as well. There wasn't anything I had to say to anyone. Not Albinita. Not Irma. And Lucio? Well, what was there to say? Where are you now, cabrón? Did you really give up La Puta as you said you would? And so why haven't you called? Haven't you heard through the chisme grapevine that I'm dying?

Okay, so I was a little melodramatic. Strap me to the bed. I was already pinned down, like a giant butterfly. A specimen of what can go wrong when you love the wrong man.

I was in a fever, burning up inside and out. I wanted to die, but I had to live to show Lucio that I wouldn't die, not for him, not for anyone.

Albinita brought me hot tea, sat by my bed and prayed.

"Dios te salve María, llena eres de gracia . . ."

"Mamá," I asked, "stay with me. Please. Don't leave. Talk to me, Mamá. Tell me stories."

"Just lay there, Tere, and rest. I'll bring a wet towel to put on your head. You're on fire. The doctor says you need to rest. If you want, I can call a priest."

"No priest. I mean, not yet. You sit there, pray for me."

"Move over, m'ija. Can you move over? Ay, you're so weak. Here, let me lift your head. I'll put it in my lap. And then I'll wipe your forehead. You're sweating so much. Whatever you have, it's coming out of you. Bendito sea Dios. Dios poderoso."

The cool washrag felt so good on my skin.

"Let me brush your hair back like I used to do when you were a little girl. There."

Albinita ran her fingers through my hair the way she'd done when I was a child. She was the only one who could stroke my hair the way I liked. She was the only one who loved me quietly, without wanting anything back. Not like all the men I've known.

Back and forth, back and forth, Albinita's fingers gently untangled my hair.

"It used to be so thick."

"I know, Mamá, now it's so thin."

"But you're still my baby."

"Even if I have canas . . ."

"Oh, there's not so many."

I wanted Albinita to hold me this way forever. Mamá, I need you, Mamá. Don't leave me. Please.

Irma also came to see me. She brought me herbal tea and a bunch of magazines, including one called *Freaks of Nature*, with an article about a woman who weighed thirty-five pounds and had given birth. Another article featured a boy of ten who swallowed a watermelon seed and died when it grew up through his esophagus and choked him.

But Irma was too noisy and too flappy. She made me nervous. She seemed flustered, overheated. She had something to tell me,

I could tell, but I couldn't look at her without feeling tired. The way she was going on about Mr. Wesley was wearing me out. And then when I thought about Lucio, I thought how tired she must be to have heard me go on and on.

"Ay, comadre, I'm sorry you're not feeling good. Pobrecita, my girlfriend! I know you're going to feel better tomorrow. You have to, Tere. Don't try and talk. You want some Kleenex? Oh, you want the basin? Here. I'll hold it for you."

A swirl of too many voices, too much movement, and me, in bed, not caring one way or another for the workings of the damned and busy world.

Nothing mattered to me. Things. Food. People.

For people who are well, everything seems to be a matter of choice. To love or not to love. To live or not to live.

I lay in bed, unable to move or speak or cry.

And if I could speak, who would hear what I had to say?

Part II: The Cojo Curse

In *Un Rincón Cerca del Cielo*, Pedro-as-Pedro is still crippled from throwing himself from the rooftop. In Part II of the saga, *Ahora Soy Rico*, he was repentant, until he meets the little snippet puta wench who was the granddaughter of the factory guard where he worked. Ay, the way she stretched out in his convertible when she bummed a ride from him! Pointing those little tetitas of hers in his direction for him to admire. And he looking all cucaracha-eyed at her, or rather, at *them*, like they really were something, instead of little baby chichis in a pointy 1952 bullet bra with the swirly reinforced stitches that you could see outlined in any outfit you wore.

You know who played the part of the young strumpet? None other than Irma Dorantes, Pedro

Infante's mistress, and his second wife after María Luisa. The marriage was annulled the week before Pedro was killed in the plane crash while on his way from the Yucatán to La Capital to try to talk María Luisa into divorcing him. María Luisa was totally against Pedro marrying Irma from the beginning, she was the one who fought for the annulment. I don't know how Pedro could have thought he'd talk María Luisa into anything.

I'll say this for Mejicanas, the first woman who grabs a man always feels that man is hers, forever and ever, come hell, high water or a puta cabrona without shame. You try and cross a Mejicana who feels a man is hers. Uh-uh. There was no way María Luisa was ever going to let Pedro go. And he knew it. He was already a broken man when he got into his small plane taking him nowhere but to the grave. He was dead before he died. If the women he loved didn't kill him, the diabetes would have.

So Irma Dorantes played Pedro's mistress in *Un Rincón Cerca del Cielo*. She didn't care about him being a cojo; all she could see was his big convertible. She had it all planned out. She needed a father for her illegitimate son. She would try to get as much from Pedro as she could. ¡Vale más! He had the money and the car and he liked her, she could tell.

"You know, Wirms," I said to Irma at Sofia's, "I think Irma Dorantes only got parts in Pedro's movies because she was sleeping with him."

The last meal we'd shared was at lunch a week ago at the Come-On-and-Drop-In, where Nyvia Ester works. Irma was busy most nights now, hanging out at the Flying W with Mr. Wesley. There was a certain tension between us because neither of us liked the other's boyfriend. Loving the wrong men had made us irritated with each other.

"You're wrong, Tere," Irma said firmly, and with a certain belligerence. "And not only that, I'll always be faithful to my tocaya, Irma Dorantes, even though she's the 'other woman,' in a culture that doesn't appreciate 'other women.'"

Irma looked at me knowingly.

What the hell, Irma Dorantes had status then, and still has status, because she was Pedro's consentida. In that same way, I still had status in Cabritoville. Not because I was special, but because I was Lucio's first major mistress, the one the song would be written about.

I was feeling cocky that night, or I would have caught myself instead of mouthing off about Irma Dorantes to La Wirms, who I could see was becoming more defensive.

"Irma Dorantes didn't have a shred of talent and you know it, Irma Granados!"

"She had talent, she always had talent. Have you seen her lately, Tere? She looks good."

"You're just saying that Wirms," I told her, "because your mother renamed you after Irma Dorantes when Pedro took up with her. You know damn well Irma Dorantes only got work because Pedro was screwing her. Although she did have a sexiness underneath it all, a smoldering Latina kiss-my-culo attitude. Mejicanos go wild for young ingenue schoolgirl types who wear bobby socks and tight skirts with little pleats in the back."

"Why do you always have to be so crude, Tere?"

"Irma Dorantes wasn't even that attractive. Well, maybe she was to some, but to me she was too cat-eyed, too obsidian-faced, a short, somewhat common-looking type, no princess, more of a handmaiden."

"Irma Dorantes had a good career going, she was in demand before and after Pedro," Irma said, her jaw hard. "So are you going to order or what?"

"Her life only changed when she got involved with Pedro, Irma. She was just a little inconsequential pip-squeak of a no-account actress who had small roles in those early days. No movie role she ever had could ever match the movie of her life with Pedro."

"You should become a movie critic, Tere. Or since you know so much about human psychology you should have a talk show. Or maybe you could become a therapist. I don't know what's wrong with you and I don't want to know. But when you start attacking Irma Dorantes, you better watch out."

"I'm only teasing. Come on, let's order. We'll start with some jalapeño poppers."

"You're not teasing me, Tere, the insults are real. I'm not hungry anymore, I'll just wait for the fan club meeting. You know there'll be food there."

"You call that food? Well, if you're not going to eat, neither am I. It's no surprise you're not hungry. I saw you in here with Mr. Wesley about four o'clock."

"I have to go to the bathroom, Tere."

I followed Irma into the room marked DAMAS. She was anxious to get away from me, but I wasn't going to let her escape. I was going to get the truth out of her one way or another.

Irma ducked into a stall while I used an adjacent toilet. I could hear her fumble with her favorite clanky old concha belt. She had so much turquoise and silver jewelry on, it was going to take her a minute to get situated. All the more time for her to listen to what I had to say.

"And not only that, I saw you having what looked like a chocolate doughnut. And all this after you and I started our Dr. Atkins diet two weeks ago. Chingao! You told me you'd be strong. So all I want to know is, did you get off the Dr. Atkins? Tell me the truth, Irma Granados."

"You know I did. I saw you driving back and forth outside Sofia's Mighty Taco checking Mr. Wesley and me out."

"Oh, you did?"

"Why didn't you just come in and sit with us?"

"Seeing you eating that doughnut almost surprised me as much as seeing you holding hands with Mr. Wesley. You betrayed our pact."

"I couldn't help myself."

"You've never gone back on me like this before, Irma!"

"Oh, grow up, Tere!"

"I just hope to God I don't have to go into Mr. Wesley's place of business and check in to check out if you're sleeping together. Tell me you aren't doing an Irma Dorantes on me."

I could hear Irma's spurty but intense urine stream. She was a fast pisser and in this session she outdid herself. I could barely keep up with her, and I flushed early to mask a number of deep, growly farts.

"You've gotten to be so nasty, Tere. You've changed since you met Lucio."

I was embarrassed to admit it was true. I'm glad Irma couldn't see my face at that moment.

Lucio thought about things as very black and white except when he was in bed screwing. I never liked that word. It's a word I picked up from him, too. Sometimes I sound like him. Words come out of me that aren't me. Like menudo butt and son of a bitchin' joto tortilla queen. I even see things differently now. Lucio's done that to me.

Irma flushed.

But did I give up and give in and admit I was wrong? Hell no, I came out of my stall like a bull seeking vengeance.

"You're so touchy these days, I hate to say anything to you. I've never told you, Irma, but I can't stand Irma Dorantes, I never could. When I see her, my Disgust-O-Meter is switched on high. I'm sorry, but that's how I feel."

Irma turned to face me. She backed me into the toilet, her eyes full of rage.

"Touchy? Me, touchy? What about you, Miss Rude and Crude?"

"I don't like the way you've been acting, Irma. We used to have things in common, but now you're too busy for me. You're either at the Flying W or gone to El Paso with Mr. Wesley to see a movie at the Plaza Theater. We hardly ever go to El Colón anymore. You didn't want me to know you were dating him, but I found out anyway. You've tried to keep the whole thing secret. Well, nothing's secret in Cabritoville, and you know it!"

"You should be talking, Tere."

"I didn't like Sal, but I sure as hell like him better now that you started seeing Mr. Wesley, whatever the hell his first name is."

Irma wiped her hands and tossed the paper towel in the wastepaper basket. I'd never her seen her look so angry.

"Tere Ávila, you stay the hell out of my way. Don't you ever insult Irma Dorantes again, not to mention Mr. Wesley, who's never hurt you or me or any other living soul. You don't know a thing about him and you've already jumped to conclusions. Mean ones at that. You think you can talk to me about what I can and can't do, when you're sleeping up and down the valley, past Anthony, on into El Paso and beyond Juárez. And the thing about it is that you aren't even sorry for hurting the Valadez family."

I looked at Irma with the cold dispassionate eyes of someone who would throw their best friend overboard for a lousy measly sniveling man who was so far up her butt that his feet were sticking out. It was a low moment for both of us. As soon as I started speaking, I regretted everything I'd said. But I was a sleepwalker. The words came out of a pain so deep I was breathless with confusion.

"I'm sorry I've wasted your time, Irma. I should have known you wouldn't understand anything. I thought you knew what it was to really love, but I can see you never have. I'll drive my own car to the fan club meeting. *If* I decide to go. And don't expect me next week for our Pedro-athon. I have other plans."

Irma looked at me as if I was a plateful of chewed-up grizzled fajita meat.

"You can call me when you're feeling better or you have some sense knocked into you, because that's what it's going to take. A semi hitting you or your roof falling in on you so you can see the sky. Tere Ávila, someday you're going to take back all the mean things you've said to me about Irma Dorantes."

I looked at her as if she was wearing a necklace of cucarachas.

"Just wait and see."

And then Irma, the old Irma, my former best friend Irma, my soul and heart sister La Wirms, looked at me with a mixture of sadness and pity.

"Wake up, Tere! Lucio's never loved you and he never will. At least Mr. Wesley loves me!"

"Mr. Wesley *loves* you? Shit, Irma."

"That's more than you can say for Lucio!"

"Lucio loves me, Irma, he does!"

"I'll talk to you later, Tere Ávila. And bring back the Pedro videos I lent you. You've had them for two months. Don't you ever return anything? And while you're at it, bring back my cookie sheet and the salad bowl you've had since last year!"

I stomped out the door in my new, still-too-tight Luccheses that I'd bought to match Lucio's and into the glaring neon brightness of Sofia's Mighty Taco. Sofia was at the cash register. She stared at me.

"You okay, Tere?" said Sofia.

"Yeah, I'm okay. Cancel my order."

"Hon, you and Irma never did order."

"I'm outta here, Sofia," I said.

Before I hurried out the front door, I yelled to Irma and to everyone else in the restaurant—that being a surprised elderly gringo couple near the window and Pinco Mondrales, who'd come out of the kitchen in his full regalia, paper chef's hat and bloody apron—"Irma Granados, call me when you realize you don't want to be the girlfriend of a dusty dried-up bovinic gabacho who everyone in Cabritoville thinks is old enough to be your father."

And with that, I stood in the doorway and flashed Irma with a defiant double-whammied sobacage. It felt dirty, it felt ugly and it felt too damn good.

"You want to know what people are saying about you, Teresina Ávila?" Irma yelled back from the middle of the room. But I didn't stick around long enough to hear her answer. I was out of there faster than you can say Irma Dorantes was a puta bitch whore whose chest wasn't all it was made out to be.

When I got inside the car, I was all huffy and puffy. I wanted to cry loud and hard, but I wasn't about to, not there. Wirms was looking out at me through the restaurant curtains. When she saw me looking at her, she closed them. I wasn't about to give her the satisfaction of seeing me lose my composure in the parking lot of Sofia's Mighty Taco, especially in front of two gringos who had an Oklahoma license plate. I was so mad I peeled out of there like a pissed-off vato dragging Main Street.

But I wasn't really mad at Irma G. or even Irma D. or even Pedro I. I was mad at Lucio V.

I knew all this, and I really secretly admired Irma Dorantes and even envied her for being Pedro's last love. I couldn't, wouldn't tell Irma how I felt. Not now. Not ever. She had wounded me deeply.

And the worst thing was that I knew she was right.

Piojos

Have you ever had piojos?
I did, when I was a little girl. I probably wouldn't
have ever gotten them if Albinita hadn't brought
that woman home from church. She was falling
down drunk and was sitting at the back of Sacred
Heart Church near the statue of Our Lady of
Guadalupe with the feet whose paint had long been
rubbed away. The rest of the statue was intact. La
Virgencita's robe was that lovely blue-green and she
had that same sweet and loving expression we all
know and adore. If it weren't for her faded, used-
up plaster of paris feet, you would have thought
she was perfect. She was loved, of that there was
no doubt. But too many people had kissed La
Madrecita's feet or rubbed them with soft moist fin-
gertips. Kiss. Touch. Kiss. Touch.

Albinita often lifted me high to kiss La Virgencita.

"Go on, Tere, touch her. She's our Mother. And she takes care of us. Remember her words to Juan Diego: 'Do not be afraid. Am I not your Mother who is with you always?' " Albinita said tenderly.

Saints and even the Mother of God have to be placed up high, where mortals can't reach them. Otherwise, the world's sorrows and mournful laments, like lapping, pounding waves, will buffet and bruise. Eventually even she, the Mother of God, will disappear in desperate kisses, overzealous love and furious hopes.

It was inevitable in a small town where feverish old women and faded dusty men still carried Jesus around the plaza in a wooden coffin on Good Friday during the Santo Entierro, the Holy Burial, at the darkest time of all, the day Christ died, that everyone still mourned the All-Encompassing Male Godhead.

That's the time the Mother of God died as well, because without her son, what was she? Nothing.

That's if you subscribe to the traditional Mejicano version of what a mother is and should be. You have to think of Pedro's mother, Doña Refugio, and place her up on the altar where all Mejicanos place their mothers, next to God. No one can imagine her sorrow at losing her favorite son, and a nation's idol.

There's a special section in my Pedro notebook that has to do with mothers. I have a list of all of Pedro's mothers in his movies, or the women who were like his mother. They're a motley assortment. There's Sara Garcia, the feisty older lady who played his grandmother in various movies. A short, pigeon-chested, cigar-smoking, gun-toting, no-nonsense woman, she was a contrast to the long-suffering Bilbiana in *La Oveja Negra*. Not only does Bilbiana have to put up with her husband Cruz's long-standing infidelity, she has to watch him humiliate and beat their son, Silviano, played by Pedro. It's no wonder that Pedro had trouble with women in that movie. His father was a bully, his mother was weak and he was playing out the only story he knew.

Don't get me started about Mercé, the black maid, in *Angelitos Negros*, who never tells her successful, educated blond daughter,

Ana Luisa, that she's her mother. What about Rosa, the long-suffering mother in *Islas Marías*, once the wealthy widow of a revolutionary hero who ends up a blind beggar waiting for her son, Felipe, to return from Islas Marías, a prison where he has been sent for the murder of her daughter's lover? Not to mention the worst of all, Pepe el Toro's mute, paralyzed mother, who sits in a wheelchair all day long and is abused right and left and can't utter a single word in her defense.

Irma told me that that's the problem with most women. We're still playing out our parents' melodramas, our ancestors' locura. We're stuck either on the altar or in the gutter.

How difficult, also, for a man to navigate between the tough Sara Garcías, who will make the men toe the line and keep it straight, and the poor, put-upon, anguished and voiceless mothers like Bilbiana who wrench him around with their immense inability to demand their rights.

After seeing so many of Pedro's movies, and trying to understand why Pedro was Pedro and why he's still so alive to us so many years after his death, Irma and I have analyzed the roles his many movie mothers have played. And in turn, we've looked long and hard at our own mothers: Bilbianas in the throes of anguished service.

I grew up in the shallow air of my mother, a woman who prided herself on the world's hottest, most flavorful red enchiladas, who lived only for me, her sole child, and whose house was a cultivated hothouse of memories, a living altar to her dead husband, and now a long-awaited God.

Prayer kept Albinita together, that and the hope of a better life to come. But she also knew that good deeds carry you faster down that ever-speeding earthly highway leading to the heavenly host.

Albinita attended early-morning Mass daily. One day she saw a woman hunched over a pew and realized right away what was wrong. She smelled liquor and knew she would take the woman home to recover.

After Mass, Albinita invited the woman to come back to her house for breakfast. The woman had been drinking all night. She took one last swig from a bottle of cheap red wine and nodded in Albinita's direction. There was no way she could get away. And besides, she needed to sleep.

Slowly, the two of them made their way across the churchyard and into the cold morning air. The drunken woman was wearing a thin red sweater under her pecheras, soiled overalls. It was January, and although they didn't have far to go, the walk seemed interminable, filled with desperate uncertainty.

Albinita called to me to get out of my bed. It didn't surprise me; she had done this before.

"Teresina, the lady needs your bed. You can go into my room to sleep."

Albinita pulled me out of my bed and guided me to her room. I fell asleep right away. It was around seven-thirty in the morning, around the time Albinita came home from the six-thirty Mass.

Later, when I woke up, I didn't know where I was. I went back to my room. I saw a very light-skinned woman sleeping in my bed. I didn't know her. Her dirty blond hair fanned my pillow. Her mouth was open and she snored loudly. Spittle oozed down her chapped lips. My special blanket was between her legs. I could see her frayed panties. The hair on her legs was long, blond. Albinita was in the kitchen. I could hear her singing "O María Madre Mía."

"Who's the lady?" I asked.

"She's staying with us for a while, Teresina. You can sleep with me tonight. She's very tired. Now I want you to go to the store and bring back some grape juice. She wakes up every now and then and asks for wine. I don't want to give her any more. She's had enough. Bring me a big bottle of grape juice from Canales' Grocery. The cheapest one. Now go."

The lady, whose name was Helen, was drunk at first, and then really sick. She stayed in my bed most of the time. She even threw up in it once. The first day she kept yelling out for wine, and Albinita would bring her a glass of grape juice. After a while, Helen caught on and started cussing. She wasn't very nice to us, she kept yelling all sorts of ugly things. Her voice was as thick as a man's. Then it turned guttural, otherworldly. It frightened me.

"Leave her alone, she has the spirit of evil in her," Albinita said. "You hear that low voice, Teresina? That's what the Devil sounds like. Listen to it now and remember it so you won't have to hear it again."

Albinita got some holy water and sprinkled it over Helen, saying, "Ayúdenos, Diosito." She began praying in Spanish, her little mantra of "Dios te salve María"s that filled the air with a thick, protective buffer against the high stream of incoherent evil that taunted and teased and buffeted us mercilessly. And as suddenly as it began, the desperate sound trailed off. The demon was gone.

Since then, I've only heard that voice a few times in life. Once when I was in the emergency room at the hospital and they brought in a young woman who was strung out on drugs. I heard it outside my house one time as well, when a man was leaning up against my wall, sick or drunk, and calling out in pain in a horrible, deep voice. I remember the ugly drowning sound from my dreams, dreams of evil and darkness. It's the voice of the lost soul, the lonely soul, la ánima sola, burning in some faraway and isolated Hell.

Albinita threw holy water in the air. Helen settled down and went back to sleep. When she woke up on the second day, she cried herself to sleep. By the third day, she was quiet and embarrassed. All she talked about was how much she loved Nestor and how she couldn't live without him.

Helen was married to a Filipino man named Nestor Macario, who worked on a farm just south of town. She had come to Cabritoville with Nestor and somehow they had gotten separated. She said Nestor took off without her. She was mad, and decided to get drunk to think things over, although later Albinita said Helen was an alcoholic and that when you are an alcoholic you need little or no excuse to drown yourself in drink. Helen had gone to the Serenata Lounge, but they'd thrown her out. But not before she'd met some man who wanted to have sex with her. She told him she didn't feel like it. He tried to talk her into going home with him. She told him to go to hell and then she'd gotten lost. She wandered around for a while and found the church open. She didn't remember too many details about the previous night. It had been cold, very cold, she couldn't forget that.

"Do you know what it's like to be left by a man?" she said with bitterness. Then she whispered under her breath, "Louse."

Albinita nodded her head yes. Yes, she knew what it was to be left by a man. Dying was the worst leaving. This poor white woman might find her man, but Albinita would never find hers.

"My daddy left us when I was just a little girl. Later on, I heard he'd died in California. We never knew what he died of. He was young, but not so young that he didn't leave a whole lot of living behind. And that meant my mama and me," Helen said.

I understood what Helen was talking about. She was talking about me, Teresina Ávila, and my father, Quirino Ávila, who'd died in his sleep and never came back.

"Nestor and I, we're married, Mrs. Aveela. That's the bitch. I'm not sure where he went to. He was following the crops. He heard about some work down the valley, so that's how we ended up here. It's a rough life, not one I'd have chosen, but Nestor is all I have. I had two little girls from my first marriage. After I met Nestor, they stayed on behind with their grandmother. No one liked him. You know how the world is. Prejudiced. What are you, Mexican? Thought so. But after I met Nestor there was no one else for me. Then we got separated. More like I think Nestor wanted to lose me. But you don't lose people, do you? If you love someone, how can you just let them go? And if you do let go, I mean, finally let go, can you ever lose them? I don't think so. Once a man's left his seed in you, whether you have a child with him or not, there's always a bit of a pull from that dark place inside. What do you think, Mrs. Aveela? I don't know if I can find Nestor. Or if he wants to be found."

Helen held court in our small kitchen as Albinita mixed her another cup of Sanka, extra strong. The two women had so little in common, but in the little humid kitchen they seemed like sisters. Two broken halves of a former whole. Helen was a rough-and-tumble sort, her hands were large and callused and with her pecheras she seemed more man than woman. And yet she was a woman who had suffered and who now cried and mourned the loss of the only man she ever really loved.

Albinita wore a dark brown dress with her familiar gray sweater over her thin flowered apron. She darted around the kitchen getting Helen another roll, then some jam and then another napkin. Albinita was at her happiest while in her kitchen, cooking or waiting on someone. The familiar walls of her home defined her and made her complete.

"I'll take you to the farm. We'll look for him," Albinita said gently. She didn't have a car, she didn't know how to drive and she wondered what she could do to bring a man back to a woman when he didn't want to be with her in the first place.

"Don't you worry, miss, we'll find your husband," Albinita said firmly.

"Mrs.—I'm married."

"Of course," Albinita said softly.

Together they would look for Nestor Macario.

"He's Filipino. We met about five years ago. In Los Angeles. He liked the way I looked."

Someone from Sacred Heart Church took all of us to the farm to look for Nestor. He was still there. Helen was relieved and delighted to see him. He, on the other hand, seemed irritated. Helen and Nestor didn't touch each other or even say hello. Helen gazed at him adoringly. Nestor looked at her coldly and said, "Leave her here."

Helen cried when she said goodbye to Albinita and hugged her hard. She even hugged me. Helen gave Albinita a statue of the Infant Jesus of Prague. It had a broken head that was held in place with a dried wad of gum. Albinita took it and thanked Helen. Helen was a Catholic, she said, and that's why she'd gone to church the morning she'd come to our house.

Albinita put the little statue of the Infant Jesus on her chest of drawers next to her candle of the Sacred Heart, her dried palm leaves and white plastic glow-in-the-dark rosary in its black case. You would have thought the statue was a treasure. As far as I was concerned, it was a lousy gift.

A few days later I started itching. Helen had given me piojos. Now that's a surprise, a white woman giving me lice. But that's what happened. I itched and itched and finally Albinita put this really strong-smelling brown liquid stuff in my hair. It smelled so bad I had to stay home from school. Albinita said, "I'm sorry, Teresina, but you have piojos."

"What's a piojo, Mamá?" I asked, afraid.

"A little bug."

"A bug?"

"They itch you and then when you put this stuff on them they go away. I'm sorry it smells so bad."

"What happens if you don't put the ugly-smelling stuff in your hair, Mama?"

"Then you can't go to school, m'ija."

"Maybe piojos aren't so bad, Mamá. I want to stay home with you. I don't like school. The kids tease me because I don't have a dad."

"Piojos *are* bad, Teresina. If you have them, your teacher and your principal will make you come home. You'll be sick with scratching and wish you weren't so full of piojos. When you go back to school, you tell the kids you might not have a father, but you have a mother who loves you."

"How big are the bugs, Mamá?"

"Look, this is a piojo," Albinita said as she showed me the comb. There, stuck in the teeth, were a few little bugs, the size of small black dots. She took one nit between her fingers and squeezed it with her fingernail.

"Have you ever had piojos, Mamá?"

"Yes, m'ija, when I was a little girl. We were so poor. We didn't have any way to clean up when we were in Kansas one time. We were following the crops, too. My father made us burn all of our old clothes. Ladies from the church gave us new clothes and then we moved on to Oklahoma. We were so poor, m'ijita, I didn't have a dress that fit me for a long time. Or shoes. I wore my brother's shoes with cardboard stuffed inside. I was very thin and everything fit me big. I'm sorry about your hair, but we have to cut it off."

"What about Helen? Will she have to cut off all her hair?"

"Yes, she'll have to cut her hair."

"What was wrong with her? I mean, she was so sad."

"She's in love, m'ija. She can't see anything but that man in front of her."

"Why does she do what she does?"

"She's weak. She drinks to forget. Except she can't ever forget."

"I don't ever want to be weak like that, Mamá."

"You won't ever be, m'ija . . . Con el favor de Dios . . . ," Albinita said, in a faraway voice. "Now hand me the scissors. We're going to make you feel better. And after that, we'll take the holy water and we'll clean and bless the house."

When I went back to school I wore a scarf. All the children laughed at me and called me Piojo Head and Lice Lady and Bug Girl and other ugly things. But I didn't care. Helen had some good stories, and it felt good to hear women talk the way she and Albinita did. Full of hope and excitement and love eternal. The stories about loving, especially for me, who didn't know what love was, were worth the piojos.

"¡Ay, esa mujer, La Helen! What business does a woman have dragging herself around after a man? And Nestor not caring for her! You could see it in his eyes," Albinita said, shaking her head.

"Yeah, and I lost all my hair because of her."

"I have no respect for women like that, Tere. Women who run after men, women who chase men down when they don't want to be found, and then try to stay with them when the staying is nearly impossible. As Father Vizcaíno from Sacred Heart says, we have to know when to 'let go and let God.' "

"Yes, Mamá."

After Helen, I never thought about my pillow the same way or my special blanket that my madrina gave me for confirmation or my bed or my room or the house. Everything was full of piojos. Everything was itchy long after the time my head stopped burning, long after I couldn't feel the little bugs crawling all around my brains. As a reminder, there was the broken and battered statue of the Infant Jesus of Prague in Albinita's bedroom looking at the world with his crooked and gummy head, a twisted white-faced baby full of illusions. He was a traitor. A liar.

Lucio is a piojo. A giant flea.

Lucio's a big black bug.

A spider in his web.

A roach on the lurch.

An ant with its bite.

A grasshopper jumping to be free.

A wasp stinging again and again.

A fly ever thirsty.

A mosquito sucking blood.

Lucio is the man I love.

My hair was once long and thick and lustrous. After Helen, it never grew back the same way. And today I have fine, thin hair, like a cat's.

I, Teresina P. (for Piojo) Ávila, sat in the living room picking at my head the way I do when I feel nervous, sometimes causing it to scab and then bleed.

I'm my own leech. I do this because my thoughts are too much
for me. They're dangerous and dark.

When it's really bad there will be four or five scabs, sometimes
more. Soon I'll start balding in certain spots.

Some people bite their nails or chew their fingers. I pick at my
head until my scalp bleeds. I swear I won't scratch, but I do, I
can't help myself. It's something a senseless child would do, a
restless older man or a person in a crazy house with nothing better to do.

When I pick at myself I remember my piojos and how I first
learned what kind of man not to love.

I sat on the couch in my living room, between faded peach-
colored walls, on my old gray couch, waiting for Irma to pick me
up for the fan club meeting. She was late. And then I remembered. I was on my own.

Without thinking, I started to twitch.

Ráscame, baby.

I've got an itch.

Minutes of the Pedro Infante Club de Admiradores Norteamericano #256

Members present: Nyvia Ester Granados, president; Irma Granados, vice president; Tere Ávila, secretary; Sista Rocha, treasurer; Catalina Lugo, parliamentarian. Members present: Ofelia Contreras, Concepción Vallejos, Elisa Urista, Merlinda Calderón, Pancha Urdialez, Tina Reynosa and Margarita Hinkel.

Members absent: Ubaldo Miranda.

Surprise guest: María Luisa Miranda.

The meeting was called to order at 7 p.m. by Madame President, Nyvia Ester Granados. The meeting was held at the home of Irma Granados. Elisa Urista made a motion that we always meet at Irma's. The vote was 11–1 for having the meetings at Irma's nice house with the large-screen TV. The one opposing vote was cast by Irma Granados.

María Luisa Miranda, Ubaldo's mother, arrived as we were ready to approve the minutes from last month's meeting. She was crying so much that we couldn't make out what she was saying. The treasurer's report had to wait until Mrs. Miranda stopped crying. Irma got her a glass of water and a couple of aspirins.

Finally she blurted out that Ubaldo was missing. She first noticed that things weren't right when she was folding laundry in the TV room and watching *Siempre en Domingo* with Raúl Velásquez.

Mrs. Miranda fainted. It was a good thing she was on Irma's pink divan. Sista Rocha put a cold towel on her head and she came to.

Madame President tried to reassure Mrs. Miranda that Ubaldo was fine and asked her if she minded if we tabled Ubaldo's disappearance until the end of the meeting. Mrs. Miranda asked if she could stay, she was afraid of going home to a dark house. The vote was 12–0 in favor of Mrs. Miranda staying put.

The treasurer, Sista Rocha, reported that since the fan club met at the Speaking Rock Casino, the bank account holds $375.75.

Irma Granados introduced her new puppy, who goes by the name of Pedrito. He's a mix between a chihuahua and a French poodle. He was officially voted the club mascot, 12–0. After we all said hello to him, Irma showed us how smart he is. She told him to get his snuggy-wuggy and he went out of the room and came back with a little blanket. Then she said get your boney-woney and he came back with his bone. The same thing for the bally-wally and the little blue birdy-wirdy. Irma said she would look into ordering some Pedrito T-shirts.

This month's movie was *Angelitos Negros*. It came out in 1948 and caused quite a stir, dealing with racial issues as it did. Irma Granados led the discussion. She said that Ana Luisa, the blond subdirectora of the girls' school, who married the famous singer José Carlos Ruiz, played by Pedro Infante, should have been told by her mother (Mercé), the woman she thought was her maid, that she was black. If she had, then when their first child was born black, they wouldn't have been so surprised.

Merlinda Calderón thought Pedro's acting wasn't very good in the movie.

Sista Rocha disagreed, saying that Pedro did a great job of living with the blond wife from Hell who thought she was better than everybody else, including her long-suffering negrita mother.

The discussion of *Angelitos Negros* continued for a long time.

Elisa Urista was offended by Pedro wearing blackface, and she didn't like the subject of interracial marriage and racially mixed children.

Ofelia Contreras wanted to know why Pedro had made this movie and what he had to gain from it. If she'd known she was going to see a lot of colored people speaking Spanish, she might have stayed home to dye her hair.

Irma informed us that the only really black person in the movie was Chimi Monterrey, who played the part of Fernando, a friend of José Carlos.

Everyone started talking at once. There was a fight between Elisa and Irma, and then Ofelia and Tere, and then Elisa and Sista, who said her best friend was black.

Elisa announced, "Black, gay, it's all the same thing. A sin against God, nature and Pedro Infante." Everyone knew she was talking about Ubaldo. Thank God Mrs. Miranda was in the bathroom at that moment.

Sista called Elisa a bigot and said the movie was powerful and full of great life lessons.

Elisa stormed out of the room, taking her pumpkin empanadas with her that were supposed to be for dessert.

Sista told her what do with her dry empanadas.

Madame President stepped in and called the meeting to order.

A motion was made by Irma that we ask Elisa to leave the fan club for general insubordination. And for being such a pendeja, Sista added. The motion was seconded by Tere Ávila. The vote was 6–5. It was suggested by Irma Granados that we send Elisa a note asking her to apologize to the fan club and to serve the refreshments for the rest of the year. That vote was 11–1, Ofelia voting in support of Elisa.

Madame President said she would talk to Elisa when they got together for their weekly bingo night.

A discussion followed on whether Ubaldo was gay or not. Merlinda had no idea. Tina wasn't surprised. Pancha thought he was merely unhappy. Sista didn't care and said we should love him the way he was. Irma said that Mercé didn't have a choice about being black. Everyone was sure about Mercé. But no one was really sure about Ubaldo.

When Mrs. Miranda came back in the room, Madame President called for Old Business.

Old Business included the usual pro-versus-con on what really happened to Pedro. Did he die in that plane crash in 1957 or was it a setup?

Irma reiterated her long-standing argument that Pedro wasn't on the plane, that it was a getaway plan. He was on the run because he was having an affair with the President of Méjico's mistress and he had to disappear.

Sista countered with the idea that he was on the plane but survived. The left side of his face was mangled up like carne desebrada, so that's when he took off for parts unknown.

Concepción thought Pedro had gone to Europe for reconstructive surgery, but it didn't take, and he wasn't ever the same again.

Merlinda suggested that he was so disfigured in the plane crash that he became the famous wrestler El Enmasquerado de Plata.

Madame President said that the stress of being a movie star was too much for Pedro. Just like Padre Mojica, the Mejicano actor and singer who became a priest and left all his riches behind, the world of the flesh took its toll on Pedro.

Sista refuted this, saying Pedro liked women and women liked him. She suggested he was on the run from the Mexican Mafia. Her brother-in-law's cousin, Manolo, told her there was a contract out on Pedro and he had to disappear. She added that Manolo was a hit man in Méjico and he should know.

Catalina Lugo claimed she'd heard of a viejito in Juárez with a metal plate in exactly the same spot as Pedro who could really sing well.

The vote was 11–0 in favor of visiting the little viejito in Juárez to see if he really is Pedro Infante.

Margarita Hinkel suggested we could use her van again as long as we paid her gas. The vote was 10–1 in favor of carpooling.

The "Viejito Visit" Committee members, Catalina and Irma, will report to the fan club at the next meeting. There was a motion that we eat at the Shangri-la, because last time, when we ate at the Pollo Borracho, a few people got the runs. The vote was 8–2 in favor of eating Chinese, with one abstention.

A discussion of why Pedro continued flying after the first plane accident followed.

Irma said the metal plate never bothered her as it bothered other people. To her, Pedro was still Pedro after the metal plate. Irma went on to say that Pedro should have given up flying forever.

There was an awkward silence. Everyone knew Margarita Hinkel was taking flying lessons at Cabritoville International Airport and planned to buy her own private airplane to fly down to the panteón for the anniversary of Pedro's death.

Very New Business included the fact that Mrs. Miranda was made an honorary member of the Pedro Infante Club de Admiradores #256 by a vote of 12–0. She said that she would have to change the time of her weekly weigh-in at Weight Watchers and that she had wanted to join for years but Ubaldo would never let her come to the meetings.

Other business included the news that Tina Reynosa's baby is due next month. If the baby is a boy, she'll call him Pedro, and if it's a girl, Infanta. She reported that her husband, Willie, wasn't too excited about the names. She hoped to make the annual pilgrimage this year if Willie didn't make her pregnant again.

Irma made a motion for Tina to get an appointment at Planned Parenthood. Sista Rocha seconded the motion. Everyone but Ofelia Contreras was in favor of Tina getting on the pill.

Margarita commented that she had heard Irma was dating Mr. Wesley.

To everyone's surprise, Irma announced to the fan club members that she was engaged. There was silence for a minute, then fan club members offered their congratulations.

After a lot of hugging and carrying-on, Nyvia Ester called the meeting back to order. Irma went into the kitchen and brought out a lemon meringue pie from the Safeway to celebrate.

The last order of business was the matter of Ubaldo Miranda. Madame President asked Mrs. Miranda to share her story.

Mrs. Miranda said she first knew something was wrong when she noticed Ubaldo's chones were missing from the laundry basket! And then when she went into his bedroom she saw he'd packed all of his clothes and taken off with her suitcase that she got as a retirement gift from the hospital laundry staff.

The vote was 10–2 in favor of putting Ubaldo in the Lord's hands and on the Prayer Chain.

Mrs. Miranda wept when she said she would report back to us about Ubaldo.

The next meeting of the Club de Admiradores Norteamericano #256 will be held June 18 at Irma Granados'.

Madame President closed the meeting at 10:35 p.m.

Minutes for the monthly meeting of the Pedro Infante Club de Admiradores Norteamericano #256, respectfully submitted by Secretary Tere Ávila.

The Border Cowboy

When I gather up all the nights of my life and place them in front of me, like a deck of cards from Vegas with a hole in the middle, I have to say that the night of Irma's engagement was one of the worst hands I've ever been dealt. It beat out the time Irma and I got stuck on the Ferris wheel at the County Fair when we were ten years old and so scared we started praying the rosary. And it was far worse than the time my dad was so angry that he hit a door and broke his little finger.

I don't remember too many things about my father. I do remember he yelled at Albinita because she wouldn't yell back at him. Wherever he is now, he's probably still used to getting his way.

I was a sickly child. Afraid to breathe and always

kind of weak. Albinita used to take me to the doctor regularly to get B12 shots. The doctor said I was anemic. My dad thought the shots were a waste of money. He told Albinita I was always sick because I was necia, a spoiled foolish girl; he didn't want any daughter of his to be puny and afraid.

He was a hard man, Albinita says, a cold man. It's good he left us early on. No telling how scarred both of us would be. He never really loved her; she was too nice, too kind, too soft, too intimidated by him. And yet, would he have had it any other way?

Quirino ruled our house, the way Pedro ruled his many houses, and Lucio Valadez rules his world.

Irma has said that, from everything she's read about Pedro, he would listen to you respectfully, look at you with those big brown peeps of his and then do whatever the hell he wanted.

Once Wolf Ruvinskis asked Pedro to what, in reality, he owed his career and success. He answered, "No le debo nada a nadie y le debo todo a todos."

Pedro didn't owe anybody anything at the same time that he owed everybody everything.

The night of Irma's announcement I also felt that I didn't owe anybody anything. And that's what got me in trouble.

It was a hot July night, barely starting to cool down at ten o'clock, when Irma informed us she was getting married. I had to leave the room. Irma's swamp cooler was on the fritz, and all we had to refresh ourselves was a tiny portable fan that someone placed near Mrs. Miranda. I couldn't wait for the cool air to circulate around me, so I extricated myself from Irma's long couch that sucked you into its hot cushions. I felt like a whipped chihuahua. I'd voted for Pedrito, thinking Irma and I would enjoy lounging around with him, baby-talking and such. I had no idea she meant for the club mascot to be sharing dinner leftovers at the Flying W with Mr. Wesley.

Irma engaged to Mr. Wesley. It couldn't be true! I was astounded by the depths of her betrayal. All I could think was that her name, Irma, fit her. I knew how Pedro's wife, María Luisa, felt! The worst thing of all was that she had announced her engagement at the fan club meeting, in front of God, Ofelia Contreras, Elisa Urista and me, as if butter wouldn't melt in her mouth.

I made my way stoically to Irma's bathroom, sidestepping that mongrel mutt of hers that was sleeping in the hallway. Once inside, I felt sick to my stomach. Forced sounds of gaiety reached me: the old hens whooped it up in the living room, a donkey brayed, a cow snorted with delight and more than a few dressed-up dogs scratched themselves with glee while an ancient coyote howled with joy. How could Irma keep me in the dark for so long?

I pulled a huge wad of pink Kleenex out of a pink plastic dispenser and snuffled back my sorrows. No one was going to see me cry in front of them, least of all Irma. And besides, I had to take the minutes. When I returned home, I promised myself, I would take a hot bath and get drunk.

Somehow I made it through the rest of the meeting and excused myself before it was time for the refreshments, pleading fatigue. To my credit, I even went up to Irma and gave her a perfunctory, halfhearted hug. Ofelia saw how I winced and smiled at me. To tell the truth, I didn't care. I last saw Irma pushing the swinging kitchen door aside with her leg as she came into the living room with that lemon meringue pie held aloft as if it were a precious offering to a god of abundance.

I drove home in a stupor.

Once home, I checked the mail and picked up an old tape of Lucio's. He had gotten in the habit of sending me cassettes in the hope I would play something other than Mejicano music, especially by Pedro Infante. I had the tapes all lined up on the bathroom shelf. I liked listening to music when I took my bath. No showers for me. I like a long hot bath to calm the nerves. To get the juices flowing to where they needed to flow. Showers were like bad sex. Over before you knew it, leaving you slightly wet, but never satisfied.

I always filed Lucio's tapes on one particular shelf. He liked "soft sounds" from the old Italian guys—Perry Como, Vic Damone, Al Martino, Jerry Vale—all those smoothly oiled middle-aged men with lubricated vocal cords, or ladies' men such as Tom Jones and Engelbert Humperdinck. I couldn't bring myself to listen to them, in the same way that I couldn't stomach the tapes Ubaldo had given me to counteract the evil he felt was running rampant in the world.

Ubaldo was a spiritual groupie. Most of his tapes were of people talking. Almost all of them were white men with high nasal voices or ethnic people I had trouble understanding. Rarely did I listen to them. Their titles didn't much appeal to me either: *Swami Muchanalga and His Divine Flute; Your Lives: All of Them; So What Is It? Life Eternal? Or the Hurried Now?*

The last time Lucio and I had spoken, he tried to talk me into forgetting all about him and I tried to tell him why that wasn't a good idea.

Our conversation ended on a strange note: him bitter about something and me wondering about what.

I took the tape out of its plastic case. It was "Release Me" by Engelbert Humperdinck.

The man was not subtle.

I decided to run a hot herbal bath, and as I did so, I listened to Pedro sing "Sé Que Te Quiero."

The water was too hot. I scalded my feet. I sat on the edge of the tub and turned on the cold water. I swirled it around as best I could with my two hands and my two still-aching feet.

I took up my washrag and eventually moved into the hot water, breathless from the heat. It surprised me and charged me all at once. That's what I love about a hot steaming bath, the surprise of letting go.

I eased myself into the tub and closed my eyes.

When I was a little girl, a bath was the only time Albinita gave me any privacy.

Although I didn't want to bathe and would rather have been doing anything but bathing, the actuality of it was wonderful.

It was so good to feel the warm water on my skin, as I submerged myself and then torpedoed upward with a swish of water. My old soft pink washrag became a mermaid that swam gracefully around the pylons of my brown feet, wrinkled and whitened by the sloshing flow of water that curled around my slithering dolphin body.

The last remainders of that outdoor skin were washed away, of socks worn all day long, arms dirty with the remnants of somersaults and slides down to the dusty ground. The rapidly darkening water was comforting, generous, and it left me with the fresh new skin of an underwater sea child, glorious and free.

No one bothered me as the water grew cold, as the mermaids did one last dive and I got sleepy and lay back against the smooth tub and dreamed myself another life, with someone, that someone to love.

That was what a bath still did for me.

It was hard to get out of the water. I had finally adjusted to the temperature. But I did get up, and hopped over to the cassette player, dripping wet without house shoes, hoping that I wouldn't electrocute myself turning it on. I didn't want to think about Lucio, the way I didn't want to think about my bathroom rug. Viejo. Peludo. Full of hidden things. Too many lives lurked there. There were traces of Diablo and Angelita, and my own self, shedding skin, nails, hair, the odors and juices of another day's work. Wet footprints on a dark blue rug.

It was still early enough. Eleven o'clock. Suddenly, I knew what I would do. No mistake about it. I knew who I was. I knew who my mother was. I knew who my grandmother was. And I knew where my place was in that long line of women that stretched into an eternity of loving that had to be paid in full, and reckoned with.

I broke into song beside the tub.

"Pa' que veas lo que se siente
pa' que sientas lo que siento
yo sí juro por mi madre
que me las vas a pagar . . ."

Que sufres, baby, que sufres. I want all the world to know you're a cabrón—especially your mother. Para que sepan, puto, just how you did me wrong. Yeah, you. Pinche vato motherfucker, well, maybe not in this case, but you get my drift, desgraciado infeliz from Chuco Town.

I don't have anything against El Paso, don't get me wrong. It's just that you live there with her. And not with me.

I love the Franklin Mountains. I love the plaza with the alligators in the middle. I love El Colón. I love Ciudad Juárez and the mercado and La Basílica de Nuestra Señora de Guadalupe and the carnicerías and the pastelerías and the loncherías and my gente that live on both sides of El Río Grande on La Frontera. I love everything about my border world, except you. Condenado.

After my bath, I set out my clothes, my white boots, resurrected from the back of the closet, the Luccheses relegated to the far corner. I pulled my black miniskirt and furry red halter top out of retirement at the back of the closet and laid them on the bed, sacramental vestments for a sacred journey.

I put on my makeup carefully, looking at my face in the mirror. I liked the cast of my light brown eyes, the faraway but clearly centered look, the steady jaw, the pursed but generous lips, the way my hair dripped down my back, sleek, fresh like a mermaid who knew in what waters she swam. I was ready for anything that came my way. And it would, the world could be assured of that.

I went back to La Tempestad, as if I'd never been there. Irma was probably at the Flying W watching *The Beverly Hillbillies* with Mr. Wesley. I saw Graciela out of the corner of my eye. She was with her fiancé, a guy with acne-pitted skin. They were laughing in the corner near the end of the fishpond. A private joke of some kind. The regulars were all there: Pollo, the bartender, who flashed me a giant smile; Wimpy and Popeye, hunched over a couple of Coors, trying to gather courage, no doubt, to pick up someone;

María González, who was slumped at a far table, sleeping near a bottle of Bartles & Jaymes. Lupe Báez was arguing with a big tall vato about the two-dollar cover charge. Louie "El Baboso" looked at me with hungry eyes and waved. I waved back. And lo and behold, the owner, Tino "El Cuate" Sotero, was sitting at a table with Cabritoville's chief of police, Panfilo "Tuche" Zertuche.

There was no way anyone was going to get in my way. Not tonight. Louie had the good sense to stay in his sector. He crawled back into the darkness and I never saw him again that night. I slithered over to the bar a 'lo todo stay-out-of-my-way.

"Hey, Pollo!"

"Tere! So, girl, what's new? Where you been keeping yourself?"

"I'm back, Pollo. So let me have the usual."

"What'll that be?"

"Oh, I don't know. How about a Cuba Libre, no, make that a Daiquiri, no, make that . . ."

"Let me fix you something special, Tere . . ."

"Good idea."

"Where's your sidekick? La Ethel?"

"Ethel?"

"La Lucy y La Ethel, get it?"

"She's with her boyfriend. Hey, you heard she's getting married?"

"I heard."

"Who'd you hear it from? Ah, shit. Well, I'm not getting married, not me. I'm footloose and fancy-free."

"Yeah, I can see that. Well, you better watch out, girl, you're so hot, you're on fire."

"So what's happening here?"

"Chago's back from California. He's over there playing pool with those college girls."

"Chago who?"

"Good girl. Here's your drink, Tere. On the house. The Devil's Machete."

"Just what I wanted, Pollo, thanks. Hey, don't worry about me. I

just came in to see old friends. I'm not staying long. And as for
Chago, send him a beer on me for old times' sake."

"I wouldn't do that if I were you, Tere."

"Ay, tú. You're as bad as Irma. Just send Chago the damn beer
and give me a glass of ice water. What the hell you put in this
drink anyway?"

It was around that time that Santiago "Chago" Talamantes
caught my eye and I caught his. I have to tell you he looked pretty
good for someone you used to think you loved and still harbored
ugly resentments toward until you realized why the hell you liked
him in the first place. He was ugly as sin and in that ugliness so
handsome it was even more sinful. He wasn't a pretty boy like Pedro or Lucio. But there was something big and masculine and out
of control about him.

Chago put down his pool cue, leaving the college girls to fend
for themselves as Wimpy and Popeye saw their chance and moved
in. He headed in my direction, but slowly, stopping to jostle a
friend or two and pat Tuche on the back as if they were lost brothers. He took his time getting over to me. I sipped my Machete
through a red straw and nibbled on my lime.

Before I knew it, Santiago "Chago" Talamantes stood next to
me breathing in my breath as I breathed in his. He looked at me
and I looked at him. When he took my hand I didn't resist. I put
the Machete down and stood up.

I don't know what I was thinking. I wasn't thinking. The little
red furry halter top was as itchy as I was itchy. I wanted to go
somewhere and be alone with someone who thought I was beautiful and desirable.

Chago paid his respects to Tino, who winked at us. He then
adiós'ed and high-fived the whole room, which took a while. I
stood near the fishpond like a dolled-up manikin looking for the
two lover fish, nowhere to be found.

My hand tucked into Chago's massive paw, he led me toward
his old Ford truck in the parking lot. It was still hot outside, a
night that would never cool down, it seemed, a night that would

lead into another hot day of temperatures over 110° F. I should have known this and stayed at home, stretched out naked on my bed, swabbing myself with a cool washrag, the portable fan blowing air over me.

After a long hot kiss outside Chago's truck, I hiked up the half mile to the seat, landing with a thud. I couldn't get my seat belt right. Chago tried to help me and finally, devil-may-care, I flung it over the back and said, "So, where we going?"

We hadn't seen each other in over a year. We'd hardly spoken since we left Tino's La Tempestad. I liked the fact that he didn't have any excuses and neither did I. He was the type of guy you could sit next to for hundreds of miles and not worry about talking to him. It felt good to have all the windows rolled down as we sped through the night on the old highway surrounded by miles of pecan orchards. You could feel the temperature was at least ten degrees cooler in the trees. At one point Chago turned off the car lights. It was something he loved to do, to drive blind like that, on a little-traveled road, in darkness, the only light coming from the moon, intermittently, through the thick overhanging trees.

I didn't know where we were going, and I didn't care. I knew I would be as safe as I wanted to be. Chago, despite his size, wasn't an animal. He wasn't the brightest kid on the old bloque, but he didn't use force on women. At his best, he was steady, a good companion; at his worst, he was as exciting as an imperturbable leech.

We ended up at the Noa Noa bar in Juárez. On the main drag by the Santa Fe Bridge near a lot of liquor stores whose shelves were mostly lined with rum, tequila, Kahlúa and vodka, it was where people went to dance to the latest rock-and-roll band. The groups who played were never good, but they were loud. The Noa Noa was popular with young people and adults who wanted the club life up close and steamy. It was dark in there, and humid, as

couples clung to each other, propping each other up at that late
hour, almost one o'clock.

Chago liked to dance, and the Noa Noa was one of his favorite
places. Once on the dance floor, undulating to some kind of sexy,
unchained border music, tunes whose names you can never identify and will probably never hear again in your lifetime, we made
out like everyone else. It didn't matter that lips mashed against
each other or that teeth got in the way. We rubbed and ground our
pelvises into each other, not minding anyone around us, because
everyone else was doing the same thing.

We drank all sorts of watered-down drinks with rum. I stumbled back to the bathroom several times to lift a trembly arm up
to the cracked mirror to put on red lipstick, bringing it down to
hoist up my limp halter top. It was beginning to look like a de-
flated fox, the fur moist, mashed down. I wore no bra and the sim-
ulated fur was beginning to drive me crazy. I was also getting
really tired. And when I get that kind of tired, I get itchy, a different kind of itchy than before. I knew it was time to go home. A
woman rushed headlong into the bathroom, bobbing and weaving,
her outraised hand guiding her like a homing device to the nearest
stall, where once inside, she sighed with contentment.

I headed back to the spawning ground. Chago and I were
salmon headed upstream, without regard for tomorrow. Tommorrow? You get the drift. I allowed myself to be pulled headlong into
the water of no regret, at least not now, full of witless bravado.

In my inebriated state, I wanted Chago and he sure as hell
wanted me. I could tell he had missed me.

We tried to hold a conversation underneath the harsh pounding
rhythm of Los Guapos del Norte.

"I forgot you had those boots. Remember when you wore those
boots for me that time?"

"Yeah, I remember."

"Remember that time? It was good."

"Yeah, I remember."

"Remember, it wasn't me who didn't want to see you anymore."

"Yeah, I remember."

"Me, too. Did you think about me when I was in California?"

"No."

"I remembered your boots."

"Yeah?"

"I was pissed off."

"Yeah, well, so was I."

"I never wanted to see you again."

"Yeah?"

"But then I remembered those boots."

And that's when he leaned over and kissed me real soft and I remembered how he was and how much I really had liked him, maybe even loved him.

And I kissed him back as hard as I could. Thinking if I remembered anything, then maybe I could forget everything. We stayed at the Noa Noa for a while, dancing and making out, and then Chago changed course on me. I knew it was coming. A big man like him has his needs.

"I'm hungry."

"It's about time for you to say that. So what is it, Fred's?"

Fred's was a sandwich place in Juárez where everyone went to sober up. They also had an incredible selection of tortas, sandwiches a 'la Mejicana. Fred's was the most popular hangout on the late-night hunger circuit and sold many a meal to college kids, soldiers from Fort Bliss, tourists who were going native, as well as lovers who were trying to find some dark excitement, people like Chago and me, who should have been home, asleep in separate beds.

But we didn't go to Fred's.

"What you say we call it an early night, Tere?"

It was past two-thirty in the morning and I was having trouble staying awake. I started yawning and to my surprise so did Chago. I also began to feel really old, and I guess Chago picked this up as well, because we rattled back across the border, not having any trouble crossing when La Migra asked us if were American.

"American citizen," I said, and Chago mumbled the same. No one asked to look in the truck's cabin. It was easy, all of it, too easy. No smuggled mangos, no Mennonite cheese, no Kahlúa to declare other than what was in our bodies, no pink or white Chiclets or mother-of-pearl jewelry or black-and-white onyx chess sets, nothing to hold us or root us to who we were just hours ago.

Chago headed toward our old stomping ground, a place he loved almost as much as Fred's and the Noa Noa.

The Border Cowboy Truck Stop was some twenty miles outside of Cabritoville, just off the highway. A big barn of an all-night truck stop this side of the state line, it was always busy at this time of the morning, when all the bars had closed and the twitchy insects began to find their way back to their nests. It was a lively place, loved by truckers and the locals alike, known for its big servings of good, hearty food as well as its service.

Long strips of brightly lit panels crisscrossed the ceiling. It was like being inside a slot machine. There was noise all around, a lot of jangly movement from all sorts of mismatched people cruising the night and stopping for late-night eggs over easy and hash browns. The coffee filter was always being changed. It was a place that didn't serve decaffeinated, only huge metal pots of industrial grade that would make your teeth curl. Not a place for the faint-hearted. Chago loved it and had to eat there at least once a week.

I'd known the Border Cowboy Truck Stop intimately, and once I was inside, all the memories came rushing back. Marva, the cook, was in the kitchen yelling to her crew of new busboys to get out there and "Hustle, hustle, how you say it? Andale. Pronto. Pronto." They were straight from the border, like most of her hired help. Her long-standing cook, Ramón, stood guard over a hot grill covered with eggs, hash browns and steak. He'd been with her for over twenty years, once coming under that barbed-wire fence and crossing the not so mighty river at a point of entry known as "La Rinconada." Shorty, her husband and co-owner, with a missing leg from a tractor accident on an Iowa farm, sat with a bunch of truckers near the large picture window, his

wooden leg propped up on a red plastic chair. Daria and Wuanita with a W, the veteran waitresses, not a sprayed hair out of place, were in control of a room full of ravenous rednecks, sleepy-eyed Chicanos, a host of horny truckers, a few dazed travelers who were pulling all-nighters, as well as a few errant, surreptitious early-morning lovers. We were all in search of nourishment, something to tide us over, bolster us up.

Rosaura, the crotchety cashier, was at her post, chewing a wad of gum as she rang up a passel of bills. A line stood before her counter. As soon as someone left, another moved in place.

Wuanita, a large-boned gringa with a huge name tag, greeted us. She was carrying a large pepperoni pizza that she delivered to a female trucker and her companion, the world's largest lesbian, well over three hundred pounds, each breast a hefty sandía. "Y'all want some jala-peenies on that?" she asked, holding a shaker of dried red chile flakes.

Since when had the Border Cowboy started serving pizza? Times *had* changed.

The Border Cowboy offered down-home, country-style cooking with endless cups of coffee that could bring the dead back to life. Greasy-looking merchandise was on the wall for sale: white caps with Border Cowboy across the front in red, white and blue letters, white cotton T-shirts with the restaurant logo: "Where the bullshit ends and the service begins." The T-shirt said it all.

It felt like home and it would have been, if I didn't not love Chago. I could see he still cared for me. If I didn't now love Lucio, who didn't love me at all, and if I still had a best friend who loved me the way I loved her, Irma La Wirma Granados, maybe, just maybe I could have learned to love Chago again.

I ordered the Border Cowboy Roundup Special: chicken-fried steak, two eggs over medium, hash browns, a side of buttermilk pancakes, and coffee. I was starving. To say I was depressed doesn't do justice to how I felt. If I'd had a gun I would have shot myself right there and then.

But Chago was pleased to have me at his side. I could see his eyes light up. I always knew that he felt paternal toward me. As if I were a little girl. He was a big man and big men feel that way about small women. Not that I'm that small. I was big for Lucio and small for Chago. He was probably the world's tallest Chicano. And he knew it. His size made up for his speaking skills. He was so big no one expected much from him. When I'd danced with him earlier, I realized how good it felt to be with a man who wanted to take care of you. He would have carried me around if I'd wished. And dancing with him to that slow music, I could feel his entire body turning into me, the way a blackbird heads into the wind, knowing the force will carry him along. His body wanted me, and for a short while, on the dance floor, I had wanted him.

And in the Border Cowboy, I wanted to give him my dictionary. I'd left it at home and its weight was now a phantom part of me. "Chago," I wanted to say, "you need some words. And if you had those words, maybe then I could love you. The way I love Lucio, who has no words for me."

I had to go to the bathroom. If I got there, I knew I would be able to think. I would find some modicum—*a moderate or small quantity*—of peace in there. A moment of rest before the bullshit hit the proverbial—*well known as through frequent observation or mention*—fan. I couldn't help it. Even though we levigated—*to rub, grind or reduce with or without the addition of a liquid*—on the dance floor, my cells had oscillated—*to swing or move to and fro*—like it or not. I had been Lucio-fied. All to me now was meaning, and at the expense of sense.

And then I saw Diolinda Valadez in the rest room, leaning up against the automatic hand dryer, drunk as the proverbial *small black-and-white North American mammal of the weasel family.* Her smudged almond eyes were tiny pinpricks of light. She was dizzy on her feet, punch-drunk and reeling like an animal who's been hit by a speeding car, no longer glamorous or classy, just another woman waiting for her hands to dry. Lady Macbeth of the Border Cowboy, she wrung her hands with exaggerated motion, while outside, waiting for her, was some man who would surely be her downfall.

She saw me come in. I'd seen her before and she knew who I was. Now we both knew who we really were, and it was a shock.

Diolinda was there with someone other than Lucio. Could he be her lover? And I was with someone other than her husband. And if that was so, and it was, where the hell was Lucio? The lightbulbs went off at the same time. It was a moment of sickening awareness. We smiled to each other, tortured Mona Lisas with shit-eating smiles of recognition and complicity as we swallowed the ugly pill of reality.

Lucio was with his other woman and I was with my other man and Diolinda was with her man and Andrea, well, she was fast asleep somewhere in El Paso with a babysitter who was surely getting overtime.

"What the hell are you doing here?" Diolinda asked me.

"I'm here with a friend."

"It's not my husband, is it?"

"Don't worry about it. What about you, who are you with?"

"You leave my husband alone. You hear that? I'm going to report you to the principal at Cabritoville Elementary. No one like you should be working with children. And don't bother telling Lucio you saw me here. He'd never believe you. Now get out of my way, bitch."

"You know what? I love him . . . And he loves me . . . ," I stammered as she flew out of the room, but I don't think she heard me.

I tumbled toward the safety of the stall, dizzy with knowledge.

For a second, I wanted to yell at Diolinda that I was sorry. But I was too tired, and I wasn't really sorry. I emerged, too nervous and strained to pee anything. I peered out the bathroom door to see her arm in arm with someone taller than Lucio, a young guy, probably someone just out of college, someone ready for a wild ride. It wouldn't last, and that was the point of the whole thing. I had to do some quick thinking. Surely Lucio would find out about me and Chago. I could tell him about Diolinda, but then I would have to confront the fact that he was probably with Mary Alice.

Nothing had happened with Chago, not yet. And up to the moment I saw Diolinda, things could have gone either way. When I went into the bathroom, I wasn't sure if I was going to hook up with Chago. Now I knew I wasn't. And it made me sad. Because Chago was out there in the dining room eating as if there *was* a tomorrow. It took so little to make him happy. A small woman at his side. A steak. A few dances around a slippy-slidy dance floor with someone you loved. A late-night drive in pitch darkness with a woman you could spend the rest of your life with, if only she would let you.

Could I get out the back door? If I could make it out, I'd call Irma from the pay phone booth around the side. She would come and get me and take me home. It wasn't something she was beyond doing. That is, if she still wasn't mad at me. It was worth a try. I would call her and see how she was feeling. Hopefully, the slate of friendship didn't have my name stricken out.

Chago wouldn't miss me for a few minutes. He'd ordered the Cattleman's Special, all the steak you can eat with home fries. It came with a side of beans. And in addition, he'd ordered sides of tomatoes, one of grits and a bowl of Marva's famous chile con carne, extra hot. By the time he'd hit his gravy and biscuits, I'd have reached Irma and she'd be headed down I-10 to the rescue.

But it didn't happen that way. The line was busy. And then I got scared. What was Irma doing on the phone at three in the morning? It had to be an emergency, the perfect excuse. I rushed out of the bathroom and found Chago finished with his meal and working on mine. He had eaten most of my hash browns with sour cream and chile, a concoction Ramón fixed especially for me.

"Chago, there's an emergency. I have to get home, *right now.*"

"What happened?"

"I don't know. But I know something is wrong. I can just tell."

"Is it your mom?"

Believe it or not, Albinita liked Chago, hulky, overpowering silent specter that he was in her small doll's house, and he adored her.

"I don't know. I don't think so, I mean, that's not the vibration I'm getting."

"Vibration?"

"I'll explain it to you in the truck."

"So what happened?"

"The phone was busy."

"Whose phone?"

"Irma's."

"Irma's? Now let me get this straight . . ."

I tried to explain to Chago that La Wirms and I had this mental telepathy thing going between us, and that if something was wrong, the other one knew about it immediately.

"La Wirms is a great transmitter of soul energy. Her chakras run very deep and she's got powers and can see Signs. She's full of *desde*."

Chago almost knew what I was talking about. He was descended from some Indios around Chimayó and knew what power, that kind of power, could be. He'd touched the Holy Dirt that cured sinners and saw the proof of discarded crutches and body braces on the wall of the little back room of the Santuario. He saw the milagros giving testimony to the healing of eyes, breasts and lungs. He read the testimonials and poems and stories and knew what it was to have faith in a power greater than yourself. And he was respectful toward Albinita and my comadre, Irma, because big men like him are respectful, knowing their real power and how they don't have to show it all the time, because they have other gifts that no one sees.

We arrived back in Cabritoville in record time. When we got to Irma's, the light was on and most of the fan club members were gathered in the living room, in all states of nighttime attire, some with bathrobes thrown over their flimsy nightgowns, others fully dressed in mismatched outfits they'd grabbed in a hurry. Tina Reynosa was wearing a T-shirt that said "Baby On Board," with a ratty pair of black shorts. Ofelia Contreras was in full makeup, her hair in curlers. María Luisa Miranda was wringing her hands as Sista Rocha tried to console her. I smelled coffee.

"Where the hell have you been?" Irma said to me. Then she saw Chago come in behind me and clammed up. There was a

happy little smirk on my comadre's face. She felt I'd be better off
with Chago than Lucio, she'd told me many times. I felt the same
way about Sal. Better him than Mr. Wesley. Only Sal was dead
and Chago was standing there, all six feet four of him—to the embarrassment and infernal gossipy joy of several of the fan club
members, who were fanning out now, keys in hand, to scour the
local motel parking lots in search of Ubaldo Miranda, who'd
called his mother to say he was going to kill himself.

"What?" I screamed. "Oh no, not Ubaldo!" Chago propped me
up with his large, solid body.

"When did this happen?" I asked Irma, who seemed the most
levelheaded of the group. She had gathered the troops and they
were headed into battle. It was a sight to see. Elisa and Ofelia
were huddled in prayer in the middle of the living room, while
Tina Reynosa was changing the batteries in one of Irma's flash-
lights. Merlinda came in with a thermos of hot coffee and pre-
sented it to Irma, who put it in her backpack.

"About an hour ago I tried calling you at home, but you weren't
there."

"I went dancing with Chago," I said guiltily.

"I see that."

"It's not what you think."

"Get ready to defend yourself to Lucio and half the town. You
know Ofelia and Elisa. Have Gums, Will Travel."

Chago, meanwhile, was apprehended by Concepción, who realized one of her tires was nearly flat. Chago had gone outside to
put his headlights on Concepción's car.

Sunrise was still a ways off, but despite the hour everyone
seemed alert. The overriding thoughts were group thoughts, ant
thoughts of saving the nest, and one of our own. La Reina, Nyvia
Ester, sat in the kitchen, drinking coffee and giving Irma ideas
about where to look for Ubaldo.

"Sheck behind the Come-On-and-Drop-In and also behind
the carnicería where the chavalos hang out where it's all spray-
painted. Don forget the shurch parking lot. I seen people sleeping
there under the árboles."

Irma gave everyone their orders.

"Check all the motel and hotel parking lots. Don't forget to go to the office to see if Ubaldo's checked in. Elisa, you and Ofelia take the Holiday House Motel on Highway 478. Merlinda and Margarita, you head toward Anthony and the Merry Manor. Don't forget to check the side streets. Concepción, take the Holiday Inn and the Sheraton. Pancha, drive by the Lariat and the Desert Sky. Tina, check the Plains Motel. And the Cactus Inn. I'll cover the Lazy T and swing by the Flying W on the way back, and you, Tere, you take the Sands."

"The Sands?"

"Everyone, report back here. Mrs. Miranda, you stay here with Sista and Nyvia Ester. I'll stop by Tuche's to see if he can help us."

"The last time I saw him he was with Tino at La Tempestad."

"Bad news, you know what a sound sleeper he is. If I can't wake up Tuche, I'll call the Border Patrol. Your cousin Junior still works there, doesn't he, Pancha?"

"He's the custodian. He's only working there part-time while he's finishing the Police Academy."

"Does he know CPR? We'll need someone who knows CPR."

"CPR!" screamed María Luisa Miranda, as Sista took her into Irma's bedroom to lie down.

"I know CPR," I said as I headed out the door, only to realize I was without a car, and without Chago, out there in the dark street.

The Shifting Sands

It was hard as hell getting away from Chago. The man stuck to me like chicken fat on an old burned sartén. He was well-meaning, and that's what made you give him the chance, but once given the chance, he had a way of insinuating himself into your life so completely that you forgot what freedom meant.

Concepción's tire was flat, and because of the urgency of the mission, she doubled up with Tina. They sped off, leaving me facing Chago Talamantes. I knew I was in trouble.

It was four o'clock in the morning and still warm. The red fur on my halter top was sweaty and my boots were scuffed and getting tighter by the minute. A woman can't wear go-go boots for more than a few hours without wanting to burn them. My arches were hurting me and my legs were tired.

"Can you take me home, Chago? I need to get my car."

"I'll take you wherever you want to go."

"It could take a while."

"I got time."

"Well, I've got to get to work in a few hours. I thought I'd go home, change, look for Ubaldo and then go to work from there."

"Where?"

"Wherever I am. Listen, I don't have time to argue, take me home."

"No."

"No?"

"I'm going with you. You might need help."

"Dammit, then, let's go to the Sands."

I didn't have time to argue with Chago. We were loud, I know I was, and I was afraid someone would complain. It was a family-type neighborhood where everyone knew and loved Irma and too many people knew enough chisme about me to make things uncomfortable.

Imagine the state of my mind: Had Ubaldo really called his mother to say his last goodbye? Had he really told her that he was going to kill himself? Had Víctor De La O left him? Ubaldo kept telling me that Víctor was the one, the only one, and that this was his last chance for love and all that crap. And that if it didn't work, he didn't know what he'd do.

I couldn't think. My heart was pounding. We drove over to the Sands. The early-morning light was spreading across the sky. I jumped out of the truck in one bound, as Chago parked in front of the office. It was dark in there.

"I'll ring the bell. You check for Ubaldo's car, Tere. I'll meet you out front."

There are about twenty rooms at the Sands, and it looked like they were all filled. There were license plates from all over: Texas, Arizona and even one from California. I didn't see Ubaldo's red Camaro.

We had so many things in common, Ubaldo and I. We both loved the color red. We weren't pink people, like Irma. We both liked the chisme. We both laughed the same way: an explosive burst, followed by a trail of honking chortles.

Ubaldo didn't really want to kill himself over Víctor, did he? Yet I knew I had once felt the same way he did about Lucio.

As if in a dream, I saw myself running around the back of the Sands, peering through the opened windows of whatever rooms I could, sniffing now and then to get a whiff of Obsession for Men, Ubaldo's favorite cologne. I was crazy and out of control, given the long, long night and too many drinks.

And this is where the dream part comes in. I could see how absolutely ridiculous I was, running here and there, looking for Ubaldo at the Sands, hoping not to run into Lucio, who wasn't expecting me, hoping not to find him, while Ubaldo was possibly bleeding to death, or laying in the noxious fumes of a room full of carbon monoxide, a suicide note nearby on the cheap pressed-wood table. Alternately, I thought horrible thoughts about Lucio, in our motel, with another woman. Then I imagined Ubaldo crying somewhere.

I ran up and down the wooden ramada that sheltered the motel rooms, knocking on doors, asking for Ubaldo. The motel was full and the sleeping residents greeted me grumpily, some with downright hostility. I ran to No. 17 and pounded on the door. No answer. Again.

"Lucio! Lucio!" I yelled. "I mean Ubaldo! Is Ubaldo Miranda there?" I hit the door hard, with both hands. My strength startled me.

"Are you there, Lucio? Dammit, answer the door. If you're in there, you better open the door. You can't hide. I know you're inside. I know you hid your car down the street! Are you in there with her . . . that . . . that . . . fake"—and here I spit out the word—"blond?"

An unapologetic blond with dark roots showing. It was such a betrayal. I knew how the poor Indita felt in La Mujer Que Yo Perdí. Lucio had a way of making you feel so inferior. Where do people go to learn that skill? He had to have learned it from Cuca.

Standing there in front of No. 17, the ratty wooden door I knew so well, with its tricky lock that you had to lift to the left that last second before opening, as if you were shaking a stick, I knew how all of Pedro's rejected brunet lovers felt when they realized that, once again, he'd turned his back on them to take up with a blond.

I heard stirrings. Someone got up slowly, turned on the light, but not before knocking over the digital alarm clock that had one lazy number that never flipped over, no matter how much you jostled the clock, and stumbled to the door. An older man without teeth, his thin gray hair sticking up, peered out behind the dead bolt.

I backed away quickly, as Chago walked toward me. I took his arm, which surprised him, and led him away from the room. The parking lot was quiet, all the rooms were still and my heart was pounding so fast I couldn't see straight.

"Ubaldo isn't here," I said trying to hide my emotion. I had to ditch Chago and come back and look for Lucio.

"He wasn't checked in, Tere. I asked."

"Take me home, Chago. Please."

"I went through the register."

"You did? Anyone you knew?"

"Not a soul."

"I need to get to work."

"If you want . . ."

"Just take me home. We'll talk later."

"Hey, this is for you. I forgot to give it to you."

Chago handed me a Border Cowboy T-shirt. It was a 6XXX. I don't know what the man was thinking. He'd probably bought it for himself and then decided to give it to me. I took it limply, thanking him, swearing to myself I'd never wear it.

Chago drove me home. It was hard to convince him that I would be all right. But he finally did leave, after I promised to call him at his mom's once I got out of work. I peeled off the sticky tank top. I smelled my armpits. I promised myself that I would never wear those white boots again or that halter top or that black imitation-leather skirt. I'd burn them later when I had a free moment.

I took a quick shower. And then I made the mistake of lying down for a few minutes and promptly fell asleep, dreaming of Lucio and Ubaldo, Ubaldo and Lucio. Two terrible karmic bookends. When I woke up it was nearly eight. I called work in a panic to tell them I would be late. The receptionist, Dorinda, said that Mr. Perea wanted to see me.

But first I had to check in with Irma. I dashed over there, still thinking of Ubaldo. I felt terrible, knowing there was something I should have done for him.

Irma wasn't back yet from her rounds, probably waylaid at the Flying W. Nyvia Ester was in the kitchen making her morning atole and María Luisa Miranda was asleep on one end of Irma's couch, snoring loudly. Sista had gone home. Nyvia Ester greeted me.

"Tere! Everybody sheck in but jew. We can no find Ubaldito. La Señora Miranda, chee fall asleep praying the Sorrowful Mysteries. Irma, chee go to the sheriff's office to file a People Missing Report. You want some atole, m'ija?"

Nyvia Ester was holding a bowl of breakfast cereal made out of ground blue maize, flour and water. It looked delicious.

"Ubaldo wasn't at the Sands, Nyvia Ester."

"Ay, m'ija, que Dios lo cuide. I knew Ubaldito was in troubles and that he would only get worse from them."

"I have to get to work, and I'm late. Can I use the phone?"

"Como no, m'ija. Vente a comer, María Luisa, you need your estrength," Nvyia Ester said to María Luisa Miranda, who woke up suddenly with the noise. She was on autopilot and did what she was told to do. Nyvia Ester laid a bowl of atole on the dining-room table for both of us.

I called Lucio's apartment in El Paso. And then his office. And then his house. Nothing. No answer anywhere.

When I got to Cabritoville Elementary, I made a beeline for Mr. Perea's office. Susanna, his secretary, ushered me in.

Mr. P. had his back to me. He was reaming out his right ear with the end of a Bic pen. He heard me and turned around with embarrassment.

"Have a seat, Miss Ávila."

I sat across from his large walnut desk. Mr. Perea sat down, but not before he popped a Life Saver into his mouth.

"Care for one?"

"No, thank you."

Mr. Perea was very neat. His papers were laid out in an orderly manner, one cream-colored file atop another. There was a Father's Day card on the table with a kid's scrawly writing. The wall behind his desk was covered with family photos. His children were in the ugly, big-tooth stage. Most of their supposed pearly whites were snarly, yellowed, and seemed to be hanging from a thread. There seemed little hope for improvement.

"Do you know why I've called you in, Miss Ávila?"

"No, Mr. Perea. I'm sorry that I was late. A friend of mine, well, he's missing. His mother can't find him. We've been looking for him all over town."

"Who is that?"

"Ubaldo Miranda. His mother worked at the hospital."

"What happened?"

"To tell you the truth, no one knows. He's disappeared."

"I'm sorry to hear that. I know his mother. Buena gente. I worked with Ubaldo when I was a coach at Cabritoville High. Couldn't dribble worth a damn."

"I'm never late. We were looking for him."

"Miss Ávila, I called you in here because we've received a complaint."

"Who? Who complained?" I said, getting up. The office was stifling, a noisy overhead fan did little to circulate the air.

"I can't tell you that. But I will have to ask you to take a leave of absence."

"Why?" I asked in disbelief. "What have I done? There must be some mistake."

"I wish it were, Miss Ávila, Terry. This has nothing to do with your work. It's . . . It's . . . I don't know how to say this, Terry, but it's about your personal life."

"I don't have a personal life. I mean . . . I work hard . . . I'm here all the time and when I'm not . . . I love my kids, Mr. Perea. I'm a good educational assistant."

"It's about you and Lucio Valadez."

"Oh." So he knew.

"I have to ask you to take some time off. We'll talk again in August."

"Does this mean I don't have a job?"

"It means," said Mr. Perea, getting up and unloosening that coiled-up belly like a water hose settling down, "it means that you are on leave. I wish I could tell you otherwise. It's not something I wanted to do, but, Terry, Miss Ávila, you have to . . . Listen, the best of luck. You're a good aide, that's not it. I'll make sure you're still on the insurance plan, until, you know . . ."

"I have to go, Mr. Perea."

"I understand. It has to be hard to lose a friend."

"Ubaldo's not dead, Mr. Perea. He's very much alive some-where. I can feel it. Now, if you'll excuse me."

I stepped away from Cabritoville Elementary for possibly the last time. The halls were quiet. The dark blue linoleum floors were shiny and devoid of tiny footprints. The great machine of the school was at rest.

Later on I would call Mrs. Durán, the Head Start teacher I was working with, to let her know I'd been put on leave. I'd tell her. Just tell her. That. That I was hopefully coming back to my kids and please, tell them hello from Miss Terry.

I went back to Irma's. She sat on the couch going through the phone book. María Luisa was listening to the news on television.

Nyvia Ester had gone to work at the Come-On-and-Drop-In. The other fan club members were on call. Someone had put Ubaldo on the Prayer Chain and Sista had come over with a devil's food cake. The food had started rolling in, as if there had been a death in the family. And yet no one knew anything. No one had heard from Ubaldo or seen anything on the news that showed any signs of foul play.

I entered Irma's living room warily and perched on a chair, not sure if I was coming or going. Or whether I was welcome.

"So, you want something to eat?" Irma asked.

"I'm not hungry, Irma," I said.

"You have to eat."

"What I have to do is sleep."

"Too busy partying, huh?"

"Chago's back, but it's not what you think. Any sign of Ubaldo? Oh, God, I don't know how he could do this. I feel terrible, Irma. I could have helped him. Poor Ubaldo!"

"Nobody could have helped him, Tere. He was sick."

Just then we heard a giant roar, like a supersonic plane flying overhead, breaking the sound barrier.

"What was *that*?" Irma asked, as we both paused to listen. The noise had been incredibly loud; the walls of the house seemed to vibrate.

"I don't know. Hell, what *was* that, Wirms?"

Some minutes later, while drinking some iced tea in the kitchen, we heard the squeal of police sirens.

Irma got up to look out the door. A fire truck was hurrying to get to its destination.

María Luisa went to lie down on Irma's bed, now her bed for the duration, and I got up and turned on the radio, hoping to find out the cause of the noise.

"That was some explosion, whatever it was," Irma said, coming back.

Irma settled into the couch, took up her glass and asked, "Do you have anything to say to me, Teresina Ávila Ambriz?"

"Friends?"

"Is that all? Is there anything you have to say to me?" she repeated.

"Like what?"

"Like you're sorry you insulted my tocaya."

"Okay, I'm sorry I insulted your tocaya."

"Say her name."

"I'm sorry I insulted Irma Dorantes. Happy now?"

She paused, as if to consider whether my response met with her satisfaction. Then she asked, "So, what did you do last night?" looking at me out of the corner of her eye.

PART V

¡VIVA MI DESGRACIA!

Burning

I camped out at Irma's all day and went home heartsick that night; I couldn't get to sleep, worrying about Ubaldo. No one had heard any news despite the hivelike activity of the fan club members. I moved to the living-room couch around two in the morning to think more clearly. I can't think in bed, and since I couldn't sleep, the least I could do was think. I thought about Lucio. Then I thought about Ubaldo. And lastly I thought about me.

Just when I was falling sleep I heard a car with a bad muffler drive up. It was Tina and her son Sammy delivering the *Cabritoville Chronicle*. I went out to get the paper in my Border Cowboy T-shirt. When I bent over to pick up the newspaper lying in the cactus, I made sure I stooped with my butt side facing the house.

Then I came upon the headlines.

EXPLOSION AT THE SANDS MOTEL

A 9 a.m. explosion shook the Sands Motel at 390 North García Street. Manager La Vonda Mungler heard a tremendous blast and called 911.

A badly burned man was pulled from the flames of his room by elderly motel guest Perry D. Winkler from Shallow Water, Texas. Winkler said he had been awakened by a young woman pounding on his motel room door around 4:30 in the morning.

"It's a good thing she woke me up," Winkler stated. "I couldn't go back to sleep. So I was watching television when I smelled gas and then heard the explosion in the room next door. I got up and ran outside. I heard someone moaning in there. That's when I kicked in the door and pulled out a man that was on fire. There wasn't anyone else in there. Just him, lying on what used to be the rug. The room was all broken up, furniture thrown this way and that. When I pulled him out of there, he was still on fire. He tried to talk, but he was too weak. I could see that he was losing ground. There was no way to give him CPR. It was terrible. I'll never forget it as long as I live."

The chief of police, Captain Panfilo Zertuche, stated, "We're looking into the cause of the explosion. There were tools near the heater and it seemed as if it had been tampered with," he said. "Things could have been worse if the force of the blast hadn't gone out the back window." He reported the power of the explosion moved the walls a few inches. A suicide note was found nearby.

Police have not identified the man whom Winkler pulled from room 16 at the Sands Motel. Damage to the motel is estimated at $50,000. The unidentified man was airlifted to the burn unit at Presbyterian Hospital in Albuquerque.

I called Irma. She reported the story to Nyvia Ester, who was in the kitchen getting breakfast ready. Then Nyvia Ester went in to wake up María Luisa Miranda, who was sleeping in Irma's room. María Luisa started screaming and Nyvia Ester had to calm her down. Irma called the fan club members. Then she called the burn unit in Albuquerque. By this time, I had pulled on a pair of jeans and was headed over to Irma's. I was still wearing the Border Cowboy T-shirt Chago had given me: "Where the bullshit ends and the service begins."

The news that came back to us from the hospital was that the man was burned so badly they had no way of identifying him. Irma called the police department, and Captain Zertuche recommended that María Luisa go to Albuquerque; there was an all-points bulletin pending for Ubaldo. He said she could help determine if the man was Ubaldo. Sista Rocha offered to drive her to the hospital. They took off in midmorning after a frantic meeting with the fan club members. Sista promised to call us when they got there.

By this time, all the fan club members were praying in the living room. Ofelia Contreras was on her knees, propped up against Irma's long couch, leading the rosary. Everyone was quiet, and the prayer responses were listless. I had cried so much my eyes were nearly shut and I had a terrible headache. I also felt as if I had a concussion. I was afraid to lie down because I knew the pain would be more intense. I slumped in a chair near the door and tried to pray. No use. Irma's swamp cooler was still on the fritz. Every once in a while someone would cry out, "¡Ay, Ubaldo!" It was terrible. After the rosary, Irma put on *El Album de Oro de Pedro Infante, Volume I*, and the fan club members lay on the rug and meditated on Pedro Infante, Ubaldo, the transitory nature of life. When "No Volveré" came on, a loud wail went up and even Ofelia broke down. Eventually, the cries subsided and through muffled sniffling you could hear Merlinda snore. I snuck out to the kitchen to make a call.

I dialed Lucio's number. No answer. I left a message, against all better judgment. I had to tell him about Ubaldo. There was nothing to do but wait. I was beside myself. Was the man in the motel room Ubaldo? ¡Ay, Ubaldo!

It would take Sista about five and a half hours to get to Albuquerque.

I walked back into the living room. Elisa was massaging Ofelia's head as she cried without restraint. She had never liked Ubaldo and her crocodile tears were so hypocritical to me. Tina suggested the club members take a prayer break and head over to Arby's. Everyone was in agreement. They left with promises to return. Irma and I were left alone at last.

Irma looked at me and said a little uncertainly, "Wes is coming over."

"Wes?"

"Mr. Wesley."

"Oh," I said finally. "Mr. Wesley."

"He's very upset about Ubaldo."

"Now listen, Irma, we don't know for sure if it is Ubaldo."

"It has to be, Tere. Who else?"

"He's not the type to do this, Irma. I know Ubaldo. It's a terrible mistake."

"Wes will be right over. But he doesn't have to come over now. I did want him to meet my Maid of Honor."

"Me?"

✺

Mr. Wesley was an older, rugged-looking cowboy who still had the remnants of early good looks. If he hadn't seen so much sun and too little shade he would really be something. Take a young Roy Rogers about thirty-some years down a hot, dusty road. Mr. Wesley was lean like that, but tall. He had that Texas punch that made him a man's man and a woman's best friend. He was what Nyvia Ester called propio, lots of "Yes, ma'am"s and "Excuse me"s. But he wasn't weak, I'll grant you that. He wasn't at all *desde*, he just needed a little updating.

He walked into Irma's house, familiar with the layout. They greeted each other, kissed, and then Irma said, "Tere, this is Wes Wesley."

"Howdy, ma'am," Wesley said.

"Howdy to you," I said. Irma flashed me a dirty look.

"So sorry to be meetin' yuu under these circumstances," Mr. Wesley said consolingly. "I understand Ubaldo was yer friend."

"One of my best friends," I said, looking at Irma.

"Oh, Wes! Honey, I don't know where to begin . . . ," Irma started in. It was nauseating to see them lace their arms around each other like braided lassos.

Irma continued, "Mrs. Miranda took off with Sista Rocha and my mother to go to Albuquerque to see if the man is Ubaldo. Oh, I can't believe it. It's such a horrible thing to happen just before our wedding!" Irma said, folding into her dusty dude.

Wesley stroked Irma's cheek and then pulled her close.

Irma popped up with a cheerful "Wes, honey, are you hungry? We have plenty of food in the kitchen, don't we, Tere?"

"You know we do, Irma," I said caustically.

"Honey, you want some lunch?" Irma said.

"I'm not sure, darlin', what kind of vittles you got?"

"I don't know, baby. How about some enchies? Red with an egg."

"Yep. Might do."

"I also have some chile con carne," Irma said, pronouncing "carne" the gringo way, "carney." I winced. La Wirms was losing her roots!

When they finally stepped into the kitchen, Irma swung the door closed with her foot. I put on *El Album de Oro, Volume II*. They were in the kitchen a long time cooing and carrying on like cucuruc'ed palomas. I could hear them. When they finally came out, Irma's lipstick was gone.

"Come on, Tere," Irma said. "Come and join us at the table."

"I'm not hungry, Irma."

"You can at least have something to drink, Tere. Come on!"

It was worse when El Wes started eating. They hardly let up on each other, holding hands whenever there wasn't a fork moving toward their mouths, or if Irma wasn't wiping food from his face. They nibbled from each other's plates.

Mr. Wesley had a bad habit of talking when he ate. Bits of half-chewed food came flying at you every which way. You didn't want to sit across from him, much less on his side. Irma was always wiping food off him, some fleck of meat, or flicking a kernel of corn off the table.

And the worst thing was that she didn't even seem to notice that she was doing it. They had a sign language all their own; when she ran her fingers to the right or left side of her mouth, signifying, "Food on the right, watch out," or "Food on the left, clean it up," he would automatically lift a corresponding hand and wipe the affected side.

Not that I was critical of him.

Let's just say I was feeling all *desde*.

Irma paid keen attention to Mr. Wesley's spewing and whistling. You could see she was attentive to all the things that women have to do to keep a man groomed and presentable in public.

For instance, more women should pay attention to their husband's ear hair. I noticed a number of hairs in Mr. Wesley's ears. I'm surprised Irma hadn't dealt with them already. Once they got married, she'd get him under control.

To see him and La Wirms carry on across the table with her "honey this and darling that" was revolting. I realized with astonishment I was celosa and then envidiosa.

When Irma excused herself to go into the kitchen, Mr. Wesley turned his attention to me, and we had our first real talk.

"Irma has been tellin' me jest how much yuu've helped her out," he began. "She really thinks the world of yuu. I wanna thenk yuu for bein' such a good friend to her, Tere."

He pronounced my name "Teddy."

"We've been best friends for years. We met in grade school."

"Irma's been tellin' me. Now, I was right sorry to hear about yuu-all's friend Ubaldo."

(There's no way I can approximate what Mr. Wesley did with the name Ubaldo.)

"We're all very worried," I confided to Mr. Wesley. And why not? I *was* worried.

"Irma's beside herself, yuu know."

I wouldn't say that, I wanted to say to Mr. Wesley, knowing how shabbily La Wirms and most of the fan club members had treated Ubaldo in the past. But it was some consolation to see them regretting—if only out of guilt—their prior actions and rallying around the cause, which in this case was Ubaldo's disappearance.

"Ubaldo was, well, he was having problems. We're not sure if it was him in the motel room or not."

"If yuu all need any help, I mean it, please call on me. The motel's at yer service, I mean, if you need to put up kin at the funeral."

I bent my head and sobbed. Mr. Wesley handed me a wad of napkins from a dispenser. They were stiff to the touch, but it was better than nothing.

"Irma says yuu-all have had some hard times."

I wondered if Mr. Wesley was talking about Ubaldo or me.

"Now lookee here, things are gonna get better, Tere. Yuu put yerself on that path, and it cain't help but rise up again to yer feet."

Don't tell me he was Born Again. Not that! Anything but that. I knew I'd thrown away my red fur halter top for a reason.

I nodded to him without too much conviction.

"I don't know if Bunny told yuu . . ."

"Bunny?"

"That's my pet name for Irma. I told Bunny I'm lookin' fer some help, and wondered if yuu'd be interested. Irma says yer a people person. I need a manager. It's a good part-time job. I'm talkin' about the Flying W. Yuu okay, Tere?"

"Of course. I'm not sure, Mr. Wesley. Can I think about it and let you know?"

Things were moving too damn fast!

"Take yer time, Tere. We're closed for renovations until after the wedding."

I shook my head. Irma came up and they kissed and hugged and then she hunkered down next to her man.

I was grateful to Mr. Wesley. But I wasn't sure I could work at the Flying W. The lobby was so old-fashioned and the rooms were so ugly. No, I couldn't do it.

Mr. Wesley made idle chatter, about Irma, the wedding.

"I want yuu to know, Tere, that Bunny and I both care for you very much. We want yuu to know how happy we are that yuu'll be our Maid of Honor."

"Will you excuse me?" I said, getting up suddenly.

"Go right ahead now, Tere. We'll be right here, waitin' for yuu," Mr. Wesley said with immense compassion.

It always seemed that I was slinking off somewhere to get out of someone's way.

I made my way to Irma's pink bathroom.

I rinsed my hands with warm water. They were trembling. The soap in the dispenser was empty. Irma was so distracted with Ubaldo's disappearance, she'd forgotten to refill it. It was so un-like her. There was no way I could wash my hands. I toweled them dry and looked at myself in the mirror.

I felt like Cruz, Pedro Infante's deluded father, when he stared at himself in that all-seeing mirror in *No Desearás la Mujer de Tu Hijo*. There was no way I would ever be Lucio's wife. Andrea's adopted mother. Or Cuca's daughter-in-law. I was barely anyone's friend. And somewhere, Ubaldo Miranda was crying.

Instead of a thirty-something-year-old woman, this is what I saw: A Little Girl. Nine Years Old.

I was standing in front of the checkout counter at Cabritoville Drugstore. The woman behind the counter was talking to my dad, Quirino. Then they were laughing. I'd never met her before. She was neither old nor young. I can't remember exactly what she looked like.

"So, you're Teresina," the woman said. "I've been wanting to meet you. I'm a friend of your daddy's. These are for you."

I was too shy to say thank you. I wanted to run away and hide. I wanted to tell her that I didn't want any gifts from her. I didn't know her. I had a mother and she was waiting for me to come home. And the more I stood there, the longer that wait would be. Somehow I knew if I accepted any gifts from her, it would mean I didn't love my mother. I loved my mother and she loved me. No woman, not even one with gifts, would come between us.

Her name was Consuelo, she worked at the drugstore, and I saw her once or twice after that. We never spoke again. She was my father's lover. She almost died aborting his child, but no one spoke about it. It was only when I was an adult that I learned the story.

Inside the paper bag was a girl's toy vanity set, with a small compact with a hazy aluminum mirror, orangish lipstick that tasted funny and a vial of cheap, stinky perfume.

The woman in the mirror knew what the little girl didn't. That eventually, over time, all things would work out for the best. They had to.

I wet one of Irma's pink washrags and put it across the back of my neck.

Andrea was a strong little girl. She wouldn't understand what everything meant, until one day she would look in the mirror and see things as they really were. And at that moment she would grasp the unvarnished, illusionless reality of those characters who made up the movie of her life.

I made my way back to the living room. Irma and Mr. Wesley were glad to see me return. La Wirms smiled at me, the resurrected pinche cabrón fénix with a wet towel on her neck.

"What's that?" Irma said.

"Oh," I said, balling up the towel.

"Don't yuu worry, Tere, everythin' gonna to be all right," Mr. Wesley said calmly.

Mr. Wesley smiled at Irma. She patted his hand lovingly.

I wanted to tell Lucio Valadez to take a Flying F, but instead I contemplated my possible career as the new manager of the Flying W.

I'm a good person—who is sometimes bad.

That day, Mr. Wesley rose up big in my mind like a giant Macy's balloon and stayed in the sky for a long, long time. He was the kind of man who helped you stay calm when the world was all firecrackers and old smoke.

It seemed natural for Irma to be marrying Mr. Wesley. He would never hurt her. Not him.

I decided to go home to rest.

I had so much to think about. Who was the person who had been consumed by flames?

Rabia

We were in the lobby of the Flying W Motel, where la comadre was cleaning the display case. Wes was out of town and la comadre had invited me over for a Pedro-athon. She suggested we throw a couple of potpies in the oven and relax in the motel's sunroom on some blue lounge recliners and stay up all night.

I felt uncomfortable. Irma feverishly cleaned the room, as if it was already hers.

The decor was Early Wagon Wheel. You know, that canned-corned-beef version of the West: big wagon wheel lamps suspended from ornamental rope, a front desk made out of wagon wheels, John Wayne-sized chairs with wagon wheel backs and a huge neon wagon wheel sign in front of the building blinking: "The Flying W Motel. American Owned."

"I just can't get over it, Irma. María Luisa getting all the way up to Albuquerque to the burn unit to find that the only part of the man's body that wasn't burned was the crotch area and the bottoms of his feet."

"I feel sorry for her, I really do."

"You can imagine how awful it was trying to figure out if that was Ubaldo's como se llama after not seeing it for so many years. She did know what his toes looked like and that Ubaldo was a size ten."

"María Luisa said the toes were different."

"Ubaldo couldn't have tried to kill himself. Not Ubaldo!" I said with disbelief.

My eyes teared up.

"Dammit, Ubaldo! Where the hell are you?" I cried out. "How could you do this to me? And what about your mother? She loves you, cabrón!"

"Sista told me the man is in an induced coma."

"Híjole, Wirms, I didn't know they did that."

"They do that to people who are badly burned, the pain is so bad. They have to, Tere."

"How about the handwriting? Why couldn't they analyze it?"

"The note was typewritten."

"I don't think it's Ubaldo. He couldn't type."

"I don't know, Tere. He *was* pretty crazy."

"Not *that* crazy. No, it's not Ubaldo and that's all there is to it!" I said with stubborn determination.

I stared out the large picture window at the blinking red Flying W sign.

"What I want to know is why people go out of their way to say their businesses are 'American Owned.' It gets me, Wirms. The only people who say 'American Owned' are white people with an ax to grind about being American or white. Or worse yet, white and American. You don't see any Mejicanos saying Mejicano Owned, or better yet, Mexican-American Owned, do you? Not that we don't own or aren't proud of owning. It's just that Mejicanos don't flaunt owning things the way American Americans do."

"What are you trying to say?"

"Life is just too strange."

"The sign was here before Mr. Wesley bought the business, for your information, Tere. One thing I'll say about Wes, he's not one of those America-Love-It-or-Leave-It types."

La Wirms had taken everything out of the display case and put it in several collapsible gift boxes for men's shirts from Penney's. The boxes were flimsy and punched-in already, but they were the only ones she could find. All I could think about was that they were probably left over from some gifts to Mr. Wesley: some plaid flannel pj's or a gray viejito-style polyester cardigan that would start bunching up the first time you accidentally washed it in hot water. Either that or she had given her consentido several boxes of white cotton handkerchiefs.

When she finished with the boxes, Irma tried to drag a huge bearskin rug that was on the floor across the room. I got up and helped her hoist the thing out the lobby door.

"We'll leave it there a while to air," Irma said, trying to catch her breath.

"Hopefully someone will steal it," I said.

"Wes shot it in Alaska."

"Comadre, how can anyone *deliberately* kill a bear, unless, of course, it was attacking you, and then have it stuffed? It's too weird," I said, cleaning off my hands from dusty bear sobacage. "Speaking of strange, I swear, last night I thought I heard Ubaldo calling my name. Then this morning I heard him singing his favorite Pedro song, 'Cien Años.' "

"I think you need some sleep, Tere."

I walked around the room, looking at various hides and animal heads and mounted fish on the walls with little silver engraved signs underneath: "The Gila 1974," "Montana 1963," "The Gulf of Mexico 1955."

"How are *you* going to sleep with all these animals out here? Knowing they died for no reason at all except to be someone's trophy."

"I don't like them either," Irma confessed. "But you have to go slowly with these things. I'm inching my way toward the southwestern look, one ristra and Kokopelli at a time. Before you know it, we'll be up to our eyeballs in howling coyotes."

Irma rushed around the room. She was now in a cleaning frenzy, spraying the wood with wax, cleaning the glass on the counter, and not once did she break stride. Despite Irma's frantic movements to and fro, I felt pensive.

"I should have gone to Albuquerque with them," I said. "I could have identified Ubaldo, *if* it was him that was burned."

"Oh yeah?"

"Yeah, I once walked in on him in your bathroom. He was playing with himself."

"During a fan club meeting? In *my* bathroom?"

"You asked."

"So . . ."

"So?"

"What did it look like?"

"Let's just say I could identify him and leave it at that."

"So now you're all clamp-mouthed? You know, you could save María Luisa a lot of grief with this information."

"No one is lining anyone up for identification. And besides, I only caught a quick look at it from the corner of my eye."

"Oh yeah?"

"Distance distorts size."

"Like how?"

"It was big, okay? Now leave me alone, Irma. So, do you want me to help you or not? I'm just sitting around and you're doing all the work."

"Just sit there and talk to me. Tonight it's just you and me, Tere. Like old times."

"Only we're not in your house on your couch in curlers and you have to worry about a dog and a fiancé. And not only that, nothing around us is pink! What are you going to do about your house, Irma? How can you stand to leave it?"

"I'm not sure. I think one of my nieces is moving in," she said. "I'll bring my things over to the motel little by little."

I was happy for Irma, don't get me wrong. But our future as co-madres was uncertain. Would we still have weekend-long Pedro-athons where we cooked up a storm and then fell asleep feet to feet on her long couch? Would La Wirms listen to me the way she always did, offering consejos, a back-cracking, a glass of red wine or a glass of Alka-Seltzer, whatever was needed, day or night? Would we still go to El Colón to see Pedro's movies with Nyvia Ester and then go to Sofia's Mighty Taco to eat the Deluxe Chimichangas until our panzas stuck out like spare llantas? Who would I call up at 3 a.m. after the familiar nightmare where I was looking for my coat in that same small room full of caca? How about the one where all my teeth fell out and I kept trying to put in my now bloody implants? Would Irma still join me for our monthly visits to Salón de Belleza Maritza to have our mustache hairs bleached blond and our dry heel skin shaved off with a razor? What about our annual trip to the hot baths at T or C, where we stocked up on smoked oysters and saltines and A&W root beers?

"So which one of Pedro's movies are we going to see?" I asked Irma. "I know I don't want to see *Un Rincón Cerca del Cielo.* When you think you can't stand any more poverty and heartbreak, when you think you can't stand to see Pedro and his wife, Margarita, climb that ratty set of stairs up to their dingy attic apartment without heat and running water one more time, then you have to sit through the part where their son dies because they can't get the medicine until too late and Pedro has to steal it but the son dies anyway. I don't want to see anyone cry, Irma. Besides, the movie was one of Ubaldo's favorites."

"Well, then we can't see *Nosotros los Pobres* either, Tere. There are too many scenes in it where Pedro cries. Especially the scene where he cradles the burnt body of his little son, El Torito."

I turned away, too sad to say anything. Irma realized she had said the wrong thing. I sat down on the cowhide couch. She came over and put her arms around me.

"You know . . . ," Irma began, and I knew I was going to hear something profound. Other people's "you know"s are so, you know, *desde*. But Irma has a way of waking you up and making you snap to attention. And after her pronouncements, you actually *do* feel that you know whatever there was to know, or at least at that moment.

". . . The mind. It's a healer. And yet, I miss Sal," Irma confided. "I wish I remembered him more, Tere. And then I ask myself, why do I need to remember? My life is changing. Wes and I are getting married and Sal . . ."

"We should remember less, that's what I say, Wirms."

"Or more. You know what's surprising? I can't remember Sal's penis. The way it looked," Irma said with sadness. "We didn't really look in those days, Tere. At least not in Cabritoville. I mean I did, but I didn't."

"What brought this on? I mean, I know what brought it on, but why are you thinking of Sal now?"

"The thing about the past is that many of us don't really remember it the way it was," Irma said. "To tell you the truth, I've forgotten a lot, comadre. But that's good, I suppose. Love gives us forget pills."

In *La Vida No Vale Nada*, Pedro-as-Pablo wanted to believe that he could live that life with Cruz in the antique shop with her little son. He wanted to keep Cruz's father's watch and live happily ever after. But his mother was waiting for him in his pueblito. He remembered her, the poverty, their little adobe jacalito, his rough and merciless and selfish father. He remembered their ugly life and how he'd tried to get away from it and how he never could. And how because of that he'd turned to drink. And he knew how

the drink had turned on him and made him crazy. He had to forget his mother's face, push it out of his consciousness, forget that
little dusty town in the middle of the desert and his family's collective nothing. And that's why he drank: to forget. But ay, it only
made him remember more. The heat. The stench. The hard tears
of that terrible place where his mother lived like an abandoned
dog.

It was a beautiful imagined life with Cruz. But it just couldn't
be Pedro-as-Pablo's life. That's why he ran away and went back to
find his family.

And that's why Irma and I were still comadres.

"Look, Irma, I don't mind seeing *Arriba las Mujeres*. I know it's
one of your favorites, but I have to tell you I was more in the
mood for ¡*Gitana Tenías Que Ser!*"

"Okay, that's what we'll see," Irma said to me with finality.

"We will?"

La comadre put down her dustrag, the torn-up back panel of
one of her old nightgowns that I had given her, and nodded in my
direction. It was a white cotton size 2X without lace. Irma was allergic to lace.

We both liked our nightgowns large, no confining shoulders or
chests to inhibit us. In the past, I'd gotten in the habit of keeping
some of my clothes and things at Irma's. I never knew when I was
going to need them, especially if I got sleepy during one of our
Pedro-athons and I decided to stay over and then had to go to
work the next day.

What would happen after Irma's wedding to Mr. Wesley?

Would I sleep in the motel lobby on the lumpy couch near the
window with the burpy "American Owned" lights winking in the
background?

The fact of the whole stinking matter was that I was riddled
with envidia. I would have given anything, even to El Puto Mayor,
as Nyvia Ester called the Devil, to have someone love me and take
care of me the way I saw Irma take care of Mr. Wesley and Mr.
Wesley take care of Wirms.

"Promise me, Wirms," I said, gathering myself up, "if you ever redecorate, the first thing to go are the wagon wheels. And then the 'American Owned' sign."

"You're telling me?" Irma said.

I wasn't really sure what she meant. What got me was the question mark at the end of her sentence. Was Irma telling me that yes, the wagon wheels had gotten to her, too, that she knew they looked like shit? Or was she saying that she was offended that I couldn't stand the decor of her beloved viejito's place of business? I let the comment hang there in outer space as I stared at a dried cow skull over the registration desk.

I don't want to go on and on about how the place looked like an old white man's hellhole, especially since Irma was in love with the old white man whose hole it was. I didn't want to offend my comadre, but her husband-to-be's taste was, well, *bad*.

Several faded brown simulated-leather chairs faced a table made out of old license plates from Oklahoma, Texas and New Mexico. Stacked on it were copies of *Farm and Ranch* magazine and a few old *Reader's Digests*, one of them with a blaring Prostate Cancer Hot Line toll-free number on the cover. I moved around the lobby restlessly.

"What's wrong with you, Tere?" Irma asked. "I know how upset you were about Ubaldo, but at least we found out it wasn't him in the burn unit when the family claimed the body. If *you're* relieved, imagine how María Luisa feels! It's more than Ubaldo, isn't it?"

I went to my purse and took out a newspaper clipping with a photograph. I handed it to Irma.

"Lucio built a new house. Andrea's moved to a new school."

She looked at it carefully: it was the photograph of an expensive adobe house handcrafted with vigas, latillas and all kinds of details. I could imagine the inside with its very expensive one-of-a-kind ceramic Kokopelli corner light fixtures with every santo in the book in the gadzillion nichos, Saltillo tile in every room, even the one with the king-sized hot tub. Translate that to mean: I was sad and jealous as hell that a picture of Lucio's dream house had come out in the *Cabritoville Chronicle* and I was in neither.

It wasn't my house, it would never be. It was a rich American house made for a wealthy person who wasn't Mexican, much less Mejicano. It was "American Owned," if you know what I mean.

I've never known what it is to have an acre or two or a house of my own, a house that I wasn't renting or that didn't come with a sad history, a used house, a house full of other people's memories.

Lucio's was brand spanking new. No doubt it smelled good, like fresh paint and new carpets. No fingerprints on light switches, crumbling plaster around the bathtub, or cucaracha skid marks under the sink. Lucio Valadez, in the world's reckoning, had everything: a wife, a child, money, a good business, a new home.

The house was on a beautiful rise of land, a place where a family could grow and be happy. It was a place for children. It was a picture-perfect house, and it belonged to Lucio and Diolinda Valadez.

Irma knew Lucio's white truck. She looked at the photograph and wrinkled her nose. And then she reached over and hugged me hard.

"Get over it, Tere. Girl, please. Find yourself a man who will love you, and love him back. He might not be the right man, the best man, the most exotic or exciting man, but let him love you deeply. And try to love him back any way you can. With everything you can. So what about Chago? Is he back in town for good?" Irma said conspiratorially.

"There's nothing to say," I interjected.

I'd avoided Chago like the plague and yet he'd turn up where I least expected him. I even saw him at Mass! He had to go back to California to finish a job, he said, but then he'd be back. He asked if Irma's house was for rent.

"Tere . . ."

"Don't say anything. Just be quiet. If you're quiet, then I can be quiet."

And so we were quiet for a long time.

Finally, I had to admit to Irma: "If I knew then what I know now, it would probably happen the same way."

What I meant was that it was all so ugly and stupid. I painfully remembered my last, long goodbye to Lucio in the parking lot behind Sofia's Mighty Taco. Necking so hard it hurt. Empty promises to stay in touch. I'll call you, you call me. But not now. Now is not Our Time. Sometime will be Our Time. That liquid sweet *pendejo* voice coming from the crotch of his tight jeans, all his *cuerito* energy bound up in who he was and who he would be. Rich. Famous. A millionaire by age forty. Blah blah blah.

There was no getting away from the facts. The man was short. He had a small back. He was a liar. And he was mean.

And *in addition to all this*, he hated his mother. And his sister. And his sister's kids. And their dogs and cats. Who did Lucio Valadez love besides himself?

"Listen, Wirms," I finally said, "I'm tired of seeing you bounce around this lobby like an overheated goat. Let's get this lobby cleaned up once and for all."

"Okay, start taking things out of that desk drawer and put them in a box," Irma said, pointing to an old desk off to one side.

I peered inside. Old plastic combs, faded green squeeze coin purses, orange golf tees with "The Flying W Motel" printed on them.

"Does El Wes have insurance? If he does, Wirms, let's torch the wagon wheels. On second thought, how about the whole lobby?"

"Always with a joke, Tere."

Irma was in one of her "let's clean until we drop" moods, which was all right with me because cleaning made me stop thinking. I had so many serious things on my mind like: Where's Ubaldo? Is

Ubaldo alive? Where's Lucio? Who is he with? How's Andrea? How are my little kids at school? Will I ever get my job back at Cabritoville Elementary? Or will I become manager of the Flying W? What about Irma and El Wes? Will they live happily ever after? What about me, Teresina P. (for Pelada) Ávila? Will I live and then die a loveless nobody?

I said, "You know, Wirms, all this drama with the fan club members mobilizing to find Ubaldo, thinking he had committed suicide, only to discover that it was a depressed fire extinguisher salesman who killed himself instead—it's made me think about how I want to live. And die."

"Me, too. It's not that most of us have a choice about how we die, but there is a consciousness with which we can approach death. Only this morning I was thinking about how mi tío Juventino died. I never told you."

"Oh yeah?"

Irma put down her professional-style blue plastic bucket that held all her cleaning supplies: Bon Ami, Windex and a large knife she'd had for years that she swore could scrape anything off any given surface. She took off her yellow rubber gloves and sat on the hard leather couch, but not before washing it with some lemon-scented ammonia.

"He was bitten by his wife, mi tía Eloria, who was bitten by a rabid dog."

"No!" I said in disbelief.

"He died from her bite. And then when mi tía Eloria got well and found that she'd killed him, she died from a broken heart."

I stared out the picture window of the Flying W. The constant blinking of the neon sign was like a heartbeat. I could hear Ubaldo drawing breath somewhere.

"Mi tío died around the turn of the century. It was a brutal time to live. There were no rabies shots in the stomach with a needle a yard long then. This was way back when people died in the middle of nowhere at four in the morning foaming at the mouth without a doctor to help."

"Your tío Juventino must have really loved Eloria," I said quietly.
"Yes, I think he did," Irma replied wistfully.

I couldn't ever imagine Lucio taking care of me the way Juventino took care of Eloria. Oh, I could see myself looking after Lucio, pampering him and babying him, feeding him warm tapioca with a spoon and changing his adult Pampers at age eighty-four, me age eighty-nine, but I couldn't ever see him bringing me a glass of water, or my glasses, or a book, much less any food he might have cooked for me.

Irma got up, took off her apron and flung it down on top of the *Reader's Digests*. Exactly my sentiments.

"Just look at these things, Tere. I mean, would you want to buy them?"

I peered into a box of dried-out cigarette lighters and old Tums. "Hell no."

Wirms and I just looked at each other and burst into laughter. Lord, it felt good to laugh hard with la comadre. I felt relieved.

Wirms didn't care for the poor animals with their severed heads on the walls, or the dusty bearskin rug on the porch that was a piojo breeding ground.

"Wirms, there's probably someone out there who needs a hand-tooled wallet that says 'Cabritoville, U.S.A.' But I don't know. You might want to keep the Land of Enchantment back scratchers and the White Sands thimbles."

"It's okay for an unmarried man to have a motel full of bad Western art, but if you're married, it's no good. I can take the dogs-playing-poker wall hanging, Tere, maybe one howling coyote, a couple of branding irons and Mr. Wesley's spurs collection, but no way am I going to live and work in a room full of dead animals. The stuffed beaver, the deer, the mountain lion, the antelope, the snakes and the bear have to go and so do the stuffed frogs playing musical instruments. We're going New Age. Only Wes doesn't know it yet. We'll sell healthy snacks. Trail mix, a variety of nuts, unsweetened banana chips, packets of soy milk."

"I don't think Cabritoville is ready for that, Wirms. But you can give it a try. There aren't too many vegetarians around here, other than you and El Wes. Amazing how fast you both converted. The only other vegetarians in town are the viejitos with no teeth sitting on the benches near the plaza."

"We *can* change the world if we want to, Tere. Or at least we can change the way we look at the world."

"Okay. So what can I do next? Do you want me and the deer heads to watch you work up a sweat? Or are you going to put me to work?"

"Bring those boxes over here," she said, pointing to several Green Giant canned string bean boxes rescued from behind Canales' Grocery. "We'll put the combs and coin purses in there and take them to the nursing home, and as for the yellowed souvenir toothpicks with 'The Flying W' written on the side, toss 'em. Ditto the Red Man chewing tobacco. No telling how long it's been here."

"Aren't you getting tired, Irma?" I asked. She had worked up a sweat.

"Heck no! I'm just getting started, Tere. We Mejicanas don't formalize exercise, if you know what I mean. We don't make rituals of it like gringas do, with purple designer sweat suits, special running shoes, StairMasters and saunas. We don't have time to hang out in a swirling tub full of naked prunelike gabachas talking about bioflavonoids! I want to die with my boots on, working, going full tilt."

None of my ancestors died the way Irma's did: of rabies bites, or atop a horse in childbirth, or crossing a river in a rage after finding one's wife in bed with another man, later getting paralyzed mid-río on the way to confront the lovers, or still later dying on the riverbank as they foamed their last breath away in anguish articulating the One Holy Name. Most of my family had died of cancer.

Me, I wanted the grand gesture. And dying atop a horse in some remote pueblito was better by far than dying in a cold, im-

personal room at Cabritoville Memorial Hospital, the Joto brothers taking care of you: Danny/Mannie, two overweight gay nurse's
aides, soul brothers, who everyone said were each other's lovers,
God help them, each of them over three hundred pounds of pure
Morrell. Lard, that is.

(The Joto brothers, once unjustly named by none other than
Ubaldo, who said he wouldn't touch either of them with a ten-
foot dildo, were actually not brothers, but cousins, both of them
obese from birth. Their two obese mothers pushed out their obese
'jitos around the time of the very full moon.)

But if I had to die in Cabritoville, and I hoped I would, I would
sooner die of a rabies bite than of cancer, with the two Joto
brothers in attendance. Although, to be fair, it was said that
Danny/Mannie were very gentle with their patients.

I wanted to die in my boots, like Pedro and Lupe, the mother of
his baby daughter, in *Las Mujeres de Mi General*, as they blasted
their way into eternity surrounded by enemy gunfire.

The Joto brothers worked as a team, turning the patient sideways ever so carefully while changing the sheets, one half section
at a time. Danny/Mannie lifted the patient effortlessly as the
other wiped his ass or slid the bedpan underneath.

Danny/Mannie were big and strong and nothing ever upset
them, no smell was too pungent, no sight too terrible, no wailing
too painful. Danny/Mannie had seen it all and nothing about life
and dying scared or moved them. They were rocks, twin mountains, and if you had to die in Cabritoville, U.S.A., it was more
than likely that Danny/Mannie would be cleaning you up for that
long last trip through the Valley of the Shadow of Death. No
green pastures. No still waters.

I gleefully imagined Danny/Mannie putting a pañal on Lucio.

The picture was really clear now. No fuzzy channels.

Something happens when a man's juices get into your body,
when his burning lips touch yours, when his penis pushes hard

through dryness to get inside you, when his semen flows through you, a dark, hot late-night river. You wade through wetness to lay down and you beg to die by the riverbank. You've been struck. You don't know how to get up, and when you do, if you ever do, you carry a limp, an ache, some jodido scar that you know for sure will someday kill you off.

Rabia/Love is a spot on your lung.

The silent scream in your throat.

That knot in the pit of your stomach.

The bile you can never expel.

The cough that comes back to haunt you when you least expect it.

Rabia/Love is an old friend, coming to pay a visit.

Hello, friend.

Reminding you where your home really is.

The earth.

In the darkness of the sunroom at the Flying W Motel, La Wirms next to me, in front of the flickering television screen watching ¡Gitana Tenías Que Ser!, I wrote Lucio Valadez's name over and over in the palm of my left hand.

I never ran out of room as on a piece of paper. *Lucio Valadez* over life lines, love lines, children's lines, birth lines, death lines.

And when I tired of that, I wrote *Lucio Valadez* on my index finger, my eyes fixed on the small television screen, where Pedro argued with Pastora de Los Reyes.

In ¡Gitana Tenías Que Ser!, Pedro plays Pedro Mendoza, a charro turned actor who gets his big break to star in a movie with Pastora de Los Reyes, a fiery ethpañola who can't stand him. As a matter of fact, they can't stand each other and the filming of their movie is hell. And it probably has to do with the fact that she's Spanish and he's Mexican.

"Ay, comadre, I guess Lucio and I are a sad history now, huh? And that history was a trial-and-tribulation kind of thing. And it's like Pastora de Los Reyes and Pedro Mendoza in ¡*Gitana Tenías Que Ser!*?"

"Yeah, something like that," Irma said.

Even as I mouthed Pastora de Los Reyes' words to Pedro-as-Pedro Mendoza, "Me has hecho sufrir daño," my thumb traced the holy name on that seemingly endless page of thought.

Lucio Valadez. Lucio Valadez.

Who was there to see the name, know the name, understand the name except you? You. Woman Inside My Head. Girl Without a Name. The Me of Before. Listening-But-Not-Hearing Woman. Knowing-But-Not-Understanding Woman. Looking-But-Not-Seeing Woman. Stupid Pendeja Girl. Cabrona Woman. Dark Night Woman. Woman Who Knows the Terrible Power of the Endless Flowing Hidden Words.

I wrote Lucio's name on my finger one last time as the movie ended and Irma turned the lights back on.

Lucio Valadez.

Fin.

28

Minutes of the Pedro Infante Club de Admiradores Norteamericano #256

Members present: Nyvia Ester Granados, president; Irma Granados, vice president; Tere Ávila, secretary . . . etc., etc. You know who you are.

Members not present and still missing: Ubaldo Miranda.

The meeting was called to order at 7:37 p.m. by Nyvia Ester Granados, president.

Tere Ávila reported that the man in the burn unit at Presbyterian Hospital in Albuquerque was *definitely not* Ubaldo Miranda for those of you members who missed the last meeting or were out of town. The man was positively identified by a family member, as reported to us by Captain Zertuche. María Luisa said she knew it wasn't Ubaldo. And yes, he passed away. Que descanse en paz. Sista passed around a paper cup for donations for a memorial Mass at Sacred Heart Church. María Luisa Miranda broke down, and we had to stop the meeting for a while until she composed herself. She had nothing to report about Ubaldo's continuing absence.

The reason for the special meeting was a wedding shower for Irma Granados hosted by Tere Ávila. The theme for the shower came from *Tizoc*, Pedro's last movie. In the movie he plays a humble Indio who falls in love with María Félix, who plays the beautiful daughter of his patrón. Tizoc is so smitten with María Félix he thinks she is the Virgin Mary. He also mistakenly thinks she has agreed to marry him when she hands him her handkerchief, an act of commitment in his culture.

All club members dressed in costume from the period. Irma Granados, the bride-to-be, wore a beautiful traje indígena of white linen with an embroidered border she made herself that put everyone to shame. Ditto her mother, Nyvia Ester, who wore a brightly colored huipil over a long red skirt, her long black hair in two thick trenzas intertwined with ribbons.

Sista Rocha forgot to bring the treasurer's report, because, just like Madame President, she thought it was a wedding shower and not a meeting.

Merlinda Calderón gave a report on *Tizoc*, noting that Pedro won El Oso de Berlín, a Best Actor award at the Berlin Film Festival in 1957, for his role.

Elisa Urista, on probation, arrived late and started complaining about the food as soon as she was in the door. The menu was supposed to be a potluck *Tizoc*-type meal, except everybody forgot, so it was the usual Mejicano mishmash.

Madame President reminded fan club members it was a happy occasion, and if anyone had a problem, they could just put their gift on the table by the front door and leave. No questions asked.

We stopped at the end of *Tizoc* to get more food and another box of Kleenex.

Merlinda said, through tears, that the scene where María Félix is accidentally killed by an arrow was too painful for her.

Irma seconded this. She said Tizoc must have really loved María Félix. Only someone in love would pull an arrow out of his loved one's chest and stab himself in the heart with it.

Tizoc wanted their souls to enter Heaven as two doves and continue to sing to Tata Dios, Madame President reminded us.

Pancha sighed and said that nothing could be more romantic than two lovers eternally joined.

Margarita Hinkel felt it necessary to explain that there was no way Tizoc could ever cross the barrier between culture and class.

Catalina Lugo said that we don't pick who we're going to love.

Ofelia Contreras told Catalina that she's been married six times, twice to the same man, and that she should have learned by now.

Madame President reminded everyone that this was a wedding shower and not a confessional. Although, she added, whenever women get together, it *is* a confessional.

María Luisa Miranda wished Irma lots of luck.

A discussion followed about whether Mr. Wesley was too old for Irma. And what exactly did it mean to marry a much older man.

Concepción Vallejos said that her father was twenty-three years older than her mother. And that they went on to have eleven children and a very good marriage.

Madame President asked for approval of the minutes of the last meeting.

Margarita Hinkel objected to the minutes. She didn't like the way the meetings were run, with everybody always giving her a hard time just because her husband was the manager of Luby's and because they had money. Margarita said she was a member only because of Pedro and thought she was his best fan.

Much heated discussion followed from the fan club members about who was Pedro's best fan.

Irma said she'd seen all his movies . . .

Sista had been to the panteón over ten times . . .

Ofelia knew someone who had been Pedro's barber . . .

Madame President called the meeting to order again. Then she asked for Old Business.

Merlinda Calderón called for a show of hands by the people who were interested in going to the panteón for the Anniversary of Pedro's Death. She will report back to us on plane fares. She mentioned that *a woman whose name we won't mention* at AAA is working on tickets. She wants to know *for sure* how many members are joining the tour. She didn't want what happened last year to happen again. And she wasn't talking about Concepción's gallbladder surgery. She was talking about a few members who canceled at the last minute. If you sign up you *have* to go, she says.

Madame President passed out cards from the Flying W Motel, just in case anyone ever had out-of-town guests coming to Cabritoville who needed a place to stay.

Sista proposed a toast to Irma. The motion was seconded by Tere Ávila.

We're the Pedro Infante Club de Admiradores Norteamericano #256, Sista said, and no one can take that away from us. Amen!

Everyone agreed. Pink plastic glasses were lifted high in the air. Irma brought out her famous punch—spiked. More toasts followed, many of them with Pedro's name invoked.

Someone put on a Pedro Infante record, "Las Románticas de Pedro Infante."

Sista, Pancha and María Luisa Miranda brought over Irma's gifts and laid them at her feet.

The following is a list of Irma's shower gifts:

Nyvia Ester Granados: A set of "cheets"—cotton and not silk, because cotton is more comfortable.

Sista Rocha: A copy of a book written by Pedro's wife, María Luisa León, *Pedro Infante en la intimidad conmigo.*

Catalina Lugo: A set of pots and pans from the White House in El Paso.

Ofelia Contreras: A Pedro Infante T-shirt she found in the mercado in Juárez that says "Dicen Que Soy Mujeriego."

Concepción Vallejos: A bottle of One A Day Extra Support Vitamins for Mature Women, with Calcium and Magnesium.

Elisa Urista: Nothing. She said she forgot it was a shower. But she said she would bring a gift next meeting. Everyone knew she wouldn't. She's never brought gifts to the Christmas or Valentine or Halloween parties, or for anyone's birthday.

Pancha Urdialez: A pink blanket for Irma's bed. Full size. Everyone squealed when Pancha said "bed."

Sista bawled us out, telling us that most of us had scores of kids, miscarriages right and left, have known childbirth, divorce and death, not to mention drunken husbands, runaway teenager girls with drug problems, homosexual sons and a few lesbian nieces. She said we were "women who'd changed religions like hats, now Catholic, now Pentecostal, now born-again Jehovah's Witness and now New Age, not to mention the shift of political alliances from Democrat to Republican to Green Party to Democrat to finally Republican and all the crap that goes along with living in Cabritoville in this day and age and *still* you're giggling at words like 'bed,' 'sex' and 'wedding night.' "

Tina Reynosa: A scented candle. Laughter. For those special nights. Laughter.

Someone asked if it had to be only at night? Laughter.

(Madame President: I didn't get the name of who said this.)

Margarita Hinkel: One gift certificate to Luby's. Sista mentioned that it was only a gift certificate for *one*.

Tina made a motion that Margarita give Irma another gift certificate. Tere seconded the motion. The vote was 12–1 in favor that Margarita give Irma *two* gift certificates to Luby's.

María Luisa Miranda: Two throw pillows that she made with the face of Pedro Infante on the front. Everyone wanted to buy a set of pillows. María Luisa took orders for about half an hour, in the course of which the con queso cheese dip bubbled over and burnt.

Teresina Ávila: 1. A gift certificate for a deluxe dinner for two at Sofia's Mighty Taco. Including sopaipillas.

2. A tape of Pedro Infante's "Rancheras."

3. A beautiful white scrapbook with the phrase "My Wedding" on the front.

4. Massage oil. Wild banana.

5. A pink negligee. Size 2X. No lace.

Madame President asked for a motion that we end the meeting. Elisa gave the motion and it was seconded by Pancha.

The meeting was adjourned at 8:43 p.m. The shower went on until 2:30 a.m.

Minutes for the monthly meeting of the Pedro Infante Club de Admiradores Norteamericano #256, respectfully submitted by Secretary Tere Ávila. Madrina to the Bride.

The Flying U

Ilyvia Ester stood in front of a crowd of about four hundred people. Her large fleshy arms were folded over tiny breasts that belied her formidable girth. Dressed in a flowing pink sheath that gave her the appearance of an inflated doll, with an enormous corsage of pink roses that nearly hid the left side of her face, she addressed the festive group in the stentorious voice of a practiced orator.

"Thank jew for coming a mi Irmita's boda. Jew no I come to the Jew-es a trabajar an to get ahead. Empecé a trabajar limpiando casas, planchando, and ahora trabajo en el Come-On-and-Drop-In. I work muy duro to put mis keeds through el colegio. La Irma, chees my joy and pride. Estoy muy orgullosa que es mi hija. Y cuando la veo, I see all the mujeres de mi familia. Eran muy estrong. My mamá, her mamá. Como m'ija, La Irmita. Okay, I gonna estop talking. Por fin llegó el día que se la change la vida a m'ija. Bendito sea Dios. Y les weesh a los novios una vida llena de amor. Y lots of keeds. Porque m'ija, se no está pasando el tiempo, we all getting ole. Amen!"

With that amen, Nyvia Ester took Irma's arm in hers and strode down the aisle of Sacred Heart Church to the tune of Pedro's song "Paloma Querida" played by Los Gatos del Sur, who fanned out at the back of the church in full mariachi regalia, huge black hats with silver trim, black vests, black skintight pants and bright red bows. It was a festive scene as Irma and her mother moved down the aisle, stopping from time to time to hug someone or take a well-wisher's hand.

When she got to the altar, Nyvia Ester faltered a moment, gathered herself up and gave Irma's arm to El Wes, who stood there, all six feet whatever of him, in a Western-style tuxedo with a black string tie. He took off his hat, leaned down to kiss "Mamá Nyvia," his beaming mother-in-law, and took Irma's trembling hand.

I stood behind her, arranging her long train so that she wouldn't trip over it, as I had done all the way up the aisle. I was so worried about her enormous silk train that I didn't have time to really see anyone in the audience. But it didn't matter. I wasn't the one getting married, thank God.

The fan club members, minus Ubaldo, came up to the altar, all sequins and levanta chichis, all dark brown eye shadow and red lipstick, in six-inch heels, and with pink carnation corsages to put the lazo around Irma and Mr. Wesley, signifying the irrefutable ties that bound them now as man and soon-to-be wife. They retreated but not before a lot of hugging and kissing. I took a Kleenex and wiped Irma down from all the kiss marks and then stepped to her right as carefully as I could. Father Ronnie called for a moment of silence and then the Mass began.

The Mass was bilingual; Irma said her vows in English and El Wes in Spanish. I didn't know he could talk so well, but he did. And then they switched off and he said his vows in English and Irma said them in Spanish.

Irma and Mr. Wesley wrote their own vows. Irma had replaced all the "obey"s in her vows with "respect"s.

I got some good ideas from her in case—ha!—I ever get married again.

When the "I Do"s came and went, we heard a loud grito that came from Sista Rocha, who let out a giant "¡AAAAAAYYYY!" that was followed by several smaller yips and various catcalls from a group of teenagers at the back of the church.

Father Ronnie clapped his hands and the entire church broke into applause. A few people were crying—make that Nyvia Ester and a little old lady she was leaning on who wasn't part of the wedding party but who had pitched tradition overboard and sat in the first pew next to Nyvia Ester just as if she were family.

Father Ronnie performed a beautiful service. Members of the fan club gave the scriptural readings and brought up the communion wafers. Throughout the Mass, Los Gatos del Sur broke out into one or another of well-known Pedro songs like "Palabritas de Amor" and "Las Tres Cosas," as well as the usual Kyrie Eleison, the Holy, Holy, Holies, and the Our Father in Spanish.

La Wirms had dragged me to confession a few days before. I should have gone years ago, it felt so nice! Father Ronnie didn't even bat an eye during my long list of "Father Forgive Me"s. The experience wasn't an ominous sliding-door-in-the-darkness kind of thing with hovering evil overtones. We were both in cutoffs in the rectory kitchen drinking Negra Modelos. It had been so long since I'd been to Holy Communion that I had no idea whole-wheat pita bread had replaced those hosts that stuck to your palate.

Los Gatos del Sur played throughout the service, fitting in a Pedro song whenever possible. They ended on a very high note with "De Colores" as we floated out of the church and headed toward the reception at the Flying W.

The grounds of the Flying W were set up with a large number of tables with pink tablecloths. On each table was a centerpiece made by the fan club members under the direction of María Luisa Miranda. Sticking out of each pink vase was a photo collage on a wooden stick, blown up from one of those street photos that you find in Méjico taken by an ambulatory photographer. The beaming faces of Irma and Mr. Wesley were cut out and placed within a circle of hearts. In each heart was an alternating image of Our Lady of Guadalupe and Pedro Infante. On the bottom left side of the composite was a photo of the panteón where Pedro was buried. To the right was a bouquet of roses. The centerpiece was María Luisa's idea. The woman had an artistic gene that was coming to flower now that Ubaldo was gone. She was selling her Pedro pillows to a boutique in El Paso. Just lately, someone from a gallery in Albuquerque wanted to feature her in a show on textile art.

White lights were strung across the pool and throughout the surrounding motel rooms. The motel was closed for the week, to make room for Nyvia Ester's Mexican relatives, who stayed there.

The party spilled into the lobby, but fortunately the stuffed animals, heads and torsos, were gone. That cleared out a lot of space. We had pushed back the registration desk, covered it with a white tablecloth, and then put an Egyptian ankh on top of the chocolate cake, replacing the traditional white cake and the familiar sappy-looking bride and groom with the symbol of life—Irma's idea.

Sofia's Mighty Taco was set up for the catering, with Sofia herself riding herd. She was dressed in an elegant light blue pantsuit she'd bought at the Merry-Go-Round women's dress store in Las Cruces, protected by a large white apron. The food was Sofia's usual fare, only more of it, on giant steaming silver trays, and, hard to believe, better outdoors than in.

The fan club members were the hostesses. *Everyone* was dressed up. That meant everything from sequined tops to a China poblana outfit that María Luisa Miranda wore. It was a little hokey, until she got up to sing a medley of Pedro's songs including "Amorcito de Mi Vida," "Corazón, Corazón" and "Paloma Querida," and sounded just like Lola Beltrán. Los Gatos del Sur backed her up and then played for the wedding dance. Sista Rocha and her husband led the marcha in their slow, familiar, long-practiced way. You could tell they had done it a thousand times and would do it a thousand times more before they separated into their own eternal cosmic dance, or if you believed, as Irma and I did, they would finally end up together, in the dance of clouds and rain, one integral and blessed part of the many smaller and greater parts of life.

As Maid of Honor, I must admit I looked pretty cool in this hot-pink satin dress with an Empire top. Irma made all of our dresses, including hers. I'd lost a whole lot of weight—that's one good thing about suffering. No more Grand Slam breakfasts with buttermilk pancakes at 2 a.m. at the Village Inn or Roundup Specials with hash browns. Oh no. Chago was moving back to California with promises to keep in touch. We'll see.

When Chago came to say goodbye to me at the Flying W the week before the wedding, I felt something fluttery. But it just could have been something I ate for breakfast. It was around eight-thirty in the morning.

"I'm headed out, Tere," he said, standing in the doorway at the Flying W. I was at the reception desk checking someone in from Indio, California.

I first saw him out of the corner of my eye, all hulking strength in that jean jacket of his that I bought him for Christmas two years ago, wearing a tight pair of Levi's that fit him pretty good considering he was so big he couldn't find anything his size in Cabritoville. He'd be better off in California, I thought, what with all those men's Tall and Big Stores in those giant shopping malls.

"Excuse me, sir," I said to the man from Indio. He was pretty much tuckered out from driving. I could see that when I handed him the key. "Here you go, Mr. . . . Dexler . . ."

Mr. Dexler headed out of the lobby, peering up to see Chago standing in the door like a pillar of salt.

"So, you heading out?" I said, coming around from behind the desk.

"I'm heading out," he said, inching into the room.

"I see that."

"I came to say goodbye."

"Goodbye, Chago."

"Goodbye, Tere."

"Hey, good luck."

"You, too."

"Me, I always have good luck," I joked. "Nah, just kidding."

And this is where I came up close, so close I could smell his cologne. It was a grave mistake on my part. Chago came up to me, took me in his arms and kissed me, solid, the way Pedro kissed Sarita Montiel in *El Enamorado*, with an unmistakable bravado, as though he had the right, yet with a tender, almost shy respect, as though he didn't. A kiss like that can break your heart.

"So . . . ," I said, pulling away. And it was hard.

"So . . . ," he said. "I'll keep in touch."

"Ya, you do that, Talamantes," I said, surprising myself.

"Hay te watcho, babes."

And with that, the boy was gone.

Later, during the wedding reception, I almost wished Chago were there. He most certainly could have helped me, distracted me, and not only that, I would have had a great dance partner.

El Wes's Best Man was a short Mejicano from Terlingua named Al, who said he danced, but he didn't. I had to show him very basic steps and we suffered through the evening. But Al was funny. I had no idea that people from Terlingua were so amusing.

There was no way Irma could get around asking Graciela to be a bridesmaid. She came with her fiancé, the lawyer with the bad skin. He kept her occupied and out of trouble. When Los Gatos played "Tiburón," Graciela, for once, behaved.

Standing there in the middle of the lobby looking out on the flashing "American Owned" Flying W sign with the strands of white lights that looped through the fake wooden vigas that went nowhere, I could see La Wirms and El Wes sitting at the bridal table by the swimming pool. They kept holding on to each other's arms like they were life jackets. They fed each other wedding cake and even wrapped their hands around each other in that snaky way brides and grooms toast each other with champagne. (It was a little tricky to do, since Irma is so much shorter than Mr. Wesley.)

Irma's brother Butch was out there. I could see him standing by his long-suffering Bilbiana type of wife. I couldn't stand him for the most part, because when he got drunk he always came on to me, even though he'd been married for twenty-five years and had a potbelly that resembled a costal of chile.

The good thing is that no one got drunk, or if they did, they kept it to themselves and behaved like rational human beings. As a matter of fact, no one threw up in front of the motel in the bushes either. Quite civilized. No pleitos. No one smoking joints or drinking until they were all pedo, kicking random indiscriminate ass in a mixed group of Mejicanos and Anglos. The wedding was what I call mixed. That's what I love about Cabritoville, the way all the gente and la plebe and the white folks can mix if they want to.

No unpleasant people. Lots of pretty chavalitas who made you smile when you saw them making circles in their long pastel skirts, cute chavalitos dressed in dark suits digging how they looked. Women over sixty sitting in lawn chairs with folded arms over their large breasts, and loving the night air and being out of the house, away from the stove. Cleaned-up old men, hanging out with their compas and smoking an occasional Camel, remembering the good old days way back when Cabritoville was full of goats and roosters and chickens, and there weren't so many people as now and you had to walk to school but it was okay because you walked through fields of rabbits. School was far, but not so far you couldn't make it in time. There weren't any fences or barbed wire or tall houses out there to block your view. You were happy because Cabritoville ended at the back of your street. All there was was the blue sky, the white clouds that offered wonderful shade, the endless mesquite and at night a universe of stars so bright they looked like planets. You lay outside on a blanket and watched the shooting stars and an incredible meteor shower and then fell asleep, without fear, without doubts, under the endless backyard sky of your hometown. Cabritoville, U.S.A.

Los W's went on their luna-de-sticky-dripping-miel to San Diego. They drove, stopping along the way in Tucson to see the Desert Museum and all kinds of other dry, dusty desert things. They were going to make a vacation of it and take their time. Mr. Wesley hadn't had a vacation in years, and as far as I knew, Irma had never had a vacation, aside from a few trips to Santa Fe and that long cross-country trip to Pennsylvania with Sal.

While they were gone, I moved into the Flying W as the new manager. You wouldn't believe what it looks like! Irma has done so much work there. She painted the lobby a warm ocher. The display case is full of healthy snacks. Gone are the "Cabritoville: Ten Miles from Water, a Foot from Hell" postcards. Everything is fresh, clean, new.

The day after the wedding I called the cleaning staff and the desk clerks together in the lobby. It was a beautiful day, with the heat of the summer months looming strong, yet there was still something wonderful about the cool nights, the way everything was in bloom, the red-tipped ocotillo, the rose hedge around the swimming pool, the birds of paradise, the yuccas with their waxy white flowers.

As I looked around the motel, I knew why Wirms was so proud of the Flying W. Not only had the lobby been revamped, but the motel rooms had all been renovated a 'lo todo southwestern. Each room was full of desde. And Irma Granados Wesley, "La Mrs. Wes," had played no small part.

El Mr. Wes had been delighted with the new changes. He was a man who knew he'd come in from outside after a long hot day and found his shade.

That first night, I was nervous, walking around in Mr. Wesley's rooms, but after a while it felt like home because it was Irma's home. Hers and Mr. Wesley's. I do hope after all is said and done that Irma didn't hold out for the wedding night and that she'd lain down in sweet darkness at the Flying W with her dusty consentido.

When Irma's dog Pedrito slept with me that first night, I knew everything was going to be all right.

Irma had moved her large-screen TV to the sunroom of the Flying W. El Wes's two slumpy, really comfortable blue recliners were also crowded into the room, and there was a table full of game sets: Monopoly, dominoes, Parcheesi. (Who in the world still played Parcheesi?)

My copy of the autobiography of Santa Teresa de Ávila lay on one of the TV trays near a recliner. I was immersed in Chapter 2. My bookmark? The battered Blue Dot.

I checked the TV listings in the *Cabritoville Chronicle*, which had information on the two Spanish-language stations. Irma had called me earlier that afternoon to tell me she'd read in *TV Guide* that there was going to be a movie about Pedro Infante on Univisión and that I should record it for her.

At 5 p.m. *Pedro Infante, ¿Vive?* began. The movie was a modern-day love story, but with a twist. The young woman reporter and her sidekick, an older male staff photographer, show up at the panteón during the April 15 festivities for the Anniversary of Pedro's Death.

The woman reporter meets a young novelist at the panteón, and they are immediately attracted to each other. It turns out he has been researching the life of Pedro Infante and believes he is alive.

Throughout the day's events, the photographer takes random photos. Later on, in the darkroom, he notices a picture of a handsome older man at the panteón who is walking hand in hand with a lovely older woman. Inspecting the photograph more closely, he finds the man's similarity to Pedro Infante incredible, if it weren't for the scarred face.

After extensive research and interviewing Pedro's friends, he comes to the conclusion that the man in the photo is indeed Pedro!

Can it be?

The woman journalist and the novelist continue to see each other. One thing leads to another and to a small village to locate Pedro and the woman he was walking with in the panteón. The poor young novelist is in love with the well-off journalist, who is of a different class. The novelist finds out that the man in the photo really is Pedro. The journalist wants to publish the photos, but the novelist begs her not to. Despite the urging of her boss, the unscrupulous editor of the newspaper (who has a more than paternal interest in her), she decides to let Pedro and his mujer live in peace. She goes off with the novelist, who really loves her. It's a happy ending for everyone. Except, of course, the editor of the newspaper.

I sometimes think that if Pedro's out there, I might find him, or at least someone like him. That's if I want someone like Pedro. I'm not so sure anymore. Oh, I'll take someone who looks like him and sings and talks like him. As for the rest, I don't know. It wasn't a happy ending for María Luisa, Pedro's wife. Someone found her sitting at a table dead, just hunched over. All alone.

Pedro's mother, Doña Refugio, died a long time ago. The other women in Pedro's life, Lupe Torrentera and Irma Dorantes, they're still alive. Hugging their memories.

It makes me think of Ubaldo. He's out there somewhere looking for his Pedro. I can feel him breathing. And every once in a while I hear him crying. Someday I'm going to get a postcard from him, or a letter, or he's going to call me, probably collect, or send me a photograph of himself and some Pedro look-alike clone in some pueblito out in the middle of nowhere, their arms wrapped around each other. Somehow knowing that Ubaldo is still looking for his Pedro, that Chago is out there, with promises to keep in touch, gives me hope. Ay, maybe you can see the invisible p, for pendeja, on my forehead when I say that, but I don't care. No one is perfect.

Not even Pedro. I mean, he had diabetes. His hair was thin on top—don't tell me you didn't notice he wore a tupé. If he did fake his death, was it because he was so worried about getting old and he didn't want to let his fans down? Did he fabricate his own demise to save face? But then, where is he? In that little pueblito near the Sierra Nevadas where everyone knows him and protects him?

Or did Pedro look in the mirror one night and realize, like Cruz, the father in *No Desearás la Mujer de Tu Hijo*, that even he would get old and die? Did it devastate him to realize that someday women wouldn't look at him the way they used to, eyes open and fluttering with desire? Did he feel sorry for himself? Did he understand that one day he would feel unloved by people who once said they loved him? Was he sad when he thought that someday no one would be attracted to him except women of a certain age, older women who had lost their teeth, their firm flesh, their small waists, nearly all their dreams? Was it too much for him to realize that few people would be attracted to him anymore, and for the old reasons?

If that's what Pedro believed, then he was wrong. For as long as there is breath in my body, I'll always love him, just the way he was.

✻

The phone rang. I'd forgotten to take it off the hook. I thought it might be Irma, checking in on me to see if I'd taped her movie. I hoped it wasn't her. She had no business calling me on her honeymoon, at least not at night.

Four rings. Then a pause. And then it rang again.

It was Lucio. When you give up on a man, that's when he wants to get close.

I answered the phone warily.

"Tere, it's Lucio."

"How did you know I was here?"

"I heard you'd moved over to the Flying W. Pollo, the bartender from La Tempestad, told me you're the new manager."

"So what do you want, Lucio?"

"Cuca's sick."

"I'm sorry, Lucio."

"We took her to the hospital. These two big guys tied her to the bed because she kept threatening everyone. She grabbed Velia by the hair and wouldn't let go. They gave her morphine because of the pain, but even that didn't help. My stomach starting acting up, you know how it does, and I had this pain. I thought they were going to have to admit me as well. And Velia, you know how she is . . . She didn't help at all. Her boyfriend was there and that upset Cuca. Dio was acting up as well. Did I wake you up?"

"Lucio, please. I wish you wouldn't call me anymore."

"I needed to call you. And besides, we have this code."

"A code?"

"Four rings. I hang up. And then I call back. Wherever you are, you'll know it's me."

"The only code you have is that you call me whenever the hell you want."

"I thought you'd want to know."

"Thank you for calling me. I'm very sorry about your mother. Now goodbye."

"Can't we be friends, Terry?"

"No. I told you before. I don't want to be your friend. Not anymore."

"I have an appointment with a doctor about my stomach."

Lucio always had a pain in his stomach. He would probably die of stomach cancer. Or something to do with the anus.

"I'm worried, Terry. I think Dio's having an affair. Someone told me they saw her with this young guy at that truck stop, the Border Cowboy."

I laughed out loud, much to Lucio's consternation.

"What's wrong with you?"

"What's wrong with me? For the first time in a very long time, nothing is wrong with me."

"You sound strange. I thought maybe I could come over . . . I want to see you, Terry."

"You just don't get it, do you, Lucio? Please don't call me again. Don't ask me how I am, don't look for me, don't tell me how much you miss me, and don't come over! Now goodbye!"

And with that, I hung up.

I didn't want to be interrupted.

It was a quiet night and that's how it would stay.

Pedrito wanted attention. Loud noises upset him, the ringer on the phone, a sharp voice on the television. He was a nervous little dog. I wasn't used to chihuahuas. Never wanted a chihuahua in my life—not any kind of dog, for that matter. He was demanding, always craved attention. And yet he was a sweet boy. He slept in a small straw wastebasket during the daytime. At night I had to lift him up to the bed to sleep with me. He had that warm, soft, humid animal smell. A small-dog smell.

Pedrito brought me his bally-wally.

I threw his ball and he ran far—clear across the room. He jumped up in the air and caught the ball in his little mouth. Little dog. All he wanted to do was play. It was all a game to him, and he could play the game all night. He brought me the ball, I threw the ball back, he brought me the ball, I threw it back. I talked to him the way I used to talk to Lucio: I love you, baby, mi amorcito, te quiero, mi precioso, como eres lindo, my baby boy. I stroked Pedrito's fur, soothed him. He brought me the ball. I threw it. He brought it back, I threw it out again. Now he brought me his toys. One by one. The birdy-wirdy. The dolly-wolly. He was a smart little dog. I threw the ball out as far as I could, but it was never far enough. No sooner had I thrown the ball than Pedrito was running toward me again on those little short legs of his. He would never tire.

Another ring. Then another. And another. And then one final ring.

I unhooked the phone.

Pedrito brought the ball back to me. He wanted me to keep playing.

Ay, m'jito. Aren't you tired? .

The game would never end until I grew tired and finally decided to stop.

At some point you just have to stop.

You have to.

I threw the ball as far as I could. Pedrito brought the ball back to me, excited, as all creatures are, wanting more.

I put the ball away. Turned off the television. Got my car keys and headed out the door. The night was young for the very young.

No, I wasn't headed for La Tempestad. I drove in the direction of Gabina.

That great giant tree. The mother tree. I would sit there in the darkness of those deep roots for a while and breathe in the immensity of that old, steady cottonwood. I would say the prayer that had been running through my mind. That old familiar prayer. That prayer of long ago. And then I would look at the mountains, watch the sunset and head toward home.

1917–1957
"Pedro Infante no ha muerto.
Vive en los corazones del pueblo mexicano."

"Pedro Infante has not died.
He lives in the hearts of the Mexican people."

Fan club banner, Pedro Infante Club de Admiradores

Nació Mazatlán, 18 noviembre 1917, en la calle Constitución 88

Born in Mazatlán, November 18, 1917, 88 Constitución Street

My editor at Farrar, Straus and Giroux, John Glusman, says I can't have five single-spaced pages of thank-yous. I'd like to know why not. So this is the short version. If you want to know if you're on the long list, write to him.

Special thanks to the following people:
To my parents, Delfina Rede Faver Chávez and E. E. Chávez, for their love and belief in me in this life and in the other.

To my husband, Daniel Zolinsky, whose fierce loyalty has sustained me in the doubtful times and who has given me the love and space to do my best work.

La Mera Honcha, mi comadre Susan J. Tweit, who believed in this book and dreamed I danced with Pedro.

Pa' la Sandy B.—Sandra Benítez—who has wept and laughed with me so many times and in so many ways.

To Sandra Cisneros, dear friend, comadre del corazón, who loved her daddy like I loved mine.

The Jerrys, Wright and Niebles, for never giving up on their Pedro search.

Thank you to Jorge FitzMaurice and Lisa Muñoz for loaning me their Pedro movies, toditos, and for giving me places and spaces to put my books and artwork to remind me of life's beauty.

To my sisters, Margo Chávez-Charles and Faride Conway, for the catnip and the chisme.

To all the Pedrophiles, who shared their energy, stories, photographs, posters and magazines with me: Cynthia Farah, Francisca Tenorio, Richard Becker, Rebecca and Raúl Montaño, José

Luis Herrera, Dolores Dickinson and my best buddy, Rich Yañez, vecino de Chuco Town.

Thanks to Tey Diana Rebolledo, friend for many years, la comadre who helped me see more clearly and who confirmed that I wasn't so far off.

To Kenneth Kuffner. There is justice in this world, never doubt that.

To friends and artistic soul mates, Kate and Russell Mott, for their encouragement and friendship during these years of work.

To the Salom Family of El Paso, John and Marta, daughters Sandra and her husband, Jefferson, and Susan and her husband, Matt, for their incredible help and support in researching El Colón.

To Ronald and Violet Cauthon, dear friends who have taught me so much about generosity of heart, what it means to serve.

To my special girlfriends que entienden tanto: Margie Huerta, "La Comadre de Next Door," Kathleen Jo Ryan, who dared me to expand my horizons in ways I never imagined possible, Barbara Earl Thomas, la comadre who knows the wild owl in me, and of course Doña Ruth Kirk, high priestess of the natural world.

My thanks, always, to dear friends Rudolfo and Patricia Anaya. I love seeing the stars on the ceiling of your guest room.

In memory of Genoveva "Gen" Apodaca, my loving spirit guide. Thank you, Gen, for Casa Genoveva, your many consejos.

Thank you to Norman Zollinger, the finest literary brother one could ever have. Hasta luego, compadre.

Thank you to my two hometowns, the very best places to live and love: El Chuco and Chiva Town.

To the NM Arts Division, Dr. Margaret Brommelsiek, for her encouragement and goodwill.

To my sisters in the trenches at the Doña Ana Arts Council: Heather Pollard, Nancy Meyers and Judy Finch.

To Susan Bergholz, my agent, for sharing her gifts of mimicry and gauging the many moods, and for friendship and professionalism in so many ways. The best and fiercest comadre to come down the proverbial pike.

To John Glusman, my editor and friend at Farrar, Straus and Giroux. Thank you for your belief in that first wild and ragged chapter. And for staying with me all the way even when we both realized how very far we had to go.

To everyone at Farrar, Straus and Giroux, my thanks for your friendship and fine work.

My deepest gratitude to the Lannan Foundation, for their belief in my work and for giving me the time and peace to finish this book. My love and gratitude to Patrick Lannan, a visionary for this time, all times. Special thanks and love to the wonderful creative family of the Lannan Foundation: Janet Vorhees, Saskia Hamilton, David Martino and the Board of Directors.

My blessings and thanks to the Lila Wallace–Reader's Digest Fund for their support and belief in community and for allowing me to remember the stories of la vecindad, mi frontera divina. And to PEN USA and Carolina García, hermanita of the multi-colored Krishna. And to the Divine Ones, my "Divinities"—students in my oral history and writing workshop—for helping me to remember my deepest roots!

I have to stop. John won't let me go on any longer.

DENISE CHÁVEZ
Las Cruces, New Mexico